Faerie Fire

by

Silver James

Faerie Fire

Cover Art by *Rae Monet*

The Wild Rose Press
PO Box 708
Adams Basin, NY 14410-0706
Visit us at www.thewildrosepress.com

Publishing History
First Faery Rose Edition, 2010
Print ISBN 1-60154-817-6

Published in the United States of America

As soon as her fingers touched his palm,
an electric jolt ran up Duncan's arm all the way to
his brain. Alarms jangled in his subconscious. He
was vaguely aware that Margaret Steele said, "And
this is the senator's other daughter, Moira."

The young woman clutched his hand, staring at
him but not really seeing him. Duncan watched as a
fleeting series of emotions crossed her face—love,
passion, and then a look of sheer terror entrenched
itself in her eyes, turning them a dusky blue. Her
mouth opened in a silent scream. Slowly, her eyes
refocused on him.

"You," she accused before promptly fainting.

Reacting instinctively, Duncan caught the girl
with a strong arm around her shoulders and lifted
her easily, sliding his other arm under her knees.
Aware of the stares and murmurs around them, he
turned to Margaret. "Is there somewhere I can take
her?"

Margaret was too flustered to speak. Allen
stepped up and put his hand on Duncan's shoulder.
In a low voice, he directed. "The study. Follow me."

Allen quickly led him out of the room and across
the entry hall. The senator followed at his side, his
anxious gaze never leaving Moira's face. Margaret,
Deirdre, and Gemma, looking irresolute and unsure,
trailed behind.

Duncan barely glanced around the room as
Allen ushered him in. He laid Moira on a leather
couch while Margaret fussed about putting pillows
under the girl's head and shoulders. He checked her
pulse, surprised to find it racing. Most people
suffered a slow heart rate after fainting.

Though still unconscious, Moira clutched at his
hand, holding it tight, almost instinctively clinging
to him. Again, that tantalizing jolt of energy surged
up his arm. He knelt beside the couch watching her.
Moira remained deathly pale.

Dedication

A writer's journey is often solitary, so supportive family and friends are all the more important.

This book is dedicated to Greg and Clary, who often have to explain my eccentricities to colleagues and friends; to writing cohorts Justin, Heidi, Jen, and Leslie; the Beta Bloggers, and the wonderful people who hang out on my blog, Penumbra; my editor, Frances Sevilla, and the terrific people at The Wild Rose Press.

Thank you for dragging me out of my cave and reminding me that life is for living.

Prologue

The haunting trill of pipes swirled through the standing stones, echoing down through the green valley all the way to the misty, blue mountains and the white-capped sea. The forbidding sky transformed into a dark, boiling cauldron stirred by jagged fingers of lightning.

"Enough, Abhean," a deep voice murmured across the rising wind.

"You could have stopped it," the piper accused.

"Do not chastise me, Abhean," the voice roared. A clap of thunder punctuated the order.

Abhean, Harper of the Tuatha dé Danaan, played his lament again. The plaintive wail of the pipes drowned out anything else the angry voice might have said. The stormy sky slowly stilled its wild dance, and as the piper coaxed forth a mournful melody, the dark clouds wept. Grief permeated the entire realm of the Tuatha dé Danaan, and many cast a disparaging glower at the High King of Tir Nan Óg, the Land of Ever Young, though none dared do so openly. Only the Harper voiced his anguish.

Manannan Mac Lir, the high king, tried to shut out the sad tune. This legendary god of the Tuatha dé Danaan had a heavy heart and the sorrowful music tore at him. Abhean was wrong. He could not have changed this outcome. The last plaintive note sighed away on the dying breeze.

"I loved him," a voice as rich as spun sugar whispered on the wind.

"As did I." Manannan's voice filled with anguish. "And her as well."

Chapter 1

The dusky scent of horses mingled with the sharp smells of leather and dust in the gloomy stable. Duncan fought back a sneeze. The wooden door groaned like a sailor with a vicious hangover, as it swung drunkenly outward on creaky hinges. He slipped through the drab shaft of light seeping through the doorway. All his senses flared and his hand gripped the hilt of the sword at his side. Once unsheathed, the blade gleamed dully in the gray light.

He stole down the center aisle of the stable, every sense alert, his steps muffled by the straw littering the dirt floor. He stopped. A large pile of fragrant hay blocked his way. His head moved from side to side like a hound testing the air for the scent of his prey. With his nostrils flaring, Duncan turned to check the way he'd come.

Without warning, hands grabbed him from behind, jerking him down into the hay. For a few tense moments, he wrestled with his unseen attacker, grunting from both exertion and alarm. Twisting as he fought to overpower his opponent, he found his arms full of linen and lace. Warm, moist lips kissed the vee of his throat, and long fingers pushed their way inside his shirt to caress his chest.

Catching his breath, Duncan settled his brawny frame on top of the girl's willing body. Her legs parted, surrounding his thighs, and her hips cradled his hard shaft as it strained against his trews. His hands caressed her curves from hip to chest, while his lips and tongue found the soft valley between her breasts and trailed up her slim, white throat until they found the moist delights of her mouth. His lips brushed across hers gently, his tongue teasing them apart before it darted inside. He kissed her long and hard, savoring the sweet taste of her.

He finally pulled away from the kiss and rolled to one side, propping himself up on an elbow. The girl flashed him a saucy smile as her hand sought his midsection. A faint shaft of light played over her face, coming to rest across her eyes. Dark lashes fringed luminous pools of azure blue, and Duncan's breath caught in his chest from the sheer beauty of her.

"And what, bold Duncan, brings yee here?" she purred, her Irish accent both sensuous and sassy. She cocked an eyebrow at him and the corner of her mouth mimicked it.

In answer, Duncan rolled back on top of her and kissed her soundly, his tongue probing inside her mouth until it took her breath away. "As if you didn't know," he growled in her ear after breaking the kiss.

Taut, his whole body ached to his very core with the need to be buried deep within her. He hungered for her like nothing else in his life. Not glory, not riches, not life itself could take her place. As he pulled her closer into his embrace, she faded into moon shadows.

****

"Dunnie? Dunnie, wake up."

The voice in his ear sounded shrill and harsh. He tried to brush it away but encountered soft curls. Then warm lips left punctuation marks across the muscles of his chest and abdomen. Blindly, he reached for those lips, his hands fisting in the curls

4

as he jerked the lips to meet his own. He kissed them hard, demanding they soothe the ache still consuming him.

Even as he sought to quench the thirst raging within him, a warning prodded his subconscious. Something was wrong. He opened his eyes. Instead of blue eyes in which he could lose himself, a pair of faintly mocking gray eyes watched him warily.

He loosened his hold on the woman in his arms and rolled away. He would never love anyone but that other. His heart longed for the pair of eyes from his dream. "What do you want, Gemma?" Duncan demanded, irritated his dream had been interrupted.

Living with Gemma seemed a simple solution in the beginning, when he needed a place to stay. He'd moved in with the understanding he'd move on eventually. She was sexy and vowed she wanted no strings. They were perfect for each other.

His heart stuttered a beat. Had he always loved the woman in his dream? Some *where* else? Some *when* else? He shook his head at his own folly and didn't give Gemma time to answer his question. He got out of bed and strode into the bathroom for a shower instead.

****

Moira tried to rationalize what was happening. She'd awakened to pitch black darkness, in a place so stuffy she could barely catch her breath. She shivered in the dank cold as indistinct voices babbled outside. Frightened so much her fear went beyond reason, she choked back a scream as something skittered across the floor near her feet. Just a rat, she told herself. Rats were ordinary, mundane, nothing to fear. That screaming gibberish outside? Pure terror incarnate. She trembled, holding her breath and listening.

Voices quieted in hushed anticipation, the stark silence somehow even more horrifying. Rusted bolts grated and groaned as they were pulled from their sockets. Blazing light from a hundred torches flared across her dark dungeon, and she had to squint against the bright onslaught. Rough hands grabbed her, dragging her out into the open. Leering eyes raked over her. Every face filled with mad bloodlust. The smell of acrid smoke and dead roses mingled in her nose, making her nauseous.

"Please come," she whispered. "'Twas a promise." She squeezed her eyes shut, willing herself to be anywhere but there.

Trembling, Moira O'Connor huddled under her covers. The dregs of her nightmare left a bitter after-taste in her mouth and a sense of indefinable dread in her heart. Not one to run from fear, she threw off the covers and swung her legs over the side of the bed. Sitting up, she checked the clock on her nightstand. Red digital numbers glowed "4:00." Knowing she'd never get back to sleep, she snagged a plaid flannel robe and shrugged it on. The mid-March weather in Washington remained chilly, and the old house in Georgetown never seemed to get warm during the long nights of winter.

Moira didn't bother to turn on lights before she padded out into the hall. Surefooted even in the dark, she paced down the carpeted hallway and skipped down the stairs. The socks she wore left only a whisper in her wake. Years of living in this house gave her steps confidence as she crossed the vestibule and reached for the familiar feel of brass knobs. Pulling open the carved mahogany doors, she entered her father's study.

"Might as well get started on the senator's speech," she murmured, finally switching on some lights.

Soft incandescence imbued the study. A matching credenza backed the traditional cherry wood desk, and leather club chairs flanked the marble fireplace to the left of the desk. Floor to ceiling bookcases lined the wall on the right where leather-bound first editions proudly mingled with paperbacks and magazines. She bent over to turn on the gas fireplace lighter, and soon the logs crackled as the flames danced merrily in the hearth.

Settling into her father's leather desk chair, Moira goosed the mouse and waited for the computer and monitor to come alive. She took a deep, appreciative sniff of the leather next to her cheek. The chair exuded her father's essence—bay rum aftershave, cherry pipe tobacco, worn leather—all of it eloquently old fashioned and infinitely reassuring. Smiling at childhood memories of the stories he'd read to her while she sat here snug in his lap, Moira began tapping the computer keyboard, her fingers flying as the screen filled with words.

Three hours later, as she watched the printer spit out paper, a deep, resonant voice echoed from the doorway. She swiveled in the chair. Senator Patrick O'Connor strode into the room carrying two mugs of steaming coffee, one in each hand.

"Good morning, Da." Moira smiled as she accepted his offering.

"Up and about early aren't we?"

She shrugged. "Couldn't sleep." She evaded her father's real question and diverted his attention. "Here's your speech for the Irish-American Coalition." She pulled the neat stack of pages from the printer and handed them to him.

Without looking up from reading the pages, the senator unerringly sank into one of the over-sized club chairs. As her father perused the draft, Moira watched his face. She could read him like a book, and nodded, pleased by what she saw. Even at seven in the morning, Patrick O'Connor looked comfortably distinguished. He wore a creamy Irish knit sweater which perfectly complemented his charcoal cashmere slacks. Strands of silver wove a stylish tapestry

7

through his sable brown hair. A member of the press once hinted those strands might be something other than natural. Moira hid her grin by biting her lips. The word "artificial" and her father didn't belong in the same sentence. He'd even patronized the same barbershop for over twenty years.

"Excellent," the senator pronounced. "Just the right touch of blarney." He looked up to meet her gaze. "But then I knew it would be perfect. After all, I did have the good sense to hire the best speech writer on the hill."

The corner of Moira's mouth quirked at her father's praise and he smiled back. Shifting gears, he asked, "Do you have the schedule for this week?"

Moira grabbed the leather-bound planner from her father's desk and flipped it open. Delivering it to him with a flourish, she announced, "Other than the Irish dinner and speech, there's nothing major. The Steeles' house party is still penciled in for the weekend. Do you want to go or not?"

Patrick patted Moira's hand. "Margaret is determined to find husbands for you and Deirdre. If we don't attend, I suspect there will be some greatly disappointed young men."

Moira playfully swiped his shoulder. "Oh, Da," she admonished.

"Actually, I do have some things to discuss with Allen and I'd prefer to do so face-to-face. You don't have to come..." His voice trailed off, punctuated by a wistful sigh.

"Allen will have the place filled with lobbyists." Moira snorted. "I'm not about to leave you to face the wolves alone."

Moira headed toward the door, but the senator snagged her hand. His eyes seemed almost sad as he looked up at her. "I don't know what I'd do without yee, darlin'." A faint Irish brogue crept into his voice.

Moira ignored the sorrowful look on his face.

With her free hand on her hip, she danced a little jig. "Yee'd be doin' just what yer doin' now," she informed him gaily, her brogue much broader than his. Her eyes twinkled as she pulled her hand free and danced to the door. "But, me dear father, yee'd have to be payin' someone a hellava lot more if yee had to replace me." She bowed and left her father alone.

Left alone, the senator stared at the portrait of his wife hanging above the fireplace. "There are times when she is so like you, Maeve," he whispered to the smiling young woman gazing down at him. "Is it so selfish to want her with me all the time?" His eyes glistened with uncharacteristic tears. Patrick swiped at them with the back of his hand and heaved out of the chair.

Entering the sunny breakfast nook an hour later, Moira looked exactly like what she was—the top aide to one of the most powerful senators in Congress—him. Dressed in navy gabardine slacks, a tailored blouse and tweed blazer, she could be the cover model for Efficiency Magazine with her blonde hair smoothed back into a business-like French braid, and no makeup.

Moira slid into the chair across from him and poured a cup of coffee. After adding cream and sugar, she took a sip and gazed out across the small back yard. As Patrick grew engrossed in the morning paper, his breakfast sat at his elbow untouched—so did the coffee in the cup he held.

"The faeries have been busy," Moira whispered, her face and voice betraying an inner sadness.

Startled, he crumpled the paper into one hand, spilling coffee in the process. Following his daughter's gaze, he noticed the ring of soft green visible against dull, winter-browned grass in the yard. A few toadstools, their caps a drab white, peeked up from the green circle.

"'Tis early yet for a faerie ring," Moira mused. "They must be getting ready for the equinox."

"What do you mean?"

Moira turned to look at him, her face registering surprise at the sharp tone of his voice. "Why, Da," she teased, "I didn't think you put much stock in tales of the faerie folk. With St. Patrick's Day coming, I thought leprechauns would be more your style."

Recovering his composure, he presented his daughter with a smile meant to disarm. "Old habits die hard," he dissembled. "Your grandmother filled my head with frightful tales when I was a child." He noticed the involuntary shudder that ran through Moira at the mention of his mother, but chose to ignore it. "As for the little people?" He forced laughter into his voice. "As soon as St. Paddy's Day is done, they can all disappear back to the old country, unless they're registered voters in my district."

Moira laughed. "Spoken like a true politician, Senator."

Patrick covered his inner thoughts with a smile as he shoved away those memories from his childhood. Something else, though, a half-forgotten memory or the fragment of a half-remembered dream, nagged him. Before he could pin it down, a car horn blared from the street in front of the house.

"There's Darrel with the car, Da." Moira pushed back from the table, all business once again. "I have your briefcase, and your overcoat is in the front hall."

Feeling like a little boy trailing after his mother as she got him ready for school, he followed Moira to the vestibule. She helped him into his overcoat, then snagged her own before picking up two briefcases.

"What is it with you people?" a strident voice bawled from upstairs. "Some of us are trying to sleep."

"Deirdre's awake," Moira announced.

A willowy redhead, clutching a jewel-toned silk kimono around her, appeared at the top of the stairs. "Did you leave any coffee?" she grumbled, yawning and stretching.

"Mrs. Spencer just brewed a fresh pot," Moira informed her sister.

"Thank God for small favors," the redhead groused.

"Late night?" Sarcasm lurked just below Moira's cheery question. "Let's see, was it the polo player or the musician?"

"Neither, for your information," Deirdre snapped as she stumbled down the stairs.

Patrick sighed. His oldest daughter would never change. "What time did you get home?" He asked out of habit, but wasn't sure he wanted the answer.

Deirdre ignored his question. "As soon as I get my coffee, I'm going back to bed," she announced imperially.

Patrick turned to Moira who only shrugged her shoulders at Deirdre's behavior, the gesture commenting on both her sister's rudeness and her lifestyle. Shaking his head in defeat, he motioned for Moira to precede him through the door. Not for the first time, he pondered the differences between his daughters.

****

Manannan glared at the Harper. "You will not get involved," he ordered.

Abhean glowered back, his hands clenching and unclenching at his sides. "Who are you to decide?" Sparks all but shot from his rage-filled eyes.

"As High King, I am the Timekeeper," Manannan roared. "I am the one who sees all the islands in the river of time, and it is I who will decide their fate."

"T'were just dreams," Abhean hedged.

Colors swirled around the two men, angry reds and bruised purples, as Manannan's fury breathed life into the wind. "Beware the fire dreams ignite." His voice cut through the space between them, a black dagger that barely pierced the righteous swell of Abhean's chest. The high king slapped his hands together. He disappeared in a blinding flash. A moment later, as the echoing thunderclap reverberated, Abhean followed.

Chapter 2

Duncan Ross shifted in his chair, and focused his attention on the small, bespectacled man sitting across from him. The man droned incessantly about the importance of electronic surveillance while Duncan scrutinized the rest of the men circled around the conference table.

He could all but read the thoughts of the older man sizing him up from the head of the table. Bradford Williams, CEO of the Williams Company. If the look on the man's face was any indication, Duncan had failed to impress him. Duncan kept his well-schooled expression ambiguous.

He'd cultivated his look as well, keeping his thick, dark hair long so it straggled over his ears and hung several inches below his collar. The faded jeans, scuffed boots, and bulky sweater he wore were chosen to undermine the confidence of men inhabiting a world where appearances made the difference and suits with styled haircuts were the norm. Slouched in his chair with a well-practiced, befuddled expression, Duncan didn't exactly try to present a commanding presence.

He had already dismissed the company CEO. The man's expensive clothing and manicure left no questions in his mind. *Suit*, he smirked silently, putting all the disdain he could muster into that pronouncement. Suits had done more to ruin the world and Duncan's personal life than he cared to admit. The bespectacled bantam across the table from him presented another story. Named Franklin, he should have been called Napoleon. What the man lacked in size, he tried to compensate for with sarcastic bluster.

"So what is your opinion, Mr. Ross? Is the system feasible?" Franklin asked. He arched a brow and looked positive he already knew the answer to his own question.

Duncan glanced at the charts spread in front of him. "If you say so," he drawled in his thick Scottish brogue.

Franklin harrumphed, looking around the table with an I-told-you-so air. "How much are we paying this consultant?" Sarcasm dripped off his tongue as caustic as battery acid.

The men at the table exchanged uneasy glances. Without warning, Duncan sprang to his feet, a lean jungle cat eying his prey. One moment he'd been lounging in his chair, the next he stood, relaxed but deadly. No one had seen him move, just as he'd anticipated.

Still seated, the men all had to crane their necks to look up at him. At six feet four inches tall, Duncan's legs and shoulders were so well proportioned his true size was deceiving, another *something* he cultivated to his advantage. He watched Williams, amused he'd caught the man completely off guard.

"Gentlemen, you don't need me." Nodding curtly, Duncan snagged his worn leather jacket from the back of his chair and strode across the room toward the door.

"So much for so-called experts," Franklin sneered as he stood up.

Duncan stopped dead still. He pivoted, executing a classic military about-face. Like an entomologist pinning a slightly distasteful insect specimen to a board, Duncan's gaze impaled the little man and held him in place. He took great pleasure in watching the little bantam squirm.

"A boy scout with a Swiss army knife could break through your defenses. You don't need me, gentlemen. You need an army."

"One of the top firms in the business designed this system," Williams protested.

"The terrorists you seem so concerned about are also tops in their field, Mr. Williams," Duncan replied, his voice frigid. "I've seen their handiwork, gentlemen. Up close and personal. They're willing to die for their cause. Are you willing to die for yours?"

Three of the men still seated at the table glanced nervously at each other. Franklin hadn't moved since the moment he'd caught the full brunt of Duncan's glare. Of all those present only Williams appeared calm, but the fingers of one hand tapped the tabletop, belying his outward demeanor.

"I thought not." Duncan lowered his voice. "The weak link in your system is and always has been the reliance on human intervention. Men with families and bills to pay don't fare well against fanatics. Men with families want to go home at the end of their shift, alive and in one piece. Men with debts can be bought."

"That's a very cynical attitude, Mr. Ross." Williams thumped his fist on the mahogany table as if to reassert control of the situation. Too dense to understand he'd never been in control, Duncan wasn't in the mood to remind him.

"These are very cynical times, Mr. Williams," Duncan replied, keeping his voice even. He stared at each of the men, his smile mocking them. Unblinking, he returned and leaned over the CEO's shoulder. "Just ask the people of Northern Ireland." He whispered for Williams' ears alone.

15

One of the junior suits finally worked up the courage to squeak, "So what do we do?"

"Nothing." The word hung suspended in the thick silence that followed. Duncan waited a long moment, letting the men stew a bit before continuing. "The bottom line with you people is and always has been money. Your current security system and procedures are adequate for your needs. You can pat yourselves on the back at the next stockholders' meeting as you tell the investors you've saved the company a small fortune."

Another man looked up, his expression hopeful. "Are you saying we aren't a potential target after all?"

Optimistic murmurs whispered around the table.

Duncan reined in the disgust welling up from the pit of his stomach. "Only a mad dog bites the hand that feeds him," he answered cryptically. He headed for the door again, reaching it this time and pulling it open. "I'll return my fee," he tossed over his shoulder.

Williams studied the wood grain patterns of the table in front of him. Without looking up, he said, "Keep it, Mr. Ross. You've earned it."

Without so much as a backward glance, Duncan glided across the outer office, his legs eating up the distance to the elevators, not altogether oblivious of the feminine sighs he left in his wake. He ignored them, wanting only to get on the elevator and get away from the suits in the conference room.

****

Inside the conference room, nervous men waited to be told what to do. Franklin remained uncharacteristically silent. He refused to meet his boss's stare.

William Bradford continued to steeple his fingers, contemplating what had just happened.

16

When Duncan Ross, so-called security expert arrived, his first thought had been, *Ex-military, my ass.* He'd obviously misjudged the quiet, unassuming man. He would not make that mistake twice, especially in light of the cryptic message Ross whispered in his ear. How much did the big Scotsman actually know?

****

Standing on the sidewalk outside the building, Duncan gulped a breath deep enough to fill his lungs. Washington's smoggy air seemed cleaner than what he'd been breathing for the past several hours. Glancing up the street, he spotted a sign advertising a small tavern. Dealing with men like those in the offices twenty stories above him always left a bad taste in his mouth.

He pushed through the front door of the tavern and paused for a moment, adjusting his vision to the dark interior. He glanced around, assessing the place. Faux English pub. He stalked to the bar, hooked the stool with his foot, and settled his big frame onto it. He glanced at the bartender as the man slapped a coaster in front of him.

"Glenfiddich," he ordered.

A moment later, a highball glass three-quarters full of amber liquid appeared on the coaster, the glass devoid of ice. Scotch was meant to be drunk neat with a splash of water, but most Americans were oblivious to the finer nuances of taste. They wanted theirs on the rocks, the glass filled with ice. Duncan took an experimental sip, swishing the contents around in his mouth before swallowing. It was Fiddich all right. He took another long sip. The Scotch forged a fiery trail all the way down to his stomach.

"We don't get many single malt drinkers around here." The bartender opened the conversation.

"Good Scotch is like good jazz," Duncan replied,

his voice a soft hum barely audible above the whirring fan overhead. He swirled the Scotch in the glass as he admired the amber lights glinting in the liquid.

When he didn't clarify, the bartender raised a questioning eyebrow. "How so?"

"They're both smooth and smoky."

The bartender nodded. "Yeah," he agreed. "I like that comparison." Another customer down the bar caught his attention and the man left Duncan to his solitary pursuit.

He kept track of the bartender as he mixed and served the other customer. The man stayed at the far end of the bar, exchanging pleasantries Duncan neither wanted, nor had time for. He finished his drink, left a twenty on the bar, and slipped out the door before the bartender realized he'd gone.

****

Williams returned to his private office. A hulking man, dwarfing the leather armchair he occupied, impatiently awaited him.

"An' did yee learn anything new?" the man growled, his Irish brogue so thick it dripped off his tongue like molasses.

Williams eased into his desk chair and rested his hands, fingertips pressed together like a church steeple, on the highly polished mahogany desktop. He stared down at his hands for a long moment, finally replying, "Mr. Ross bears watching."

The big man harrumphed. "I told yee that now, dinnit I." With a negligent shrug of his shoulders, he added, "He suspects more than he can prove."

"Are you sure he worked for British Intelligence?" Williams persisted, still trying to reconcile his image of the man who'd just left his conference room. The big man nodded. Williams huffed out a disgruntled breath. "Well, are you sure he no longer works for them?"

The hulk snorted, the sound both disdainful and dismissive. "Aye. Yee can be sure we took care of that long ago."

"So you keep telling me," Williams retorted. "But I've yet to see proof."

"The man was disgraced, Williams. The SAS couldn't wash their hands of 'im quick enough. Any information he might pass along 'twould only be dismissed. He's considered an embarrassing lunatic now. What about the senator, Williams? My friends are getting a bit anxious."

"I told you I'd handle him," he snapped. This man and his associates were beginning to try his patience.

"Well, see that yee handle it and soon, else my colleagues will handle it their own way," the man drawled.

"You just take care of Duncan Ross," Williams demanded. He didn't appreciate the blatant threat.

"Oh, that's somethin' yee can bank on," the man vowed.

****

Gemma Todd pushed away the box of watercolors and fought the urge to crumple the sketch she'd been painting. Out of habit, she brushed her fingers through her short auburn hair, fluffing it. Exasperated, her full, sensuous lips pouted as she grimaced at the sketches littering her worktable.

"I'm an up and coming interior designer." She said the words out loud, like a mantra. A national magazine had even done a spread on her last project—a garden house for one of Washington's more prominent society matrons. She prided herself in staying away from fads, which made her current project an absolute nightmare. "The client is always right, and I have to finish these sketches." Her client wanted to frame the three-dimensional room renderings for display at her house. The corner of an ivory card peeked out from under one of the sketches. Gemma retrieved it, rereading the heavily embossed invitation.

Mr. and Mrs. Allen Steele
Request the pleasure of your company
For a celebration in honor of St. Patrick's Day
And to christen our new home
Friday through Sunday
Faerie Glen Farm
Charlottesville, Virginia
R.S.V.P.

She smiled. Even though Margaret Steele's tastes annoyed her and even if Margaret insisted the house be decorated in English Country Castle, thereby resplendent with paisleys, plaids and chintz, Gemma actually looked forward to the upcoming weekend. Margaret was positively famous in Washington circles for her parties. The social events the Steeles hosted were always attended by the rich and powerful—the very people she hoped to attract as clients. Upon discovering she had a live-in, Margaret had been gracious enough to include Duncan.

Her indulgent smile changed to a seductive leer at the thought of him. Duncan Ross was the most fascinating man she'd ever met. A surge of thwarted passion made her stomach flutter. Dark, mysterious, with a hint of danger, he could be a poster boy for Sexy Bad Boy. Since his peculiar dream several nights ago, he hadn't touched her and she planned to change things this weekend. She would see to it. She knew firsthand just how romantic Faerie Glen could be. Before Duncan entered her life, she'd tried out the Laura Ashley bedroom with the willing assistance of one of the painters. A smug cat-and-cream smirk curled her lips. She'd made up her mind she would be the one to tame the wild

Scotsman. Pushing thirty, it was time to settle down. She'd never wanted a man like she wanted Duncan. He could do things to her body, make her feel things no man ever had. Her smile grew wider. Yes, this weekend would be lovely.

Chapter 3

Patrick looked up at the light tap on his office door. "Come in," he called.

Moira opened the door and as if it were a white flag, she waved a suit bag in his direction. Patrick smiled at his daughter.

"Monkey suit," she hinted.

The senator glanced at the expensive watch on his wrist. "I didn't realize it was so late." He offered an apologetic smile.

Moira glanced at the stack of papers on his desk. "Mid-East or budget?" she asked.

"Take your pick." He rubbed his temple. As chairman of the Senate's Armed Services committee, he received daily memos on the world's hot spots. With the Cold War over and the war on terrorism hot, the United States' position in the world order was being redefined on a daily basis.

"Tonight will give you a break." Moira flashed a smile meant to encourage him. "The only thing these people want is a bit of blarney from their favorite Irish senator. Put your work way. It's time to get ready." The senator glanced at her, noticing the navy business suit she wore. He arched one eyebrow and chuckled at the look on Moira's face. She called the expression his question mark face. She rolled her eyes at him. "I'm going home to change," she admitted. "Even I know the fashion police would arrest me for wearing a business suit to a formal affair. I'll meet you at the hotel."

"I'll have Darrel drive you."

Moira shook her head. "Darrel is under strict orders to deliver you to the front door of the hotel absolutely no later than seven. I'll take a cab."

She was gone before he could protest further. As he unzipped the suit bag, he knew everything he'd possibly need would be packed there. Nothing if not thorough, Moira had even packed the green plaid bow tie and cummerbund bought just for St. Patrick's Day many years ago.

****

Moira waded into the sea of motley greens swirling through the hotel lobby. An inebriated young man stumbled up to her, a bright green button proclaiming "Kiss me, I'm Irish" dangling from his lapel. Weaving drunkenly, the man tried to plant a kiss on Moira's lips.

From a vantage point across the room, a slender man watched as she politely steered the drunk away. He wondered if everything he'd heard about the senator's daughter was true. She had her thick blonde hair twisted into a business-like knot at the nape of her neck. Small, tasteful emeralds, her only ornamentation, glimmered at her ears and throat. The long-sleeved, high-necked black velvet cocktail dress she wore looked almost chaste, even though the fitted bodice and flared skirt showed off a good figure, though one more curvaceous than the current fashion. A Kelly green rose, the same color as the satin shawl draped over her arm, accented the flounced skirt. The colorful touches did little to alleviate the austere picture she presented. The girl probably was all business and no play, as he'd heard through the grapevine.

A laughing couple pushed through the door behind her. He shared her wince at their use of theatrical Irish brogues. In a hurry and paying no attention, they brushed past. The man stumbled into her and Moira teetered on her high heels, fighting to regain her balance.

He arrived beside her in a moment, his hands steadying her as he whispered conspiratorially in her ear, "At least they're only Irish once a year, *cailín*." Moira pulled away and turned sharply to face him. "Michael Shanahan." He extended his hand in introduction.

"Moira O'Connor," she replied, taking his hand. Moira smiled as their fingers touched.

"Am I that amusin', then?" His voice came out gruffer than he'd intended, but something about her knowing smile put his guard up.

"Not at all," Moira assured. "In fact, I think you are a most studious man."

Michael looked askance, puzzled by her statement. "I guess me secret's out then, but how did yee know?"

"Know what?" Moira looked perplexed.

"That I'm a professor."

She smiled again as she shook her head slightly. "I didn't know," she admitted. "How interesting."

Michael watched her for a long moment before finally smiling back at her, even though his suspicions weren't allayed. "You must be very intuitive, Miss O'Connor." His voice carried a slight edge, and he'd dropped his broader accent. Though a true Irishman, he could wear his accent as needed. "I see your father hasn't arrived yet," he continued. "I was sent to fetch the two of you and escort you to the dinner."

He followed her gaze as Moira glanced at the clock behind the hotel concierge desk. Five minutes to seven. Before she could reply, Michael nodded toward the front door. "Ah, here he is at last. Now I won't be havin' to fight my way through these blasted pagans twice." He grinned and winked. When she grinned back, the twinkle in her eyes surprised him.

Senator O'Connor strode through the doors and immediately spotted Moira. As he walked up, she introduced the man at her side. "Senator, this is Professor Michael Shanahan. Professor Shanahan is one of our hosts this evening."

The two men shook hands. "What is your field, Professor?"

"Irish literature."

Moira chuckled. "Why does that not surprise me, Professor Shanahan?"

"Please, call me Michael," he requested, ushering them toward the back of the lobby.

Though small, Michael was quick and sure as he forged a path for them across the crowded room. As the noisy celebration faded behind them, he led them down a hallway. The jaunty notes of an Irish ditty drifted from behind closed doors at the end of the long hall, spilling out as he opened the door. A hum of conversation murmured under the music. He led his two guests to the VIP table at the front of the room, made the necessary introductions, then excused himself.

Michael settled in at his own assigned table, and listened to the conversations ebbing and flowing around him. Once she found out he had steady employment, the large lady on his left became particularly interested in his marital status. During the course of their dinner conversation, Michael learned the woman had an unmarried daughter employed as a secretary at the State Department. He filed that tidbit of information away. A few dinners and some dancing could well be worth his while. He'd be sure to get the daughter's name and number before the evening ended. He listened as his gaze roamed across the room, watching and analyzing the people in attendance. Even so, he missed one.

The dark, brooding man occupied a seat at a table in the far corner of the room. All during dinner, he covetously eyed the head table. His ego demanded he should be sitting up there with the bigwigs, even though the more rational part of his mind told him he had to stay in the background for a while longer yet. He declined coffee or tea with his meal, preferring the burning delight of straight whiskey.

Though others at the table chatted and laughed, his manner discouraged any attempts to include him. He sulked in his corner, watching the blonde sitting next to the senator. Downright plain, she still had a body that could pleasure a man. Thoughts of what he would do to her if they were alone occupied him for the first part of the evening. He wolfed down his dinner and then settled back for the after-dinner show.

The president of the Irish-American Coalition made some brief opening remarks about this being a celebration not a political rally. Then he introduced Senator O'Connor to a round of hearty chuckles and a smattering of applause.

The dinner had been better than most on the rubber chicken circuit, as Moira's full stomach could attest. Prime rib, salad, and baked potatoes definitely hit the spot. Contented, she settled back into her chair to listen. She'd timed her father's speech to last ten minutes, give or take some time for applause. She wasn't disappointed. The audience clapped in all the right places and laughed at all the puns she had intended. The senator finished to a rousing ovation twelve minutes after he'd begun. Moira smiled. Give them just enough to make them happy, but always finish leaving them wanting more. She'd learned that lesson from a veteran speechwriter and followed his advice religiously.

Their host thanked the senator and announced the open bar. The band struck up a lively air as people stood up to stretch. Most of the men headed to the bar while the ladies excused themselves. A few intrepid couples took to the dance floor.

Looking determined, Michael appeared at Moira's side. "May I have a dance with the loveliest cailín in the room?" he asked, complete with a gallant bow.

Moira studied him for a moment. A slight man in his forties, he stood only an inch or two taller. Ruddy cheeks complemented his curly brown hair while clear, blue eyes met her own with a steady gaze. She stood up and offered her hand to the little scholar. "And when did you last kiss the Blarney Stone, Professor?" she teased.

On the dance floor, Michael, quite nimble on his feet, led her through the intricate steps of a traditional Irish jig. She had no trouble keeping up with him. He looked both surprised and impressed. The jig ended and the band began a more sedate tune. Michael never missed a beat as he continued dancing with her. He twirled her away, but before he could reclaim her, a new pair of hands grabbed her shoulders.

"Time yee danced with a real man, m'darlin'," a husky voice growled in her ear.

Moira crinkled her nose at the smell of stale whiskey on the man's breath. Before she could pull away, he grabbed her around the waist, his strong fingers brutally biting into the soft flesh of her sides. She couldn't stifle the shudder running through her as the man whisked her away between other dancers. Her new partner led her in a dizzying dance across the floor, and she quickly lost sight of Michael. She stumbled and the brute pulled her up against him, molding his fleshy body to hers. Fear stabbed through her middle and she gagged.

"Let me go," Moira demanded through clenched teeth.

"What? An' let the prize of the evenin' slip through me fingers?" the man growled. "Yer daft, girl, if yee think I'm lettin' yee get away."

She glared up at him, assessing her opponent. The man had to be over six feet tall with broad shoulders and a barrel chest. His body was thick and she guessed he weighed more than two hundred and fifty pounds. Some women might have considered him handsome, with his jet-black hair and blazing blue eyes. *Black Irish, and in more ways than one.*

Enough was enough. She pressed her palms against his chest, and leveraged as much distance between them as his rough grip on her waist would allow. With a little room to maneuver now, she brought the spike of her left shoe down sharply on the man's right instep. His eyes widened with the sudden pain, but before he could react further, Moira shoved her left knee high between the man's legs. He immediately released his hold on her waist, and she stumbled back, as much from the malevolence radiating from him as from her sudden freedom.

Michael caught up to her seconds later. "Are you all right?" Panting from his mad dash through the other dancers, he could barely get the words out.

"Who is that man?"

"Seamus O'Rourke." Michael almost spat the name out as he steered her across the floor away from the other man.

She glanced over her shoulder. O'Rourke hobbled over to a chair on the edge of the dance floor. Turning back to Michael, she asked, "What do you know about him?" She glared at the little Irishman in front of her.

Michael shrugged. "Not much. He came over from Belfast about six months ago."

"IRA?"

Her question caught Michael off guard and he answered without thinking, "We can't prove it for sure."

Moira flashed him a knowing smile. "There's definitely more to you than meets the eye, Michael Shanahan." She kept her voice low and touched him on the arm. "Thank you for the dance." She had to find her father. Weaving through the throng as if she was part of the dance, she headed toward the bar. Politics in Northern Ireland were always at the boiling point, and only a fool would underestimate the influence of the IRA. The senator's stand on the Irish question was well known and the possibility an IRA agent might be present was cause for concern. Moira found him clustered with a group of men near the bar. She caught his eye and a few moments later, he excused himself to join her. He'd known from the look she gave him something had occurred.

"There's a man here by the name of Seamus O'Rourke." Moira leaned against him, her lips brushing his cheek as she spoke.

The senator nodded. "I met him earlier," he acknowledged, then added his own assessment. "A rather gruff man for his profession. He runs an Irish antique and gift shop over in Bethesda. In fact," he said, pausing to dig in a pocket, "I have his business card right here."

"Antiques may not be the only thing he runs, Da."

Her implied message was not lost on the senator. He'd learned to trust her instincts over the years. Her gut had never failed him, and she knew he'd follow her advice now. Taking her arm, they strolled over to the head table as if they didn't have a care in the world. While Moira gathered her wrap, the senator thanked their hosts. Claiming an early breakfast meeting and a need for clear heads, they took their leave.

A light rain fell as the two of them exited from the hotel. Within moments, their car rolled to a stop in the drive-thru. Using a colorful umbrella to shield the two from the rain, the doorman escorted them to the car and held the door open. Patrick slipped the man a tip as he climbed in after Moira. As soon as the doorman shut the car door, the car pulled out of the hotel drive, merging smoothly with traffic.

"Anywhere else you want to go, Senator?" the driver asked, glancing in the rear view mirror.

"No, Darrel. We're done for the evening."

"Then home it is, sir," Darrel acknowledged.

****

Two men sat in a dark sedan parked down the block from the hotel. They watched the big Lincoln pull up in front of the hotel and waited while the man and woman climbed into the back seat. The driver started the engine of the rental car. As the Lincoln merged in with the late evening traffic, the driver deftly negotiated his vehicle into a position several cars back from it. From that position, they could easily trail the senator's car without being noticed.

"'Tis a nice bit o' fluff on the senator's arm," the driver drawled, his lecherous thoughts obvious by the tone of his voice.

"Don't be daft, man," the passenger chided. "'Tis his daughter."

"Well, now," the driver mused. "Is that a fact?"

The driver didn't notice his partner's tight smile as it twisted the man's narrow lips into a grimace. "Aye," the passenger snarled, his voice low and husky. "'Tis a fact for certain."

****

Michael watched the senator's car pull away. The evening had proved to be an interesting one. Ever the consummate politician, Senator O'Connor proved not much of a surprise. His daughter, though,

30

was an entirely different story. With her blue eyes twinkling and the saucy grin she'd flashed while they danced, Moira O'Connor looked almost pretty. He brushed his fingers through his hair, a nervous gesture he made without conscious thought. What if the girl intentionally made herself look plain? He couldn't for his life understand why a cailín would want to, but then the female mind remained a mystery to him. Even as he shrugged the thought away, he decided the senator's daughter bore some watching. His gut told him there was a lot more to her than met the eye.

Chapter 4

The hair on the back of Duncan's neck bristled. Since walking through the wide doors of the barn, his sense of *déjà vu* had been in overdrive. Something about this stable seemed familiar, in a disturbing way. He couldn't put his finger on the cause for his uneasiness, so he tried to nudge it away. He glanced over at Gemma, still in deep conversation with the distinguished older man who was their host. He tuned back into their discussion.

"Did you really have the whole thing shipped over from Ireland?" Gemma gushed and flirted, hoping to score points with the man.

Allen Steele nodded, beaming proudly. "When we first saw it, the old place was all but a ruin. The farmer intended to tear it down and use the stones for fencing. When Margaret discovered it was fourteenth century, she fell in love with it." He paused for a moment and looked sheepish. With an embarrassed shrug, he added, "I had to buy it."

Gemma smiled and nodded, waiting for him to continue.

"Our contractor flew over to supervise the whole process. They numbered each stone as the place was dismantled so it could be reassembled here. Unfortunately, none of the wood could be salvaged so we had to replace all of it. I'm most pleased with the restoration."

Duncan caught sight of a pile of hay spilling out of an empty stall toward the back of the building. With acute clarity, the memory of his dream crowded out everything else in his mind. His cock hardened at the mere hint of the dream and the woman who'd shared it with him.

"Duncan? Duncan!" The shrill demand in Gemma's voice snapped him back to reality. He looked over at her. "What in the world were you thinking about, Dunnie?" She looked both vexed and perplexed. She cut her eyes toward their host, her meaning plain. *Don't mess this up for me!*

The corner of his mouth quirked in a wicked grin, but he wasn't really seeing Gemma. He shifted his stance to ease the tightness of his jeans. "Just a fondness for stables."

Gemma stared at him and suddenly blushed. Her lips curved into a seductive smile. She deliberately took a deep breath, her chest rising and falling to call attention to her breasts.

In the half-light of the stable, Allen couldn't see their expressions. He turned toward Duncan. "Do you ride, Mr. Ross?"

Duncan's nonchalant shrug implied "a little."

"Feel free to ride any of the horses while you are here, Mr. Ross. I have some very fine animals, and I'm sure you'll be able to find one to your liking. I don't ride near as often as the horses would like. Just let my stable manager know, and he'll have one saddled for you." Allen returned his attention to Gemma. "Did Margaret mention Senator O'Connor and his daughters will also be staying here for the weekend?"

"Senator Patrick O'Connor?" Duncan was all ears now.

"Why, yes," Allen replied. He seemed taken aback by Duncan's sudden interest. "Do you know him?"

He reined in his curiosity. "Not personally," Duncan dissembled. "He's been in the news recently." It wouldn't do to show his hand this early in the game.

"Interesting man," Allen mused, his expression unreadable. Duncan didn't want to play poker with this man. "He has quite a collection of antiques, including several pieces I'd like to add to my own collection."

Gemma seized the opportunity to change topics. "Are you still collecting old weapons, Allen?"

"Why of course, my dear. I have to admit, besides my wife, my weapons collection is my on-going passion."

"You should talk to Dunnie, then. Maybe he'll sell you some of those nasty old things collecting dust in my warehouse."

Allen eyed Duncan with renewed interest. "Are you a collector, Mr. Ross?"

"Please, sir, call me Duncan. And no, I wouldn't classify myself as a collector. I have a few family pieces that were handed down to me."

"He's much too modest, Allen," Gemma interrupted. She placed her hand on Duncan's forearm and squeezed. He knew she needed to impress these people for business purposes. That's all she'd talked about on the drive, reiterating how important it was for Duncan to also gain their approval. She batted her lashes at him. "What do you call that big, fat sword, Duncan? The one with the fancy handle?"

"It's a battle sword, Gemma." He kept his voice patient. She'd pulled him in too deep to gracefully retreat now.

"What century?" Allen's curiosity was piqued.

"It's believed to be the ninth. Perhaps earlier."

"Old family piece?" Allen looked incredulous. "That's what you call a ninth century Norman broadsword? Duncan, you do astound me."

He shrugged. "I didn't say it was Norman," he corrected, "and it isn't a broadsword." Allen stared at him, all but rubbing his hands in his eagerness to hear more. "It's a Celtic battle sword, handed down through my mother's family," Duncan finally added when he realized the conversation would go no further without an explanation.

Allen all but hopped from foot to foot in the effort to contain his excitement. "Now I know Patrick will be most interested in you, young man. He has a Celtic dagger I would almost kill for."

A *miodóg*, Duncan thought, putting the Irish name to the dagger. The fervor in Allen's voice was disconcerting. He shrugged and assumed a bemused look. Steele was a shrewd businessman, a ruthless opponent in the boardroom or on the playing fields. Duncan wondered what the man would do if Allen realized he carried a fourteenth century Scottish *skean dhu* in his boot even as they spoke. While most modern daggers were for ceremonial or costume use only, his *skean dhu* was a deadly weapon. Duncan needed to divert the man's attention from weaponry. "How many other guests are you expecting?"

"Quite a few, I'm afraid," Allen admitted. "Margaret is determined to fill the house to the rafters. And speaking of her, I should return to the big house to help out. Feel free to stay down here as long as you like. Cocktails are at seven with a buffet to follow."

As soon as Allen disappeared from sight, Gemma shimmied her body against him like Jell-o in a mold. "So tell me, Dunnie," she purred. "What makes you so fond of stables?" Her hands pushed past his leather jacket and jerked out his shirttail so she could press her palms against his skin.

Duncan shrank from the touch of her fingers,

but tried to hide the fact. "What has come over you, Gemma?" His voice sounded gruff on purpose.

"I saw the look you gave me." Her voice deepened, husky with suppressed desire. "I've never done it in a stable, Dunnie." She nuzzled the soft skin under his chin. "Come on," she begged. Standing on tiptoe as she tried to kiss his mouth, her hand groped his groin.

Duncan pushed her away before she could touch his erection, knowing she'd misunderstand. Gemma stumbled backwards and fell through the open stall door to land in the pile of hay. Shapely thighs peeked from beneath the peasant skirt she wore, and her poet's blouse dipped precariously over her right shoulder, revealing the top of a softly rounded breast. Gemma pouted, her gray eyes going smoky.

She missed the disparaging look he gave her. Gemma had always been aggressive in their relationship, and her behavior had suited him once. Ever since his dream, though, the thought of being with her repulsed him. In fact, the thought of being with any woman but the blue-eyed vixen in his dream was abhorrent. His feelings had changed through no fault of Gemma's and a small pang of guilt plastered a smile on his face to compensate for his lack of them.

"I have done it in a stable, and it's damned uncomfortable. That big, fluffy bed in our room seems much more inviting." Duncan reached down and hauled her to her feet. He gave her a quick buss on the mouth, playfully pushed her toward the door, and swatted her bottom. "Get thee hence, wench. You heard the man. Cocktails at seven, and I intend to have the most beautiful woman in the room on my arm."

Gemma rubbed against him like a hungry cat. "Promises, promises," she all but purred. "I'll hold you to a romp in that bed later." Her mouth puckered into a pouting moue as she batted her lashes at him. "Just remember you're mine, darling." She strolled back toward the house, her hips swaying in obvious invitation.

Duncan grimaced at her retreating figure. He uttered a low growl beneath his breath, "I'm my own man, Gemma." A soft snort and warm breath on the back of his neck made him turn around. A blood red sorrel whinnied and tossed his head through the open window on the stall door. Duncan reached up to scratch the big horse behind the ear, and the animal's liquid brown eyes shone with gratitude. Giving his new friend a last friendly pat on his muscular neck, Duncan strode out resolutely. It wasn't fair to punish Gemma for his obsession with a pair of haunting blue eyes. Besides, he owed her one for the invitation this weekend. The guest list grew more interesting by the minute. Determined to make amends, he headed through the gardens toward the main house.

****

The tires on the big Lincoln whispered against the highway pavement, the sound a muted backdrop to the sporadic conversation inside. The three passengers didn't notice the rolling countryside of central Virginia exhibited the first signs of spring. Like a Seurat painting, green buds dotted skeletal tree branches while daffodils and tulips splashed bright colors against the dull canvas of winter grass. The long trip from Washington was made longer by Deirdre's continuous whining. Even now, less than an hour from their destination, she continued to berate their mode of transportation.

"This would have been a much better trip if we'd chartered a helicopter," Deirdre groused under her breath, but still loud enough for all to hear. "We'd already be there if we had."

Moira teased her sister with a smile meant to

lighten the mood with some levity. "You just want to make a big entrance."

"And what's wrong with that?" Deidre hissed. "Unlike you, I enjoy being noticed."

"Relax, Dee. Margaret always invites more eligible men than women. I'm sure you'll have plenty to choose from at the party tonight."

Moira was ever the peacemaker and Patrick knew she wanted only to placate her sister. He gazed at his daughters. *How can they be sisters?* he wondered for the umpteenth time. Day and night. Fire and ice. That simile curled the corners of his mouth, though he hid the smile. In his last campaign, a reporter had made the same distinction, and it was very apropos. Tall, willowy, with her mane of red hair, and blazing emerald eyes, Deirdre never failed to elicit notice. Moira, with her silvery blonde hair and clear, sapphire eyes tended to fade into the background whenever the two stood together, just like the moon being outshone by the sun.

Moira was slightly shorter and more sturdily built than Deirdre. Her broad shoulders tapered to a slim waist from which muscular legs flared. Moira was built like an athlete, Deirdre a model. Moira was levelheaded and calm, serenely sailing through the most turbulent seas of his political life. Deirdre, true to her red hair, was easily provoked and quick to lash out in anger.

He watched his younger daughter. She hadn't always been so composed. He refused to dwell on that distressing and painful period in their lives.

The car slowed, and then turned onto a gravel lane. Huge stone pillars flanked the drive, and a polished brass plate proclaimed "Faerie Glen Farm" in ornate Old English letters.

"Leave it to Aunt Margaret to come up with such a corny name," Deirdre snorted. Her mood hadn't improved during the last ten miles.

"I think it's charming," Moira replied, a gentle reproach hiding in her soft voice.

"You would," Deirdre sneered. A sharp look from her father silenced her before she added any further insult.

Patrick reached over and patted Moira's hand. "Margaret will love your gift."

When Deidre snorted again, Patrick cleared his throat, favoring her with another pointed stare. Moira was proud of the housewarming gift she'd carefully packed in her suitcase. While shopping in Old Baltimore, Moira discovered the Tiffany-style lamp. She told Patrick the stained glass shade depicting a band of faeries dancing through a garden was perfect. Without hesitation, she'd bought it for the Steeles, knowing Margaret would love it.

The gravel road changed to brick as it curved around a peninsula of ancient oaks. The main house stood, displayed in all its resplendent glory, atop a low hill. Built of gray granite, mansard roofs and battlements jostled with mullioned windows in a crazy quilt of architectural styles. Norman castle, French chateau, Tudor manor house—each style found a place in a patchwork that should have been hideously Gothic but somehow, the sheer mass of the building made it intriguing and appealing instead.

"Charming," Deirdre declared, her flat tone a sarcastic echo of Moira's earlier declaration.

Patrick gaped at the house. Like her father, Moira found it a bit overwhelming, too. Up until this moment, they'd only seen architectural drawings of the structure. A vague sense of dread settled around her. She pressed her hands against her middle. Gray clouds swept across the sun, and shadows rippled over the house's facade. Moira felt weak and then she mentally shook herself. She sat up straighter and craned her neck to see out the window, watching for the garrulous Margaret Steele.

When the car rolled to a smooth stop, Patrick didn't wait for Darrel. He opened the back door and climbed out.

Ever faithful to life-long habits, Margaret waited on the broad stone steps leading to the front entry. A petite woman in her late fifties, Margaret could easily pass for younger. All the advantages of a life of wealth kept her trim and attractive. Her chin-length, light brown hair had subtle hints of sunny highlights and artfully applied makeup gave her skin a youthful glow. She was dressed in Fifth Avenue's version of a genteel countrywoman. A teal corduroy blazer with leather elbow patches topped a heather tweed wool skirt, which brushed the tops of hand-made brown leather riding boots. The boots looked almost clumsy on her small feet.

Her green eyes sparkled with good humor. Patrick waved and Margaret waved back. When Deidre emerged from the car, followed by Moira, the three of them climbed the broad steps to meet their hostess.

"Patrick," Margaret gushed as she stretched to give him a peck on the cheek. "And Deirdre," she continued, kissing the redhead on both cheeks. "You're as beautiful as ever, my darling. Moira, my sweet child. I'm so pleased all of you are here. Come in. Come in. We'll have tea and coffee in the sitting room. Or would you like to freshen up first? I forget how long that drive from Washington can seem." She prattled on, not giving her guests the chance to answer any of her questions.

As Moira crossed the threshold, that sense of dread she'd first felt upon seeing the house returned to clutch her heart. Deep down, she knew if she stayed in this house, her life would be forever changed. This was one of those rare, defining moments in her life, and she found herself rooted to the spot, unable to move.

Like a mother hen, Margaret fussed over her guests, politely herding them in the direction she wanted them to go, chattering the whole time. Almost to the sitting room, Margaret turned, counting noses, and realized one of her chicks was missing. Her gaze met Moira's. Still flustered and shaken, she stood just inside the massive front doors, her feet rooted to the beautiful inlaid wood floor of the entry hall. She couldn't breathe for the weight pressing against her chest, and she couldn't hear for the pounding of the blood in her veins.

Margaret rushed to her side. "What's the matter, dear? Are you feeling ill?" The woman clucked and fussed.

Moira forced air into her lungs and willed her heart to slow its hammering beat. "I'm fine, Margaret," she assured her hostess. "Just a little tired."

"Patrick, you're working this poor child too hard," Margaret scolded. "I know a weekend in this marvelous country air is just what you need, Moira." The woman patted Moira's hand maternally. "Why don't you go up to your room and lie down for a bit, dear. Simpson will show you the way. I'll have Cook send up a light repast to munch on while you're resting."

Moira glanced at the tall, angular man who had magically appeared at the mention of his name. In dark gray-striped trousers, black morning coat, vest, starched white shirt, and narrow black tie, he appeared the epitome of an English butler. Moira wasn't a bit surprised when, with a cultured English accent, the man asked her to please follow him.

Climbing the massive stone staircase in the butler's wake, Moira took stock of her surroundings. The front entry hall was styled after a Norman castle. Soaring from two to three stories tall, the hall made the huge tapestries depicting medieval battle scenes hanging on its walls seem small. A glut of coats of arms and ancient weapons littered the whole place. Moira smiled. No one had ever accused Margaret and Allen Steele of doing anything in moderation.

At the landing, Simpson led her up the right staircase, explaining the family wing was to the left. Moira looked up to find a full suit of armor standing guard at the top of the stairs. A quick glance over her shoulder revealed its companion on the other staircase. A little shiver ran down her back. The faceless guardians, cold and remote, looked forbidding.

Like sentinels, a series of heavy wooden doors faced each other down the length of the hallway. Thick rugs strewn across the oak floor muffled their footsteps as Moira followed Simpson. Passing one door, Moira heard giggles followed by a husky murmur. She hesitated at the door as a wave of jealousy slammed into her. The emotion was so intense, she almost fell to her knees. She actually had to squeeze her hands together to keep from pounding on the door. Unnerved by her reaction, she stumbled in her rush to catch up to Simpson.

At the door to her room, Simpson stood aside so she could precede him. Her luggage was already neatly stacked on a small chest in the corner of the room. A maid wearing a black dress, frilly white apron, and mop cap ducked through the door behind the angular butler. She carried a tray and, with great care so as not to rattle the cup or pot, set it on the bedside table.

"Will there be anything else, miss?" Simpson asked, as reserved and formal in his speech as he was in his bearing.

"No, thank you, Simpson."

The butler dipped his head, the gesture more

regal than subservient, motioned the maid to go, then backed out of the room, and softly closed the door behind him.

As soon as the door clicked shut, Moira pounced on the tray. Scones, still steaming from the oven, nestled under an embroidered cloth. She bent low and drew the scent of the hot pastries deep into her lungs. Silver pots of whipped butter, clotted cream, and lemon curd nestled next to a porcelain carafe filled with café au lait. This "light repast" was more than Moira could have asked for. She kicked off her shoes and climbed up into the tall four-poster bed, sinking into the thick, eiderdown mattress. Moira buttered a warm scone, spooned on some cream, leaned back against the comfortable pile of pillows, and relaxed.

The room was an advertisement for Laura Ashley—all ruffles, lace, chintz stripes and flowers. The wallpaper, curtains, and bed coverings all coordinated. Even the pattern of the dainty china cup from which she drank matched the wallpaper. The peach and pale green rug reflected other patterns in the room. Even the white, French provincial furniture in the room she'd occupied as a child couldn't come close to the frill factor of this room.

Moira chuckled. Leave it to Margaret to choose this room for her, the most tailored, and straight-laced of the O'Connor bunch.

Happily ensconced, she finished off the scone and her coffee. Setting aside the cup and dessert plate, she flopped back, her hands tucked behind her head as she stared up at the ceiling. Moira couldn't help but worry about the weekend. Margaret was always full of surprises. She definitely had her work cut out for this trip.

Chapter 5

Duncan lay on his back staring at the ceiling. For the past ten minutes, every extra sense he possessed had been on alert. When someone passed by the door moments ago, every synapse in his body fired. He attempted to sort out his feelings but wasn't having much luck. He could sense only a hint of danger associated with whatever had just transpired. For the first time... For the first time in ages, he felt truly and completely alive and aware. Once he admitted that, his curiosity was even more aroused.

Gemma cuddled up to his side, her fingers tracing lazy circles through the feathering of fine, dark hair sprinkled across his chest. "I've missed you, Dunnie," she murmured before kissing the hollow under his chin.

Duncan tried not to grit his teeth. He did not want to have sex, but stalling Gemma without hurting her feelings had been the hardest thing he'd done in quite awhile. In an attempt to mask his reluctance, Duncan rolled away from her to reach for his watch, which was lying on a table near the bed.

"We'd best be up and moving, Gemma," he said over his shoulder.

Gemma snuggled up to his back, her left arm snaking over his side. As her fingers played across his chest, she nipped his shoulder. "We have plenty of time," she drawled, her intentions plain.

"Later." Duncan refused to look at her. He slipped his watch over his hand. "It won't do to keep our hosts waiting." It wouldn't do to keep Gemma waiting either, but that's what would happen. He didn't believe he would be able to accomplish sex with her ever again, and for a man as lusty as he was, that was quite an admission.

****

It was pitch black. Moira knew her eyes were open but she couldn't see a thing. There were voices nearby—ugly, shrill voices, but she couldn't understand what they were saying. She only knew that the voices frightened her beyond all reason and she had to escape them. She clawed at the darkness, striving to tear a hole in it. Her heart pounded and her lungs sucked in ragged gasps of air. She was exhausted from her efforts.

"I can't breathe," she screamed but she didn't know if the words had come out or not. With her last ounce of strength, Moira pushed at the blackness. Like a flood crashing through a dam, sunlight tinged with watercolors washed over her.

Panting, she sat up and looked around. Through the ruffled curtains hanging at the wide window, the setting sun painted the clouds mauve and salmon. The evening gown she was to wear that night hung on the front of a massive cherry wood armoire.

Moira vaguely remembered the timid maid knocking at the door, asking if her dress needed to be pressed. She scrubbed at her forehead with the heels of her hands. She couldn't recall when the girl had returned the gown. She reached for the lamp on the bedside table and turned it on. Though it was barely dusk, she craved light.

Someone sang out in the hallway—a sweet, sad tune. Most of the words were indistinct but Moira caught something about faerie spirits and blackened ruins. She shuddered and pulled the fluffy down comforter up around her shoulders. The song ended with a light tapping at her door.

"Come in," she called.

The little maid poked her head around the door. "G'day, miss. I've come to see if there's anythin' yee be needin'?"

Listening to the lilt of the maid's voice, Moira stared at her for a moment. Dark curls sprang from beneath her cap and a light dusting of freckles across her nose added spice to her hazel eyes. "Ellie, isn't it?" Dimples appeared on the maid's cheeks, making her look even younger. "Was that you singing out in the hall?"

The dimples disappeared, and Ellie looked anxious. "I hope I wasn't disturbin' yee, miss?"

Moira smiled, hoping to alleviate the girl's concern. "On the contrary. You have a lovely voice."

Ellie's cheeks flushed a warm shade of rose. "Thank yee, miss."

"How long have you been in America?"

The little maid blushed even more. "I come over about six months ago. The missus hired me when she and the mister were in Dublin." Ellie moved across the room to the armoire. With delicate strokes, she fingered the rich sapphire blue taffeta skirt of the gown. "Will yee be needin' help to get dressed, miss?"

"No, thank you, Ellie. I can manage."

Disappointed, Ellie caressed the velvet bodice. "'Tis a lovely dress. Me thinks you'll look like a princess, miss."

Moira started to laugh. Her? A princess? Before she could retort, all the color drained from Ellie's face, and the girl flinched as if she'd been struck. She cocked her head as if listening to something.

"Do yee hear it, miss?" the little maid whispered, moving to the window to stare out.

Moira got out of bed. Standing at the window, she strained to hear something, anything. Almost as an afterthought, a few notes of music—a strange, haunting sound—drifted up from below. It sounded a bit like bagpipes, but like a harp as well.

Ellie's face was ashen. "'Tis the faerie folk," she murmured. Moira looked at her, her forehead furrowed in consternation. "They be callin' to someone," the little maid continued as she quickly crossed herself. "God have mercy upon this house."

Moira stared out the window. Far across the open lawn, a dark band of trees huddled in deepening dusk. Small flickers of light danced among the shadows. It was much too early in the year for fireflies—they didn't appear until early summer.

Dread crept up Moira's spine. Refusing to give into it this time, she turned away from the window. A moment later, Ellie did the same. The girl's fear was apparent as she glanced up at Moira. "Will there be anythin' else, miss?"

Guessing the maid wanted to escape "below stairs," she replied, "No. You can go now, Ellie." The girl practically trotted to the door.

"By the way," Moira called after her, "you can call me Moira."

The girl stopped dead in her tracks and genuflected again. Concerned, Moira took a step toward her. "Ellie? Is something wrong?"

The maid turned to face her, her hazel eyes wide. She reminded Moira of a frightened fawn. "I didn't know, miss, honestly," Ellie stammered.

Moira felt completely confused. "Didn't know what? You aren't making any sense, Ellie."

"'Tis an old tale, mum, about the fair Moira. She took a faerie lover and then..." Her voice trailed off.

Moira's breath caught in her throat but she swallowed around it. "Go on, Ellie."

The girl cleared her throat. "Not even her faerie warrior could save her, so the story goes. And when she died, he burnt the village to the ground to avenge her."

Moira's laughter bubbled out, rich and deep. "Oh, Ellie," she declared. "What makes this story different from a hundred other Irish tales? Why should you apologize because you know a story with my name in it?"

"The song, miss, the one I was singin'. 'Tis the song of Moira and her hero. I dinnit mean t'be disrespectful," Ellie explained.

Though intrigued because she'd never heard this tale, Moira still sought to reassure the girl. "You had no idea of my name, Ellie. But, you do have my curiosity up. Would you sing the whole song for me?"

Before Ellie could reply, the booming chimes of a clock hidden deep within the house counted off the hours. If she wanted to be dressed in time for the evening's festivities, she would have to forego the song.

"Never mind, Ellie. Another time, okay?"

The maid ducked her head in response and retreated through the door like a banshee followed hot on her tail. She all but slammed the door behind her.

Moira went to the luxurious bath adjoining her room and opened the taps to the tub full blast. She stripped out of her clothes and leaned over to test the water. A hot bath was just what she needed.

She stepped into the tub, sat down, and turned off the taps. The haunting notes swirled in through the window and a shiver skittered down her spine. Sinking up to her chin in the steaming bubble bath, she shook a determined fist at the window. "Yee can call all yee want, but I'll not be answerin'," she challenged the music. "Faeries indeed," she harrumphed, not realizing she'd spoken in Gaelic.

****

Abhean smiled, but it didn't reach his eyes. "Aye, cailín, yee'll be answerin' soon enough. And him as well." He spun around and dissolved into a shaft of sparkling lights. The fireflies danced off into the woods and disappeared.

Manannan stared into the center of the standing stones and sighed. He'd warned the Harper, but the fae would not leave well enough alone. The time had come to clip Abhean's wings.

****

Deirdre smiled at her reflection in the antique cheval mirror. Aunt Margaret knew her so well. Pulling a lock of her bright hair over her forehead, she studied the result. She rather liked the coy effect created when she peeked out from behind the curl. She'd spent the last hour achieving the studied wildness of her magnificent mane. She'd finally gotten it just right. Smoothing the emerald green satin gown over her hips, she posed once again for the mirror. She pasted a coquettish pout on her face, delighted with the whole image.

Strapless, gold sequins encrusted the bodice, which showed daring décolleté. The gown's sensuous, satin skirt hugged her slim body all the way to her ankles. When she moved, the satin whispered seductively, like a lover's sigh in the dark. Deirdre cocked her left knee slightly, parting the sheath to reveal a slit running well up her shapely thigh. Gold-sequined stiletto heels completed the outfit.

All she needed now was jewelry. She crossed to the dressing table and opened her jewelry case. From the velvet-lined box, she pulled out a heavy gold choker—a modern piece fashioned to look antique. A large, square cut emerald surrounded by diamonds hung from the center. Pawing through the top tray of the case, she found the matching earrings. The last treasure she uncovered was a diamond and emerald ring. Deirdre slipped it on her slim, right ring finger. She wanted the men assembled tonight to have no doubts as to her availability. She clipped on the earrings and fastened the choker around her neck. Deirdre moistened her cherry-red lips with the tip of her tongue. Giving her hair a final fluff, she crossed to the door and went out into the hall.

****

The senator had just come out of his own room when Deirdre emerged. A moment later, Moira exited her room and joined them in the hallway. As his daughters stood side by side, Patrick was again struck by their dissimilarity. Tonight, Deirdre more than ever resembled the sun. If a man gazed too long at her radiance, she might blind him.

Moira, on the other hand, looked even more like the moon. Her heavy blonde hair, swept up and twisted into an intricate knot on top of her head, was held in place by an antique silver comb. Fittingly, white moonstones adorned the hairpiece. She wore a sapphire taffeta and velvet gown the color of the midnight sky. Off the shoulder sleeves set off the milky smoothness of her chest and long neck to perfection. The softly gathered taffeta skirt rustled like a balmy night breeze passing through pine trees. The delicate diamond drop and matching earrings Moira wore glittered like the first stars in the evening sky.

The senator had to admit when they stood next to each other like this, Moira's plain beauty paled when compared to Deirdre. In many families, the disparity would have created a great deal of sibling rivalry and hurt feelings. Once again, he thanked his lucky stars Deirdre's flamboyant beauty never appeared to bother Moira. His younger daughter's talents lay in other directions and she seemed content with her role in life. He was grateful, as he depended heavily on her to keep his life running smoothly.

"Here, Da," Moira said, as if reading his mind. She reached up to straighten his black bow tie. Satisfied, she pressed her cheek against his to avoid smearing the pale lipstick she wore with a kiss.

Patrick gazed at his daughters. "How could a man have two such lovely women under his roof?" he asked. Offering his elbows, the three linked arm-in-arm, and he escorted the girls down the hall to the main staircase. *At last,* he thought, *Deirdre will get her grand entrance, but now she'll have to share it with Moira, and my moon will have a chance to shine, too.*

****

The doors along one side of the massive entry hall had been thrown open. As they descended the steps, the sounds of clinking glasses, an occasional recognizable word, and the merry din of celebration floated up to them. Beneath the murmur of conversation, Moira's sharp ears picked up other sounds. Those same haunting notes she'd heard coming from the woods earlier in the evening now emanated from behind a closed door to the left.

Hiking up her skirt, Moira skipped down the stairs. Her high heels played a sharp, staccato rhythm on the inlaid wood floor as she marched across the foyer. Determined to get to the bottom of the mysterious music, she threw open the door.

Startled, the four people sitting in the darkly paneled room swiveled their heads toward the door as it banged open. The small man cradling an odd collection of plaid wool and wooden spikes grinned, recognizing the intruder.

"Well, Moira O'Connor. Fancy meeting you here." He looked like a jovial innkeeper welcoming a favorite guest.

Moira's blush heated her skin to the roots of her hair. "You appear at the oddest times, Professor Shanahan," she dissembled in an attempt to regain her composure. Arching a brow, she eyed the contraption in his arms. Skeptical about Shanahan's presence, she deflected her doubt by focusing on the thing he held. "What's that?"

"*Uilleann*n pipes." The professor adjusted the instrument and squeezed out a few wailing notes. "A cousin to the more recognizable bagpipe," he explained.

The girl sitting next on the couch next to Michael grimaced as he played a few more notes. She plucked the strings on the small harp in front of her, listening intently. "Wrong key," she told Michael with a grin.

Ignoring the girl's sarcasm, Michael looked at Moira. "May I present the Celtic Connection, Miss O'Connor. This lovely thing with the indisputable ear is Sheila. That young man with the bodhran drum who is trying so valiantly not to blush is Kevin. And the quiet lass over there is Sinead." Each of the three young people nodded as Michael introduced them.

With obvious curiosity, Moira stared at the instrument resting in Sinead's lap, a long, triangular wooden box tied up with strings. "And that?"

Sinead explained. "'Tis a bowed psaltery," she said quietly, her Irish accent understated but discernible. Only then did Moira notice the object, similar to a violin bow, clutched in Sinead's hand.

"We're the entertainment this weekend," Michael interjected.

"We're students at Georgetown," Kevin added. "We play gigs on weekends to earn money," he hinted.

"And that's a blatant advertisement," Sheila finished boldly.

Deirdre appeared in the doorway beside Moira. "Oh, jolly." Her bored voice dripped sarcasm.

"My sister, Deirdre," Moira introduced the other woman, her voice apologetic.

Michael and Kevin stared, both trying to keep their mouths from gaping open. Michael couldn't believe these two were sisters. Deirdre was magnificent. He heard Kevin gulp. Forget youthful hormones, his middle-aged ones were rampaging as well. All thoughts of Moira had fled from his brain.

Margaret Steele, resplendent in red silk, swept through the doorway. "So this is where you've been hiding," she scolded. Her sweet smile belied the reproach, though. "Deirdre, I've got a room full of attractive men just dying to meet you." She linked her arm through the redhead's and led her away. "Come along, Moira," she called over her shoulder.

"Nice to see you again, Professor. I'm looking forward to your music this evening," Moira said before turning to follow Margaret and her sister. "So much for Ellie's faeries," she muttered under her breath.

Michael caught every nuance of their exchange. The undercurrents in the O'Connor family were of rip tide proportions. Though Deirdre took his breath away, there was something about Moira he couldn't quite put his finger on. Someday, he promised himself. Someday he'd peel back the layers and discover what lay beneath her calm facade.

Men were stacked three deep around Deirdre by the time Moira entered the great hall. There was no other way to describe the room. Massive squared timbers buttressed the soaring arches of the ceiling. Brightly colored banners depicting the heraldry of England, Ireland, and Scotland hung in rows from the beams. Though the chairs and couches were massive in proportion, they seemed lost in the vast reaches of the hall.

Unnoticed, Moira slipped around the edge of the room to a heavily laden buffet table. While a bartender poured white wine into a fluted crystal stem, she nibbled a canapé. A burst of salt from the caviar teased the creamy sweetness of the lobster sauce before the crispy crunch of the cracker finished the delicacy. She savored the taste for a moment. Moira then took a tentative sip of the wine and swirled it over her tongue. Crisp, with a tart hint of pear, the wine perfectly complimented the lobster and caviar. Allen boasted about an impeccable wine cellar for a reason.

She spotted her father near the massive stone fireplace at the far end of the room. As she circled around the room to join him, snatches of conversation drifted around her.

"That Deirdre O'Connor is quite a catch," one heavily made-up matron spouted to another. "My Eddie is right by her side, and I'm sure he'll have made a date with her before the evening is over."

The other woman stared at the group of men surrounding Deirdre. "Your Eddie would have better luck chasing after the plain one," she replied, not quite sniffing in her disdain.

The smile on Moira's lips faded. "Well, someone in this family had to get the brains," she muttered as she moved away from the two women, both of whom were oblivious to her presence.

Michael Shanahan and his group took their places at the other end of the hall. They began their set with a contemporary Irish song, and within a few measures, couples filled the space cleared for dancing. Deirdre and the panting Eddie led the way. In the swirl of bright evening gowns and black tuxedos, Moira spotted her father dancing with Margaret.

Several young men stood around the perimeter of the dance floor, all of them watching Deirdre twirl by. No one noticed Moira, much less approached her to ask for a dance. Even polite conversation seemed out of the question. She cringed, her back pressed against the stones of the wall. Cut from granite, the blocks refused to radiate anything but cold. Moira shivered, chilled to the bone. Feeling very much like the proverbial wallflower, she tried not to let her hurt feelings bubble to the surface. Despite what she felt in her heart, her foot tapped to the beat of the music.

Chapter 6

Duncan shrugged on the black, double-breasted suit jacket over his white silk turtleneck. The jacket and matching pleated slacks were the only concession he would make to the black-tie affair downstairs.

Gemma fluffed her bangs then daubed her favorite perfume behind her ears. Smoothing her black cocktail dress over her hips, she turned to him. "How do I look?"

He noticed her hesitancy as he studied her with a practiced eye. Her dress was just a slip with intricate straps crossing her chest, shoulders, and back. Stopping above the knees, the straight skirt had a small kick pleat in back. "You look fine," he assured her.

"I don't know," Gemma vacillated. Duncan recognized the beginning waffle about her choice as she turned to face the mirror. "While you were in the shower, I heard voices in the hall so I peeked out," she admitted.

"And what did you see?"

"Two women in formal gowns." Gemma didn't quite wail but her tone was close.

Duncan walked up behind her and on impulse, kissed the nape of her neck. "So everyone will be admiring your legs instead of theirs."

"Oh, Dunnie!" Spots of color appeared on

Gemma's cheeks. Turning, she threw her arms around him and kissed him, her lips locking against his for a long moment. Stepping back, she brushed invisible lint from his jacket. Her happy look changed to one of indecision.

Duncan schooled his voice as he asked, "What is it now, Gemma?"

"Are you wearing your hair like that?" Her doubt and skepticism were plain to see.

His thick, dark hair lay in loose waves across his shoulders. Deciding to humor her, he went into the bath. Brushing his hair back, Duncan pulled it into a ponytail and secured it with a sterling silver ring worked with Celtic knots.

"Is this better?" he asked, stepping back into the bedroom.

"Most handsome," Gemma declared. "I'm sorry, Dunnie." The apology was meant to placate him. "I really need to make a good impression on these people and most of them are quite conservative."

Duncan looked at the ornate Louis XIV furniture filling the room. "You could have fooled me," he muttered.

Gemma applied fresh lipstick and took a last look in the mirror. "Okay. I'm ready," she announced.

****

The Celtic Connection was taking a break and a hum of conversation filled the room. Moira stood silently at her father's side, listening to his discussion on the capital gains tax with Allen and another man. Margaret joined the group, smiling prettily as her husband hammered a point. Moira looked up to see Deirdre sailing across the room, the ever-persistent Eddie dogging her the entire way.

As Deirdre joined the group, Margaret interrupted Allen. "Mr. Williams," she said, turning to the third man in the group, "have you met the senator's daughter, Deirdre?"

While Bradford Williams gushed over Deirdre, Moira whispered in her father's ear. Something about the man's demeanor didn't ring true. She couldn't pinpoint just what troubled her about Williams so she just warned her father to be wary. As Williams returned his attention to Allen and the senator, Patrick gave her arm a little squeeze. She knew he'd be watchful.

Deirdre looked bored. Nothing more than a frisky puppy tripping after her, young Eddie was not her sister's type at all. Moira suspected Dee had joined the group in order to dodge the persistent man. She noticed Deirdre glance first at Eddie and then her gaze slyly appraised Moira. She knew her sister too well. The second Deirdre decided to "keep" Eddie was written all over her face. Not that Moira had any interest in him. His boyish enthusiasm focused on Deirdre was much preferable. Movement by the main doors caught her attention, and Deirdre's too.

"And just who might that be?" Deirdre purred.

Margaret's gaze followed Deirdre's to the two people who had just entered. "Oh, Gemma Todd," the woman explained. "Her work on the Hamilton's house was in that magazine. Oh, which one? Well, you know the one I mean. Gemma helped me decorate Faerie Glen."

"Not her," Deirdre hissed. "Who's that gorgeous hunk of man candy with her?"

"Oh," Margaret replied, a bit taken aback. "His name is Duncan Ross." Deirdre's eyes narrowed and she all but licked her lips prompting Margaret to quickly add, "He's spoken for, Deirdre. He's dear little Gemma's friend."

"Well, dear little Gemma may just have a run for her money before this weekend is over," Deirdre vowed. "Dear, mousy, little Gemma had best have her hooks sunk deep," she added under her breath.

"Deirdre, pull in your claws. I will have none of your nonsense this weekend," Margaret declared. Her sharp tone left no room for debate. "There are more than enough eligible men here tonight and more coming tomorrow. Set your sights on one of them."

"Oh, you can be sure I will," Deirdre promised, her lips twisting in a predatory smile.

Moira watched the exchange between her sister and Margaret then focused her gaze on the subject of their debate. She didn't recognize the woman Deirdre skewered with her glare. She glanced at the man, and her knees buckled. Only determination kept her upright. She studied his face. Did she know him? There was something familiar about him, but she couldn't for her life remember if they'd met. His face had smooth, angular features yet seemed rugged—as if carved from stone. Still, his face had a certain softness—no, she amended—a goodness showing on it. His eyebrows were thick and full as were the lashes framing his soft, brown eyes. His hair was dark brown, almost black, and pulled back, setting off his broad shoulders.

Margaret waved to the newcomers, motioning them over to the group. Moira quickly stepped behind her father. Her heart raced, and she brushed damp palms down the side of her dress, smoothing the material over her thighs. There was something about this man, and until she figured out what, Moira wanted to stay well clear of him.

As they crossed the room toward Margaret Steele, Duncan couldn't help but notice the tall redhead beside their hostess. The girl was undeniably beautiful. All show but no stamina, he decided. The corners of his mouth twitched at the thought of comparing the breathtaking girl to a horse. Gemma noticed his scrutiny of the gorgeous woman, and took his arm possessively to remind him of her presence.

"I saw that look, Duncan Ross," Gemma hissed.

Duncan glanced down at her, bemused by her reaction. Recognizing the jealous squint to her eyes, he patted the hand clinging to his arm. "As my father would say," Duncan told her, his Scottish brogue thick, "'She'd be all flash an' no glory.'"

Gemma's brow knitted in puzzlement. "I have no idea what you mean."

Her grip on his armed loosened a little so he must have mollified her. He led her across the room where they were welcomed into the group by their hostess.

Again, Margaret interrupted the men's conversation. "Patrick, I'd like you to meet Gemma Todd. She's that wonderful decorator I've told you so much about. Gemma, Senator Patrick O'Connor. And this is our dear friend, Bradford Williams. Brad, this is Gemma and her friend, Duncan Ross."

Williams ignored Gemma, glowering instead at Duncan. "We've met," he growled.

Duncan simply stared at Williams, ignoring the man's implicit challenge. His expression never changed.

Everyone in the group noticed the uneasy atmosphere developing. After a moment, when neither man had offered to shake, Patrick slid into the breach. Proffering his hand, he smiled at Duncan. "Mr. Ross," Patrick acknowledged. "Allen tells me you have quite a collection of antique weapons."

Duncan ducked his head in a show of modesty. "I suspect that's rather an overstatement. I have a few minor pieces."

"A few minor pieces," Allen sputtered. "Patrick, this young man has a ninth century Celtic battle sword."

The hair stood up on Duncan's arms. A cold, rustling sound, like a snake slithering through leaves, whispered nearby. He looked up to find the brassy redhead standing there, smiling seductively. "Before my father embroils you in a tedious discussion of antiques, let me introduce myself. I'm Deirdre O'Connor." She presented her hand with a haughty flourish.

Duncan ignored her gesture. His arched brow mocked her as he smiled perfunctorily. "Miss O'Connor," he acknowledged with an all but imperceptible nod.

Still in the senator's shadow, Moira watched, her attention focused on the by-play. Bradford Williams did not like this man, and in Moira's book, that counted as a plus on the stranger's side. She stared at Duncan, deciding she liked the way the short hairs at the nape of his neck curled away from his ponytail. Were they as soft as they looked? *What am I thinking?* She shook such thoughts out of her head.

When Duncan blatantly ignored Deirdre's play for his attention, Moira relished her sister's discomfiture. Was it possible there actually lived a man immune to Deirdre's charms? Moira looked up. He stared at her and she was pulled into his warm gaze. Some small part of her brain, the only part that seemed to be working on autopilot, noted his amber eyes were flecked with gold.

"Duncan Ross," he said, extending his hand to her.

The sound of his voice broke the spell. He was just being kind to the plain sister in order to tweak the beauty. Moira understood this game. She'd been recruited to play it often enough growing up. At some point, the Celtic Connection had resumed playing, the music a soft hum in the background. The melody was sad and haunting, and eerily

61

discordant. One part of her mind recognized the sounds of the bowed psaltery and the *Uileann*n pipes. With some reluctance, she took Duncan's hand.

The thoughts and emotions tumbling through her mind made her giddy. She tried to halt the mad kaleidoscope and focus on one scene. Even concentrating, the picture appeared hazy and blurred at the fringes. She saw herself sitting on a bright sorrel horse. A man reached up for her, but she couldn't see his face. She slid off the horse and into his arms. They embraced, their bodies molding together with practiced familiarity.

Moira shook that memory loose and the next one tumbled into focus. She sat in a field of green grass and wild flowers. The same man stretched out on the grass, his white shirt open to reveal his muscular chest. He reached for her. He... Moira gasped in surprise and shock. His large, rough hand caressed her breast.

That image faded into blackness—a thick, oppressive night. Moira heard him calling. She tried to run to him, but she couldn't. She was as rooted to the spot as an ancient oak tree. Panic welled up inside her as she struggled to move, but invisible bonds held her fast.

A bright light flickered in the darkness, and Moira found herself looking down on the scene. People milled about a huge bonfire. She saw a shadowy figure charging across the field—a man on a horse riding at full gallop. She continued to watch as the man jerked the horse to a sliding stop in front of the fire. His face twisted into a mask of rage. He stared at the fire, his expression contorted by the horror of what he saw. Still detached but curious about the tortured look on the man's face, Moira looked into the fire. She screamed when she saw her own face melt into the heart of the flames.

As soon as her fingers touched his palm, an electric jolt ran up Duncan's arm all the way to his brain. Alarms jangled in his subconscious. He was vaguely aware that Margaret Steele said, "And this is the senator's other daughter, Moira."

The young woman clutched his hand, staring at him but not really seeing him. Duncan watched as a fleeting series of emotions crossed her face—love, passion, and then a look of sheer terror entrenched itself in her eyes, turning them a dusky blue. Her mouth opened in a silent scream. Slowly, her eyes refocused on him.

"You," she accused before promptly fainting.

Reacting instinctively, Duncan caught the girl with a strong arm around her shoulders and lifted her easily, sliding his other arm under her knees. Aware of the stares and murmurs around them, he turned to Margaret. "Is there somewhere I can take her?"

Margaret was too flustered to speak. Allen stepped up and put his hand on Duncan's shoulder. In a low voice, he directed, "The study. Follow me."

Allen quickly led him out of the room and across the entry hall. The senator followed at his side, his anxious gaze never leaving Moira's face. Margaret, Deirdre, and Gemma, looking irresolute and unsure, trailed behind.

Duncan barely glanced around the room as Allen ushered him in. He laid Moira on a leather couch while Margaret fussed about putting pillows under the girl's head and shoulders. He checked her pulse, surprised to find it racing. Most people suffered a slow heart rate after fainting.

Though still unconscious, Moira clutched at his hand, holding it tight, almost instinctively clinging to him. Again, that tantalizing jolt of energy surged up his arm. He knelt beside the couch watching her.

Moira remained deathly pale.

Allen stood next to Patrick, lending moral support. "We can call a doctor," he offered. He started to speak but closed his mouth as if he didn't know what else to say.

Duncan glanced up at the senator. The man stared at him, his eyes narrowed and his expression speculative. "A doctor won't help, Allen. No sense dragging one out here." His gaze never left Duncan or Moira as he spoke and it lingered on their clasped hands. The senator didn't appear too upset and Duncan wondered what the man was thinking.

"Leave it to Moira to grandstand so she gets his attention," Deirdre muttered darkly. She sprawled in a chair across the room, eyeing her sister with contempt.

Duncan noticed Gemma standing by the door watching the scene. Not quite wringing her hands, she looked anxious and unsure. Gemma glanced at Deirdre and then back to Moira. He could tell by Gemma's expression she felt sorry for Moira. He agreed. She'd seemed so quiet and shy standing there behind her father. Curled up in the leather armchair, Deirdre looked like some bejeweled serpent coiled to strike at anyone unwary enough to approach. The difference in the sisters confounded him.

Margaret stood near the couch, her hands fluttering like frantic birds. "I feel so helpless," she moaned. "Do you suppose it was something she ate or drank? What will my other guests think?"

Gemma relaxed a little and stepped over to Margaret. She put her arm around the overwrought woman. "Why don't you go back to them," she suggested helpfully. "You are such a marvelous hostess, Margaret. If you reappear quickly, no one will think a thing about what just happened."

Margaret raised her chin and nodded, visibly

relieved by Gemma's suggestion. "You are absolutely right, my dear." She fluttered her hands in the redhead's direction. "Deirdre, come with me," she pleaded. "You are always the center of attention. Come back to the party and let the men flock around you."

Duncan watched Moira's face. Like a magnet, she drew his gaze every time he looked away. Color crept back into her cheeks and her eyelids fluttered, her eyelashes casting dark shadows against her pale skin. "She's starting to come around," Duncan informed the rest, forcing himself to look up. "I think it will be safe for all of you to return to the party. I'll sit with Moira for awhile."

Gemma flashed him a questioning look. His actions confused her. He'd carefully cultivated a demeanor since meeting her, and here he was playing against type. He met her gaze steadily to reassure her. Her gaze flicked to the redhead and back to his face. If Deirdre had been the one lying there Gemma wouldn't leave, but he saw the precise moment she decided she had nothing to fear from the pale, plain girl laying on the couch.

"I'm sure Mr. Ross is right," Patrick insisted. "If Moira comes around and finds all of us hovering over her, she'll only be embarrassed. I think we should all go back to the party. Moira will join us when she feels up to it."

Deirdre slowly uncoiled from her chair, smoothing the wrinkles out of her satin gown. Once again, the image of Deirdre as serpent superimposed itself in Duncan's imagination. As Patrick and Allen ushered the women out, Gemma gave him a last questioning look while Deirdre favored him with a leer. Allen shooed them out and closed the door.

He watched Moira lying motionless until her nostrils flared slightly at the telltale click of the door.

"Are they gone?" she whispered, her eyes still closed.

"Yes." Duncan watched her closely. Her eyelids fluttered open but she refused to meet his gaze. "Would you like to explain what happened out there?" His voice sounded brusque.

"I'm not sure." Her reply sounded lame.

Duncan freed his hand from her grip. "That's not good enough," he snapped, moving away from her.

Without looking up, Moira tried another feeble excuse. "I didn't eat much today, and I don't usually drink..." Her voice trailed off.

He continued watching her for a long moment but couldn't decipher her expression. He didn't buy her alibi for a minute. He detected no strong odor of alcohol about her, and he'd watched those emotions flit across her face before she'd fainted. There was something disquieting, something haunting and familiar about this childlike woman. "Who are you?" he blurted, his voice unintentionally harsh with suppressed emotion. His reaction to her almost frightened him.

Moira's head snapped up as if he'd slapped her. Her cerulean eyes blazed angrily as she glared at him. "I might ask you the same question," she retorted, defiance rolling off her in waves.

Duncan stared at her, striving for some solid hint of recognition. The tight French twist in which her hair had been wrapped had come loose, and a silken strand straggled across her forehead and cheek. Without thinking, he reached to smooth it back. The tips of his fingers brushed her cheek. Moira's eyes closed, and she rubbed her cheek against his caress. He jerked his hand back as if contact with her skin had burned his fingers. Moira opened her eyes, and he looked into their depths— two luminous pools of blue reminding him of fire opals, which had been his mother's favorite stones. A shudder of longing ran through the whole length of him, and his cock grew hard, recognizing her before his brain did.

"You can't be," he murmured. He gazed at her, his heart full of wistful yearning. Duncan sighed. "'Twas only a dream."

"No!" Moira declared vehemently. "There was someone. It was real."

Duncan's eyes narrowed. "What was real?"

Moira shivered. "The...the things I saw," she stammered. Moira continued to shake and wrapped her arms across her chest in order to stop. "And felt," she added in a whisper.

He stared at her. The girl spoke the truth as far as he could tell. He recalled the jolts of energy every time their hands touched. He needed more information. "Tell me, Moira," he urged, keeping his voice soft and soothing. "Tell me what you saw."

A dreamy look came over her face. "But it can't be," she murmured. "You're sitting right here." She looked up at him. "But he looked just like you." Her voice quivered with the desperate plea.

Duncan took her hand and tenderly stroked the back of it with his thumb, all the while willing her to relax. "Tell me, Moira," he repeated in that same soft voice. "'Tis all right, lass, to tell me what you saw." His voice remained calm and soothing, compelling despite the brogue creeping in.

Moira took a deep, shuddering breath. Even through the closed oaken door, the strains of a traditional Irish air, bright and lilting, could be heard. Though she looked directly at him, Duncan realized she wasn't seeing him at all. Her body remained, but her mind had gone to a far distant place and time.

Chapter 7

Moira stared at the scene unfolding before her, blinked and suddenly peered through that other Moira's eyes. The village, as she watched out the window, looked ancient and her clothing and the room surrounding her belonged in the late Middle Ages. The voices wafting up from the lane below sounded lyrical to her ears, and Gaelic. Her stomach knotted and heaved for a moment as vertigo set in. This feeling of being in two places at once almost overwhelmed her. She swallowed the bile rising in her throat and closed her eyes. When she opened them, she was that other.

She leaned against the windowsill, watching and hoping to get a glimpse of him. She waited for an hour but he didn't come. Giving up, she pulled the wooden chair closer to the fire, and began sewing. He'd come. He always came.

The big sorrel, barely winded even though he'd been ridden hard for the entire afternoon, galloped up the lane scattering chickens and children in his path. His rider couldn't wait to get back. Gone for an entire day, just the thought of the woman waiting for him had his shaft so hard, he could barely sit his horse. Horse and rider clattered into the stable yard behind the inn and a boy ran to catch up the reins as Duncan swung off the big animal.

Without stopping, he hit the door to the inn at a run. The whitewashed walls flashed by as he took the stairs three at a time. The muscles in his legs bunched and stretched with each leap up the steps. He had to get to her. His need for her, to hold her in his arms and to kiss her drove him hard.

He burst through the door and grabbed her around the waist. Duncan lifted Moira above his head and spun her around the room in a drunken dance. Her long, golden hair cascaded across his face and shoulders like a silken veil. He gulped in its clean, fresh fragrance like a drowning man gasping for his last breath of air.

****

The vision faded abruptly, and Duncan realized Moira had pulled her hand free. She stared at him with eyes round with fear.

"It can't be," she protested. "'Twas too long ago. Too far away." Faint traces of an unfamiliar Irish accent clung to her words.

A terrible emptiness consumed him. He felt as if something precious had been torn from him, and he despaired of every retrieving it. Of its own volition, his hand reached out to stroke her hair.

"Show me, Moira," he demanded, his voice gruff but kind. "I have to know more, lass."

Duncan's gentle caresses calmed her, and Moira closed her eyes. Her own hands now rested folded in her lap. Duncan covered both with one of his.

****

Thunder crashed around them, reverberating through the thick stone walls sheltering them. Jagged streaks of lightning split the heavens and the wind howled like some fierce banshee. They were soaked to the skin, their sodden clothes dripping while puddles formed at their feet.

"'Twill be all right, lass," he assured her. He took her slim, cold hand in his massive paw. Raising

69

it to his lips, he kissed the back of it, his breath spreading a warm glow across her chilled skin.

Duncan studied this fragile thing he held, slowly turning her hand over. Then, looking deep into her eyes, he softly kissed each fingertip before nuzzling her palm. Still holding her gaze with his own, he allowed his lips to travel up her arm. Her skin warmed as he wove a trail through the forest of goose bumps on her skin. He kissed her shoulder, and then his tongue traced the curve of her throat. Her breasts strained against the soft linen of her bodice with each ragged breath she took.

"You'll catch your death," he whispered, nuzzling her ear. He tugged the ribbon on the front of her blouse, and the wet fabric slithered apart. He pushed the material off her shoulders just enough to reveal the soft roundness of her breasts. The battle-hardened roughness of his skin rasped her skin as his hands tenderly cupped her full breasts.

"'Tis perfect you are, m'love," he told her, a wicked grin spreading across his face. His hands stroked and pinched her breasts, hardening her nipples into sharp peaks.

Embarrassed by her body's response to him, she tore her gaze from his face. He was so tall that if she looked straight ahead, she could see only the fine feathering of dark hair on his chest. His white linen shirt stayed plastered to his sun-browned skin, and her eyes traced every hardened muscle on his chest and stomach. Shyly, she let her gaze travel lower. What she saw both delighted and frightened her.

She jerked her eyes back to his face. His full sensuous lips favored her with a smug curl at their corners. Stepping back from her, he reached up with one hand, grabbed the back of his shirt and peeled it off. When he tossed it across the room, the shirt grabbed an old wooden chair as it sailed past and hung on drunkenly, like some old salt trying to ride out the storm in the crow's nest of a ship.

His shoulders were broad, his arms long and strong. His muscular chest tapered to a narrow waist, and the muscles across his abdomen were taut. That feathering of hair across his chest dipped, narrowing as it defined the muscles of his abdomen before circling his bellybutton to dip even further, only to be lost from sight in the lacing of his trews.

Moira shivered, not knowing if it was the cold or the sight of him. He pulled her close to him, and wrapped his massive arms around her. His body radiated heat, and she pressed nearer, wanting to find the center of him.

Undressing her quickly, Duncan scooped her into the cradle of his arms. With long, sure strides, he carried her to the bed set against the far wall of the room. As if she were some precious icon, he settled her onto the feather ticking, and then stood to pay homage. The damp tendrils of her thick blonde hair crowned her face like a wild, golden nimbus against her smooth silky skin. His adoring gaze touched every inch of her even as his hands itched to do the same.

He tore his boots from his feet and stripped off his leather trews, dropping them on the floor. Stretching out beside her, he wrapped her in the warmth of his arms. His mouth found hers, and he kissed her hungrily. Her lips parted and his tongue slipped between them, probing and searching her mouth. The tip of his tongue traced along the length of hers, tasting and savoring. He teased her breasts, rolling her nipples between his fingers and caressing them with one hand. Leaving the sweetness of her mouth, his lips sought the soft skin where her neck met her jaw, and she sighed as he nuzzled her there. Before Moira could catch her breath, his shadow-bearded chin rubbed between her breasts as his tongue swirled from one rosy nipple to the other. He stole her breath away, and was arrogant enough to savor the fact he could.

Duncan tasted her nipple, suckling and pulling, and nipping with his teeth. She moaned and squirmed beneath him. Leaving his hands to tease her breasts, his lips and tongue trailed further down her body, finding the silken skin where her thigh met golden curls. Those curls caught in his rough stubble. With a knee, he parted her legs and one hand sought the secret center of her warmth. His thumb found the hard little nub in the soft folds of her sex. Moira gasped. She pulled his hand away and clamped her knees together.

"Shh, lass," he whispered as he slid up her body to nuzzle her neck and ear. "'Tis the way it should be." He took her hand and guided it to his cock, which was rock hard and ready. Her slim fingers barely circled its rigid mass. Her breath caught in her throat. "I seek only to ease its way," he murmured. "Let me love ya, lass, love ya the way ya deserve t'be."

His knee again slipped between her silken thighs and his hand caressed her once more. He found her hot and wet. With gentle patience, Duncan inserted one finger into her. Moira stiffened immediately so he kissed her, his tongue darting in and out of her mouth in mimicry of what his body longed to do to hers. As she relaxed against him, he tried two fingers. This time, when her muscles clenched, she meant to keep him from withdrawing his fingers. "Aye, you'll come to like this part, lass," he promised.

Duncan settled himself between her legs, keeping most of his weight on his elbows. Her hips cradled him like she'd been made for him and he suspected she might have been. His cock pushed and strained against her entrance, demanding access to the very depths of her being.

"I love ya, my bonnie girl," he declared, his voice thick with fervent need. "Have no doubts about my feelings for you." He kissed her again, savoring the plump fullness of her lips. His hands fisted in her hair as his cock pushed inside her. "Doona' worry, little one." He whispered encouragements against her cheek. "'Tis but a prick that will fade away soon enough."

He kissed her again, deeply, stealing her very breath as he pushed all the way in. Moira gasped in pain and a tiny tear collected at the corner of her eye. Duncan kissed the dewy drop away. He lay still, savoring the feel of her surrounding him.

Her arms finally embraced him, circling around his back and stroking his hard muscles. One of her hands became entangled in his thick, dark hair. Slowly, with great care, he began to move inside her. His mouth and tongue teased her and then his body did the same. In slow, achingly fast out, only to do it all over again. Moira began to move beneath him, rocking and arching to meet his thrusts. Her breasts rubbed against his chest and the muscles deep within her clenched around him, trying to keep him from withdrawing. His hands fisted in her hair as he drove into her again and again.

These feelings were completely new to Moira. Her middle felt like a tightly coiled ball of yarn about to unravel. Her breaths came in short gasps. He was so huge she'd been afraid he would impale her. Now her need drove her even though she knew he could rip her apart, and she'd be begging him to do so. Like a pebble thrown into a placid pool, little ripples fanned out from her center. There was something, some feeling she could almost touch but couldn't quite reach. She knew she was crying, but she didn't care. Her nails raked across his back as she thrust her hips up to meet his. Harder. Faster. Not enough. Harder still. In. Out. Draw a ragged breath. She felt his hands slide down to cup the cheeks of her bottom. He pulled her hips higher, and he drove in from a different angle. Yes, she cried. Yes. This was what she needed. She felt him explode inside her, hot liquid pumping into her very soul. She breathed his name as stars exploded behind her eyes.

Her muscles clenched and pulled at him, milking his very lifeblood. Duncan felt the shudders radiate from her center, felt his own climax create wave after wave shooting out to the very tips of his fingers and toes, only to curl back and crash into the next wave. Drained, he lay on top of her, panting. He kissed her bruised lips tenderly.

"'Tis the most glorious gift of all ye ha'e gi'en to me, bonnie lass," he murmured.

****

Duncan opened his eyes and tried to school his breathing. His hand still covered Moira's and her eyes remained closed. He could see the flush of her skin running all the way from the neckline of her gown to the roots of her honey hair. Her lips were slightly parted and her breaths came in rapid, uneven bursts. Duncan gazed down at her, fully expecting to see the evidence of his seed and the blood of her innocence staining her dress.

For the first time, he really looked at her. Her high cheekbones kept her face from forming a perfect oval. Her nose was finely drawn and straight, and the lashes fluttering on her cheeks were lush and dark. Her jaw line softly rounded into her strong chin. Startled by the total picture, Duncan realized how stunning Moira truly was. How could he have missed her beauty? An image of Deirdre flashed through his mind, reminding him why no one else would discover what he just had. That suited him just fine. His. She always had been. Always would be.

A shudder ran the length of her body, and a little gasp escaped from between her lush lips. Duncan caressed her bare shoulder, and she arched her back to meet his hand.

"Yes, there was that," he whispered huskily, the experience affecting him as much as it had her. Taking her hand, he squeezed it gently. "Show me the rest, bonnie girl. Show me what happened to us," he murmured.

****

He felt the powerful horse's excitement as it pranced between his legs. He patted its strong neck and made soothing sounds. As anxious as the horse was to be away, he had something to do before they could go. He saw her then, standing on a nearby hill. Sunlight danced in her hair, sending golden sparks up into a sky so blue he had to squint against its brightness. A playful breeze molded her long skirt to her legs. He grinned devilishly, remembering all too well the feel of those legs wrapped around his middle.

"I'll be back before ye know it," he shouted to her.

She called to him, but the wind snatched her words away before he could catch them. She blew him a kiss and waved. Reining his horse around, he lifted his arm in a last salute. Giving the horse his head, they galloped down the road into a stand of trees. He turned around one more time, but she was lost to his sight.

Already his heart felt heavy but he was a warrior. He'd been brought to Ireland to fight a war. He had to join in this one last battle before he'd finally be free to return to Moira and make her his forever.

****

As the image faded from his mind, Duncan became painfully aware of Moira's nails digging into the palm of his hand. She kept shaking her head, moaning "no" over and over.

Suddenly, she let go of him and curled her hands into fists. She flailed at the air around her, lost to any conscious thought. When one hand connected with his arm, she hit him over and over with her balled fists. Duncan gripped her wrists gently, but with enough strength to keep her still.

"Talk to me, Moira," he demanded. He realized she had gone somewhere he couldn't, and he was frightened for her. "What's happening? I can't see it. You have to tell me, Moira." She lay still for a moment, no longer fighting him. His voice seemed to have calmed her. Then Duncan felt her body go rigid. "Tell me," he cried, worried he couldn't reach her.

"It's dark," she whimpered. "I can't see. I can't breathe." Panic tinged her voice as she panted for air. "The roses..." Her voice trailed off.

"It's all right, love," Duncan soothed. "I'm here, lass. You'll be safe."

Again, Moira quieted at the sound of his voice. After a moment, she continued her narration in a flat voice. "It's so dark. I don't know where I am. Wait. I can see lights now. Bright lights. Torches. People." Her voice went up a notch in pitch. "Lots of people with torches. NO!" she pleaded even as she choked. She tried to jerk away from him, squirming and pulling, but Duncan held on firmly.

"No," she ordered, her voice stronger now. "Don't put the hood on again. I want to see you. I want to see your faces, you godly people who would hide your evil deeds behind the veil of darkness." She spat the words out.

As Duncan watched Moira suffer through her vision, defiance replaced the fear in her face. He strained to picture the scene in his mind, but met only blankness. Far off, voices whispered and he strained to hear them, but Moira had gone somewhere he couldn't follow.

****

Moira watched the large mob mill about, the flickering torches they carried painting their faces like grotesque masks filled with fear and hatred. Most of them carried bundles of sticks and kindling, which they tossed onto the growing pile of wood in the center of the broad meadow. A thick wooden post jutted from the center of that insidious mound, a pale woman dressed in white lashed securely to it. Moira blinked and the next thing she knew, she stared out from the pile of wood. Her heart stuttered. She was the woman tied to the post.

A big man, the obvious ringleader, wearing the rough clothes of a peasant turned to face the mob. In a voice more suited to the pulpit than the fields, he shouted, "Let her burn for a witch." His voice rang out, echoing off the encircling trees. "She's consorted with the very devil his self." He glanced at a hooded figure huddled on the fringe of the mob. The figure nodded, urging the speaker to continue. Before he could, her voice rang out, clear and steady above the babble of the crowd.

"If witch I be, then hell 'tis where we'll be meetin' again." Her outburst silenced the mob for a moment, but then their derisive shouts grew even louder. "I'll be damnin' your souls, and the souls of your children's children through all eternity," she shouted at them.

The big man grabbed a torch and jabbed it into the straw piled at her feet.

Flames flickered and danced around her. "So where's your devil lover now, witch?" the man screamed.

Moira struggled against her bonds, coughing as choking smoke swirled around her.

Smoke curled from the hem of her linen skirt,

and searing pain raced from her toes up to her tortured brain.

"You promised, Duncan!" she screamed. "Oh, God, where are you?"

Chapter 8

Duncan held her tightly, wincing with each sob wracking her body. He would have absorbed her pain if he could have. Moira's head nestled up under his jaw, and he rubbed the top of her head with the point of his chin. "It's all right, lass," he murmured. "I'm here now."

Her sobs slowly lessened and then, with a little hiccup, ceased altogether. Duncan knew he should let her go, but it felt so right, so natural holding her, he didn't want to. In fact, he wasn't sure he could let her go.

"I don't understand," she whispered, then hiccupped again.

Duncan tried to ease the dark mood. In a light, teasing voice, he asked "Do you do this often?" Moira pushed away from him, glaring up at his laughing eyes. "This is a hellava way to meet men," he added, chuckling.

"No!" Moira denied vehemently, the urge to slap the smirk off his face so strong she actually raised her hand.

"Whoa, lass," he soothed, holding up his hands to ward off her blow. "I was only joking." Duncan watched her, trying to read the thoughts behind her eyes. A shadow of fear still lurked there, but something else hid there as well. He got the distinct feeling she wasn't telling him something. "I think you owe me an explanation about what just happened here." He sounded as cold and sober as a judge. Or an inquisitor. He didn't like being kept in the dark.

"I don't think I can explain." She met his gaze without looking away.

"Then you'd better think again."

"What's going on between you and Bradford Williams?"

The switch in topic caught Duncan completely off guard. Openly suspicious, he watched her for a long moment. "What do you mean?" He maintained his composure, but just barely. He still sounded testy, which belied his apparent control.

"You two obviously dislike each other."

"Whatever gave you that idea?" Duncan watched her, his expression wary now.

"Beside the fact he wouldn't shake your hand, or you his for that matter?" She snorted. "That much would be obvious to anyone watching. Even before you were introduced, I had a..." She paused, searching for the word she wanted to use. "I guess you could call it a feeling."

Duncan eyed her, uncertain about her meaning. "Do you get these feelings often?" One scene remained etched in his mind and his mouth curled into a wicked grin at the thought of those feelings.

"Quite often," Moira answered, then blushed when she caught his implication. "Some feelings anyway," she clarified.

"Can you explain those to me?" Duncan remained skeptical.

Moira shrugged. "I can't," she reiterated. He started to get up but she laid a restraining hand on his arm. "Please," she added, her voice not quite pleading. "It's something I've always done. I don't know how. I don't know why. Just like you and Williams. The man is a blowhard, but he has some sort of hidden agenda. There's a darkness to him. Your hackles rose the moment you recognized him. You turned territorial, wanted to challenge him. Thus, no handshake." She squinted at him, gazing up from the corners of her eyes, her thick lashes framing them with mystery. Her right shoulder lifted in a small shrug. "I just know people."

"Know them? Know them how? Are you some sort of mind reader?" Duncan smirked, hoping to mask his consternation at how close she'd come to the mark.

"No. It's not like that," Moira argued. "I just know. It's like I sense what is inside them."

Duncan's brow arched and his grin turned lascivious. "And what do you sense about me, lass?"

Moira's face flushed, the crimson color suffusing her cheeks. "More than I want to," she muttered darkly.

Duncan laughed, a hearty burst of merriment. He was enjoying her discomfort. Moira glowered at him, and he decided to let that particular part of their recent experience slide for the moment. "So tell me about these other feelings of yours," he prompted. "How does it work?"

Again, Moira shrugged, a subtle lift of the other shoulder. "It doesn't work. It just happens. I get feelings about people. What they are like. You know, what kind of people they are—whether they're sincere or false. I seem to automatically know if someone is lying."

"I'm sure your father finds this talent very useful." Duncan's sarcasm returned.

"He does," Moira affirmed.

Duncan stared, his gaze raking her face. He'd been joking, but she obviously wasn't.

Her chin came up at his look and she added, "My talent has served him well on many occasions."

"Well, you're certainly one to take credit."

"I take credit where credit is due, Mr. Ross," Moira replied hotly as she reverted to formality. "The senator works hard for his constituents. He is a very capable politician."

Duncan would have to be blind to miss the stubborn jut of her chin or glints the color of cold steel in her eyes. "Don't get your nose out of joint, Miss O'Connor," he snapped.

Moira suddenly turned contrite. "I'm sorry, Mr. Ross." She'd retreated to formality, likely finding it safer there. "This evening's events have me rather unnerved."

Your father is not the only politician in the family, he thought. Out loud, he asked, "So what about this evening's events?"

A look of melancholy so wistful it made his heart turn over crossed her face. He wanted to reach out and gather her into his arms, to promise her that whatever had frightened her, whatever had hurt her would never be able to do so again. Instead, he fisted his hands and remained still.

"I don't know," she answered after a long pause. "It's never happened like this before. It's like..." She hesitated, once again searching for words.

"Like what?" Duncan watched, curious about what excuse she'd create. He shifted to a less constricting position when he realized more than his curiosity was aroused.

"It's like I became her...or she me. I saw what she saw. Felt what she felt." Moira blushed again. Before Duncan could reply, her eyes, full of mischief, flashed as she leaned forward and boldly kissed him on the mouth.

"Ah, Duncan Ross," she purred. "Your Gemma 'tis the lucky one."

Duncan was too flustered to react. She bounced off the couch, and danced over to the door. The French twist in her hair tumbled down to catch in a loose knot at the nape of her neck, and the sides spilled completely free. Soft waves of golden silk framed her face. At the door, Moira paused. She flung a coy look back over her shoulder. Her blue eyes twinkled like sunlight dappling the aqua blue surface of the loch near his boyhood home in Scotland. Her cheeks were pink and her smile saucy. The child was gone and a woman had taken her place. The muscles in Duncan's stomach clenched, and he felt dizzy for a moment when all his blood rushed to his groin. She looked so fetching, his whole body ached for the feel of hers.

Her brazen smile held a hint of sadness now. "Tell your Gemma to beware," she cautioned. "Deirdre's claws are sharp and there's not much she wouldn't do to get what she wants." Without warning, her smile changed to one of sassy malice. "And that, Duncan Ross, 'twould be yourself."

Still speechless, Duncan sat on the couch staring at the empty doorway. The faerie maiden who'd stood there only a moment before had disappeared. "She's not mine, lass," Duncan whispered. "'Tis only you now."

Gemma stood in the doorway. "Dunnie?" she called to him. "Is something wrong? Where's Moira?"

Completely oblivious to her presence at first, Duncan finally shook off Moira's spell. *Maybe she is a witch,* he thought, recalling snatches of the whispered conversation he'd heard but not seen. That would be one explanation for recent events. For the moment, it seemed as plausible an explanation as any others he had. To Gemma he said, "I think she's gone to her room."

"Is she okay?" Gemma stepped into the study. "Why did she faint?"

Duncan stared at Gemma, then his mood mellowed as he recognized her genuine concern. "She said she hadn't eaten all day, and explained she isn't much of a drinker." Moira's own lame excuse rolled easily off his tongue. It made far more sense than the truth. "Cocktails on an empty stomach..." He shrugged, letting Gemma come to her own conclusions. He met her gaze as she studied his face.

He knew Gemma realized he was hiding the full truth from her. He'd never pretended to be a boy scout, and there had been others before her in his life. She'd never asked how many, and hadn't cared until recently. Only when he began to distance himself from her emotionally did it matter. Now, she seemed to cling to him, to want a future when he'd never even promised her a present.

"Do you know her?" Gemma's voice sounded tight and constrained.

Duncan stared forlornly out the door. "Not anymore," he whispered.

****

The evening's events fascinated Michael Shanahan. Duncan Ross's arrival caught him off guard. When they'd started playing, and he'd looked up to see the big Scot, he'd almost missed his note. The damn man was liable to turn up anywhere. Michael hadn't even known Ross had returned to the States and he wondered if anyone else knew the Scot was back in town.

He had expected Bradford Williams. All the players were sitting down at the card table, but Ross presented a wild card Michael hadn't counted on. He hoped Ross could be trumped when the time came, but Michael rather doubted it. There was a reason he played bridge instead of poker.

The episode with Moira O'Connor and Ross's participation caused him some concern. When the others returned without the two, Michael wanted to go searching, but he had to monitor Williams, Steele, and the senator. At the band's next break, Michael sent Sinead to check on the couple. She reported back. Moira appeared to be resting on the couch while Ross talked quietly with her.

He'd spent the rest of the evening watching Steele and Williams gang up on Senator O'Connor. Steele's name got added to his mental notebook. After a few minutes of particularly heated conversation, the Senator had excused himself and danced with Margaret Steele. O'Connor studiously avoided Williams for the rest of the evening. Moira did not return though Ross did, with his girlfriend on his arm. Steele and the Senator had disappeared at some point and, to his chagrin, Michael couldn't say when. Ross and his girl left a bit before midnight. Williams left a few minutes later, right after the band stopped playing. Michael was glad he would be in residence for the weekend, figuring this house party would likely shape up as a most interesting occasion.

****

From the shadows of a pillar on the outer side of the portico, Duncan watched Bradford Williams' limousine pull up. A moment later, Williams himself appeared framed in the massive doorway of the house. As his driver leaped out to hold open the car door for him, Williams marched down the front steps. He concentrated on each step, meticulously putting one foot down on the next riser before the moving his other foot. The man collapsed into the back seat as the driver slammed the door and climbed into the driver's seat. The car smoothly pulled away.

Duncan watched until the big car disappeared from sight. He found it interesting that Williams had imbibed too much liquor. He slipped around the house and entered through a side door. Unerringly, he found the entry hall and climbed the massive staircase. At the landing, he took the left branch. Gemma would be wondering why he'd disappeared, but she'd just have to wait. Hopefully she would already be asleep. If not, he'd come up with some sort of explanation. As Duncan slipped down the hall of the family wing, double teak doors loomed up on his right. He paused outside, straining to listen through their massive thickness.

****

Comfortable in the back of his limousine, Bradford Williams chewed on the stub of an expensive cigar as he mulled over the evening's events. Duncan Ross's appearance had nearly taken the wind out of his sails. He'd been relieved to discover Ross was just as surprised to see him. Margaret Steele mentioned Ross arrived as the guest of her interior decorator. He remained unimpressed by Ross, though he wouldn't count the man out just yet.

After her fainting episode, Moira O'Connor had not returned to the party, a boon to his plans. He knew her reputation—shy, retiring, but a hellcat when it came to protecting her father from those she considered unworthy. Her absence allowed him more access to the senator and in addition, he'd been able to discuss matters in depth with Allen Steele. Steele would make an excellent ally.

With the O'Connor girl out of the way, he'd stayed close to the senator, though the tone of their conversation had not been to his liking. Even using his most persuasive boardroom tactics, Williams noted O'Connor remained reticent. Even after reminding the senator of his Irish Catholic roots, he'd been unable to secure an answer from the senator. He hoped Steele had better luck.

He sighed and sank deeper into the plush leather of the back seat. Allen Steele's whiskey had flowed freely, and he'd sampled more than his share. He'd worry about fulfilling his promise another day. There was still time before the Senate voted.

****

Gemma paced the confines of the bedroom she shared with Duncan. Since he was a physical fitness nut, she hadn't been surprised when he'd changed into running clothes. "Be back shortly," he'd told her.

"Shortly, my ass," she groused. She retrieved the bottle of wine she'd purloined from the bar and popped the cork. She might have to wait, but he always seemed ready for serious fun whenever he took a long run.

She took a swig straight from the bottle. Their brief encounter earlier had only whetted her appetite for what she planned to be the main attraction when he returned. Duncan Ross remained the sexiest man she'd ever encountered, and Gemma had encountered her fair share of the opposite sex. She now wanted a band of gold on her left hand, and she wanted Duncan to be the man to put it there.

She plopped on the bed and took another swig. Duncan was pulling away from her but she couldn't fathom why. She smiled around the lip of the wine bottle. This afternoon had seemed like old times. Maybe she was just imagining things. Gemma took a long pull from the bottle. She still hadn't figured out what had transpired between Duncan and the O'Connor girl, but she'd coerce it out of him before the weekend ended.

Before long, she'd emptied wine bottle. Keeping her eyes open turned into a major battle and now she couldn't find her watch anywhere. She had no idea how much time had elapsed since Duncan had gone jogging. She stretched out across the bed and crinkled her toes until they popped. Chilled, she crawled under the covers. At least she could warm the bed for him. It had to be cold outside. Now that she was warm and comfortable, her eyelids drooped and she snored softly.

****

Duncan crept away from the door, the senator's muffled declaration still resonating. The man planned to vote against the Senate resolution. That took guts, given he was Irish Catholic. Certain puzzle pieces had also dropped into place while he'd listened to the conversation between O'Connor and Allen Steele.

He flitted between the pools of light dappling the hallways between the family and guest wings. Unseen, he arrived at the door to the room he shared with Gemma and crept into the dark room. Her snoring covered the sound of his soft footfalls. Relieved he wouldn't have to face her until morning, he slipped out of his clothes and tossed them over the back of a nearby chair. Naked, he turned to the bed. She stirred, restless in her sleep. Suddenly, the thought of lying naked in the bed next to Gemma made him uncomfortable.

Instead of crawling between the sheets, Duncan snagged a comfortable pair of jeans from his duffle bag. His sweats were sweaty, so he opted for the jeans. As he eased down on his side of the bed, Gemma stirred again. He patted her bare shoulder. Satisfied, she rolled over and her breathing regulated once again. She sighed in her sleep, and Duncan puffed out a shallow breath in relief.

Stretched out on his back, his arms tucked behind his head, Duncan stared at the ceiling. He knew if he closed his eyes, two damnably haunting blue eyes would taunt him. He tore his thoughts away from Moira, focusing instead on the snatches of conversation he'd overheard outside the study. The senator obviously understood the motives of the IRA, but Allen Steele's business ties made him wonder on which side of the fence the financier sat.

Despite his best effort to stay awake, Duncan drifted off. Blue eyes didn't haunt him, though. The growling throb of diesel engines underscored the clanking treads of a Royal Marine tank and two armored personnel carriers. The sounds reverberated through his mind and body. The sharp retort of small arms fire, muffled at first, added a brisk staccato to the snarling diesel engines. From a vantage point high above, Duncan watched the scene unfold.

****

The tank clanked around the corner, and a Molotov cocktail exploded on the rough pavement just in front of it. Impervious, the metal-plated monster lumbered on down the street. Men, only half-seen shadows, raced up the street firing blindly at the tank and its entourage. As heavy caliber bullets slammed into their armored sides, the three vehicles ground to a stop.

Duncan could see inside the first Armored Personnel Carrier. He watched the Royal Marine major check a clipboard and then peer out one of the side ports. Bullets pinged against the APC's outer hull, but the major didn't even flinch.

"This is it," the major radioed to the tank. "This is the address."

"No!" Duncan yelled. "It's not. You have the wrong information." His voice dropped to a whisper. "Oh, God," he pleaded. "Stop. Please stop. I gave you the wrong information. That's the wrong address."

The tank swiveled its turret and leveled its 105 mm cannon on the building. The APCs maneuvered into position, ready to spit out their human cargo.

"Bloody IRA scum," the major muttered as the first shell blasted through the outer wall and exploded in the bowels of the red brick building.

Other screams mingled with Duncan's. Then there was only silence. Dead silence. Cordite smoke drifted across the street, permeating the air with the acrid stench of gunpowder. His nostrils flared and his eyes watered as the ghostly tendrils wrapped around him.

He walked through the ruins now. Mangled bodies lay strewn about the room. Children. Every last one of them. He knelt beside one of the bodies, a little girl in a pink party dress, her blonde hair matted and encrusted with blood and plaster dust. Duncan willed his hands to stay glued to his sides, but against his orders one of them reached out to turn the child over. He stared into the child's sightless dead blue eyes. Moira's blue eyes.

Duncan jerked to a sitting position, sweat pouring from every pore. He swung his long legs off the bed, shivering uncontrollably. He grabbed a sweater and struggled to shove his arms into the sleeves and pull it over his head. He hadn't dreamed The Dream in a long time. A very long time. He fumbled around in the dark until he found Gemma's briefcase. Rummaging through it, he found her cigarette case and lighter. He jammed a cigarette into his mouth and lit it. Several long drags later, his hand quit shaking. 'Tis a bloody bad habit, he thought, but bless you, girl, for havin' it.

****

Though most of the guests had departed, Eddie still dogged Deirdre. Giving up, she invited the puppy to her room. It didn't take long before she figured out she'd made a major mistake. Deirdre put up with his clumsy groping for a few more minutes before calling a halt to his oafish fondling.

"I think I hear your mother calling," she whispered.

"What?" Eddie jumped to his feet like a guilty schoolboy. His trousers puddled around his ankles and his white boxers all but glowed in the dark.

"Good grief," Deirdre muttered.

Eddie stumbled as he tried to pull up his tuxedo pants. She could hear him fumbling around in the dark. "Do you need a light?" she asked. Her mouth pinched shut like she'd swallowed vinegar.

"Good lord, no," Eddie's voice hissed through the gloom. "She might see."

Deirdre got out of bed and all but pushed him out the door. "Goodbye, Eddie." Frost formed on the words as she shut the door in his bewildered face.

She listened to his dejected footsteps echo down the hallway before stripping out of the few pieces of lingerie she still wore. Pulling on a silk teddy, she climbed into bed and burrowed under the covers. Her thoughts turned to Duncan, just a few doors away. She speculated about what he was doing, the image of Gemma lying beneath him an unwanted intruder in her fantasy.

"Dear, sweet little Gemma," she spat. "Enjoy him while you can. It will be my turn very soon."

****

Moira tossed and turned, unable to get comfortable. She couldn't get Duncan out of her mind, especially those disturbing images of the two of them together. She was so tired she only wanted to sink into a deep, dreamless sleep. Her thoughts were so agitated she knew falling asleep any time soon was a pipe dream. What had happened tonight? Where did those memories come from? Who was Duncan Ross? His presence was dangerous to her, but in spite of her gut reaction, she was drawn to him—drawn to him like she'd known him all her life. Moira wanted him to go away. Far away. She wanted him to leave her in peace. Her heart pounded in her chest. No. She'd never find peace, not with him away from her.

She desperately wanted to talk to someone about her thoughts and feelings. Deirdre would only turn up her nose at her "fantasies." Her father, while sympathetic, remained cloistered with Allen in the other wing. Though she'd never known her mother except as a portrait, Moira longed for her presence.

Giving up on sleep, she slipped out of bed and curled up in the window seat. Bright stars twinkled in the midnight sky like handfuls of diamonds scattered across black velvet. As she gazed out the window, lights sparkled in the woods down by the stables, only this time no music teased the air. Moira realized the vernal equinox, what some still called *Alban Eiler,* was Sunday.

"Are ya gettin' ready then?" A soft lilt danced in her voice. She remembered well the half-whispered stories she'd heard as a child. Stories of faeries celebrating the coming of spring and midsummer. Stories of unwary mortals seduced by the fae. At *Alban Eiler*, all of Faerie gathered to dance the night away. Any mortal, she'd been told, unlucky enough to chance upon the festivities became enchanted, plucked up and whisked off to be lost forever in the land of Faerie. Tir Nan Óg, Nanny had named the land of the fae. The Land of the Ever Young.

Lying in the thick darkness, peeping over the edges of her comforter, she'd whispered, "Was there any chance?" In a voice fearful yet excited, and savoring the delicious tingle running up her spine, she'd asked, "Can you be saved from the faerie spell?"

"Mayhaps," Nanny had replied. "If the mortal be pure of heart and brave beyond all things, the faerie king or queen might take pity upon their poor soul."

With her eyes as wide as saucers and filled with wonder, she'd gasped. "What then?"

"Why, at the next gatherin' of the Faerie Folk, Midsummer's Night's Eve 'twould be, then the poor mortal was brought back to the earthly realm and given the choice. If he stayed beyond Midsummer's Night, then he was lost forever, but if he left right then, he traveled back to the mortal world." Nanny always told her the truth and she'd shivered with delight, scared but tempted by the dark allure of the faeries.

The lights below her winked out, and Moira shivered in the dark. She climbed back into bed, huddling under the covers. Warm now, sleep seemed easier to grab hold of.

"There's no such place as Tir Nan Óg," she murmured.

"If yee be sayin' so," Nanny's voice whispered in her ear. "But yer own mother was a Traveler and she'd have the true knowin' of it. Don't be goin' out, she'd tell yee herself, she would. Don't wander far on that night or the Faerie will find yee and keep yee fair certain."

Her eyes were so heavy, Moira could no longer keep them open. Drifting off, the strange music of the *Uilleannn* pipes and bowed psaltery swirled around Nanny's voice.

"No," the child Moira promised Nanny in her dream. "I'll not be goin' out."

"Ah, but yee must, Moira O'Connor, for all will come to naught if yee don't," a voice as sweet as spun sugar whispered.

Chapter 9

Saturday morning dawned bright and fair, driving away the dark anxiety generated by the night. A warm breeze rippled playfully across the landscape, holding the promise of spring as it carried the scents of freshly turned earth and green growing things on its back. The pastel palette of the sun's first rays painted the few plump clouds floating in the opaline sky the color of Peace roses.

Duncan strolled out through the French doors onto the wide stone terrace. He paused to gulp great breaths of the fresh air, ready to enjoy a day already unseasonably warm. Shedding his leather jacket, he tossed it across the back of a wrought iron chair parked nearby. He wore a simple white shirt cut full and black jeans. With legs apart like he was braced to ride on the deck of a ship, he stood scanning the wide expanse of landscaped lawn.

He glanced behind him at a small clattering sound. A tray with thermal carafes and stoneware mugs had mysteriously appeared on a wrought iron buffet table. A second tray, covered by a linen cloth, exuded wonderful scents that perfumed the morning air with cinnamon and other spices. He ambled over, poured a cup of the hot, black coffee and snatched a cinnamon roll. It tasted every bit as good as it smelled, the yeast and butter in the dough melting into the sugar and cinnamon of the filling. The treats had appeared so magically, Duncan wondered briefly if the little people had been involved with their delivery. He grinned at his whimsy. He knew full well there were no faeries, nor elves, nor leprechauns. His brow furrowed for a moment. Nor witches.

Settling into a wrought iron chair more comfortable than it first appeared, he sipped hot coffee and ate the roll. Gazing across the landscape, he watched and listened as the world around him stirred to life. After a moment, he hooked another chair with one booted foot, and pulled it around so he could prop his feet up in it. Mind and body were both at peace.

Patrick O'Connor stared through the leaded glass panes of the French doors watching Duncan. He'd made a few phone calls last night, but none of the conversations gave him any real peace of mind. He'd discovered the British Army had placed Duncan Ross on a classified administrative leave, and it had never been rescinded. Patrick's contact at the British Embassy had been extremely reluctant to discuss the matter.

Moira's instincts had always served him well, but he thought she might be in over her head this time. Every woman at the party last night had positively salivated over the man. He wondered if Ross was aware of the effect he had on the opposite sex. The man seemed oblivious. Was it possible his obvious charms clouded Moira's judgment?

Patrick hadn't spent most of his life in politics without learning a thing or two. In his experience, the more sincere a man acted, the more duplicitous he most likely would be. The senator wanted to get to know Duncan Ross better so he could judge for himself. Making up his mind, he pushed through the French doors, and stepped out on the terrace.

"Good morning, Mr. Ross."

Duncan turned his head slightly. "Senator."

While he poured a cup of coffee, he could feel Duncan's gaze on his back, studying him. He'd dressed in fawn riding breeches, knee-high leather riding boots and a tweed jacket. Patrick's mouth twitched. Without meaning to, he'd played right into the stereotype of a rich, country gentleman. He carried his cup to the table and eased into a chair across from Duncan. "You're up early, Mr. Ross. Didn't you sleep well?"

"I slept fine, thank you," Duncan replied, his voice a bit testy and Patrick wondered what thought had prompted the tone. He sipped his coffee and gestured with his free hand. "This morning is too grand to waste."

"My sentiments exactly." Patrick took a deep breath, savoring the warm breeze. Mornings like this were rare in Virginia this time of year. Coming to a decision, he smiled at Duncan. "I was about to take a ride, Mr. Ross. Since you are the only other person in the household astir, would you care to join me?" He waited for Duncan's reaction. Slightly embarrassed in case he put the younger man in an awkward position, he added, "If you don't ride—"

"I've been known to sit a horse when the occasion demands." A slight grin twitched at the corners of Duncan's mouth.

"And this occasion?" Patrick arched an eyebrow.

"'Tis a bright, fair mornin', Senator. I think Mr. Steele's horses might appreciate a bit of exercise."

"Splendid." Patrick finished the coffee in his cup with a gulp. "Shall we?"

As the two men strolled through the gardens, neither noticed the shadowy figure behind a curtain in an upstairs window.

"I'm surprised Moira wasn't with you on the terrace," Patrick hinted, watching Duncan's reaction out of the corner of his eye.

Duncan seemed surprised by the suggestion. "Oh?"

He smiled to himself. At least they didn't spend the night together. "Normally, Moira is the first one up and about," he explained. "Deirdre, on the other hand, would sleep the day away. Moira's up at first light as a rule. In fact, we usually ride together when we visit the Steeles. She's quite an equestrienne." He stopped when he realized he was babbling.

Duncan appeared to ponder this information but made no comment. He matched his long-legged stride to the senator's.

Patrick didn't enjoy mind games. He believed in being direct and as a result, he didn't quite know how to get the information he wanted from this man. "What kind of work are you in, Mr. Ross?"

"I'm a consultant."

"That can be lucrative," Patrick commented, keeping his voice conversational. "What field?"

"Security."

The man surely wasn't giving him much to work with. Patrick pressed on. "Personal, private industry, or government?"

"All of the above."

"With terrorism on the rise, I'm sure your talents are in great demand," he continued, ignoring the irritation in Duncan's voice. Patrick found it interesting the other man seemed to be dodging his questions. "Have you been in the States long?"

"About six months."

"You travel here often?"

"As my work demands it."

Duncan gave up no more information than necessary and Patrick almost started to enjoy the cat and mouse game. Before he could ask another questions, they arrived at the stable and a stable hand led out two horses—one a dark bay and the other the big sorrel Duncan had befriended the day before. The sorrel nickered as he recognized Duncan.

"Hello again, big 'un." Duncan greeted the horse with a soft voice.

"Thinking Moira would ride with me this morning, I requested two mounts last night. She always rides Flaming Star when we're here," Patrick explained, nodding toward the sorrel. "He's high spirited, and she enjoys him."

Duncan stepped over and checked the girth on Star's saddle. "Silly name they've stuck you with, big 'un," he whispered to the horse. He glanced over the horse's withers. "I hope you aren't too disappointed with my company," he said to the senator.

"I don't think I shall be, Mr. Ross."

Duncan rode in silence, thinking about the inquisition the senator had subjected him to. The transparency of the questions amused him. Typical father. *First he wants to know if I've damaged his daughter's reputation, and then he wants to evaluate her prospects.* The men rode a short way up the road before turning onto a wide path leading into the trees. The path extended just wide enough for the two of them to ride side-by-side.

"I hope my daughter didn't upset you last night, Mr. Ross." Patrick sounded hesitant, as if he picked his words carefully.

Duncan refrained from looking at him. Instead, he shrugged his shoulders. "Why should she have upset me?"

"Deirdre has always... Well, let's just say she has always enjoyed the company of the opposite sex."

Duncan cocked an eyebrow. The direction of this conversation was 180 degrees off. He'd thought the senator meant to discuss Moira. This reference to Deirdre came out of left field. He hadn't given the redhead a second thought since meeting her.

"And," the senator continued, "I hope Miss Todd

wasn't too perturbed."

"Gemma can handle her own." He kept his answer intentionally cryptic.

"I'm sure she can." Patrick hedged by adding, "An attractive young lady." The statement hung in the air between them.

Duncan wanted to ask about Moira but bit his tongue, knowing he should bide his time. The senator obviously had his own agenda, and Duncan willed himself to follow the other man's lead. He left the senator's last comment alone and since the man now seemed content to ride in silence, Duncan followed suit. For several minutes, the soft clop of the horses' hooves as they walked along the leaf-padded path provided a gently percussive background. Not even a breeze penetrated this serenely isolated area.

"Thank you for assisting Moira." The senator spoke so softly Duncan almost missed what he said.

Now that the subject was out in the open, Duncan replied, "If you don't mind my asking, Senator, your daughters seem as different as night and day." Patrick's rumbling chuckle surprised Duncan.

"You are not the first to use that very apt analogy." Patrick smiled genially.

"Well, it is hard to believe they are sisters." A rueful grin hovered about his own lips.

"Different mothers," Patrick replied bluntly. Duncan cocked both eyebrows. Patrick's smile turned rueful. "It's never been a secret, Mr. Ross." He remained silent, digesting the volumes the senator's statement spoke. "Deirdre's mother was an actress. Stunningly beautiful. Deirdre obviously inherited her looks. But, I was young. I learned too late looks aren't everything."

Duncan ignored the wistful look in the senator's eyes. "And Moira's mother?" he asked.

The wistfulness changed to a sad yearning as Patrick recalled his wife. "Ah, Maeve. An Irish girl I met in London. Quiet. Shy like a wild deer. But she had a twinkle in her eye..." The senator cleared his throat and swallowed hard before continuing. "She was beautiful in her own way." He paused for a long moment. When he spoke again, Duncan had to lean toward him to catch the words. "We tried for years to have a child."

"Is that when Deirdre was born?"

"Most astute, Mr. Ross. Yes, I had a brief, ill-fated affair with Deirdre's mother. Maeve never let on she knew. I hurt her deeply, Mr. Ross. The day Maeve told me she'd conceived Moira was the happiest day of my life. Deirdre was not quite one." Patrick grew quiet, lost in his memories.

Duncan hated to disturb the man's reverie but his curiosity had been aroused. He had to know more. "When did Maeve learn about Deirdre?"

"She never did. She knew of the affair, but not the child." Once again, the Senator coughed to clear his throat. "Maeve died the night Moira was born."

"I'm sorry, Senator." His condolences were sincere.

"Moira is much like her mother—quiet, shy, efficient." The senator's voice turned brusque.

Duncan sensed Patrick had more to say. "And?"

"And, like her mother, she has a certain feyness." Duncan wondered about the senator's choice of that particular word, old-fashioned and seldom used in modern times. "Moira has always been a great help to me, even as a little girl," Patrick continued.

"You mean her gift?"

It was the senator's turn look startled. He reined in his horse. "She told you?"

The big sorrel stopped a few paces further down the trail. Duncan twisted in his saddle to look back at Patrick. "Does that surprise you?"

"It certainly does, Mr. Ross," Patrick insisted. "Moira has always been rather reticent when it comes to her ability. Even as a small child, she seemed to see right through people. She was..." His voice trailed off uncertainly.

"Wise beyond her years?"

"Precisely." The senator seemed lost in thought as he spoke. "We had a housekeeper once. The woman crossed herself every time the child entered the same room. Her own grandmother called her 'that cursed faerie child.'" Sadness settled around Patrick like a heavy overcoat. "Moira was a strange child. Those big blue eyes too large for her little face peeping out from under her thatch of blonde hair. She was always out of doors, always dragging home one creature or another. She even loved storms. She reveled in them. We'd force her to come inside, and she'd run to the highest room in the house to watch from a window. Aye, strange she was. Wild and fey."

Duncan tried to reconcile the description the senator had just given him with the girl he'd met last night. The first thing he'd noticed about Moira as she'd stood in her father's shadow was how tightly she controlled herself. "That hardly describes her now."

"She tamed herself, Mr. Ross, when she was twelve. She locked away her feelings, and never let anyone have the key. She so tightly controlled her emotions she became the perfect child. It didn't matter. People still whispered." Bitterness honed a sharp edge on Patrick's voice.

Duncan gentled his voice as he asked, "And Moira? Did she hear the whispers?"

Patrick nodded sadly. "Oh, most assuredly. As a child, she'd just laugh and dance away. Ah, her laugh was like a song..."

"Or the spring thaw dancing over the rocks in a

brook after a cold, hard winter," Duncan whispered, hearing the echoes of her laughter in his mind.

"Since that day, she's never really laughed again." Patrick's eyes mirrored the sadness in his voice.

The more Duncan learned, the more intrigued he became. "Which day?"

"The day she turned twelve," Patrick replied, his voice hard and unemotional.

Duncan's gut knotted. He knew he didn't want to hear but he had to. "What happened?" The question came out reluctantly.

"Moira found Maeve's journal and read it. Maeve wanted a child so desperately. She wrote in that damned diary..." He cleared his throat. "She wrote the words, 'If I have to, I'll make a pact with the faerie folk or even the devil himself to have Patrick's child.'" Patrick spat out the words as if they were the foulest things he'd ever tasted. "For Moira, it only confirmed in black and white what everyone had been saying about her."

Duncan tried to picture Moira at twelve, reading those words and hearing the hateful whispers replay in her mind. The woman-child he'd encountered last night became all too clear to him now. Yet, there were other pieces to this puzzle still unexplained. "Where does Deirdre fit into all this?"

Patrick sighed. "Garnet tired of playing the role of mother when Deirdre turned eight. She signed custody over to me and I've raised her ever since." Patrick gritted his teeth and clinched his mouth shut. He rubbed his forehead. "I'm not quite sure what's come over me. I don't discuss my daughters, especially not with a stranger."

Duncan quickly reassured him. "You needn't worry, Senator. I'm not in the habit of discussing my private conversations with anyone."

Patrick stared at Duncan long and hard. "Just

what tie do you have to my daughter, Mr. Ross?"

There it was at last, that question, a final missing piece. Duncan met the senator's stare with a level gaze. "I wish I knew, Senator."

Patrick appeared to be satisfied with his reply. "I have no reason to do so, but I trust you, Mr. Ross." He glanced at his watch. "I must apologize. I'm expecting some calls and I need to get back. Would you like to continue your ride alone or ride back with me?"

Duncan desperately wanted some time alone to mull over the past twenty-four hours. "If you don't mind, sir, I think this fellow would like to stretch his legs a bit more." He patted the big horse's neck affectionately.

"Star knows the way home." Patrick nodded toward Duncan's horse. "Just in case you get lost," he added with a smile. "Though I doubt that will happen. You seem to be a most capable man, Duncan Ross." He turned his bay around and headed back the way they'd come.

As the senator rounded a bend and disappeared, Duncan nudged the big horse with his heels. Lost in thought, he let the horse find his own way.

Chapter 10

As the sorrel ambled along, Duncan rehashed the previous evening's events. When he and Gemma had entered the great hall, he'd noticed Deirdre. With that mane of red hair and the reckless gold and green gown, what man could have missed her? Dismissing her as a man-hunter, Duncan had declared he was no prey for her by acknowledging the shy girl hiding in the senator's shadow. He'd suspected his actions would tweak the beautiful redhead. Moira's reaction to his touch had shocked him, not to mention his own reaction to her. His fingers still tingled from that jolt of electricity. He smiled, remembering how natural he'd felt carrying Moira into Allen Steele's study. She'd fit perfectly in his arms. What he didn't understand was the why of it.

Star whinnied softly, reminding Duncan of what he was supposed to be doing rather than mooning about the wee blonde lass. Off in the distance, he heard the faint splash of water spilling over rocks.

"Thirsty, are ya?" he asked the big horse. "Well, have a go then, if ya can find it."

A few minutes later, the sound of the water grew louder. The horse pushed through some underbrush into a small, shaded hollow. The stream, like Duncan's thoughts, cascaded over a series of falls, bubbling merrily across moss-covered boulders.

Ancient oaks ringed the glade, the grass already tinged green in this enchanted valley. Daffodils, crocuses, and snowdrops bloomed in profusion. A deer stopped grazing to stare, wary and hesitant, at the horse and rider but Duncan barely noticed the timid animal. It was the faerie maiden sitting on a rock at the edge of the stream who captured his attention.

Silky blonde hair shone like a golden aura, its waves undulating halfway down her back. When the maiden turned to face him, he noticed the creamy white blouse she wore tied loosely in front, revealing her soft curves with every breath. Her cerulean eyes locked onto his. She cocked her head to one side as she studied him, and then she slowly smiled.

"And what are you looking at, sir?" she asked, her voice sweet and sassy.

"I'm looking at you, miss," he answered, his voice choked with admiration.

"And what is it that brings yee here?" The faerie's laughter bubbled up under her words.

Duncan stepped off his horse, letting the reins trail. He walked toward her as if in a dream. "I've found something that interests me."

"And who, pray tell, might you be?" She arched a haughty brow.

"Just a man."

In the back of his mind, Duncan knew this sense of *déjà vu* all over again. This had happened before. Some other where. Some other when. He knelt in the soft grass before her rocky throne and drank in her beauty. A dainty chain of flowers lay in her lap. She tenderly crowned his loose brown hair with it before resting her hands lightly on his shoulders.

"Might yee be King of the Faerie?" Gold and silver lights danced in eyes the color of the dawn sky. She leaned over and her exquisite lips touched his. The tip of her pink tongue swirled against his teeth, enticing him to open to her tender assault. Lust, like a red-hot sword, sliced through Duncan's middle. "No," his queen mused. "Methinks yee are a man right enough."

Duncan's brain dragged his voice up through his dry throat and forced it out through parched lips. "Don't do this, Moira," he begged. His voice sounded ragged as he fought to be honorable. It was all he could to keep his hands from touching her.

Moira jerked upright like she'd been slapped. "I'm sorry, Duncan. I'm sorry," she stammered, not quite able to meet his gaze.

The red heat in his middle turned to cold iron twisting in his gut as he watched her. The anguish on her face became almost unbearable. "What is it, Moira?"

"I'm not like this!" She shivered. "This isn't me. It's..." Her voice broke and Duncan watched her fight back tears of anger and frustration. "Something happens," she continued in a whisper, fighting to deny the words. "Whenever you get close to me, this other person is lurking inside, and she climbs out and takes over. She wants things. From you." She kept her eyes lowered.

Duncan briefly entertained the thought Moira might be schizophrenic but discarded the idea immediately. She was too shaken by what she'd just done, and those memories he'd experienced with her, shared memories of that other place and time, were too fresh in his own mind to discount them out of hand.

He carefully schooled his voice so no hint of disbelief echoed in it. Moira worked to regain control. He didn't want to make it harder for her. "What does she want when she takes over?"

Moira blushed crimson from the neckline of her blouse to the roots of her hair. Duncan watched for a long moment as he guessed at the direction of her thoughts. Secretly, his ego was pleased. In a soothing voice, he continued. "Are these feelings hers? Or yours?"

Moira shook her head vehemently, looking shocked. "They must be hers."

Duncan rocked back on his heels. He understood now, recalling his conversation with her father. As another conversation echoed in his mind, he realized why she seemed so distressed. "'Tis a most glorious gift…"

He stared at her. In a voice filled with wonder, he asked, "Are you a virgin?"

He had to give her credit. Her gaze met his steadily. Only her voice quivered as she answered, "After last night, I'm not sure any more."

Duncan was astounded. Without thinking, he took her hands and pulled her down to him. He cradled her in his lap and nuzzled the soft nimbus of her hair. "'Tis nothing to be ashamed of, love," he whispered.

Her body tensed. "That's what he told her. But then he left her…" A sob choked off her words. "He left her to die."

Duncan wanted to shake her, and had to refrain from doing so. "What are you talking about, Moira?" His voice sounded harsh in his ears. "What do you mean he left her to die?"

Moira's tear-filled eyes were luminous fire opals as she gazed up at him. Her hand trembled as she cupped his cheek, her thumb resting gently atop his carotid pulse. She took a deep breath, perfectly timed to his own. The softly lit glade melted away into darkness.

****

The night was pitch dark but for the road glimmering dully under his horse's hooves. Fear's cold fist clutched his heart with icy fingers. He spurred his horse to greater speed. He could smell the acrid, woody odor of smoke. He whipped the tiring animal, something he'd never done. Up ahead, through the trees, he could see flames leaping and dancing. Shadowy figures pranced around the fire in some pagan ceremony.

His horse began to falter. "Come on, laddie," he urged. "Just a wee bit further now." He felt the horse leap forward in response. They burst into the clearing. Through choking clouds of smoke and angry orange flames, he could barely make out a figure trapped in the heart of the roaring bonfire. He saw her mouth open and the name she screamed hit him like an avalanche.

"Duncan!"

He couldn't say her name. To say it would mean the end.

"You promised," she screamed. "Oh, God, where are you?"

"Moira!" His scream tore from his mouth like a thousand banshees.

"I love you, Duncan," she cried. "Nothing can keep us apart. Not now. Not ever."

The fire exploded. Sparks shot into the air, a million fireflies dancing up to the stars. He blinked, banishing the after-images of the shooting stars behind his eyelids. Duncan looked at the fire. She was gone.

"Moira," he called, but there were no banshees this time, only the whisper of the unseen wind. The grotesque shadows noticed him then. They raised their scythes and axes, surrounding him menacingly.

"There he is," yelled a big man in rough clothes. "Her faerie lover. Kill him. Send them both to hell!"

Duncan drew his sword, brandishing it above his head. "Let us see how brave ya be facin' someone besides a defenseless woman," he challenged.

A gust of cold wind raced across the dying bonfire sending more sparks streaking across the pale, cold face of the moon. "Now and forever," the wind whispered. "Now and forever."

The mob shrank back from the mask of terrible fury his face had become. They huddled together, seeking bravery in their numbers. Before they could summon up the courage to attack, a single bolt of lightning split the air around them. The big man stared in disbelief. Blue sparks flew from the dark warrior's sword and both he and his horse were bathed in the eerie blue light.

"God preserve us," the man moaned as he sank to his knees. "What have we done?" He hid his face in his hands, too afraid to witness what was happening. When he finally found the courage to look up, the dark stranger was gone, and the fire had grown cold.

****

Duncan became aware of the fact something firm but yielding cradled his head. Next, he was aware of soft breaths drying the tears trailing down his cheeks.

"Moira," he whispered, the name torn from the very depths of his soul.

"You couldn't have saved her." Her soft voice sounded reassuring.

"I tried," he cried in anguish.

"Shh."

He closed his eyes as she started to hum. Then, as clear and sweet as the stream beside him, she started to sing. Gaelic it was, the old tongue, and that was reassuring, too. He let the melody dip and sway around him. He opened his heart to let the healing touch of words only his deepest memory could understand caress his pain away.

His cheek found warm skin, and he turned his head to kiss it. His mouth followed the dainty curve of her neck before his lips found hers. Duncan kissed her gently, full of wonder. Not for his life could he explain what had just happened but he didn't care. He was here. She was here. He reveled in the taste of her kiss, in the feel of her soft body next to his. He wanted to crush her to him, but his strong arms held her like the precious gift he knew her to be.

"Ah, Duncan." Her breath teased his skin.

He wondered which Moira called to him, then decided it didn't matter. The here and now was all he cared about. Past and future had ceased to exist, unifying all the threads of time to weave the present.

"Moira." The sound of her name on his lips, like her kisses, filled him with a joy beyond all knowing.

Across the glade, the big sorrel snorted and stamped one foot. Duncan came instantly alert. The horse looked at something sensed but unseen, his ears pricked forward. Duncan stiffened and his nostrils flared as if he could scent the danger. Moira started to speak, but Duncan shushed her with one gentle finger against her lips. She froze as he whispered in her ear, "There's someone nearby."

Duncan stood up and pulled Moira to her feet. He wrapped his arms around her, kissing the throbbing pulse point of her neck. "We're being watched." His slow and sensual actions belied the whispered urgency in his voice. "Act like we haven't noticed."

As nonchalantly as they could, they walked arm-in-arm to the sorrel, and Duncan caught up the reins. He checked the girth, then swung up into the saddle. Leaning down, he caught Moira around the waist and lifted her to the saddle in front of him. A branch cracked nearby, sending a flock of birds winging skyward. Moira squeezed Duncan's muscled forearm.

"'Tis all right, love," he whispered. The endearment rolled off his tongue without a thought.

Surefooted, the horse moved through the trees to the path. Duncan's arm tightened around her waist as he urged the big horse into a canter. Though precariously perched sidesaddle in front of him, Moira found the horse's rhythm and naturally moved with it.

After putting a good distance between them and the glade, Duncan slowed the horse to a walk. His grip on Moira's waist slackened only slightly. He enjoyed the feel of her in his arms. A playful breeze teased her hair and coaxed a strand free to caress Duncan's cheek.

"What happened back there?"

Duncan looked at her, trying to decipher the question. A lot had happened back there, most of which he had no explanation for.

As if sensing his confusion, Moira asked another question. "How did you know someone was there?"

He shrugged, glad for safer territory and a more clearly defined subject. "The horse," he replied. "He knew before I did."

"It was probably one of the Steeles' farmhands. Why did we have to leave?"

Duncan looked at her, his gaze locking on her face, drinking in every feature. "Because you were in danger."

Moira looked askance. "In danger? From who?"

"I don't know." Duncan refused to feel sheepish. She had been in danger. In fact, his gut still rumbled with fear for her.

A saucy smile tweaked her lips. "Maybe it was only my virtue that was threatened."

Duncan glowered at her. "That's a gift to be cherished," he admonished. He took a deep breath. "No, someone watched in the woods, Moira, and it was you they were interested in."

Her expression sobered a bit and turned wry with an arched brow. "It seems I'm not the only one with a sixth sense. Who are you, Duncan Ross?" When he didn't answer, she mused out loud, "Maybe you are the King of Faerie."

Her teasing caused him to smile. "No, little one," he replied. "I'm just a man."

Moira knew exactly what squirming against him would cause. His reaction pressed against her, immediate and hard. He groaned and she giggled. "Aye, that you are, Duncan Ross."

Duncan squeezed her waist in a vain attempt to stop her gyrations. "Be still, woman," he growled. "Lest I take you here and now."

****

The silent watcher followed them as best he could on foot until the horse climbed out of the woods onto the main road leading back to the house. This morning's encounter disappointed in a way. When the girl had slipped out of the house before daylight, he'd followed in hopes of getting at her. However, there'd be another time in another place, he decided. He'd learned some very interesting things this morning—very interesting things indeed.

Chapter 11

Gemma, despite the warming temperatures, appreciated her choice of gray tweed slacks and a lightweight heather sweater as she sat on the terrace sipping coffee. A muffin waited uneaten on the plate in front of her. She'd awakened what seemed like hours ago, and Duncan's side of the bed had been cold. *The man positively radiates heat,* she thought bitterly. He must have left her bed quite some time before she awakened. Duncan continued to slip away from her, and she felt helpless to stop him. She rubbed her temples and adjusted her sunglasses. Her hangover didn't help matters or her mood much either.

Deirdre remained inside talking to Margaret about plans for the day, but no one seemed to know Moira's whereabouts. None of the servants had seen her, though her room was empty. Gemma had checked, on the pretense of seeing how she felt. Simpson, the butler, reported seeing Duncan very early before the sun was even up.

Movement down by the stable caught her eye. Even at that distance, she recognized Duncan's broad shoulders and long, dark brown hair. Her expression twisted into a scowl as she recognized the person riding in front of him. She stood up to get a better view, and as she watched, Duncan swung Moira off the horse. His broad back masked what he was doing but Moira was held suspended by his side for a long moment. Gemma's eyes narrowed to angry slits as Duncan let Moira slide to the ground, suspecting he'd kissed the girl.

She didn't wait to see any more. Gemma hurtled through the French doors and clattered up the wide stone steps to her room. She slammed the door with enough force to echo down the long hall. Viciously, she twisted the lock.

****

Moira waited while Duncan led the sorrel into the stable. Together they walked up the path to the house but neither made a move to touch the other. On the terrace, Moira paused, turning to face him.

"Duncan..." She hesitated, but he knew she wanted to say more.

"What is it, lass?" he prompted.

"What's happened, Duncan?"

This time, he knew she asked about those unseen but deeply felt things passing between them. "I don't know," he answered honestly.

"Who are we?"

He reached deep within, searching for the answer. "I don't know." He curled the fingers of one hand around the nape of her neck and pulled her to his broad chest. "As a boy, I knew I had to be a soldier when I grew up. There was no choice for me. My father wanted his heir groomed to run the family estates and to someday take his seat in Parliament. But I had to be a soldier." Duncan took a deep breath before he continued. "There was a sword, Moira, passed down for centuries in my mother's family. The first time I touched it..." His voice trailed off.

She waited for him to finish. When he didn't, she looked up at him. "Tell me, Duncan." Her voice coaxed him to continue.

"When I picked it up, it was like I'd held that

sword for my whole life. It became a part of me." He paused again. She remained silent this time, as if sensing he needed time to choose his words. When he finally continued, he whispered the words. "The same thing happened last night when I touched your hand. That same jolt of recognition. I don't believe in reincarnation or any other New Age hocus pocus, but I cannot deny this. You are a part of me, Moira. I don't know how. Or why. But you are. If I were to lose you..." His voice cracked.

She took a step back and looked up at him. Before she could ask the question poised on the tip of her tongue, he hushed her with a gentle kiss on her soft lips. "No more questions, Moira O'Connor," he told her. "You are who you are, and I am who I am. We're together. Does anything else matter?"

Moira's smile looked tentative. "This is all new to me, Duncan."

"I know, lass." He brushed his lips across hers. "For me as well. But I'll be here for you each step of the way."

Movement in a window on the second floor caught their attention. Moira stared up at the house for a long moment trying to decide who occupied that room. She'd felt the implied fear again in the pounding of his heart against her cheek when he spoke of losing her. His hands pressed against her back, urging her closer. She resisted, searching his ruggedly handsome face for some clue, some hint, some assurance. Her chest rose and fell as she took a steadying breath.

"What about Gemma?"

"What about her?" Duncan's voice registered surprise.

"Duncan, I..."

"Hush, little one." He took her hand and kissed the exact center of her palm. "Gemma and I had a relationship of convenience. For both of us. I will not hurt you, Moira. Not now. Not ever."

She was not about to be put off. "But..."

He shook his head. "No buts. I will take care of Gemma. Now that I have found you, I will never let you go. Never." His voice sounded harsh, but she recognized the fervent emotion behind it. As she looked into his eyes, she trusted the promise shining there.

Still holding her hand, Duncan led her into the house and up to the second floor. He stopped at her door. She didn't want to let him go, but she needed time to sort out everything that had happened. Ellie's appearance made the parting a little easier.

"G'mornin', miss. Sir," the little maid greeted them in her broad brogue. "Missus says luncheon will be served shortly so yee need to freshen up. Oh, goodness, Miss, yee've gotten grass stains on your lovely blouse. Mayhaps I can get 'em out if I put it to soakin' right away."

"Would ya be needin' any help changin', Miss?" Duncan whispered, his lips twitching in a wicked smile.

Moira sputtered for a minute, and then answered his bawdy suggestion with a curt, "I'll see you at lunch."

She opened the door to her room and entered, Ellie close on her heels. Before Duncan could follow, Ellie blocked the way, a little bantam hen protecting her chick. "Miss said she'd be seein' yee at lunch," she declared, shutting the door firmly in Duncan's face. Turning to Moira, Ellie sighed, "Aye and he'd be a handsome one."

Moira smiled at the closed door, warmth flooding her cheeks. "Aye, that he would, Ellie, m'girl."

****

Duncan continued chuckling as he approached the door to the room he shared with Gemma. He'd plainly heard both declarations from behind Moira's door. He didn't exactly reek from the smell of horse, but the odor was strong enough he wanted a quick shower and change of clothes. He turned the knob, but the door didn't budge. He tapped lightly and called, "Gemma? Gemma, it's me. Let me in."

He could barely hear her muffled voice as she called, "Go away, Duncan."

Duncan leaned against the door to hear her better. "Gemma, what's wrong?"

Her voice, harsh and accusing, came clearly through the door this time. Duncan guessed she stood just on the other side. "I saw you with Moira." She all but screamed the words. "Did you leave my bed to go to hers?"

Duncan didn't want this discussion while he stood in the hall with Gemma barricaded on the other side of the door. "C'mon, Gemma. Unlock the door so we can discuss this in private. You wanted to make an impression on these people. I doubt this is the one you meant."

"I saw you kiss Moira." There was no mistaking her accusatory tone.

He wanted to end her tiresome game. "I don't know what you think you saw, Gemma. I went riding with Senator O'Connor. He came back early, and I bumped into Moira while she was out walking. I gave her a ride back. That's all," he lied. "Please unlock the door so we can talk about this."

"I don't want to talk," she screamed. "Go away!"

Duncan shrugged and turned away from the door. There would be no dealing with Gemma until she calmed down. Indecisive, he considered returning to Moira's room. The distinctive click of a door closing snapped him out of his reverie. Looking up and down the hallway, he saw no sign of activity. He hoped the click hadn't come from Moira's door, and that she hadn't overheard what he'd said while trying to placate Gemma. He was still trying to decide what to do when Simpson appeared at his elbow.

"If you will follow me, sir?"

The butler led him down the hall to a room across the hall from Moira's. Opening the door, Simpson ushered him inside. Duncan felt like he'd stepped into a room at one of his father's houses. Paneled in dark, rich walnut, the large room seemed cozy. The tartan plaids and paisley linens tumbled across the huge four-poster bed. But for the green and blue of the Black Watch tartan, this room could be almost an exact duplicate of one at the house in Inverness. Simpson quietly withdrew while he looked around.

He wasn't surprised to find his luggage on a chest in the corner and his shaving kit in the spacious bath. He'd long since given up trying to outguess those who worked and lived "below stairs." They saw all, knew all, and covered all exigencies. In this case, Duncan was grateful. It would save a scene with Gemma later. As he pulled out a pair of casual khaki slacks, he wondered how Simpson had managed to retrieve his belongings. The man had accomplished it, which was all that mattered. Adding a soft cashmere sweater the color of the sky just before sunset to the stack on the bed, he realized it was the only article of clothing he'd brought Gemma hadn't picked out. *It's exactly the shade of Moira's eyes when she's aroused.* The thought curled one corner of his mouth as he kicked off his boots, then shed his jeans and shirt. He padded into the bath, turned on the shower, and adjusted the spray to cold. With Moira on his mind, not even the chilly water could dampen his spirits.

****

Suddenly exhausted, Moira wrapped her old flannel robe around her tighter and sank gratefully into the plump pillows on her bed. The past twenty-four hours had left her senses reeling. Ellie puttered around, clucking like a little hen over the stains on Moira's blouse.

"Would yee like me to draw yee a bath, miss?" Ellie asked solicitously. "Them shadows under yer eyes make yee look pale as a ghost, miss, if I may be so bold to be sayin' such."

Moira shook her head.

"May I lay out somethin' for yee to be wearin' to lunch then?"

Moira smiled tiredly and shrugged. Fashion was the last thing on her mind. "Any old thing will do, Ellie."

"Well, I don't know if 'tis any old thing, but this arrived for yee a bit ago." The little maid's smile brightened as she held out a large, white box.

Curious, Moira sat up. The name of a Charlottesville clothing store was embossed in gold on the top of the cream-colored box. "I wonder where this came from."

Ellie shrugged as she lifted off the top and pulled back the crisp tissue paper. A soft mound of material tinted a pale shade of peach snuggled inside. Ellie lifted out a long knit tunic made of a luscious blend of silk and cashmere. She noticed a second item nestled under another layer of tissue paper. She laid the tunic across the bed, and then unfolded the next item—a long, slightly flared skirt in a dainty floral pattern of soft peach, green and cream silk.

"Oh, miss," Ellie sighed. "'Tis a grand color with your golden hair and skin." Moira leaned over to touch the soft fabric. "And yee've got them brown boots in the wardrobe." Ellie all but clapped her hands. "Aye, 'tis a grand statement yee'll be makin' fair certain. Just like a fashion magazine."

Ellie's enthusiasm made her giggle. Deirdre had

always been the clotheshorse in the family. Catching a glimpse of her reflection in the dressing table mirror, she peered closely at her reflection. For perhaps the first time in her life, she really studied her image in the mirror. Her features, which up until now, had never seemed to fit together quite right. She saw a completely different picture. The woman returning her earnest stare seemed a stranger. *Why, I'm almost pretty.* The revelation startled her.

"Are you sure about the boots?" she asked, turning back to Ellie.

"Oh, aye, miss. 'Tis the latest look. I'll take 'em down and have one of the boys put a grand shine on 'em."

Moira sank back against the pillows as Ellie slipped out the door. Only one person she knew would be thoughtful enough to order her a new outfit. She'd be sure to thank her father when she saw him at lunch.

****

Margaret Steele flitted about the room she referred to as the conservatory. Built like a Victorian solarium, the multi-faceted glass windows allowed ample sunlight to pour in, spotlighting the myriad tropical plants clustered profusely about the room. Even a pair of exotic birds cooed in an ornate gilt cage. Margaret loved this room, having planned it as a place to entertain with casual luncheons. As two maids set the table, she fussed over the seating arrangements. One guest had declined at the last minute, leaving an odd number with more men than women.

The day had also turned out fair after a week of cold rain. For a moment, Margaret worried about the menu. The first course of lobster bisque might be too heavy for the weather. The fresh green salad and Cook's special key lime chicken would be perfect, though. Deciding the bisque would suffice, Margaret went upstairs to change. Her other guests would be arriving soon and she wanted to be ready to greet them.

Chapter 12

The big Land Rover clawed up the gravel road as it had been built to do. The barrel-chested man at the wheel chuckled to himself. This vehicle was the only thing the British had ever done right. He powered the big SUV into a turn, sending up a spray of gravel. As the Rover straightened out, its wheels found firm purchase on the brick drive. The massive granite house loomed up ahead.

"Bloody rich robber barons," the man spat as he looked at the huge edifice.

He parked the Rover among several Lincolns, a couple of BMWs, a Mercedes, and a little Rover TC2000 sedan. His Land Rover dwarfed the smaller vehicle but its presence delighted him. Climbing out, he spotted Margaret Steele waiting for him on the broad front steps. Plastering on his most charming smile, he crossed the parking area to meet her.

"Mr. O'Rourke," Margaret gushed. "We're so pleased you could join us."

"But not half as pleased as me to be here, Mrs. Steele," he answered, charm positively oozing from every pore in his body.

The dimples on Margaret's cheeks crinkled. "Oh, Mr. O'Rourke," she dissembled. "You are so charming."

"'Tis the company, madam. A beautiful woman always brings out my best."

"Oh, you," she tittered as the massive front doors were opened by unseen hands. Margaret ushered him inside. "The men are hiding in the study. If you'll follow me?"

He followed the petite woman across the vast entry hall. *Not even noon yet and she's drippin' in diamonds,* he grumbled to himself.

Margaret tapped lightly on the door before opening it and entering. "Allen, dear," she called to her husband. "Look who's arrived."

He strode through the door, pausing to study the group. Allen Steele advanced across the room, his hand outstretched. Senator Patrick O'Connor and that professor, Michael Shanahan, both looked uncomfortable about his presence. If he hadn't been watching closely for reactions, he would have missed the slight narrowing of Duncan Ross's eyes and the flare of the Scotsman's nostrils. Two younger men rounded out the party but as they were strangers, he paid them little attention. He plastered a genial smile on his face.

"Seamus, good to have you here. I'd like you to meet my other guests." Allen's handshake pulled O'Rourke into the center of the room. "Seamus O'Rourke has been instrumental in building up my antique weapons collection," he explained. "He's the one who discovered the dirk I showed you last night, Patrick. Senator Patrick O'Connor, Seamus O'Rourke. Professor Michael Shanahan. Ward Winston. His father owns Wintech Manufacturing, Seamus. This is John Murray, a fine young attorney originally from Alexandria."

O'Rourke acknowledged the two younger men. They remained of no particular interest. The quiet man across the room? Now he was worthy of his attention. "And you, sir?" O'Rourke asked pointedly as he stared at Duncan.

"Oh, I'm sorry, Seamus," Allen interjected. "This

is Duncan Ross. He's here with Gemma Todd, our decorator."

"Yes," O'Rourke said, his smile quirking a bit. "I know Miss Todd." He played an excellent hand of poker, and he'd noticed the almost imperceptible narrowing of Ross's eyes and the slight intake of breath at the mention of Gemma's name.

Margaret interrupted any further conversation when she tapped on the door and peeked in again. She smiled sweetly at her husband, and then beckoned to Duncan. "Excuse me, dear," she told Allen, "but I need to borrow Mr. Ross for a few minutes."

Duncan stood up and walked to the door. Margaret took his arm and escorted him out of the room. Closing the door behind them, she turned and smiled contritely. "I'm sorry, Mr. Ross, but Gemma won't come out of her room. She seems to be very upset even though she insists she isn't. I've tried talking to her to no avail. She's locked the door so I know something has to be amiss. Would you mind checking on her?"

His equilibrium already reeling from O'Roarke's arrival, he wondered about the games being played here. Duncan was not a happy camper. First Bradford Williams and now this brute. He'd feigned disinterest when Allen Steele greeted the big man, and he'd managed to hide his surprise when O'Roarke mentioned knowing Gemma. How could he not know that? O'Rourke recognized his name and face, which in itself would have been enough to put Duncan on alert. He was more than familiar with O'Rourke. He'd tracked the man across the Atlantic six months ago.

As he explained why he'd be the last person Gemma would talk to, Gemma herself appeared at the top of the stairs, precluding his explanation.

"There you are, Duncan," she called down. "May

124

I have a word with you?"

He stopped mid-word, dumbstruck by her tone of voice. She sounded so sweet and contrite, he became immediately suspicious. Could this be the same woman who had locked him out earlier? Since her mood had changed so drastically, maybe now she would listen to him.

He followed her back to her room. Duncan didn't want to hurt her feelings, but he knew their relationship was over. He would never share a room with her, would never touch her again. Not after last night. Not after this morning. Not when the mere thought of Moira made him go weak in the knees and grow hard as a rock.

Gemma shut the door behind them. When she plopped down in a chair, Duncan granted her a measure of respect. As a rule, she used her body to get what she wanted. A wave of relief hit when she refrained from trying to seduce him. She was one of those women who believed a man's brains hung between his legs, and sex became her sure-fire way to get what she wanted.

"You wanted to talk, Duncan?" She purred at him.

He hid the wince shimmering under his skin. When Moira said his name, it rolled off her tongue like a caress. When Gemma said it, it sounded harsh and crude.

"I'm not sure where to start." He hesitated. How to explain he'd fallen in lust with a dream, and then the dream appeared in real life? He loved the dream, both real and imagined, and by whatever stretch of the imagination, a seven-hundred-year history colored that love. Thinking of Moira made him grow hard again. He shifted his stance so his arousal wouldn't be so obvious. "There are things going on here, Gemma. Things you wouldn't understand," he finally admitted.

"Try me," she urged coldly, about to lose her temper.

Duncan's thoughts tumbled, sorting through the options as he looked for the right tack to take. "I have a job to do, Gemma."

"Does that job include seducing the senator's daughters?" she spat, losing her battle with her temper.

"Gemma!" he admonished.

She jumped up and paced the floor. "What am I to think, Dunnie? One throws herself at you, and every time I turn around, the other's in your arms."

Before he retorted, a light tap on the door interrupted him. Ellie's muffled voice announced, "Lunch is served, Mister and Miss."

"Look, Dunnie," Gemma preempted him. "Let's just get through this weekend. We'll talk about all this nonsense when we get home." Before he could stop her, she headed out the door.

He felt a little guilty he hadn't made her stay and listen to him. He wouldn't be going home with her, nor would he be spending the rest of the weekend with her. He should have insisted she stay until he finished the discussion. He liked her well enough, but he'd known from the beginning there would never be anything permanent between them. She'd always given him the impression she felt the same. He wondered when she'd changed her mind.

Gemma awaited him at the door to the conservatory so he had no choice but to enter with her. He glanced around as he came through the door. The three young musicians from the previous night played softly in a nook across the room. The lawyer and the rich boy vied for Deirdre's attention, while Allen Steel and Seamus O'Rourke were in deep conversation with the senator. Professor Shanahan chatted with Margaret, or rather, he listened politely to Margaret's small talk. Duncan would have known without looking Moira was not present.

While talking to Michael, Margaret counted noses and kept track of her guests. Gemma and Duncan entered together and she let out a little sigh of relief. Everyone had arrived but Moira. She decided everyone could be seated while they waited so she ushered Michael to his place at the table. To her consternation, someone had tampered with the place cards. Deirdre was seated next to Duncan with Gemma at the far end of the table. After Deidre's declarations last night, that just wouldn't do. Before she could rectify the situation, Deirdre slipped into the seat she had purloined.

Well, that damage is done, Margaret reasoned, but she did her best to salvage the situation by surreptitiously moving Gemma's card back to the other side of Duncan. In her maneuvering, she failed to realize she'd created a triangle with Duncan caught in the middle between Deirdre and Gemma, while Moira formed the apex directly across from him.

Moira slipped into the room just as the men moved to their seats. Margaret gaped, shocked at the girl's transformation. She glanced around the room. Duncan blinked rapidly, looking like someone had opened heavy curtains in a dark room and glorious sunlight now spilled in. Margaret smiled. Moira appeared positively radiant. Her golden hair shimmered in loose waves across her shoulders and down her back. The long peach tunic and silk skirt she wore clung in all the right places. Her cheeks glowed and her blue eyes were the color of the spring sky.

Patrick stared at his younger daughter. "Maeve," he whispered. Margaret heard the pain in the murmured name. Her throat constricted with memories from the past, as she suspected Patrick remembered them, too. Margaret knew he'd ordered the outfit for his daughter and as soon as the clerk had described the color of this outfit, she'd known it would be perfect.

Margaret almost enjoyed the expression on Deirdre's face as the redhead suddenly realized her sister had changed dramatically. How would she feel now that Moira might actually provide some real competition?

"So the mouse has found her roar," Deirdre muttered darkly. "Well, let the games begin, sister mine."

Gemma stared first at Moira and then over at Deirdre. Margaret couldn't read her decorator's expression but suspected she bore no good will toward either of the O'Connor sisters. Considering the circumstances, Margaret couldn't really blame her. Her attention returned to Moira and Duncan. The two exchanged a knowing look Margaret found puzzling. He took a step forward, as if to claim Moira, but Gemma laid a restraining hand on his arm. His gaze never left Moira's face as the blonde crossed the room.

Once everyone found their seats at the table, Margaret realized the error she'd made. Even now, Duncan couldn't take his eyes off Moira. Convinced something dreadful was going to happen and unable to eat for fretting, she barely touched the lobster bisque even though Cook had sprinkled caviar on top of the thick soup.

Trouble arrived with dessert. As Deirdre was served, she turned to Duncan. "So tell me, Mr. Ross. Did you enjoy your ride with my sister this morning?" Poison dripped off her tongue like honey.

Gemma flashed Duncan a hurt look. He, however, only had eyes for Moira.

"Actually," he said, nodding in Deirdre's direction, but his gaze on Moira, "I went riding with your father, Miss O'Connor. I didn't run into Moira until later." Duncan's face remained poker-straight, but his eyes danced with reckless amber glints. "And yes, we had a most enjoyable conversation."

Deirdre leaned over, pressing her breasts against Duncan's right biceps. He glanced at her, blinked as he noticed she also showed him her ample cleavage, and then ignored the show. "That's about all my sister is good for, Mr. Ross. Conversation. If you are interested in something more substantial, someone who isn't all talk and no action..." Deirdre paused to let the implication sink in. Gemma took his hand possessively. Deirdre saw the gesture and without missing a beat, she continued, "Or when you decide you want a real woman, I never lock my door."

"Deirdre," Margaret snapped, horrified. "That is completely uncalled for." Turning to Gemma, she smiled apologetically. "Gemma, please ignore Deirdre. She seems to think she can have whatever she wants, including any man who catches her fancy."

Gemma stared at Moira before she answered, "Deirdre is not my concern."

"I'm so glad, dear." Margaret's relief gushed out with her words. "I wouldn't want her antics to spoil your weekend."

Though replying to Margaret, Gemma aimed her point at Duncan and Moira. "I'm sure they won't."

Relieved the meal had finally ended, Margaret, the ever-diligent hostess announced, "Coffee will be served in the parlor. We have a few minutes to freshen up but hurry back. I have something most interesting planned." As she ushered everyone toward the door, she fervently hoped she could use the afternoon's entertainment to dam the undercurrents swirling through the room during lunch.

Chapter 13

After a few minutes, Margaret gathered up all her strays and herded them into the parlor. Duncan had wanted to talk to Moira after lunch, but Gemma remained glued to his side. As they entered the parlor, she steered him as far away from Moira and Deirdre as she could. As Duncan's gaze roamed the room, it kept settling on Moira, checking on her, adoring her.

Margaret's taste appeared abundantly clear amid the flowery chintz and ruffles. Where the study had been very much a man's room, this was the domain of the lady of the house. Duncan smiled as he settled back. Though frilly, the large, overstuffed furniture sat comfortably, even for a man. Across the room, Moira shared a striped loveseat with the lawyer, John Murray. Jealousy burned in his gut. He should be the one sitting next to her. With effort, he controlled his resentment. He realized it didn't matter where she was or who she was with. Moira would always be his, just as his heart would always belong to her. Secure with this thought, he relaxed.

Almost as if he'd willed it, the lawyer stood up and moved to the sideboard at the end of the room to get coffee. A more sinister presence immediately took his place next to Moira. When a look of fear flitted across her face, he willed himself to stay still. He could not tip his hand. Not yet. Even as he watched, her fear passed. Her eyes narrowed and her chin came up in a show of sheer defiance.

That's my bonnie girl, he applauded mentally. Her reaction to the big man only confirmed his own.

****

She'd been so full of Duncan at lunch she'd ignored the warning prickle on the back of her neck when she'd entered the conservatory. A part of her mind registered the fact Seamus O'Rourke sat at the other end of the table as she took her place, but Deirdre's predatory nature put her on immediate guard. O'Rourke could do nothing in a roomful of people, which included her father and Duncan. As the big man settled in beside her, she realized having people around didn't matter. She now wished she'd paid more attention to her own instincts.

"So we meet again, Miss O'Connor," O'Rourke said gruffly, barely loud enough for her to hear. She glared at him. "You won't be slippin' through me fingers so easy this time," he promised ominously, his leer so intense she felt he undressed her.

Her gut churned. Evil clung to this man like the smell of stale smoke. She gritted her teeth, refusing to give him the satisfaction of knowing he had rattled her. The threat buried in his words revealed more went on than the fact she'd injured his pride earlier in the week. Try as she might, she couldn't imagine why he'd targeted her.

"If you will excuse me, Mr. O'Rourke," she said haughtily as she stood up. "My cup seems to be empty."

His meaty hand clamped onto her wrist. She gasped as searing pain shot up her arm. Her skin felt like it was burning away where his fingers squeezed her bare skin.

Duncan bolted to his feet, shaking off Gemma's clutching hands. Striding across the room, he faced down O'Rourke. The two men glowered at each other. "Let her go," Duncan ordered in a voice rimed with frost.

A thin, cold smile stretched O'Rourke's mouth. His grip on Moira's wrist loosened but before she could slip free, his fingers tightened again. "Another time, Miss O'Connor." His snarl turned his words into a vicious promise.

She jerked free and almost fell backwards. She wanted nothing more than Duncan's arms around her, wanting only to rest her head against his muscular chest, and listen to his heart beat in a rhythm matching her own. Every eye in the room focused on them so instead of giving in to her own desire, she held her head high. She slipped around behind Duncan, and as her hands brushed across his low back those now familiar electric shocks danced up her arms.

"Thank you," she whispered to him before walking quickly to the sideboard.

Despite her outward show of calm, her cup rattled on its saucer as she tried to pour coffee from the carafe. Setting the saucer on the table, she took a long, deep breath to calm down.

"Allow me," a softly burred voice said at her elbow. Michael Shanahan took the carafe from her and filled both their cups. "Trouble with Mr. O'Rourke again?" He sounded concerned.

She spilled some sugar as she spooned it into her cup. She was glad he pretended not to notice. Filling her lungs with another deep breath, she kept her voice soft as she demanded hotly, "Why does that man keep showing up?"

"The proverbial bad penny," Michael told her with a smile. "He turns up when you least expect it."

She eyed the little professor speculatively. "Sounds a lot like someone else I know." The words came out as pointed as she'd meant them.

"Aye, doesn't it now," Michael replied, staring

across the room at Duncan.

Margaret claimed center stage by calling for everyone's attention. Moira moved away from Michael and settled on the plump arm of her father's chair. With Moira safe next to her father, Duncan moved back to his original seat next to Gemma. He didn't necessarily want to sit there, but he had a good view of the room and all the guests from that vantage point. When everyone's attention focused on her, Margaret explained they were in for an afternoon of Irish history and stories.

"But, before Professor Shanahan begins to regale you with tales of the past, we are going to play a little game." As the guests exchanged puzzled glances, Allen slumped deeper into his chair, looking disgruntled. Margaret noticed and made a show of ignoring him. "I find names fascinating," she explained. "Both their linguistic roots and their meanings or translations." She smiled prettily at her husband. "Allen absolutely detests this little game so I shall start with him."

"Allen is Irish Gaelic and means handsome." The little woman blew her husband a kiss and added, "As I'm sure all the ladies will agree." Allen had the good graces to blush. "Steele is English and the meaning is obvious. Now, Margaret is Greek in origin and means pearl-like." She turned to her husband. "Just so you know, Allen, when you shop for my birthday present next month." She winked at her guests and everyone chuckled along with her. "This is how my little game works so who wants to be next?"

John Murray raised his hand. "I'm game, Miss Margaret," he said. After getting coffee, he'd moved to sit beside Deirdre. Volunteering gave him a good excuse to drape his arm over the back of the sofa he shared with her.

"Oh, you are easy, John." Margaret smiled until

her dimple showed.

"I've heard that," Ward chuckled from the other side of Deirdre.

Margaret pouted at him even though her eyes crinkled at the corners. "Murray is Gaelic for seaworthy and John is from the Hebrew meaning gracious gift." Margaret paused for a moment, pondering what she'd just said. "Does that make you a gift from the sea?"

"Like tuna?" Ward quipped. Everyone chuckled.

Margaret turned to Ward. "Since you are so outspoken, Ward, I'll pick on you next." He let out a facetious groan. "Winston comes from the Old English *windes-tun*, from the friend's town. Ward is also Old English—*Weard*, meaning watchman or guardian." Margaret glanced at John, one brow forming a graceful arch over her twinkling eye. "That means you should be very watchful when your friend is in town."

John grinned at Ward and feinted a punch to the other man's jaw. "You can be sure I will, Miss Margaret."

Margaret obviously enjoyed herself now that her guests were getting into the game. She gazed around the room, seeking her next target. Michael caught her eye. "Professor Shanahan, how about you?"

Michael's chin jutted out stubbornly. "I'm well aware, Mrs. Steele, of me own namin'," he told her with a great deal of dignity.

"Then please enlighten us, sir," Margaret teased.

Michael sat up straight in his chair and nodded to her. In a voice long familiar with lecturing, he said, "Shanahan is Irish Gaelic. Originally, it was *seanahan*, meaning small, wise one."

Snickers erupted from more than one mouth and then became snorts as people tried to choke them back. "It's okay, Michael," Moira spoke up. "It's not the size of the package, it's what's inside that counts." The snickers built, becoming peals of laughter rolling across the room. When she realized her encouragement came out as a double entendre, she turned crimson.

"Ah, 'tis true, Miss O'Connor," Michael exclaimed, "...as all me lady friends will attest."

The game turned quite ribald, and Margaret looked delighted. "Shall I do, Michael?" she asked, one corner of her mouth quirking in a little grin.

"You'd do me very nicely, madam," Michael enjoined, making even Margaret blush. As the hoots and catcalls finally subsided, he continued in a rich, sonorous voice. "Michael is a derivative from the Hebrew language, though it seems we Irish have appropriated it for our own. In its Hebrew form, Michael translates into he who is like God."

John looked at the little professor. "I always knew God would look more like George Burns than Charlton Heston." He fought back a snicker.

Allen finally jumped into the fray. "You're wrong, John. It's Moses who looked like Charlton Heston. God has always looked like George Burns."

Margaret was losing control. Her hands fluttered as she tried to still the catcalls. Over the noise, she asked, "Mr. O'Rourke, are you game?" At his nod, she continued. "Rourke is Irish Gaelic for illustrious ruler. The Irish addition of the O changes it to mean of the ruler or from the ruler. *Seamus* is the Gaelic form of James, from the old Spanish Jayme, meaning supplanter. As a supplanter of the ruler, I suppose the monarchy should be worried about you, Mr. O'Rourke."

A cloud of anger drifted briefly through O'Rourke's hard, blue eyes, turning them a dark gray. Duncan and Michael both watched the man's reaction. *Damn but the woman's hit close to the mark*, Duncan thought.

A charming smile lit the lower half of O'Rourke's face but it never reached his eyes. "Since America is a democracy, I'll just have to vote the bloody buggers out."

Everyone laughed, but a few eyes turned toward Patrick waiting for his reaction.

"I think he means you, Patrick," Margaret giggled. "I guess that makes you my next victim."

Duncan winced inside. Was Margaret aware of all the undercurrents swirling through the room? Could she possibly know more about the players than he had given her credit for? He gazed over at Moira. She watched the byplay as intently as he.

Margaret blithely continued the game. "O'Connor, of course, is a famous Irish clan. Connor, or Conor with one 'n', traces, back to the Gaelic *conan*, meaning wise and heroic."

"Or barbarian," O'Rourke muttered.

"Patrick, as we all know, is the patron saint of Ireland, and the name comes from the Latin *patrice*, or nobleman."

The senator seemingly overheard O'Rourke's comment, and obviously decided it would be better to play along so he wouldn't appear intimidated. He raised his voice so everyone would hear. "I suppose that makes me a noble barbarian."

Margaret's face went blank for a moment, then she smiled as the light bulb went on. "Oh, of course! Conan the Barbarian." She blinked. "Wasn't that a movie or something?" The group got a good chuckle out of her naïveté and a few applauded the senator's willingness to poke fun at himself. Margaret scanned the room again. "Who am I leaving out? Oh. Dear little Gemma. How could I forget you? Gemma is Italian, of course. A small jewel, and you are, my dear. I can't wait until you've finished decorating the entire estate. Now, Todd is Middle English, meaning fox."

Across the room, Ward let out a wolf-whistle. "She sure is," he declared, leering at her good-naturedly.

The other man's attention surely pleased Gemma, and Duncan noticed from the corner of his eye that she smiled back. She glanced at him to see if he'd noticed there might be competition for her affections. His gaze brushed over her as he continued staring at Seamus O'Rourke.

"What about me?" Deirdre piped up. She looked perturbed by the attention Gemma had garnered.

"Well, I've already done O'Connor," Margaret answered slowly, hesitant to continue. Duncan noticed her reluctance and wondered at it. Everyone had enjoyed the game so far. He wondered again how much she knew.

"Deirdre is a famous heroine in Irish legend," Michael interjected. "The daughter of King Conchobar, who just happened to have been an ancestor of Clann O'Conor."

"Why was she famous?" John Murray asked as he teased Deirdre's hair with his hand.

"She eloped with her lover and fled to England. Her father had forbidden their marriage," Michael replied.

Deirdre giggled, likely enjoying her namesake's notoriety.

"Sounds just like her," Gemma remarked, her voice acidic enough to turn metal black.

Margaret waved a hand, ready to move on, but Duncan spoke up. He owed Deirdre one, and he meant to pay her back right then. "When King Conchobar discovered the two lovers had returned to Ireland, he had them arrested. He had the lover executed, and it is said Deirdre died of a broken heart." Margaret glowered at him but he ignored her wrath.

"Let that be a lesson to you, my girl," the

senator called to Deirdre. He waggled a fatherly finger in her direction. "Time to mend your wicked ways."

Deirdre cuddled up to John, and he grinned to show his delight. "But Daddy," she pouted prettily, "that's sooo boring." She turned to Margaret. "What about Moira?" Spite added a subtle shade of malice to her question.

"Moira is rather difficult," Margaret hedged.

"Amen," Gemma murmured.

"There are several schools of thought concerning the name," Margaret continued. "One says Moira is the Gaelic form of Mary. Mary could mean star of the sea in Latin."

"Not more tuna," Ward groaned.

"No, doofus," John retorted. "That's 'Chicken of the Sea'."

Ignoring the young men, Margaret proceeded with her explanation. "Or, it could be from the Hebrew *marah* which translates as rebellious. However, I tend to lean toward the last school of thought."

"Which is?" Moira's soft voice still managed to penetrate the conversational hum in the room.

Margaret smiled at her, saying, "That Moira is a derivative of Maeve." Moira felt her father stiffen beside her. Ignoring Patrick's pained look, Margaret continued. "Maeve in Gaelic is *meadhbh*, meaning mirth and joy."

"Shakespeare translated *Meadbh* to *Mab*, who was the Queen of the Faeries in his *Midsummer's Night Dream*," Michael added.

Gemma appeared desperate to take Moira out of the limelight as she called to Margaret. "What about Duncan? Do Duncan, Margaret."

"I'd like to do Duncan," Deirdre murmured, her green eyes narrowed to feline slits.

"Of course. Mr. Ross, how could I forget you?"

Margaret gushed, smiling across the room at him. "Clan Ross is very famous in Scotland."

"So my father tells me."

"Ross is Scottish Gaelic meaning from the headland." Deirdre opened her mouth to comment, but Margaret shushed her. "I'm warning you, Deirdre, don't go there." The young men on either side of Deirdre chuckled. Clearing her throat, Margaret continued. "Duncan is also Scottish Gaelic."

"Good grief," Ward interrupted. "Irish Gaelic. Scottish Gaelic. Didn't those Gaels ever stay home in Gaeland?"

"There's no such place, *Weard*," John asserted, using the Old English pronunciation.

"Where was I?" While mostly rhetorical, the question gave Margaret a chance to gather her wits. "Oh, yes. Duncan. Translated, Duncan means dark warrior." She smiled. "Duncan was also a king of Scotland in the eleventh century."

"Ten thirty-four to ten forty," Michael clarified. "His was a bloody short reign." Duncan knew the professor watched him to see how he would react.

"Professor Shanahan, I thought your field was literature, not history." Margaret sounded a bit perplexed as she stared at the little man.

"'Tis difficult to study one without the other, dear lady. Since you've named us all, I suppose you're about to remind me it's my turn to perform." He stood up and took her place in the center of the room. He hadn't decided what tale to relate, but as if someone whispered in his ear, he suddenly knew. "The story of Deirdre and her lover reminds me of another Irish tale. Of course, if you talk to any Irishman for longer than two minutes, he's sure to tell you nothing but tales. As you all know, there's not a true Irishman alive who hasn't kissed the Blarney Stone to get the gift of gab." Michael looked over to Patrick. "Isn't that so, Senator?"

Patrick took the gibe in good humor. "Nor a politician neither, Professor," he answered with a grin.

Michael took a deep breath and slowly scanned the room, looking everyone straight in the eye, including Seamus O'Rourke. In a voice as rich and sweet as spun sugar, he began his tale.

Chapter 14

"Long ago, long before the true knowin' of it even, back in the misty memory of time, this tale has been sung. In the land of Éire fair and bright, there lived a lovely cailín with hair of spun sunlight, and eyes the color of the sunset sky. So comely she was, they say the flowers would hide their blooms in shame, though this might be a little lie. But whether or not it be right, I'll tell yee the tale this very night.

"'Twas the first of spring when the land did awaken that the fair young maid was by the Faerie taken, or so the story goes. In all of history, there be only two who would have the true knowin', and 'twould be the cailín and her lover. But, ahead of m'self I be gettin'.

"Out in the woods she was on this spring morn, on the very day this tale was born. She came upon a stranger dark as he waited in a glade. Bewitch him she did, the fair young maid. Though there be those 'twould say 'twas the other way, that the stranger did the enchantin' of the maid. Not that it matters what people say, for lovers they became right there and then in the misty faerie glen, and lovers they stayed for a full moon and a day.

"But alas, the pipes and drums did call, and bein' a warrior born and all, the stranger had to answer the summons. There was a battle bloody and fierce to be fought, and the warrior's blood did run

141

deep. So a promise he made to his true love, a promise made to keep. Then the dark warrior rode far away, never knowin' what his leavin' had wrought.

"The fair cailín returned to her home all wild and fey, so her people turned her away. Faerie they had branded the stranger and much worse, and the villagers crossed themselves to avoid his curse. When they discovered she carried the demon's seed, 'twas evil fear that knowledge did breed.

"Far away across the land, a message came to the warrior's band, and with his maid he longed to be. Across valleys green and mountains blue, he rode to claim his bride, and all his due. As he drew near, dire whispers did he hear, whispers of a black deed that caused him to ride with all speed.

"He nigh killed his horse but still arrived too late, or so goes the story of that fateful date. Tried she had been and judged as well, so the old wives do tell. Burned at the stake for a witch was she while her dark warrior looked on in agony. And when she was gone in a puff of smoke, hell's own vengeance 'twas that broke. With thunder and lightning by his side, the dark warrior did avenge his bride. Unmerciful was he with his sword stained blood red, and rested not until all were dead. Or so the story goes.

"And even now, to this very day, so the storytellers say, on Midsummer's Night, faerie hoof beats can be heard to race across that misty glen 'twas their secret place. Their laughter is heard in the bubbling brook, and their faces you'd see if you'd but look in the face of the moon's sweet serenity. For 'tis there the dark warrior and his maid are joined together now and for all eternity."

****

Gemma had been so enthralled by Michael's voice and the tale she hadn't noticed, halfway through the telling of it, when Duncan got up and moved to stand behind Moira. Moira knew instantly. As he stopped behind her, she stood up and leaned against him. He curled one arm over her shoulder, resting that hand on her side. His other arm encircled her waist.

"Seems we're famous, bonnie girl," he whispered into the sweet smelling mass of her hair. She answered by brushing her cheek against the softly knitted weave of his sweater. He dropped his chin to rest gently on the top of her head. Neither of them moved again for the duration of the little professor's performance. It felt so natural standing there together like they were, as if they'd stood there since time immemorial.

They were still standing there when Michael's story ended, and Gemma finally looked up. Her mouth tightened, and her gray eyes turned the color of steel. Duncan realized Gemma glared at them but he didn't care. The sooner she figured out she no longer had a place in his life, the better off they'd all be.

****

Gemma wasn't the only one who noticed Duncan and Moira. O'Rourke watched them like a fox eyeing the hen house. His tale had not impressed the big Irishman.

"Poetic drivel," O'Roarke muttered then grinned viciously. His expression made him look like a cat watching captive birds. What was that old saying about two birds with one stone?

His last word still echoed in the hushed room. Margaret sat cradled in her husband's arms as tears streamed unabashedly and unheeded down her cheeks. Allen dabbed at them ineffectually with a monogrammed linen handkerchief. Ward and John each held one of Deirdre's hands, and her eyes were a little misty as well. Patrick looked stricken and he swallowed convulsively as if something blocked throat.

Michael stared across the room at Moira and Duncan, his eyes soft and dreamy. *The dark warrior and his faerie queen.* He shook the thought out of his head. *Yer becomin' a sentimental, daft old fool. And with what's sure to happen this weekend, yee need all your wits about yee.* He rolled his head on his neck, relieving some tension and continued to study the other people in the room.

****

Duncan didn't want to move now that the story was over. Holding Moira safe within the harbor of his arms, Michael's words had simply washed over them.

He could have stood there for the rest of eternity so long as Moira's head rested against his chest and his arms held her. Every part of him touching her felt electric. Not sexual, though. Not this time. The feelings he had for this woman-child had a life of their own.

Margaret, swiping at her tears, finally broke the spell. "Oh, Professor Shanahan," she sighed. "What a beautiful story. I've never heard that one."

Michael smiled at her. "'Tis a sad tale so not many tell it any more. There's a song about the dark warrior and his maid, too. I'll have the kids play it tonight if you wish."

"That would be lovely, Professor," Margaret replied, her face lighting up. "And, speaking of tonight, there will be lots of music and every opportunity for dancing. John, you and Ward wipe those lascivious leers off your faces. It's not that kind of dancing. Tonight, those of you who don't know how are going to learn every traditional Irish dance ever invented. I've got an Irish dance troupe from the University of Virginia coming in to teach you."

The two young men groaned, and Deirdre looked

aghast. "Aunt Margaret," she whined. "Whatever am I going to wear?"

"I'm sure you will find something in all that luggage you brought," Margaret replied, her voice calm and unruffled but with a hint of reproach.

"I've got to go shopping," Deirdre proclaimed. "Can someone drive me into Charlottesville?" she wheedled, batting her eyelashes in the direction of John and Ward. John almost fell over himself trying to pull his keys from his pocket.

Duncan watched the by-play. Once Ward noticed Gemma sitting alone, he moved into the breach Duncan had left. The boy had watched Gemma during lunch and he'd seen the way Ward's eyes lit up when he called Gemma a fox. Duncan had to admit she was a looker but now he'd met Moira, no one compared. Ward glanced over at him and he gave a brief nod of his head, permission as it were for Ward to make his move. The kid didn't disappoint him.

"Would you like to go, too?" Ward asked Gemma. "We can make a party of it."

Gemma started to decline, then noticed Deirdre eyeing her, the redhead's expression daring her to accept. Her chin lifted with the stubbornness Duncan was accustomed to and she smiled cattily. "I'd love to go, Ward. I'll get my purse."

Ward, with Gemma on his arm, John, and Deirdre clattered noisily out of the parlor. Deirdre complained men had it so simple—a pair of pants, a shirt, and a jacket, they could go anywhere.

Duncan finally stirred. Leaning down, his lips brushed Moira's ear. "Take a walk with me, bonnie girl."

They walked out hand-in-hand, leaving Margaret quite flustered. "But," she said turning to Patrick. "I thought he was Gemma's friend."

Patrick chuckled. "He was."

His emphasis was not lost on her. She stared thoughtfully after the couple, and a cold chill teased icy fingers up her back. *The dark warrior and his faerie maid.* The words echoed in her mind. She shook the thought away. Glancing at the senator, she said, "Patrick, I have to tell you something. With her hair down and wearing that color, Moira reminds me so much of Maeve."

"That she does, Maggie," Patrick replied. He put his arm around her shoulders and gave her a gentle squeeze.

Margaret watched Duncan and Moira exit through the French doors opening to the terrace. Like the first rose bud of spring, Moira had blossomed overnight into a beautiful woman. Her transformation had been a long time in coming, and Margaret almost felt sad. Then she smiled to herself. It was time.

****

"Is everything ready?" Seamus O'Rourke growled into his cell phone.

"Aye." The muffled reply echoed hollowly.

"I'll let you know when." O'Rourke snapped the phone shut. He'd been patient long enough. After all, he prided himself on being a man of action, and he didn't much care whether that action was right or wrong. This waiting game gnawed at him, fraying his nerves to the breaking point. The others had always known sooner or later, he would do things his way. That's why he was in charge of this operation. He'd given everyone else ample opportunity to succeed, but they had all failed. It was time.

****

Michael watched through the window as Duncan and Moira strolled through the gardens. They looked for all the world like lovers, yet Michael would bet his last Guinness Stout the two had not met before last night. What sort of dangerous game did Ross play? Whatever it might be, he wasn't pleased the man had chosen to involve Moira. She seemed a sweet girl, deserving of better.

The girl had surprised him, though. At the St. Patrick's Day dinner, she'd seemed rather prim and business-like, even in the cocktail dress she wore. The lovely girl who'd appeared at lunch today was someone quite different. Michael wondered which persona was the true one. Had he missed all the signs hidden behind her senatorial façade? Then he remembered the doubts he'd had about her from the beginning. "Aye, cailín," he affirmed. "'Tis is a lot more to you than met my eye."

As Michael watched, Ross bent his head closer to Moira, his dark hair mingling with her fair. He recalled the tale he'd recounted earlier, and a cold shiver ran down his spine. He still couldn't fathom why he'd chosen to tell that one. For all his gift of Irish gab and his study of literature, Michael was not a superstitious man. Yet something about those two and the truth behind the tale buried in the dark recesses of Celtic history gave Michael the eerie feeling history might be about to repeat itself.

He turned away from the window. Enough of this nonsense, he chided himself. The girl seemed to be occupying all of Ross's attention, which suited his plans nicely. He had much to do to prepare. Things were coming to a head and deep in his gut, he knew it was time.

Chapter 15

Moira and Duncan drifted through the garden. Every time he looked at Moira, he thought his heart would burst through his chest. He'd never been one to believe in reincarnation or any other New Age mumbo jumbo but that was before—before last night, before this morning, before now. Duncan had never felt so at peace in his life and certainly not in the two years just past. Not since the horror of Belfast. The memory of that day sent a shudder through him.

Moira noticed immediately and stopped to gaze at him. Her liquid eyes, so soft and blue, spoke volumes to him. After he'd been debriefed following the incident, he'd never spoken to anyone about it. It was time, he decided, to put the nightmare to rest. His gut told him he had to lay this burden off on Moira's soft shoulders, but his heart feared to do so.

They'd wandered into a wild part of the garden and discovered a wooden bench tucked back into a vine-covered arbor that would soon be dripping with the fragile elegance of wisteria blooms. The place was quiet, secluded. Just the place he needed.

"Moira." He said her name like a prayer. Maybe it was. "We have to talk." She nodded, her eyes glowing with trust. "Come sit over here." He led her to the bench and they both sat down. He lifted her hand to his lips and kissed the back of it. Pain

148

radiated in his chest. "You know nothing about me, lass."

"I know what I need to know." She sounded confident.

Duncan stared at her, knowing he had to trust her, trying to decide if he could. He was entrusting her not only with his heart but his life. "I've never talked to anyone about this. I have to tell you."

She covered the big hand holding hers with her free hand. "Whatever it is, it won't make any difference."

"Hear me out first, Moira," he asked. She nodded, waiting for him to continue. "I told you that when I was a boy, I knew I had to be a soldier when I grew up. Well, I became one. A captain in the SAS." He paused to look at her. She nodded her understanding of the acronym—Special Air Services, the highly specialized branch of the British Army. Satisfied she understood, he continued. "I served several tours in various places. Then I was assigned to Northern Ireland." He had her attention but her face betrayed nothing of her feelings. "I'd just returned from a long tour on embassy duty in the Middle East, and the powers that be decided the local IRA probably wouldn't have the foggiest idea of my identity. They placed me on special undercover duty assigned to infiltrate one of their cells. It took me almost a year, but I did it. I even made it into the area cell's inner circle." He paused, drawing in a ragged breath.

She gently squeezed his hand and offered him a small smile. "Go on, Duncan," she urged, her voice steady even though he could feel her pulse pounding. Her eyes never left his face.

"There was a man the British desperately wanted to catch. He'd been running arms and explosives into Belfast for several years. The man was a bloody ghost. No one ever came close to catching him."

"Who was he?"

Duncan shook his head. He stared down at Moira's hands wrapped around his. "We didn't know. We only discovered his code name—Brian Boru."

"Boru? The legendary Irish king?" Her voice sounded calm, more senatorial chief of staff than lover.

"Precisely." His voice assumed the clipped tones of a military officer making a report. "I received information from my IRA contacts that Boru was in Belfast. They told me he'd brought in a load of automatic weapons and several hundred pounds of plastic explosives. He supposedly was staying at a house near our headquarters. As I'd been ordered to do, I passed the information on to my superiors."

Cold sweat broke out on his forehead, and he shuddered again. It all came back to him, only this time in the harsh light of day, not some half-remembered nightmare. Daylight made it more terrible somehow—more terrible and more real.

Like a chameleon, Moira changed back into the lover. She lifted his hand to her lips, and kissed the back of it. Duncan twisted his hand so he could trace her sweet lips with his fingers. Her lips parted, and he bent his head swiftly to kiss her. Once he'd finished his story, this might be the last kiss he'd ever receive from her. She said nothing, waiting for him to speak.

"The commanding officer ordered a raid," Duncan finally said. No longer the soldier, only the wounded warrior, he struggled to keep his voice from breaking. "Boru and his men were said to be heavily armed, and we knew they wouldn't surrender without a fight. We sent a platoon of Royal Marines riding in APCs along with a Challenger 2 tank." He glanced at her to make sure she understood he was talking about an Armored Personnel Carrier and she nodded.

Duncan squinted his eyes closed trying to shut out the sight. "There was a running battle down the street. When the Armored Personnel Carriers and the tank came to the house, they opened fire." He clinched his teeth and the line of his jaw hardened. His eyes were open now, but he only saw the past. The sun flashed in his eyes, giving them the appearance of brittle amber.

"Did Boru get away?"

"He was never there." Duncan spat and his rage threatened to engulf him. He jerked his hand from Moira's grasp and leapt to his feet. Pacing like some wild cat caught and caged, he continued. "A family lived in that house—an innocent family celebrating their little girl's birthday."

The horror of it swept over Moira. "Oh, God," she whispered, the words more a prayer than an oath.

Duncan's agonized voice dredged up words from the very depths of his soul. "They were all killed. The parents. The grandparents. The little girl. All the children who were there for the party. Fifteen people died that day. Fifteen innocent people died because of me."

Moira jumped up, and wrapped her arms around his unyielding body. Tears trickled unheeded down her cheeks. "You couldn't have known," she whispered.

Duncan shook off her embrace. "I should have checked," he argued. "I should have bloody well checked." He took a few steps then whirled to face her. In an icy voice filled with self-condemnation, he continued. "But no, not me. Not the infallible Captain Duncan Ross. I'd gotten closer than anyone. Not even MI5 had operatives in as deep. But it was all a setup. The IRA knew I was so bloody cocky I wouldn't stop to double check the information they fed me. The bloody bastards knew we wanted Boru no matter what the cost." His voice broke and his vision blurred. "But the cost was too high." He sank to his knees in the winter grass as a dry sob wracked his body. "Too bloody high." He bowed his head and wept.

She rushed to him. Taking his face in her hands, she bent to kiss his cheeks, his forehead, his mouth. "'Tis all right, my love," she murmured over and over. "'Tis all right. You only followed orders, Duncan. You were a soldier. It doesn't matter. You didn't do anything wrong."

He slowly relaxed against her, but the harsh golden lights returned to his eyes. He let out a deep, shuddering breath. "They put me on medical leave, Moira. Said I was unfit for duty."

"Shh," she whispered, kissing him again.

Duncan pulled her down in front of him and wrapped his hands in her silken hair. He stared deeply into her eyes for a long moment and she met his gaze. His voice grew husky as he told her the rest. "You don't understand, Moira. I have to find him. I will find the bastard." She knew he would keep this promise or die trying to fulfill it. "I love you, Moira. I don't know why or how you've come into my life but I know that I love you more than life itself. There's no rhyme nor reason for it and you've every right to call me a bloody sod and run like hell away from me." He gulped in a breath and clutched her tighter. "God, lass, but I'd walk through bloody hell to keep you safe. But as long as Boru is out there..." His voice trailed off.

"What can I do to help?"

Duncan couldn't believe his ears. Moira didn't condemn him. She didn't hate him. She didn't try to make him leave off his quest. In her clear, wonderful voice—as if she heard this kind of confession every day, as if this was a normal part of life—she'd asked him what she could do to help. Duncan crushed her to his chest. "Moira, my bonnie girl, just love me." His voice clogged with emotion.

"I do, Duncan," she promised. "Now and forever."

****

Unseen, the watcher flitted back into the tree line. That damned Ross had been a thorn in his side for too long. In his heart-wrenching rendition, Ross hadn't mentioned to the girl about MI5 using him. Need to know and all that, he supposed. Obviously, she didn't need to know. Then another thought struck. Maybe Ross didn't know. God, that was rich and so typical of British Intelligence. Odd, though. He actually seemed to be in love with the girl. Couldn't blame him. She had a body made to cradle and comfort a man through the long dark night.

His thoughts made him squirm. Had they done it yet? He settled into another hiding place deeper in the woods. Nay, probably not. He almost got to watch the dirty deed this morning in the woods. He hadn't been able to hear much of their conversation because of that bloody stream, but he'd heard enough. He knew what to do now. Ross had missed the chance to catch him and wouldn't be allowed another try. He'd fix the damned Scot—and the others. It was time.

****

Moira hesitated at the door to her room and shyly glanced up at him. They'd stayed in the garden long enough for him to regain his composure, and then they'd slipped back into the house. Duncan sensed her hesitancy. Rather than stepping through her door, he pulled her into his room across the hall. He kicked the door shut as he wrapped his arms around her. He instantly grew hard with wanting her, knowing he'd never be able to touch her without needing her, needing to be buried deep inside her.

153

Instead of throwing her on the bed and taking what he wanted, what he needed desperately, he simply stood there, holding her, his chin resting on the top of her head.

His work wasn't finished. As much as he wished he could just spend his life learning the depths of the woman he held in his arms, he had to finish his mission. Without loosening his hold on her, he said, "Moira, I have to know something."

"What?"

"Seamus O'Rourke."

Moira grimaced. "What about him?"

"You tell me, bonnie girl." He felt a shiver run through her. "What do you sense about his black heart?"

She took a long moment to think. Duncan hated forcing her to recall the sensations and feeling the man evoked in her. "I met him the first part of last week," she began.

"At the Irish-American Coalition dinner."

Moira looked surprised, then realization dawned. "You've been tracking O'Rourke." At his nod, she continued. "Yes. He tried to dance with me. There was... I don't know." She shrugged. "He seemed evil. And..." She faltered.

"Tell me, lass." He tightened his arms around her, yet he kept the embrace tender.

"I'm not sure I can explain it, or make sense of the impressions I received." She closed her eyes for a long moment and kept them closed as she spoke. "It was like two men inhabited the same body. Like someone standing in front of a mirror, only the mirror image reflected the true man, and the man before me was the image. Is he IRA?"

"Yes."

Moira nodded. "Michael Shanahan said the same thing."

"Shanahan? The professor?" This bit of

information surprised the hell out of Duncan.

"Don't underestimate him, Duncan," she cautioned. "There's more to him, too, than what you see."

He chewed on that information for a moment before asking, "What do you know of him?"

She shrugged. "Beyond a gut level reaction, nothing. But, I will," she promised.

"Moira," he admonished too late. The wheels in Moira's head were already spinning. He could almost see her thoughts.

She pulled away slightly so she could look up into his eyes while still in the comforting circle of his arms. "I don't know what's going on here, Duncan. There's something you won't or can't tell me." Moira started ticking off items on her fingers. "First, there was Bradford Williams here as a guest last night. Michael Shanahan is in this up to his little leprechaun ears. Now Seamus O'Rourke appears. And then there's you. I'm not an idiot, Duncan. This all has something to do with my father and the Irish vote." She stood on tiptoe and kissed the corner of his mouth. "I'll be back," she said, slipping out of his arms.

He was too stunned to grab her. "Moira?"

"I'm not my father's chief of staff for nothing, Duncan," she explained, staying an arm's length way. "He sure didn't hire me for my looks. If you'll excuse me, I have a few favors to call in." He didn't want her involved any more than she already was. He glared at her. "Don't be tryin' to talk me out of this, Duncan Ross." She put her hands on her hips and jutted her chin stubbornly. "I have access to people and information that can help."

Duncan surrendered. In his arms, she was so soft and yielding he forgot how strong she actually was. "Go make your calls." He wanted to call after her as she danced out through the door, to tell her to be careful, to tell her he loved her, but she disappeared in a twinkling.

Moira went straight to Allen Steele's office in the family wing. Banks of computers and electronic equipment covered one wall. Not many people knew of the satellite dish cunningly concealed on top of the house. Allen had worldwide holdings and he had never been a man to delegate authority.

Fairly certain she'd find at least one secure telephone line, if not several, in the bank of lines on the communications console, she studied the set up. After a few minutes of study, she discovered both the secure telephone line and the computer line as well. Unfortunately, Allen had the computer password protected and she didn't have time to guess it. She searched a little longer and found the secure fax line. These lines were encrypted so only someone with highly sophisticated equipment and a great deal of luck would be able to tap into them.

She plopped into Allen's desk chair and dialed up the first number from memory. On the third ring, a pleasant female voice answered.

"Mrs. Abbott, this is Moira O'Connor, Senator Patrick O'Connor's office. I hate to disturb you at home, but I need to speak to Harry."

Moira waited while Mrs. Abbot summoned her husband to the phone. After a few minutes, a softly southern voice said hello.

"Harry, I need a favor," Moira said without preamble.

Harry Abbott snagged a kitchen stool with one foot, and pulled it over to him. He sat down hard. He'd been playing the Washington game for years, but never, in all the time he'd known her, had Moira O'Connor ever asked for a favor. Without betraying his surprise, Harry replied, "Shoot."

"Seamus O'Rourke." Moira dropped the name without preamble.

"Who's that?" Harry asked, trying to make the question sound innocent.

"Don't play games, Harry," Moira chastised. "Is he on the list or not?"

"Does this have to do with presidential security?" His voice took on a hard edge. "Or national security?"

"The president, no. My father? Probably. National security? Again, probably."

"Have there been threats?"

"Not directly." He could tell she was hedging. "Harry, you know as well as I do that the vote on censure is coming up. I have to know if O'Rourke is IRA."

He paused briefly before asking, "Are you on a secure line?"

"Duh, Harry," Moira snapped, sarcasm dripping from the two words.

He looked around his kitchen as if he expected to find someone hovering in the pantry eavesdropping on his conversation. *I've been in Washington too long,* he decided. Grinning at his own paranoia, he continued. "We don't know for sure, Moira. We did the usual background check when he applied for a visa last year. It turned up zilch. All his papers seemed to be in order."

"Seemed to be?"

Harry grinned again. She was sharp. He'd tried for years to recruit her for the Service. "There are some excellent forgers out there, Moira, and the IRA employs only the best."

"What about his antiques business?"

"We've intercepted a few of his shipments, both coming and going, but found nothing." He took a slow, measured breath. "Moira, what are you involved in? How do you know O'Rourke?" Years on the job had his gut churning. He wanted the bottom line.

"O'Rourke keeps popping up in the oddest places," Moira replied, pointedly ignoring his first question.

He wasn't about to back down. He'd been with the Secret Service for almost twenty-five years and every instinct he had developed went on red alert. "Moira, are you in the middle of something we should know about?"

She hesitated. "I don't know, Harry," she finally replied.

"Where are you?"

"Charlottesville."

"Is your father there?"

"Yes. We're at Allen and Margaret Steele's country place, Faerie Glen Farm. They're having a house party."

"Moira, you have to tell me what's going on." He wasn't asking.

Again, she hesitated. "Harry, I'm not sure anything is going on. I just have this gut feeling. Things aren't quite right and since that's all I have to go on, I don't want anything official made of this. I appreciate the intel, Harry. Thanks."

He realized she was about to break the connection. "Moira, you will keep me posted," he growled. It wasn't a request, it was an order.

"I promise," she conceded.

"Call me, kiddo." Harry's voice remained gruff but affection tinged his tone.

"I will, Harry. Tell the missus I'm sorry I disturbed your weekend."

Harry replaced the receiver and stared out the window into his backyard. His wife was weeding a flowerbed and his son played catch with a friend. The wheels in his brain clicked along like an express train. He headed to the door to tell his wife he was going to the office.

****

"Well, so much for the Secret Service," Moira muttered. Harry might sound like a gruff old grizzly bear but he was really just a sweet ol' teddy bear. She rubbed her temples. Even so, the nuances in Harry's voice had her hackles rising. She'd been in Washington her whole life. Too often, it wasn't what was said so much as how it was said. Perhaps she saw conspiracies where there were none. She had only her instincts to rely upon. Even so, she couldn't turn away from Duncan. Not now, not after the things he'd told her in the garden. Her feelings for him left her as baffled as he felt about her. Later. She'd sort them all out later when she had time. Right now, she had information to gather.

She punched in the next number on her mental list. After the first ring, a crisp voice with traces of a Chicago accent answered, "Yazkowski."

"Ski, Moira O'Connor."

"Do you work every Saturday?" Ski asked, his voice teasing.

"Why not? You do," Moira retorted, teasing, back.

"So what can the FBI do for the senator's chief of staff today?" Ski kicked back in his chair and let his mind roam for a minute. He'd once considered asking Moira out on a date. Though plain by his standards, she did happen to be extremely intelligent with a dry sense of humor that appealed to him. Somehow, though, he'd never gotten around to the asking.

"I have some names I want to run by you."

"Hold on a minute." His chair squeaked as he leaned forward to reach the keyboard. A few clicks of computer keys and he said, "Okay, I'm ready."

"Seamus O'Rourke," Moira began. "S, E..."

"I know how to spell it," Ski cut her off. "Next."

He heard the deep breath Moira took before she added, "Bradford Williams."

Ski whistled. "Next."

"Michael Shanahan."

"Moira, just what are you up to?" He sat up, the hairs on the back of his neck prickling.

Moira didn't answer his question. She just dropped the next name on him. "Brian Boru."

This time, Ski almost dropped the phone. "Shit, Moira, you've got some heavy hitters here. I want to know what's going on."

"Nothing," she replied all too nonchalantly to suit him.

"What do you mean nothing?"

"Just what I said, Ski," she replied firmly. "Nothing's going on. These names keep cropping up in conjunction with my father. With his position on the Irish question, I just want to know exactly who these people are."

"Okay," Ski finally agreed even though it wasn't. "Any more names you want to hit me with?"

Moira hesitated. "Just one. Duncan Ross."

Ski looked over the list of names emblazoned on his computer screen. "I can tell you right now, Moira, this info is classified."

"As chairman of the Armed Services Committee, my father has clearance, Ski. And if you'll look up my file, so do I."

Ski winced at the tone in her voice. Now he remembered why he'd never asked her out—she was all business, all the time. "I'll give you what I can. Where are you so I can send it to you?"

"Virginia. I have a secure fax line but no computer access."

"You positive it's secure?" He wasn't convinced.

"I'll put it up against any in the Bureau." She sounded positive.

"Okay," he agreed. "I'll start sending you the reports as soon as the computer pulls this stuff up. All these names may not be in the computer, though."

"Yes, they are, Ski, but nice try." She chuckled. "Thanks. I owe you one."

"I'll remember that." And he would. It never hurt to hold an IOU on a senator's chief of staff.

Ski looked at the names on the monitor. He added a name to the list Moira had dictated to him— Senator Patrick O'Connor. Sighing, he picked up his phone and punched a number. No longer attracted to Moira, he did have a grudging respect for her. He was sorry to see her caught up in this mess. "We need to talk," he announced when his call was answered. "It's time."

Within a few minutes, the fax machine started humming and pages began sliding out. Moira glanced at her watch. She would only be able to give the information a cursory glance. Dinner was at seven and she couldn't afford to be late. Besides, the info arriving from Ski would have to be culled, separated, and redefined before she could assimilate it enough to read between the lines. Eventually, she'd get to the heart of the matter. She'd dealt with FBI reports before. They contained as much implied information as info stated in black and white. Her lips curled up in a wry smile. She'd gotten an expletive out of Ski. Interesting. She felt a little guilty about adding Duncan's name to the list she'd given the FBI agent. Her heart might be convinced it was unnecessary but her head insisted. She needed answers, needed to find out what was going on. It was time.

Chapter 16

After Moira left, Duncan began his own investigation. He forced himself to think about the here and now. Moira distracted him completely. She filled his heart and his head until there was room for nothing else. Too many loose ends dangled currently, and he needed his wits about him. There would be time enough later, when he'd finished with Boru, for Moira to fill him up.

He listened at the door two rooms beyond his own. Hearing nothing, he turned the knob and slipped inside. The only luggage he found was a small valise. No personal items were visible in the room or the bath. The antique wardrobe and drawers were all empty. Duncan checked between the mattress and springs and under the pillows. Nothing. He checked a few less conspicuous spots to no avail.

"You travel light, my friend," he murmured, sarcasm heavily coating the endearment.

Duncan had one more room to check. Seamus O'Rourke wasn't the only suspicious character around this weekend. O'Rourke's room sat at the end of the hall. The back stairs were just beyond. Duncan listened, eased open the door, slipped out, and took the stairs three at a time. On the third floor, he had to try several rooms before he found the one he needed. Voices drifted down the hall as he shut the door behind him. Moments later, Sinead and Sheila passed by.

It didn't take long to check Michael Shanahan's possessions. Duncan would have been doubly surprised if he'd found something incriminating. He had a good idea of who the little professor actually worked for. Back in the hall, he discovered the door to the girls' room remained open, and it would be tough to get to the back stairs unseen. He headed toward the front stairs but Shanahan's voice wafted up the stairwell. He stopped cold, caught between the proverbial rock and hard spot. He tried the knob of the door at his back and discovered a storage closet. He ducked into his new-found refuge but to his chagrin, the professor and the young man from the group stopped in the hall to talk. Moments later, the girls joined them. He checked his watch, hoping he wouldn't be stuck very long. Time was running out.

****

Moira returned to the guest wing and went immediately to Duncan's room. He was gone. She couldn't wander the house trailing faxes behind her so she returned to her room. She tossed the stack of papers on her bed, and stood for a moment to get her mental bearings. Like fog rising from a bog on a cold night, a sense of dread crept over her. Suddenly, the walls of her room felt like they were closing in on her. The curtains were open, and the turbulent sky caught her eye. A storm was coming.

A light tap on the door startled her. She stared guiltily at the faxes scattered on her bed. "Just a minute," she called, stuffing the papers under plump pillows. She smoothed the comforter and called, "Come in."

Margaret Steele opened the door. "Are you alone?" she asked. Moira looked surprised. "Well, I thought maybe...well, never mind what I thought."

She looked uncharacteristically indecisive and wandered around the room for a bit, stopping in front of an old cedar chest tucked in the corner. She brushed her hand across the top, nodded curtly, and then turned to Moira, apparently making up her mind. "It's time we had a talk, Moira."

Moira choked back a giggle. Margaret's question now made sense—she'd expected to find Duncan in her room. Through the years, the older woman had tried, in a friendly way, to be a surrogate mother. Margaret had been the one to take her shopping for her first bra, her first pair of high heels, and had, in her own embarrassed way, explained the changes puberty brought to the female body. Having no children of her own, Margaret had no experience but she'd tried vainly. Moira now suspected Margaret planned to explain about men.

"Uhm, Aunt Margaret?" She bit her lips a moment, to hold back a giggle. "I already know about the birds and the bees."

Margaret looked indignant. "Well, good gracious, I should hope so. You're almost thirty, Moira." A warm smile crept across her face. "You really like him, don't you?"

Moira felt heat rushing into her cheeks and knew she blushed pink. A liquid pool of heat gushed low in her middle at just the thought of Duncan. She prayed her thoughts weren't flashing across her forehead like a neon sign. "Is it that obvious?" She turned a darker shade of crimson when her voice squeaked.

"Only to someone looking at you," Margaret replied dryly. The older woman crossed over and patted her arm. "That's not why I'm here. You are more than old enough to make your own decisions in that regard. Sit down, dear." The two of them sat on the edge of the bed and Margaret cleared her throat. "What do you know about your mother? What have you been told about Maeve?"

She searched her memory. The sweet, serene face in the portrait hanging in her father's study seemed as familiar as her own. "I know Da met her in England, brought her back to Boston, and married her." Her voice hardened. "I know Gladys despised her."

Margaret winced at that name. "Did you always call her Gladys?"

She flashed a caustic smile. "Granny somehow never seemed appropriate." Sarcasm choked every word she said, as she remembered the imposing matriarch who had been her father's mother.

Margaret's smile turned rueful, as if she shared Moira's memory of the woman. "But what of your mother, Moira? What do you know of Maeve? Her personality? Background? Her family?"

She shrugged to show her ignorance, and to cover her sense of loss. "Da never talked about her."

"Did you ever ask? Did Patrick never talk about Maeve? I mean, especially to you, her daughter."

"I asked once or twice. It made him sad so I quit asking." Moira paused, her expression growing hard. "I knew better than to bring up the subject with Gladys." A moment later, she added, "Da did mention once that she came from an old Irish family."

Margaret patted her arm again. "It's time for you to learn about your mother, Moira. The truth. Not Gladys's bitter lies, or your father's wishful thinking."

She didn't say a word. In fact, she held her breath and then had to remind herself to breathe. She was going to learn something very important, something about her mother, about herself. Maybe she would finally learn why she was cursed.

Margaret settled herself more comfortably on the bed. "Patrick and Allen had just graduated from

Harvard. Allen and I were engaged at the time. Gladys manipulated Patrick unmercifully so he would marry the daughter of one of your grandfather's business partners. To stall her, Patrick, dragging Allen along, went off to London to finagle some business deal. Allen came home in three months, but Patrick stayed. He came home at Christmas but returned to England before the New Year. Gladys was absolutely beside herself. She begged Allen, as her son's best friend, to convince Patrick to come home."

Another rueful smile tinged her expression as Margaret shook her head, remembering Gladys and her entreaties. "Allen and I flew to London that summer. My aunt Olivia lived there and had wanted me to come for a visit for years. Allen decided the situation provided the perfect time for us to get away alone." A saucy smile curved Margaret's lips for a moment. Somber again, she added, "That's when I first met Maeve."

Moira finally interrupted, unable to keep quiet any longer. "Was she as beautiful as her portrait?"

Margaret smiled at her. "No one is as beautiful as a portrait. And your mother was not a beauty in the conventional sense. Her cheekbones were too high, her chin too pointed, her jaw too strong. But her hair?" Margaret sighed. "It was the most glorious shade of coppery blonde. I remember Patrick saying once that the sunset had become entangled in her curls."

Bemused, Moira tried to picture her no-nonsense father waxing that poetic without a speechwriter to spin the words.

The older woman didn't notice her expression as she continued. "Then there were her eyes. They were the color of lilacs when they first bloom in the spring, and the sun kisses them with gold. And they tilted up at the corners. Their color and shape were so unusual they gave her an elfin look." Margaret paused. A dreamy look stole across her face as she gazed back into the past. "It was obvious Patrick adored her and she him. But..." The timbre of her voice changed. "There was Gladys. Patrick knew Gladys would be a problem."

"I don't understand," Moira interrupted. "Gladys always flaunted her Irish ancestry. If Maeve came from an old Irish family..."

Margaret brusquely cut her off. "She did, but not the right kind of family." Moira felt even more puzzled. Margaret's eyes were sad as she explained, "Maeve's family were Irish Travelers."

"Irish Travelers?"

"Gypsies," Margaret clarified. "They've been around for centuries. They're peddlers, horse traders, fortunetellers. Thieves, some of them. They're a law unto themselves. There are those who believe the Travelers originated in Romany, like the Hungarian gypsies, since most Travelers have black hair."

"Do you mean like Black Irish?"

"In a way. That term has come to mean a black-haired, blue-eyed Irishman."

"Like Seamus O'Rourke?" She used the first example she could think of.

Margaret looked taken aback. "Mr. O'Rourke? He's not black Irish."

"But he has black hair."

"His hair is dyed," Margaret stated flatly.

She blinked, aghast. "No way!"

"Way!" Margaret smirked. "I'm certain of it."

Moira filed that fact in her memory. Could the hard glint in the man's eyes be produced by contacts? As much as the thought repulsed her, Moira would have to get close enough to the man to check. She wondered if Duncan had returned to his room. She really needed to pass along all this information. However, Margaret wasn't through with her yet.

"Your grandfather's health began to fail." Margaret continued the story. "Patrick knew he had to return to Boston sooner than later. He decided to marry Maeve in England, and bring her home with him. Confronted by a *fait accompli*, Gladys could do nothing."

"But I remember wedding pictures with Gladys and Grandfather O'Connor in them." She remained puzzled.

Margaret blew out a disgusted snort. "Gladys was so incensed over the elopement she insisted on a full ceremony after they arrived back in Boston. I remember their real wedding. It happened the first of August, and there was a bonfire at the Travelers' encampment. Maeve wore Irish lace and embroidered linen. Her parents, or at least I think they were her parents, gathered the encampment around the fire."

"Wait a minute," Moira interrupted, confused by what Margaret had just hinted. "What do you mean, you think they were her parents?"

"They must have been at least seventy, with Maeve not yet twenty. Despite their gray hair, I could tell both of them had been dark-headed. They were dour, somber people, distrustful of outsiders. Everyone in the camp could have been related. They were all dark—dark clothes, dark hair, dark eyes, dark skin. But Maeve? Ah, Maeve was full of light and laughter. She'd never met a stranger, and loved with a heart true and pure." Her voice turned harsh. "Then she came to Boston. Patrick thought ahead. Even though the Travelers had their own binding ceremony, Patrick insisted the village priest also marry them. Without the certificate from the Church, he knew Gladys would cause even more problems."

Margaret's story intrigued her since all this had been hidden from her. "So what happened in Boston?"

"Just as Patrick predicted, Gladys was in a royal snit. But, Maeve was already pregnant so Gladys could do nothing to annul the marriage. Not that she didn't try."

"Pregnant?"

Looking terribly sad, Margaret told her, "Maeve miscarried. The first of several, I'm afraid."

"I didn't know." Her words came out in a breathless whisper.

"After the third miscarriage, Maeve's health declined. She was so pale and listless. Her doctor told her to stop trying, but she wouldn't listen. Gladys was always around, sniping at her." Margaret's voice changed in timbre and tone as she imitated Gladys. "That blasted gypsy witch. She's put a spell on my sweet Patrick. Well, thank the good Lord and all the Saints above us that He's seen fit not to let her spawn any of her demon children in our midst."

Moira shivered. Margaret's mimicry of her grandmother's hateful voice touched too close for comfort. She carried too many memories of that voice for it not to affect her. Deep in the recesses of her mind, she once again heard voices raised in anger but muffled by the clothes hanging around her. The smell of mothballs had filled her nose, making her want to sneeze. She pulled her knees to her chest and pinched her nose, willing the sneeze to go away.

"You are still a young man, Patrick," Gladys O'Connor scolded her son. *"Your political career is just beginning. You need a wife—a suitable wife—by your side."*

Patrick wavered. *"Moira does need a mother."*

"Moira! That cursed faerie child," Gladys spat.

"She should have drowned with her mother. We all would have been better off if she'd never been born."

Little Moira cringed in the dark closet, her fists stuffed in her mouth to keep from crying out. She'd run there to hide when she'd seen her grandmother coming up the front walk. Now she wished she could get out of there, and just keep running forever. I hate you, her mind screamed. The child quickly crossed herself, and said a hail Mary for her sin. She strained to hear what her father would say, but she only heard the sounds of his footsteps hurrying away. After a moment, she recognized the sound of the front door slamming shut.

Terrified her grandmother would discover her hiding in the closet, Moira held her breath. Fortunately, Gladys soon moved away from the door. Moira took a tiny breath. That little gasp turned into a sob, and the sob into quiet hysterics. Having cried herself to sleep, she was still in the closet when Nanny discovered her hours later. Nanny rocked her back to sleep, singing her Gaelic lullabies.

"How did my mother die?" She was almost afraid to hear the answer.

"When Maeve learned she was pregnant again, she took to her bed, determined to carry this baby to full term. After eight months, the doctor said the worst had passed, that as long as she took it easy, she could get up. At the time, your parents lived near the Strand in Boston. Maeve loved to stroll along the Charles River. She'd save bread to feed the ducks nesting along the riverbank." Margaret shivered and her voice dropped in pitch. "She might have been caught in a sudden storm, but no one really knows what happened. A man saw her floating face down in the river and jumped in to save her." Margaret choked back a sob. "Your father attended a political rally and hours passed before someone notified him." Margaret didn't have to come right out and say that Gladys had kept the news from her son. Moira knew.

In hushed tones, she continued. "Maeve was in a coma when he finally got to the hospital. The doctors decided to perform a cesarean. They held no hope for Maeve but thought they could save you." Margaret smiled at her. "I remember the first time I saw you. You had your mother's cheekbones and her little pointy chin. You looked like a little elf. Your hair was the palest blonde I've ever seen, and such curls! Patrick loved you from the first moment he laid eyes on you. With Maeve gone, I don't know what he would have done if you hadn't survived."

Margaret smiled even though her eyes glistened with unshed tears. "Even with you to look after and to love, Allen and I were afraid he'd do something foolish. He'd go down to the river, and stand there watching the water go by for hours. We just knew he'd throw himself in one day. Thankfully, he never did." The two sat silently, each one lost in thought, mourning for what might have been. Margaret recovered from the melancholy first. "I have something for you."

With a grace belying her age, the petite woman slid off the bed, and crossed over to the cedar chest in the corner. She pulled out an old-fashioned key from her pocket, and unlocked the lid. "Come see, Moira," she invited, stepping back. Curious, Moira knelt beside the chest. With two hands, she cautiously lifted the lid, and the warm, spicy-fresh scent of cedar wafted out.

"This hasn't been opened since the day of Maeve's funeral," Margaret murmured. "I had it sent to my house before Gladys could get her hands on it."

Moira looked inside the chest. With great care, she lifted out a fringed linen shawl. Threads in a myriad of jeweled tones were delicately woven into the soft fabric. Laying it reverently to one side, she lifted out a blouse. Wide, full sleeves ended in long lace ruffles at the cuffs. The softly shirred neckline had a field of embroidered flowers, worked in the same colors as were on the shawl, forming a garland along its edge. Moira found the skirt next—yards of linen and lace. Wrapped in tissue paper, she discovered a pair of white, satin slippers with smooth leather soles.

"Maeve saved these things for you. After she was gone, I kept them for you. The time has come, Moira. Somehow, your destiny is tied up with these things. You have to wear them tonight." She held up her hand when Moira opened her mouth to argue. "No ifs, ands, or buts, and I don't give a hoot about what your father might think. If things need to be altered, Ellie has a deft needle. Here."

Margaret handed one of the leather slippers over and Moira slid her foot into it. The shoe fit perfectly. Longing washed over her, threatening to drown her. She nodded. Margaret was right. Something beyond her control insisted she wear her mother's wedding attire tonight. *Albun Eiler,* a voice whispered. *Almost as sacred as Lughnasadh.*

Margaret gathered up the outfit and left her kneeling next to the chest. She never noticed the woman slipping out of her room.

A small box tucked into the corner of the cedar chest caught her eye. Ornately carved from rosewood, it was slightly bigger than her palm. The wood glowed with a rich patina that only hinted at its true age. She inspected the clasp and hinges. *This isn't just old, it's positively ancient.*

As she studied the intricate carvings, she found a unicorn tucked in behind some flowers. On one side, two sprites flitted through a magical garden on delicate wings. A dragon slumbered on the front. She unlatched the clasp and lifted the lid. Nestled on once-red satin, now faded to a pale rose, a large translucent stone in an elaborate, heavy gold setting winked up at her. She gazed at it in rapt amazement. This was the largest fire opal she'd ever seen, the stone as large as her thumb. A soft iridescent blue, the gem winked gold and silver in the light. The gold encircling the stone was worked in a pattern of Celtic knots and the pendant hung from a heavy gold chain.

She pushed up off the floor and crossed over to the dressing table. Looking in the mirror, she held the necklace to her throat. She smiled at her reflection, tilted her head, and nodded imperceptibly to the unseen figure hiding behind her in the mirror. Moira placed the necklace back in its box. Somehow, she knew this gift had not come from her father. This had come from her mother's people, handed down for countless generations, from mother to daughter through the ages.

****

"Ha!" Abhean sneered at Manannan as fog enveloped the scene inside the standing stones. "And yee told me I couldn't get involved." The Harper pulled his cloak around him, preparing to disappear.

"I said I could not save her," Manannan reminded him. "What was could not change what is to be, Abhean."

"Yee also failed to mention that Meadhbh meddled." The Harper pressed his point.

"The choice was hers to make. Leave it be."

"Ah, but who was the hero that fateful day, I wonder?" Abhean wouldn't desist. "What mortal dared brave the icy waters to save her?"

"Enough, Abhean," Manannan barked. "Yee have interfered abundantly this time. Do not pursue the path yee have put yer feet upon. Yee cannot change what will be."

The Harper disappeared in a swirl of mist. "But

I can try," his sweet voice whispered on the wind.

Manannan's shoulders slumped. "Nay, Abhean. No matter how hard yee try, this life is already written."

Chapter 17

Shanahan and his musicians finally retired to their separate rooms. Duncan gave them a few heartbeats to completely clear the area, then he was out of the closet and down the front stairs, two at a time. On the second floor landing, he composed himself, and sauntered around the corner. Laughter drifted up from the entry hall, and he recognized Gemma's voice.

"Guess the shopping spree is over," he muttered, slipping down the hall to Moira's room. Before knocking, he pressed his ear to her door. He could make out two separate voices from her room so he slipped into this own, shutting the door just as Gemma came down the hallway.

Gemma tossed her bags on the bed and kicked off her shoes. "Damn my feet hurt," she mumbled, massaging them. She'd done some marathon shopping in her time but Deirdre was world class. She grinned ruefully. If circumstances had been different, she and Deirdre might have been friends. Ironic that.

Soaking in a hot bath sounded like heaven, even knowing her feet would have a break tonight. Dancing the night away had never been an option with Duncan. He seemed to detest the activity, and she fully intended to keep him company while he watched from the sidelines.

Deirdre seemed contented with the attention John Murray lavished on her all afternoon. Besides, she reasoned, John should be more to Deirdre's taste anyway. Handsome in a GQ kind of way, and cocky to boot, he also had lots of money to spend on her. Duncan, quiet and likely disinherited by his family, along with his wild hair and penchant for faded jeans, came nowhere close to fulfilling Deirdre's expectations. She still couldn't believe Deirdre had allowed John to pay for the outfit she'd picked out.

Thinking about Deirdre's getup brought a grin to her face. She had to admit there weren't many redheads who could wear scarlet, but Deirdre had looked gorgeous in the form-fitting bodysuit topped with a sheer lace peasant blouse. The silk skirt had just enough flounce to show off her legs. She eyed her own purchases as they spilled out of their bags. Ward had certainly perked up when she'd modeled the black lace mini-dress. Like what the red skirt did for Deirdre, this dress showed off her best asset—her long legs. If Duncan didn't realize what he'd lose when she appeared tonight dressed in it? Well, perish the thought.

A sharp rap on the door interrupted her contemplation. "Duncan," she cried gleefully. She quickly stuffed her purchases back into their bags. "Come in," she called sweetly.

"We need to talk," Seamus O'Rourke growled, bursting into the room.

"Seamus, what are you doing here?"

"Worried yer boyfriend will catch us?" O'Rourke snorted his derision. "I wouldn't. Seems he's otherwise occupied at the moment." The big man leered at her so she'd have no doubt as to his meaning.

She glared back at him before glancing at the bags on the bed. *Maybe for now but there's always tonight.*

****

Ski Yazkowski favored Matt Curtis with a dour look. The stocky FBI agent had flown into Richmond by helicopter less than an hour before. He'd never been particularly fond of choppers in the first place, and today's trip had been an even rougher ride than normal. When asked, the pilot had muttered something about a weather front and narrow isobars. He was not in a good mood, and the Secret Service agent's last statement hadn't helped alleviate it at all.

"Are you saying I flew in here for no reason, Curtis?" Ski asked glumly.

As the chief Secret Service agent in the Richmond field office, Curtis was used to such confrontations. "To the contrary, Ski. I put my men on alert right after Washington called." Ski cocked an eyebrow in silent query. "Our office, Ski, not the Bureau. Your people didn't call until later. Anyway, my guys are on their way to Charlottesville even as we speak."

"What about the local authorities in Charlottesville?"

"They've been notified. The Steeles' estate is located in an unincorporated area so there's a question of jurisdiction. The state police barracks is pulling in extra men. You guys better be right about this deal, Ski. Their commander is not happy about all this overtime."

"You've seen the list?"

"Yeah, I've seen it. Your Washington office faxed it over. We know Williams isn't there. He's at his house in Alexandria." Ski's eyebrows started dancing a tango. Curtis hastened to explain. "We have a court order for the surveillance." He swore under his breath for sounding so defensive. He didn't owe the FBI an explanation. His instructions stated the

Bureau rode shotgun this time around with the Secret Service in the driver's seat.

"What about the others?" Ski actually scribbled notes on a yellow legal pad.

He shrugged. "We know Senator O'Connor and his daughters are still there. We'll run checks on the license plates of the vehicles parked out there once we get surveillance in place. We still won't know exactly who's there, but at least we'll have a better idea."

"What about Ross?" Ski continued with the third degree questions.

With his temper under control, Curtis managed a nonchalant shrug. "Your guess is as good as mine. I've got to tell you, Ski, we'd sure like to know how your source came up with these particular names."

Ski shrugged in turn. "I wish I knew. If the source calls again, my office has instructions to forward the call here," he hedged.

Curtis glanced at the sheet on his desk. The typed names begged for comment. "This is a hellava list, Ski. We've been trying to put them together for months. And now you get a source calling them in all at once? We gotta know, dude. Who's your source?"

The FBI agent shook his head. "Wish I could say, Curtis. It's a confidential source, and I'd have to kill you if I told you." He flashed a lop-sided grin and winked.

"Can you at least tell me what kind of credentials the source has?" Curtis didn't back down, continuing to push because the answers were too important.

Ski looked his counterpart straight in the eye. "Impeccable," he declared.

"Where does the Bureau fit into all this? This is domestic stuff with ties to terrorism. I thought you guys would be leading the charge." Curtis had too many years of federal service under his belt not to wonder at the FBI's reticence. Despite 9-11 and Homeland Security, inter-agency rivalries were still active. Why would the FBI suddenly want to play second banana on this deal? Suspicious by nature, his hackles stood straight up. He'd caught Ski's hesitation and the way the agent dissembled to answer his questions. He also figured Ski had to be chafing since the Secret Service led the way.

"We've got agents on standby," Ski assured him. "Since Senator O'Connor is involved, Washington decided Treasury should take the lead. Senatorial security does fall under the Secret Service, Curtis."

"Senatorial security, my ass," Curtis muttered under his breath as he stared at the list again. "No offense, Ski, but why is the Bureau so all-fired interested in this Ross guy?"

Ski rummaged in his briefcase and pulled out a file. He slid it across the desk. "See for yourself."

Curtis grabbed the file and opened it. In typical FBI orderliness, the page fastened to the inside left cover listed Ross's vital statistics with a grainy photograph of a man in uniform attached to it. He stared at the photo, wanting to recognize the man when he saw him. Positive he could now ID Duncan Ross, he read the information.

NAME: Duncan Glendon MacDermot Ross
AGE: 34
HEIGHT: 6' 4"
WEIGHT: 220 LBS
HAIR: Brown (Dark)
EYES: Brown
FATHER: Lord Alister Glendon Campbell Ross
MOTHER: Lady Cicely Alys MacDermot Ross (DECEASED)

He looked over at Ski, debating the clout Ross's father might have with the British authorities if push came to shove. The father was a lord. That would be like going after a senator's kid here in the

States. Ski's face remained noncommittal so Curtis continued his perusal of the file.

Ross had graduated with honors from Sandhurst, the British military academy. He'd served one tour as a lieutenant with the Royal Marines before being selected for SAS. As Curtis read the list of Ross' accomplishments, he let out a low whistle of admiration. The guy was a pilot, the Harrier fighter jet among his ratings. He'd been picked for Special Air Service, in many ways the equivalent to Green Beret, Navy SEAL, and Army Ranger training all rolled into one. He continued reading and discovered Ross had undergone training for all of those, too, and had even been a guest instructor at the SEAL school.

"This guy is good, Ski. Is there anything he hasn't done?" He didn't look up.

"Keep reading, Curty."

The next several pages detailed the Irish fiasco and Ross's breakdown in its aftermath. A full page described the man's psychological profile. He looked up this time. "Is he really this wacko?"

Ski shrugged. "You tell me."

He finished reading the last few pages, all stamped across the top in red:

CLASSIFIED—CONFIDENTIAL—MI5.

"Should I ask how the Bureau got these?" he asked.

"MI5 sent them to us when Ross entered the US after Belfast."

Alarm bells went off in Curt's brain. Cynicism blatantly bled from his tone as he asked, "British Intelligence sent us something for free? We didn't request this info?"

"You know what they say about gift horses," Ski dissembled.

He was still uncertain. "Did you corroborate this information?"

Ski shrugged. "Four of those people are confirmed dead. The fifth is still missing."

"No body?" He had to be sure.

"No nothing for over a year. No body. No contact. No trace," Ski verified. "But just because we haven't found a body doesn't mean there isn't one."

He flipped back through the last three pages. Istanbul. Beirut. Colombia. Montreal. London. He looked across the table at Ski. "I'd feel better if these reports came from Interpol."

"So would we," Ski replied agreeably. "There's nothing to tie Ross to those murders except MI5 and his psych profile. We know what he's trained to do, so he's capable of it."

"So how is Senator O'Connor involved?" His gut rumbled.

Ski's voice sounded very calm as he announced, "We think the senator may be Ross's next target."

"Damn." He closed his eyes and rubbed his forehead. "If this guy's as good as they say, we'll need a SWAT team."

Ski grinned. "One step ahead of you, buddy. The Bureau of Alcohol, Tobacco and Firearm's Rapid Response Team is already on it way."

He started counting up the manpower available to them. His tally came to forty or fifty men, depending on just how many the Virginia State Police would spare. That seemed like a lot of firepower until he looked at Ross's file again. "I'd feel a lot better if we had a company of Marines."

"Quantico isn't that far away," Ski retorted.

He glanced sharply at the FBI agent but couldn't decide if Ski was joking or not. He closed the file and pushed it back across the desk. "I guess all we can do now is wait."

The phone on his desk buzzed and both men jumped. They grinned sheepishly at each other, sharing the mutual rush of adrenaline and enjoying the tingling surge. They both knew it would be time to retire if the feeling ever went away.

He picked up the phone. "Yeah?" He listened for a moment. "Right. Call if there's any activity." He hung up the receiver. "Surveillance is in place."

Ski nodded. "Any coffee? This could be a long night."

"I'll check."

In the break area, Curtis put on a fresh pot of coffee, then caught the elevator down to the parking garage. He pulled his Kevlar vest from the trunk of his car, stripped down to his undershirt, put on the vest, and put his shirt and tie back on. The big boys in Washington wanted Ross's head on a platter to serve up to the British. Ross wouldn't go down without a fight, and he fully intended on making it home to his family.

****

Bradford Williams stared out the wide picture window at the manicured landscape of his estate. The draft of his company's quarterly report was spread out on his desk, though profit and loss were the last things on his mind. He'd tried his damnedest to lobby O'Connor's support, but the man had proven to be obdurate. Williams's failure to gain the senator's cooperation galled him. He could not abide failure—not in his subordinates, and certainly not in himself. Somehow, there had to be a way to get to the senator. The man possessed impeccable ethics, and whatever youthful indiscretions of which he'd once been guilty had long since been disclosed and thereby rendered impotent. No hint of dishonor had ever attached itself to the O'Connor family.

He considered the O'Connor daughters. The redhead was a scandal just waiting to happen. She was a wild one, often featured on the society page. The media and public wouldn't get too worked up about any of her peccadilloes. His thoughts turned to the other one. He tried to remember her name but couldn't. He knew she worked in the senator's office so she might be the one to go after. The senator was well known for his anti-drug stance. Drugs in her possession would make huge headlines.

The phone at his elbow beeped softly, disrupting his reverie. He punched a button to activate the speaker phone. "What is it?" His lip curled into a snarl, irritated by the interruption.

"Is your passport in order?" a whispery voice asked through the phone's speaker.

"Who is this?"

"People say this is an excellent time of year to visit Rio," the voice suggested, the faint trace of an Irish brogue barely discernible.

Before he could reply, the mysterious caller hung up. He stared out the window again. This was it then. The decision had been made, the situation out of his hands. His alliance with certain factions had been most lucrative, but the time had come to cut his personal losses and run. Business was business after all.

He jerked open the center drawer of his massive desk. His passport sat right on top. He retrieved it and a thick leather pouch. He had travelers' checks and cash stashed in it, enough to keep him comfortable in Brazil until the heat was off.

****

The radio earphone dangling loose over his shoulder crackled faintly, and the man looked up at the sound of the static. A small woman, her hair tucked up into a knit cap rushed to his side. He held up one finger to silence her as he fit the earpiece into his ear. He fiddled with some dials on the small radio transceiver clipped to the front pocket of his camouflage shirt. After listening for a few seconds, he spoke softly into the skinny microphone attached to the earpiece he wore.

"'Kay," he replied, looking over at the anxious woman. "Just a radio check. We're to stay out of sight until we get the signal."

The young woman hunkered down, her disgust plainly evident. "I'm tired of the waitin'," she groused.

"Brian knows what he's doin'," he replied patiently. "If he says to wait, we wait."

The woman viciously tore the clip out of the AK-47 assault rifle lying across her knees. She cleared the bullet in the chamber, and prepared to strip the weapon.

"Easy, cailín," he soothed. "I doubt we'll be needin' that."

"Better safe than sorry," she spat.

"The guns are to scare 'em, cailín, nothing more," he cautioned. She muttered something under her breath. *The new ones are always so ready for bloodshed,* he thought. But, they all forgot their blood ran just as red as the enemy's, a fact he'd learned over and over in the last ten years.

He sat down and leaned his back up against the gnarled trunk of an old tree. This spot appeared as good as any for the wait. They had a good view of the stable, and were nearly invisible in their camouflage. He squinted at the sun, estimating hard dark was still a couple of hours away, even with the clouds moving in. With the zealous girl to corral, it would be a long wait.

****

He crept through the woods, flitting like a ghost from one late afternoon shadow to another. The assault teams were in place—fourteen handpicked operatives armed with automatic weaponry and smoke grenades. They were here only for diversionary purposes and as a last resort, a contingency to provide cover for his escape if his plan went to hell. His mouth twisted into a grimace meant to pass for a smile. He had every confidence in his plan.

As much as he thirsted for it, a massacre would not help his cause. He just wanted O'Connor to realize not even a member of the United States Senate was safe. A few uninvited guests at this little party in the heart of Virginia should be enough to convince even the stubborn senator of the error of his ways. If they didn't? Well, there was always Plan B.

When he'd first learned Ross was in attendance, he'd had some qualms. Then, after mulling over the situation, he'd decided the Scotsman's presence could be worked to his advantage. Ross had such a hero complex he would have to intervene in tonight's little venture. The man grinned cruelly. If Ross got in the way, so much the better. He'd like nothing better than to permanently deal with the big Scot.

He looked up as a van slowly rounded the curve, and headed toward the main house. He glimpsed young, laughing faces behind the vehicle's windows. As the van passed his position, a Kelly green bumper sticker with white letters caught his eye. *Éirinn go Brách,* it announced. His eyes narrowed pensively. Too cold and uncaring to be superstitious, the bumper sticker was still a portent too ironic for him to dismiss. "*Ireland Forever* indeed," he whispered.

****

Simpson met the van in the driveway. After a brief conversation with the driver, and some shuffling of bodies, Simpson climbed into the front passenger seat. The butler directed the driver through the portico, and around a row of tall evergreens. The trees were so full, they screened a pool and cabana from the main house. The van pulled up next to the building and stopped. Eight college students—four boys and four girls—spilled from the vehicle. The size of the cabana left them awestruck. Replete with buttresses and stained glass windows, the cabana was a small replica of a Norman fortress.

"When you said a pool cabana, I expected a tent," a girl giggled at Simpson.

"This should be adequate for your needs," Simpson informed them. "You will find all the amenities inside. Did you eat before leaving Charlottesville?" Another girl shook her head. "Excellent. Your supper will be delivered shortly." He turned on his heel, and marched sedately toward the main house.

"Adequate?" the driver laughed. "I should think so. Let's get our stuff unloaded." He looked up at the sky. "Get a move on before it starts to rain." The young people grabbed their bags from the van and still laughing, headed to the door.

Inside, two men dressed in dark camouflage scrambled for cover. "In here," one hissed, pulling his companion into a storage room filled with the chlorine scent of pool chemicals.

As the front door spilled the eight students into the main room, the door to the storage area clicked shut.

"What was that?" one boy asked, looking around suspiciously.

"What was what?" a girl asked.

"I thought I heard something," the boy replied.

"Must be your imagination," a pert redhead replied.

The third girl plopped down in an overstuffed chair. "I just hope these guys are lighter on their feet than the last bunch."

The driver stretched out on a couch. "I just hope the women all weigh under two hundred pounds."

The tallest boy in the group grinned at his friends. "You guys don't ask for much, do you? Look, the lady paid us five hundred dollars apiece, and in advance."

The redhead sank to the floor.

"For that kind of money, I'll dance with the devil himself."

Chapter 18

Wrapped in her old flannel robe, Moira stared forlornly at her reflection in the mirror. Far from feeling glamorous as she'd hoped and intended when embarking on this task, she felt hideous instead. Using every bit of subterfuge she possessed, she'd sneaked into her sister's room, and borrowed some cosmetics from Deirdre without her knowledge. Glumly facing reality, she'd goofed. No doubt about it. No matter what she'd tried, nothing worked. The finished effect looked garish—more Kabuki theater than fashion runway.

"I look like a clown," she moaned, fighting the tears threatening to spill over and take the mascara caked on her lashes with them. Her bright pink cheeks made her look like some mad toymaker's idea of a doll. She never wore makeup, had never worn makeup. She didn't have a clue and finally admitted it to herself. A gentle tap on the door sent her into frenzied scrubbing at her face with a handful of tissues, fearing Duncan would catch her looking like this.

"It's just me, miss," Ellie called as she poked her head around the door. She sucked in her breath as she caught sight of Moira. "Lord love a duck, miss, but what have yee done to yerself?"

She turned her mascara-streaked face to the little maid. Ellie tried to stifle her giggle but didn't succeed. The one giggle turned into a whole passel of giggles and soon Moira giggled, too. Ellie first hung up the clothes she'd brought in with her and then went to her.

"Here, miss, let me help," the girl offered. Ellie opened a drawer in the vanity and pulled out a jar of cold cream. "Slather that on yer face, miss, and we'll get you cleaned up so we can start over." She did as Ellie instructed. A box of tissues later, her face was clean. "Now," Ellie instructed, "go rinse yer face with tepid water. Once all the cream is off, splash some cold water on it." She obediently stood up, and went into the bath. "Mind that yee pat yer face dry, now. Don't be rubbin' with the towel." Ellie's order was loud enough to be heard over the sound of running water.

With Moira in the bath and ever mindful of her duties, Ellie straightened the coverlet on the bed. Hearing papers rustle, she looked under the pillows. Giving the papers a quick glance, she folded them tightly, and stuffed them into the trash beneath the tissues. The sounds in the bathroom ceased and a moment later, Moira emerged, her face now fresh and clean, glowing with a just-scrubbed look. She smiled approvingly at the change.

"'Tis much better, miss. Yer skin 'tis too fine to be layered up with all that gunk. Now sit yerself down here and let me have a go at it."

Moira did as she was told and Ellie went to work on her. After a base of moisturizing cream, she grabbed a compact. She brushed a fine dusting of light peach blush across the tops of Moira's cheekbones. With a light hand, she traced the base of her lashes with a silvery blue pencil. After dabbing on a hint of mascara, she stepped back to survey her handiwork. Next, she added a pale gold under Moira's brows, leaving just a hint of color in the brush's wake. Once more, she surveyed Moira's image in the mirror.

"Yee need a bit o' lipstick," she declared. After rummaging around, she found a color that suited. She presented the lipstick to Moira. "Once yer dressed, put this on, miss," she ordered.

Moira stared at her reflection, pleased with the results. This was the effect she'd anticipated when she'd raided Deirdre's makeup kit. Reaching up, she tugged on the ponytail clip in her hair, and the wavy strands fell across her shoulders. "Now all I have to do is figure out what to do with this mop."

Picking up a sterling silver brush, Ellie smiled at her. The maid counted a hundred strokes as she brushed. "Me mum brushed my hair like this every night," she reminisced. After the hundredth stroke, the maid brushed up the sides and front, leaving the back to trail free across her shoulders and down her back. With deft fingers, Ellie wove a braid from the crown of her head and tied it with a blue satin ribbon.

This time when she looked at her reflection, she smiled and her chin lifted imperceptibly. For the first time in her life, she had confidence in more than just her intelligence. *Not that looks are everything,* she silently chided herself.

****

Duncan pulled the white poet's shirt on over his head and tucked it into his black jeans. At the time, she'd declared he'd look so romantic in the shirt, she claimed she couldn't resist the urge to buy it for him. He glared at his reflection. Gemma had insisted on packing for him, and this was the last clean shirt fit for company he had with him. He buckled on his leather belt, plain but for the Celtic knot buckle.

Reaching up, he gathered his hair into a tight ponytail, using a woven silver ring to secure it. His gut rumbled ominously, but not from lack of food. For what wouldn't be the last time, he wished he'd stopped by Gemma's warehouse before this trip. He had more than antique weapons stored there. His search of the rooms occupied by the two men turned up no weapons, but that didn't necessarily mean O'Rourke and Shanahan weren't armed. Besides the *skean dhu* tucked in his boot, he had nothing but his own wits, and the best training that both the British and American armed forces could provide.

Far off, thunder rumbled like the echo of distant cannon fire. His nostrils flared as the sound of nature's bass drum faded. He could almost smell the danger lurking without. Every sense alert, he slipped out of his room and lightly paced down the hallway.

****

Ellie picked up the trashcan and smiled at Moira. "If yee need help gettin' dressed, I can come back after I empty this."

"No, thank you. You've done the hard part, Ellie," Moira assured her with a smile.

"If yee be needin' anything else, Miss Moira, just ring for me."

"Thank you, Ellie. I will. You have no idea how much I appreciate what you've done already." Moira all but glowed.

"Think nothin' of it, miss."

She slipped out of Moira's room, clutching the trashcan like it held gold. As she neared the back stairs, a rough hand grabbed her by the arm. Before she could react, she was jerked into a darkened room.

"Did yee get anything?" a gruff voice demanded as the door shut behind them.

"Let me loose, Seamus," she scolded. "Yee just scared me out of ten years of m'life."

"Give it to me, Ellie," the big man commanded.

She shoved the container into his hands. "An' not a please nor thank you to be had. Yee've been livin' above stairs for too long, Seamus." She meant the accusation.

"You'll be joinin' me soon enough, cailín," he vowed.

"Ha!" She sneered. "There's no easy way to get rich, Seamus O'Rourke, 'ceptin' to be born to it."

"No sister of mine is going to wait on bloody rich bastards anymore."

"An' why not?" she snapped. "'Tis good, honest work and 'twas good enough for our mum to put clothes on our backs and food in our mouths." Before Seamus could retort, she opened the door. "I don't know what yer plannin', Seamus O'Rourke, but yee leave Miss Moira out of it." She shook a warning finger at the big man.

Ellie stomped down the hall, refusing even to flinch when he slammed the door to show his displeasure. The big Irishman quickly turned on the light and dumped the trash out on the floor. Grabbing his prize, he unfolded the pages and began reading.

All the threads were coming together. All he had to do now was weave them into the whole tapestry. The Scotsman's file held his attention and then he perused his own. He smiled, but no warmth showed in the expression. He'd kept his nose clean, and it paid off now. The FBI's information on him remained sketchy at best, made up mostly of speculation and unproven allegations. He'd stayed on the fringes trying not to attract attention. For a while, that had suited him just fine. Tonight, though, everything would change. Tonight he would finally take his rightful place. Pasting on his most charming smile, he left his room.

****

The men gathered in Allen's study. At the bar, Allen poured cocktails for John and Ward. Duncan noticed the untouched glass of Scotch at the senator's elbow. He watched O'Rourke finish his drink in several gulps, and head to the bar for a refill. He swirled the Scotch around in his own glass, making the ice cubes clink against the Baccarat crystal. He took a small sip, savoring the smoky taste for a long moment before swallowing. As much as he hated to waste good Scotch, he still needed all his wits about him tonight. He knew from experience it didn't take much alcohol to affect a man. For that reason, the Scotch he tasted tonight came served on the rocks with a splash of water.

Simpson arrived to announce the ladies were waiting in the dining room. Jovially, the men finished their drinks and followed the butler out. The last one to leave, Duncan noticed both his and the senator's glasses were still full. That gave him pause.

Even though the night was unseasonably warm, a fire crackled in the huge stone fireplace at the far end of the dining room. A massive wooden table seemed lost in the middle of the room. Only ten places had been set with Margaret Steele's stylishly formal dinnerware, though the table could seat more than twice that many.

Only a part of his brain noticed these details. He'd tried to brace himself before entering the room, but his heart stopped and he thought his chest might burst. Moira stood in front of the fireplace ringed by a golden nimbus of firelight. Standing there, she looked like a faerie princess or, Duncan decided lasciviously, like the promise fulfilling his every fantasy.

He strode across the room, his long legs eating the distance hungrily. As he stopped in front of her, his golden vision peered up at him solemnly. Her big, blue eyes searched his face looking for some hint of his feelings. Duncan took her hand and raised her palm to his lips. He kissed it in the exact center and then placed it over his heart.

"Moira," he breathed, his voice husky with suppressed emotion. She smiled then, evidently reassured by his actions and expression.

Moira looked as lovely as Margaret had anticipated. The look on Duncan's face when he first laid eyes on her was more than she could have hoped for. Moira had chosen to wear Maeve's fire opal, as she suspected the girl would. The only other jewelry Moira wore were tiny gold hoops in her ears, hoops formed by two hands holding a crowned heart—each an Irish claddagh, the ancient symbol of love and hope. She glanced over at Patrick. He'd stopped just inside the doorway at his first glimpse of Moira. He appeared stunned and he blinked several times. Margaret wondered if tears lurked in his eyes. As she watched, he shook himself, gulped a deep, steadying breath, and exhaled. She'd thought the same thing he had, when she first saw Moira. Despite the similarities between them, it wasn't Maeve standing across the room.

Having fussed all afternoon over the seating arrangements, Margaret now watched the place cards like a hawk to ensure no hanky-panky. She urged her guests to take their places at the table. The musicians and dancers were warming up in the great hall and she was anxious to get the evening's festivities started. She wanted Moira and Duncan to have every chance to get to know each other better. To look at them, though, one might think they'd known each other forever.

She arranged the table so five guests sat on each side facing the five on the other. Deirdre was seated between Seamus O'Rourke and John Murray. Gemma sat on the other side of John with Ward next to her. Across the table, Allen faced O'Rourke, with Margaret, Duncan, Moira, and Patrick. Margaret was determined Duncan and Moira would sit next to each other tonight and she would allow no one to interfere.

Simpson and Ellie served the first course, a rich French onion soup topped with melted Provolone cheese. The little maid glared at Seamus as she placed his soup bowl in front of him. She knew her brother only too well and his cocky smile made her nervous. Until he did something, though, all she could do was watch and wait.

Moira leaned around Duncan to speak to Margaret. Duncan caught of whiff of her perfume—clean, spicy and as fresh as a field full of wild flowers after a gentle spring rain. His stomach muscles tightened, and he had a hard time sitting still. He fought the urge to squirm against the constrictions of his jeans. He'd grown hard so quickly his jeans were strangling him. *Aye,* he thought, *and where's my kilt when I need it?* He worked hard to focus. Tonight of all nights, he had to control himself. At the same time, all the memories they'd shared rushed through him leaving him hot and wanting. Woven over and through the feelings Moira evoked in him, a sense of foreboding continued to grow. He didn't need to look at O'Rourke to catch the wave of malevolence radiating from him.

"Margaret," Moira whispered behind Duncan's back. "Where's Professor Shanahan?"

"He's warming up with the musicians." Margaret whispered back, then straightened, her smile encompassing the whole table. "I just know we're in for a special treat tonight," she promised.

Simpson and Ellie cleared the soup bowls and served prime rib, roasted potatoes and Caesar salad. Ellie managed to poke Seamus sharply between the shoulders to let him know she watched him.

Gemma tried unsuccessfully throughout dinner to catch Duncan's eye. Both Ward and the senator tried to engage her in conversation, but all she could think about was Duncan. She glared across the table at Moira. Why did the girl have to look so damned virginal, and why was Duncan so smitten by her? Very much a man of the world, his tastes in bed had always been demandingly erotic. She glanced at him again, favoring him with a mocking smile. She'd let him have his fun—for now. Later, he'd be hers again. She made the promise to both of them.

Ward said something so Gemma turned to him, her smile an invitation not quite reaching her eyes. Ward mentioned his mother wanted to redecorate their summer house in Newport Beach and she lit up. Newport Beach, Rhode Island, was the home to many of the rich and famous. Business first, she decided. The pleasure to be gained from breaking up Duncan and Moira would come later. And it will, a little voice whispered to her.

****

Warmed by the good Irish whiskey in his belly, O'Rourke enjoyed his game of cat and mouse with the big Scot. Neither man had spoken directly to the other but that didn't matter. Even now, he leered at Moira and was rewarded by the hard glint of gold in Duncan's eyes. He hadn't quite figured the ins and outs but he'd guessed enough to know Moira would be the Scot's Achilles' heel. The senator's ugly duckling had turned into a swan right before his eyes. He smiled grimly. He'd have the bird and his revenge on the Scotsman. His smile twisted even more, knowing taking the swan would be only the beginning.

****

Margaret was acutely aware of the undercurrents. The unspoken byplay between Duncan and Seamus would have unnerved a less intrepid hostess. Deirdre remained focused on John Murray—a good thing. A rake, and both handsome and rich, Margaret knew John would appeal to

Deirdre as she actually got to know him.

Margaret surreptitiously studied Duncan's profile. His looks were too rugged to be considered handsome in the classical sense. Many women, though, would prefer his looks to a "pretty boy." He was intense, and his dark hair and eyes were sure to elicit immediate feminine attention. He'd certainly captured Moira's. She hid the smile her heart wanted to share with the room. Duncan seemed equally taken with Moira. She fantasized about the beautiful babies they'd make, and then blushed as she thought about them making those babies. *Yes, Duncan Ross,* she admitted, *you do have a dark magnetism that can attract even a stodgy old matron like me.* She and Allen had been married for almost forty years. They'd reached a stage of middle-aged security in their relationship. For a brief moment, she once again hungered for the fire and passion fueled by the energy of youth.

Glancing down the table at Gemma, she felt a slight twinge of guilt. She'd invited Gemma for practical reasons, wanting to show off both the decorator and her designs to other guests. When Gemma had mentioned a boyfriend, she included him in the invitation as a matter of course. Not to mention, it meant one less eligible man she had to supply. The last thing she'd considered was Moira and Duncan becoming an item. She wondered briefly if she'd known, would she still have included him? Watching the couple, their heads bent together, dark and light, she knew. Nothing she did, or might have done, would make any difference. These two were meant to be, and no mortal man, or woman either, could change that fact.

Simpson served coffee and dessert, a rich Black Forest cake, while Ellie cleared the dinner plates. Moira sipped the dark roast coffee appreciatively, tasting the subtle bite of chicory. The New Orleans style drink helped steady her reeling senses. Sitting next to Duncan had turned dinner into an ordeal of self-control. Every time she'd brushed against his muscled arm, she'd gotten lightheaded. Her desire— to feel his arms around her, to kiss him—became palpable. Even the sound of his voice sent shock waves radiating out from her middle where they settled low between her legs with an achy longing.

Is this what love is? she wondered. *This desperate need to be touched, to be held. To feel him deep within me. How is it possible that I need him so much?*

Her hand shook slightly as she raised the cup to her lips. She concentrated on keeping it steady. She knew that until she and Duncan became truly one, the tension would not go away. It was time.

****

Duncan dreaded the end of the meal. He had to keep Moira at arm's length until O'Rourke's game came to its final conclusion. Even now, the hairs on the back of his neck prickled in warning. To his dismay, every other part of him ached to feel Moira's skin pressed against his own. *'Twill be time enough later for the two of us,* he reminded himself. He and Moira were destined to love. He was as certain of that fact as he'd ever been of anything in his life. He only had to keep them both alive, and he was just as certain of that fact.

His life had been on the line since Belfast, the sense of danger a part of his every-day existence now. This new, unseen threat to Moira had him wary. He had to stay focused on it. Until he knew she was safely out of danger, he had to remain vigilant.

His resolve disintegrated as he held her chair after dinner. When she stood up, he could feel the heat radiating from her, could smell her sweet scent. Margaret shooed everyone out toward the great hall.

He held his arms rigidly to his sides. If he touched her at this moment, or if she touched him, he'd sweep her into his arms, and carry her off to bed without a moment's hesitation. Any sense of morality or propriety could be damned. As if realizing his dilemma, Moira turned to her father, linking her arm through his. Patrick escorted her out and he followed a few steps behind them, every one of his senses on alert.

He knew something would happen tonight. What, he didn't know and that had him concerned. He suspected O'Rourke meant to harm Moira in some way, but his mind recoiled from the exact nature of it. Thunder rumbled again, a little closer this time. Again, his nostrils flared. Danger lurked out there somewhere. Waiting. Hiding. Anticipating the approaching storm. His heart stuttered for a beat as he hurried to catch up with Moira and her father. He vowed not to let her out of his sight. Not this night. Not ever.

Chapter 19

The Celtic Connection occupied the same alcove they had the previous night. As her father led her across the huge room, Moira suddenly realized she'd met Duncan a scant twenty-four hours ago. A shiver ran its icy finger down her spine as a flood of memories washed over her. Just a day, this life, she corrected.

A large area in front of the alcove had been cleared of rugs and furniture. She enjoyed traditional Irish dancing. The rollicking music and partner changes felt more comfortable to her than dancing in one man's arms for the duration. She smiled. There was one man's arms she could be comfortable in for an eternity. Still, she looked forward to the evening.

At some point during dinner, she'd made up her mind. She would give herself to Duncan. Having so resolved, though, now left her feeling shy in his presence. She clutched her father's arm and Patrick glanced down at her with a worried look in his eyes. She smiled up at him.

"I'm okay, Da."

"I know you are," Patrick replied, his voice filled with pride. "My caterpillar had become a butterfly." He fingered the soft material of her shawl and his eyes reflected the unresolved sadness in his voice when he added, "Margaret saved these things for you."

Like a diamond on glass, her father's sorrow cut right through her. "She insisted I wear this tonight," she quickly explained in hopes of dispelling any notion he might have that she meant any disrespect.

He patted her hand. "I'm glad, Moira, truly I am." They both knew in their hearts he was. He looked across the room. Duncan stood guard just inside the door. "Maeve would be proud of you, darlin'," he said, nodding toward Duncan.

Moira felt close to tears as she fingered the gold chain draped around her neck. "Do you mind me having this?"

The smile he bestowed on her looked both sad and fond. "It belonged to Maeve. Her people gave it to her the day we were married. Her legacy they told us." He glanced over at Duncan again. "It's your legacy now, Moira."

She stood on tiptoe and planted a kiss on his cheek. "I love you, Da."

The Celtic Connection launched into a rollicking air and eight dancers burst into the room catching all the guests by surprise. Before he could reply to her, one of the boys had claimed her, sweeping her onto the dance floor.

"I love you, too," he whispered after her.

The boy who'd chosen Moira looked amazed as she perfectly matched his intricate series of grapevine and quick steps. "You've done this before," he accused good-naturedly.

"Once or twice," she giggled in reply.

Duncan reluctantly let himself be pulled onto the dance floor by the insistent little redhead. *Besides,* he reasoned, *Moira's already out here and I'll be that much closer if something happens.*

The first dance ended much to everyone's breathless relief. After a round of good-natured applause, Margaret introduced the Irish dancers, all students from the University of Virginia in Charlottesville. "In case you haven't noticed," she continued, "this weekend has had a rather Irish flair." Her guests chuckled appreciatively. "Since St. Patrick's Day occurred just a few days ago and this is the night of Alban Eiler, the vernal equinox, Allen and I decided this would be the perfect way to christen our new home—Faerie Glen Farm."

A few people looked bewildered so Margaret hastened to explain. "For those of you unfamiliar with the lore of the Faerie Folk, the four sun positions—the vernal and autumnal equinoxes and the two solstices, winter and summer, were of great importance to the faerie. Alban Eiler ushers in spring, the time when all those from the magical lands awaken, and come to join with us mortal folk for a celebration of the coming season. We are so pleased all of you joined us for our celebration welcoming spring here at the farm. We invite all of the faerie folk who might be in the neighborhood to join us also."

An icy finger skittered down Moira's spine, and she shivered. Margaret's mention of faeries made her uneasy, and she remembered the lights she'd seen in the woods last night. Sheila plucked an eerie note on her harp to begin the next song. She shivered again then chided herself for being silly.

Michael's guitar joined the harp and the dancers performed a caprice. The dance was sedate but lighthearted, and even Deirdre, who proclaimed her dislike of the folk music of her ancestors loudly and often, appeared charmed.

As the applause faded, the musicians began "The Road to Lisdoonvarna," a traditional air, and once again the dancers urged the guests onto the floor. Moira skipped from one partner to another as the lively music dictated. Suddenly, she found herself face-to-face with Seamus O'Rourke. She was so intent on studying him she missed Duncan's reaction as he watched the two of them from across the room.

With the light just right, she could discern the brownish streaks in O'Rourke's hair where the black dye had begun to wash away. Before she could get a good look at his eyes, he moved to another partner, and Moira now danced with John Murray.

"I'll never get the hang of this," the attorney groused while grinning like a goofy puppy.

"You're doing fine," she encouraged. She glanced over her shoulder at her previous partner. *Next time,* she promised.

Without pause, the musicians played "The Drunken Gauger," another traditional melody. Before Moira got the chance to dance with O'Rourke again, he'd been replaced in her set by her father. Though not as spry as he once had been, Patrick could still step a jig with the best.

The next song slowed, meant for couples to actually touch while they danced. Moira danced with her father. As he put his hand on her waist to lead, he teased, "I haven't seen you dancing with Mr. Ross."

She blushed all the way to the roots of her hair. Was it possible her father had read her mind? Even though she was almost thirty, he was still her father. Her virginity and the possible loss thereof was not something to be considered in his presence.

The song ended and she left the floor on her father's arm. She settled into a chair to catch her breath and regain her composure. She knew the minute Duncan appeared behind her. She also knew if she looked at him, he would read her mind. She blushed again, and her stomach started doing weird little flip-flops.

Moira stiffened a moment when he fingered the satin ribbon in her hair. She could feel his hand shake slightly at the contact, as if even that brief touch overwhelmed him. She heard his breath catch in his chest and the rasp of denim as he shifted position. Could he be as anxious as she?

Duncan stood behind Moira's chair. He watched her cheeks pinken as his breathing raced to match hers. Vaguely aware that Michael put down the guitar and took up the *Uilleannn* pipes, he listened to the first mournful notes of the haunting melody. He glanced briefly at the musicians and the college dancers, watching them exchange puzzled glances, as if they were unsure of what Michael was doing. His gaze flicked to Sinead and she stared at him for a long moment before putting down her fiddle and picking up the bowed psaltery. Kevin beat a slow tattoo on the bodhrán, and Sheila, in a voice even sweeter than Enya's, began a soft chant.

The college dancers gathered on one side of the dance floor, listening to the odd, eerie melody. As if everyone in the room had suddenly been bewitched, no one moved. No one spoke. Breaths were barely drawn. There was only the sound of the music and Duncan was trapped in its spell.

He had no idea what possessed him. He took Moira's hand and led her out onto the floor. As if hypnotized, she followed him without a word. She began to dance and he matched her steps. As they moved simultaneously to the music, the four walls around them faded into a dark haze. The room and all the people in it ceased to exist.

He was only aware of the music—the music and Moira. A vision of white and gold, she drifted first at his side and then in front of him. Their steps and bodies stayed in perfect harmony, though they hadn't touched since the dance began. The music changed slightly, and he pulled her into his arms. Their hips brushed together as their feet followed the intricate steps neither had ever danced before. Each time their bodies touched, he could see blue sparks jump between them. The music changed again, and Moira moved away from him. He followed, powerless to do anything else.

She turned to him, and he stopped. She brushed against him now and then as she dipped and swayed around him, all the while keeping time with the sensuous music. His breath quickened, and he grew so hard he thought he would burst. He had to touch her—to touch her bare skin with his own. He swept her off her feet, and cradled her to his chest. Even as he held her, his feet were compelled to dance. He swore grass grew beneath them, and that stars shone in the midnight sky above him as they danced through the shadows cast by standing stones.

He felt her heartbeat quicken to match his own. Her breasts strained against the linen of her blouse. His arm brushed across them, and her nipples jumped to his touch, forming hard peaks. The tip of her tongue moistened her full bottom lip. He groaned. Lifting her high, he offered her up to the stars and the full moon as a perfect tribute to the gods. The night wind caressed his cheeks. Words whispered in his ear, words he didn't understand.

****

"By the life that courses in my blood and the love that resides within my heart," sang a voice as sweet as spun sugar. "Take thee to my hand, my heart, and my spirit, to be my chosen one."

"Abhean!" a voice full of thunder and fury roared.

Duncan pulled Moira closer, sheltering her within his arms and the curve of his body. They were lying on grass, both of them naked. As he stared at her, he forgot all about that voice. She was perfect. He kissed her soft lips as one hand cupped a full breast. Moira moaned and pushed against his palm, her tongue sparring with his own. His other hand trailed down the silky skin of her ribs and traced her narrow waist to her softly rounded hip. His hand rested there and a small part of his brain marveled that her hip fit perfectly beneath his palm. He kissed her hard, bruising her lips, and she kissed him back, matching his fervor with her own.

His shaft pressed against downy curls seeking entrance to her most secret place. A sweet sigh escaped her lips as her hands traced the hard muscles of his back. He broke their kiss to trail his tongue down her neck, across her fair shoulder, and at last to the valley between her breasts. His shadow beard prickled her soft skin as she arched against him. The down at the top of her thighs teased and sweetly tormented the tip of his cock as she pressed against him, trying to fit them together.

"Yes," she sighed as he pulled her rosy nipple into the moist cavern of his mouth as his shaft slid between her legs to find moist heat. "Oh, yes."

"Send them back to An Domhain, Abhean," that thunderous voice whispered.

The Harper stared at the King. "No."

"'Twill do no good, Abhean. What was written will come to be," Manannan replied sadly.

"At least give them the binding," the Harper argued.

"They cannot seal the binding here."

"They sealed it before but had not the words. Give them the words this time."

"I cannot. They must find the words for themselves."

"Bah. If you will not, then I will," the Harper grumbled.

"I forbid it, Abhean," Manannan commanded.

"You said you loved him," Abhean wheedled.

"I do. Do not meddle in this affair, Abhean," the King ordered.

The Harper disappeared in a swirl of iridescent mist.

Manannan Mac Lir, King of Tir Nan Óg, the Land of Ever Young, felt his heart break. "I love her more, Abhean. I will not see her heart broken again."

"Then give them the words," Abhean's dulcet voice whispered on the breeze.

****

As the music sighed its last whispered breath, Moira slid from his grip only to hold herself pressed full length against him, her arms wrapped around his neck. His lips found hers. Soft and sweet her kiss, as full of life and promise as spring itself. The room slowly came back into focus. He blinked in the bright light, suddenly aware that every eye stared at the two of them. He kissed the tip of her nose and gently set her on her feet. He gave her a courtly bow, turned on his heel, and marched out of the room. If he didn't get some air fast, he would do something beyond foolish. If he'd held her another moment, had so much as touched her again, he would have laid her down on the floor. He would have taken her right there in the middle of the room, and it wouldn't have mattered who watched.

The room held its collective breath as Duncan left, and Moira dreamily floated back to her chair. She gazed around, bemused. Michael shook his head looking stunned, as if he wasn't sure what had just happened. She glanced at the other musicians and realized they were just as confused. The very air was charged with sexual tension and everyone in the room seemed affected.

Moira felt like she was sleepwalking. She knew she sat in a chair in the great hall at Faerie Glen, but the sweet perfume of the air from that other place still filled her lungs and her cheeks still felt the lingering kiss of the night wind. The warm glow that had been Duncan was gone but she knew he lingered nearby. She could feel him, and knew he'd return to her in a heartbeat if she but willed it.

Lost between the two worlds, she still heard the haunting music, and knew, deep down, this was no dream or half-remembered memory. What she'd just experienced had yet to occur in this life. Moira's fingertips brushed her lips in wonder. *My God, but the man can kiss.*

****

Gemma watched Duncan make a spectacle of himself with Moira, rage gnawing at her insides. He'd practically screwed the girl on the dance floor, right there in front of God and everyone. He'd been a conquest, a man she wanted to keep just for that reason. Now, though, she realized he would never be hers—in fact, never had been. That knowledge made her even more spiteful. If she couldn't have him, no one would. The musicians returned, and cranked out a lively jig. Making up her mind, she joined a set of dancers. When Seamus caught her around the waist to swing her about, she smiled at him coldly. Her eyes held a wintry glint as she mouthed the word, *Midnight.* He nodded his understanding before swinging her into the arms of one of the college boys.

Chapter 20

Duncan found himself out on the back terrace. Instead of the cool air he sought, the atmosphere felt warm and humid, the air so thick it became hard to breathe. He had no explanation for what had just happened inside. *Then again,* he thought ruefully, *I haven't been able to explain anything that's happened since I met Moira.* Even so, something about the incident tonight seemed more disconcerting than all the rest.

Though the atmosphere was thick and oppressive, Duncan sensed an undercurrent of electricity running through it. Far off on the horizon, faint flashes illuminated a heavy bank of clouds. About to decide the approaching storm fueled his uneasiness, he suddenly went on full alert. His soldier's intuition told him someone watched him.

Using that sixth sense, he cast it out, searching for the invisible watcher. Like a hound following the scent of his prey, he located the unseen sentinel's position down in the garden. Before he could pinpoint the exact location, the feeling of covert surveillance disappeared. He waited a few minutes, hoping to see or hear something more. Unable to discern any tangible threat in the thick darkness, he returned to the house. He tried to convince himself it had been some nocturnal animal he'd sensed, but to no avail. His sense of foreboding became even more pronounced.

****

Damn but that was too bloody close, he thought. He'd forgotten how good Ross could be. Reminded of his old enemy's skill, he wouldn't make that mistake again. Like the ragged clouds scudding across the face of the full moon, he flitted through the garden. Ross would be taken care of, he'd see to it. But for now, there were far more pressing matters demanding his attention.

****

When Duncan returned to the great hall, the musicians were taking a break. Shanahan was missing from the group but O'Rourke stood across the way tossing back a double whiskey. Moira was nowhere to be found, and he almost panicked before realizing most of the ladies were absent. She'd just gone to the ladies' room. A moment later, Simpson appeared at his elbow and wordlessly handed him a folded note. After Simpson walked away, he unfolded the heavy paper and read the lacy handwriting: *Duncan, meet me in the stable at midnight—Moira*

As his fingers folded the note and slid it into his pocket, he gave in to the wave of heat washing over him. Unbidden, the memory of another stable flashed in his mind. As much as his psyche continued to enjoy the memories of that encounter, he was determined not to repeat it in real life—at least not this first time. He'd head to the stable a little before midnight so he'd arrive first. If Moira had some sort of surprise arranged, he'd nip her plan in the bud. He would convince Moira to come back to the house. If something did happen tonight, she'd be safer in his room anyway. He chuckled, noting the ease with which his resolve capitulated to that bit of logic.

****

Gemma held her emotions in check as she

210

waited in the small sitting area adjacent to the powder room. One part of her brain noticed the understated elegance of the subtle mauve and peach tones she'd chosen for this room. The other part frantically plotted a way to keep Moira occupied until shortly before midnight.

Moira emerged from the inner room. She glanced around but Gemma made sure only the two of them remained. Moira's raised chin and defiant stare were hard to ignore but unfazed, Gemma schooled her voice. "Can we talk?" she asked, forcing her voice to sound sweet and sincere.

"About what?" Moira's tone and stance were both defensive.

"About the only thing we have in common," she answered coolly. "Duncan."

"Don't you think you should be talking to him?" Moira countered.

Gemma studied the other woman for a long moment, remembering the spectacle she and Duncan had made of themselves on the dance floor. "I think this is between the two of us."

Moira arched an eyebrow, not saying a word. After a few moments, she regally walked to a chair and sat on its edge.

Gemma hid her smirk. Moira wouldn't be acting like a princess much longer. She pasted a condescending smile on her face. "There are some things you should know about Duncan," she began. She hoped to shade her voice with just the right mix of concern and amused patience, as if she'd held this conversation many times.

Moira inclined her head, still every inch the royal lady.

"Duncan and I have been together for a long time, Moira," Gemma continued. She added a bit of condescension to her tone.

"So?" Moira sounded bored and rolled her eyes a

little as if to underline her disinterest.

"So, this isn't the first time he has strayed." Gemma paused to let her statement sink in. She caught a flicker in Moira's eyes. "And," she continued, pressing home her advantage, "I'm sure you won't be the last."

She watched Moira's resolve waver, and it suddenly became clear. Moira had been in Deirdre's shadow for so long, she didn't realize how beautiful she actually was. Gemma continued her attack, now knowing her opponent's weakness. "Moira, you aren't the first to fall for him like this. Duncan is a man who..." She trailed off deliberately then cleared her throat. "Well, he's a man of many appetites, to be blunt. He enjoys sampling what other women have to offer, but he always comes back to me to fill his plate." She paused, letting her words sink in. Then, in an insinuating voice, she added, "If you know what I mean." She waited while Moira stared at her. When the other woman finally spoke, she was ready.

"Why are you telling me this?" Moira asked.

Gemma sighed and in a voice cloaked with sincerity replied, "You seem like a sweet girl. Now, if you were Deirdre, I'd say you deserve what you're about to get. But you aren't her, and I don't really want to see you get hurt. You can have your little fling with Dunnie. He's well worth the ride. Just don't get your hopes up about any sort of future with him. Come tomorrow, Dunnie will be leaving with me, and you will soon be forgotten as just one of his conquests." She stood up and smoothed her black lace dress over her hips. Walking over to the door and opening it, she glanced back at Moira. "Just a little friendly advice, Moira."

Just as Gemma had hoped, Moira stayed in the sitting room. She glanced at her watch. She'd have to hurry. She had to be in place before Duncan arrived and he was notorious for being early. She didn't have much time.

****

Moira had been playing with the big boys on the Hill for so long, she figured Gemma Todd would be no match for her. After Gemma left, she sat silently, mustering her thoughts. Gemma had caught her completely off guard. Accusations of betrayal, outrage, jealousy? She'd expected those, but not this calm, matter-of-fact acceptance of the attention Duncan paid to her. Was there something to what Gemma had said?

She'd sat there stoically, staring at Gemma in fascination, as if the other woman was some sort of hypnotic snake. She hadn't been able to tear her gaze away from the cold glitter in Gemma's eyes. She'd finally found her voice to ask why, pleased and relieved her voice sounded so firm.

Moira stared at the striped cushions on the chair Gemma had vacated. Her head remembered its misgiving that afternoon when she'd talked to Ski at the FBI. Her heart refused to listen. Her gift wasn't infallible, but it had never failed her when it really mattered. She tried to apply cold logic, to be analytical, but memories of both past and present kept getting in the way.

Their strange dance from earlier left her feeling achy and longing for his touch. She'd felt his obvious arousal, and understood why he'd walked away. If he'd touched her, she'd have been on him like a ten-dollar hooker on a Las Vegas conventioneer. Duncan could not be playing her for a fool. Not even Sir Laurence Olivier could act that well.

Until he'd entered her life, she had been logical and calculating, not allowing emotion to play any role in her day-to-day existence. *Well,* she decided, *I'll be just that.* The logical thing to do was ask him about Gemma's allegations. She'd know from his answers which of them lied. Her mind made up, she went in search of him.

The musicians were playing again as Moira passed through the entry hall toward the great hall. She hesitated at the door, and Simpson appeared at her side.

"Excuse me, miss." He handed her a folded note.

"Thank you, Simpson." She waited until he'd disappeared behind the massive stairwell, and then looked all around to make sure she was alone. Positive no one watched, she unfolded the note. Bold, black letters stared up at her: *Meet me in the stable at a little past midnight—Duncan*

She stared at the words flowing across the crisp paper. The stable was just as good a place as any to talk. She glanced up at the massive clock near the front doors. Not quite midnight. She didn't want to return to the party, knowing that if she disappeared so quickly after making an appearance, her absence would likely be noticed. Yet if she didn't return, her father was sure to worry.

Simpson reappeared from under the stairs bearing a fresh decanter of whiskey. As she approached, he smiled at her. "May I help you, miss?"

"Simpson, would you tell my father I'm tired, and have decided to go to my room?" Moira hoped he wouldn't notice the hesitancy in her voice. She'd never been a good liar. *Poker player, yes, but not a liar.*

"Of course, miss." Simpson tilted his head in her direction, a very formal and almost regal gesture.

"Thank you." Without thinking, she touched the butler's arm in gratitude. She turned to go up the stairs so she missed his raised eyebrow at her gesture of familiarity.

In order to give her lie some semblance of truth, Moira went all the way to her room. Once there, she decided to retrieve her shawl. Ellie had brought it up for her during the dancing. She thought the evening air might be cool, and wanted it just in case. The shawl was folded neatly across her bed. She tossed it around her shoulders, enjoying the rich luster of the linen as it slid through her fingers. She paused to look in the mirror. "You've changed, girl," she told her reflection. "Let's hope it's for the better."

Moira paused in the hallway, looking both ways to make sure the coast was clear. Satisfied, she darted to the back stairs and headed down. The big clock boomed out twelve times. "The witching hour." She resisted the urge to cross herself.

****

Duncan's senses shifted into high gear as he scrambled down to the stable. Clouds rolled in on a quickening wind, and the only light came from an intermittent moon. All too soon, this night wouldn't be fit for man or beast. He had to find Moira and get her back to the house quickly.

He remembered the stable had a motion-activated security light above the door, but it didn't come on as he approached. The door stood ajar, opening into the gloomy interior. He slipped through it, and as he passed through the faint square of light cast by the moon at the entry, the hair on his neck stood up. "Déjà vu," he muttered, reaching down to pull his *skean dhu* from his boot.

The big sorrel nickered as he neared. He stopped to pat Star's neck. "Is she here yet, big 'un?" he whispered to the horse. The sorrel twitched his ears, looking toward the back of the stable. He gave the animal a final pat, slipped his dagger back into his boot, and prowled through the shadows toward the rear.

"It certainly took you long enough, Dunnie," Gemma drawled, her figure a vague shadow in the darkness.

"Gemma," he snarled. "What game are you playing now?" He couldn't believe his gullibility. He should have recognized her handwriting. Turning on his heel, he headed back to the front door. Suddenly, light flooded the interior of the stable.

Gemma stood at the fuse box on the back wall, her hand still on the main breaker. "Since you are dumping me for that simpering little sheep, I thought I should be able to say goodbye in my own inimitable way," she purred.

"Put your clothes on, Gemma."

Boldly, she stepped up to him. "Make me," she dared, her gray eyes snapping.

He found her black dress draped over a stall door, and tossed it to her. "You're making a fool of yourself." He felt disgusted by her.

"Do I care? Come on, Dunnie," she wheedled. "One last fuck for old time's sake."

He stared at her, his voice flat and cold as he announced, "The game is over, Gemma."

Several things happened almost simultaneously. Gemma threw her dress in his face and launched herself at him. He found himself momentarily blinded while his arms and hands were full of naked female flesh.

A tiny gasp from the doorway set everything into slow motion. He shook the dress off his head, and turned to find Moira standing just inside the door staring at them. Gemma had her legs wrapped around his waist, clutching him as she tried to kiss him. He avoided her lips, cognizant only of the hurt and betrayal mirrored in Moira's eyes.

"Moira," he called, his voice agonized, only now realizing the full scope of Gemma's duplicity.

Without a word, Moira turned on her heel and walked stiffly away. He caught sight of tears glistening in her eyes as she picked up her skirt and ran. He stared after her. Wrenching Gemma's arms from his neck, he unceremoniously dumped her onto the straw covered floor.

White-hot rage built in his gut. Looking up at him, Gemma shrank back. For the first time, she seemed to realize how dangerous he was. His hands stretched toward her, clenching and unclenching like they had a life of their own. If he fastened them around her neck, they would snap it as easily as a wooden matchstick.

As bad as he wanted to throttle Gemma, Duncan knew he had to find Moira. Spinning on his heel, he sprinted to the door. She'd fled only seconds before, but there was no sign of her. "Moira!" he called, his desperation turning her name into a plea.

Guessing she'd headed to the house, he ran. A bright white flash and an echoing boom stopped him dead in his tracks. This was no natural thunder and lightning. The sharp staccato reports of automatic gunfire quickly followed the explosion. The house was under attack.

"Moira!" This time he turned her name into a scream.

With reckless disregard, he raced through the garden. His head told him to slow down, to reconnoiter the situation before plunging in headfirst. His heart told him Moira was there somewhere in the middle of the deadly gunfire. His heart won the debate, and his pace quickened.

His body acted purely on instinct when a dark figure loomed up in front of him. One part of his brain recognized the fact that the dark form carried an AK-47 in one hand, and then it registered the dull glint of a combat knife raised to attack. His right hand slashed at the shadow's throat. As his victim crumpled, he grabbed the assault rifle and knife. The brief encounter barely delayed his forward motion.

As he neared the terrace, Duncan spotted

another dim form kneeling in the shadows. He'd become silent death, vengeful and terrible. Without hesitation, he rushed the obscure form, and plunged the knife into the base of the terrorist's skull.

Springing over the terrace wall, he dashed across the stone floor as his brain surveyed smashed windows and doors hanging drunkenly on broken hinges. Without slowing, he crashed through the doors. A small shape dressed in combat gear spun around to meet his attack. A woman, his brain registered. His slight hesitation was all she needed. She leveled her nasty-looking weapon at his chest. Before she could squeeze the trigger, Simpson loomed up behind her and she slumped to the floor. He recognized the object in Simpson's hand—a medieval mace. He grinned at the dapper butler.

"There's life in this old relic yet, sir," Simpson proclaimed proudly.

He briefly wondered if the butler referred to the antique weapon or to himself, but he didn't have the time to contemplate it for long. "Where's Moira?"

Simpson shook his head. "I don't know, sir. I haven't seen the miss."

"Where's the senator?"

"This way, sir," Simpson directed him. "They're barricading themselves in the study."

He hoped for good news as he asked, "Have you called for help?"

"Landlines are dead, sir," Simpson replied gloomily. "Cell phone coverage is spotty at best out here. Mr. Steele tried the satellite computer lines. Nothing."

Cursing under his breath, Duncan assessed their situation. They were miles from the nearest house, and even further from Charlottesville. Three of the terrorists were accounted for, but he had no way of knowing how many were left. He had the purloined AK-47 and combat knife along with his *skean dhu.* Simpson had an eleventh century mace plus the girl's machine pistol. Their odds weren't looking very good.

He motioned for the butler to wait as he checked out the entry hall. When he gave the all clear, the two of them dashed across the open space. The door to the study opened a hair's breadth, and they slipped through the crack. Frightened faces greeted him as he scanned the people assembled there. Gemma was missing, along with O'Rourke and the little professor, Michael Shanahan. His heart sank when he realized Moira was absent as well.

Another explosion rocked the outside of the house. He refocused on the situation at hand. Most of the women were huddled against the back wall. Only Sinead, the harpist, remained dry-eyed, her face a glazed mask of horror. He made a wild guess she'd been through some of the violence in Northern Ireland. Post Traumatic Stress Disorder was a terrifying thing when it reared its ugly head.

Margaret dabbed at a cut on John Murray's forehead with a handkerchief. The woman he once thought flighty turned out to have a steel rod for a backbone. The attorney didn't look so cocky any more, but determination glittered in his angry eyes. He was game.

"Mrs. Steele, will you see to the girl?" He nodded toward Sinead.

Margaret followed his gaze and knew immediately who he meant. She motioned to Kevin, the other musician to help her. Together, they got Sinead into a chair and wrapped her in a tartan afghan. Kevin held Sinead's hand and spoke soothingly to her. Margaret looked around for the next crisis.

He evaluated the rest of his troops. Allen Steele looked madder than hell after Simpson told him about the phones. The senator appeared grim but calm. Ward, the rich boy, looked as white as a ghost, but his jaw was set. He might be scared, but he was determined to go out with a fight. Ellie, the little maid, tried to comfort the college girls. They were terrified, but relatively calm. The four college boys were huddled together in front of the girls like a pack of rugby players. They'd stand and fight to protect the girls. He'd seen first-hand how capable Simpson could be. This rag-tag bunch wasn't much but they'd do. They'd have to.

****

The radio crackled with static, and the state police dispatcher spoke into her microphone. "Repeat your message," she stated as she flipped a switch.

An excited voice erupted from the loudspeaker in her console. "The Steele farm is under attack," the voice responded through the static. "Explosions. Heavy caliber weapons. Repeat. All hell is breaking loose out here. We need help now. Can you read me? Over."

The FBI agent looked at his Secret Service counterpart. "Shit," Yazkowski muttered.

"Has hit the fan," Curtis finished for him.

Ski looked at the man sitting next to a bank of telephones. "Call Richmond," he directed.

"Call Washington," Curtis countermanded.

The dispatcher pulled off her headphones. "Call the Marines. They've got a war going on up there."

Chapter 21

Everyone watched in fascinated horror as Duncan swiped the bloody blade of the combat knife against the back of his thigh then shoved it through his belt. Clearing the AK-47, he dropped the magazine clip and checked it. Two-thirds full, the automatic rifle held only twenty bullets. Allen had counted the bullets as well. Duncan looked over at him. "Have anything a bit more modern?" he asked, nodding toward the mace in Simpson's hand.

"Yeah," Allen replied glumly. "I do. However, everything is locked up in a gun safe in the basement where they aren't doing us any good."

"I'll go get them, sir," Simpson volunteered.

Before either man could respond, a heavy caliber round tore through the door, smacking into the far wall.

"Down!" Duncan commanded. "Everyone on the floor."

No one hesitated to obey as they scrambled for cover. Sinead whimpered though Kevin had her cradled beneath him on the floor.

Margaret crawled over to her husband. "What do they want?" she whispered. Allen had no answer.

The senator stared at him. "Where's Moira?"

"I don't know," Duncan answered, attempting to keep his voice firm even though his gut churned. "I was hoping she'd be here."

"Simpson told me she'd gone to her room. A few minutes later, all hell broke loose." Patrick noticed the tiny waver in Duncan's gaze. "When did you see her last?" His voice cut through the din, sharp with fear.

"About midnight. At the stable," he replied. He wouldn't lie to the man now. "She ran out. I thought she headed back to the house." The senator's displeasure at this news radiated out toward him.

Margaret had also made her own head count. "Where's Gemma?" she inquired of no one in particular.

"I left her in the stable," Duncan replied quietly, unable to meet the disapproval in Patrick's eyes. What had occurred at the stable didn't really matter right now. He'd explain it later—if Moira was safe, if they survived the night. Ifs. There were too many. His head jerked up as he listened to something only he could hear, except he didn't hear it so much as feel it. Simpson listened, too. "Chopper," he named the vibrations disturbing the air. Simpson nodded in agreement.

The others could hear the throaty whump-whump-whump now. "Ours or theirs?" Patrick wondered aloud.

"Blackhawk." Duncan identified the helicopter by its sound.

"Then it must be ours," Allen asserted. Duncan merely shrugged in reply.

Faintly, they heard an amplified voice announcing, "We have you surrounded. Throw down your weapons."

The chatter of small arms fire sounded like angry magpies, and in the background, the growing wail of sirens added to the cacophony. Duncan crawled to the door and cautiously looked out. The entry hall appeared empty now. All the gunfire came from outside the house. He gathered himself for the sprint across the entry and up the stairs.

A hand touched his arm. "Where are you going?" the senator hissed.

"To find Moira," he promised.

He sprang through the door like a jungle cat. He leaped up the stairs, taking them three at a time. His long legs galloped down the second floor hall to Moira's room. The door stood wide open. He slipped into the room, every sense on guard as he checked every hiding place—the closet, the bath, under the bed. The room was empty. Holding the AK-47 at the ready, he checked the rest of the second floor guest rooms. Like Moira's, they were all empty. He felt sick inside. Where was she? He closed his eyes, picturing her face in his mind. She was out there. Somewhere. He could feel her.

He was standing on the main stairs when a squad of uniformed men burst through the door. "Drop the weapon!" their leader commanded.

Very slowly, very carefully, he leaned down to put the assault rifle on the step next to his feet. Just as slowly, he straightened up, his hands extended out to his sides. "Senator O'Connor, it seems your Marines have landed," he called.

Cautiously, the door to the study opened, and Patrick emerged with Allen fast on his heels. Ward grinned from ear to ear as he came through the door with John and Margaret. "Boy are we glad to see you guys," he gushed.

"We aren't really Marines," the squad leader explained. "Lieutenant Pierce, Virginia State Police."

Ignoring him, Patrick rushed to the foot of the stairs. "Did you find her?" he demanded, his face hard but his eyes pleading for good news.

Duncan shook his head slowly. "There's no sign of her, Senator," he replied morosely.

The state trooper strode across the hall. "Who's missing?" he demanded.

Patrick glared at him. "My daughter, Lieutenant. No one's seen her since the shooting started."

"Description!"

"Long blonde hair, blue eyes. Five six, one hundred forty pounds. She's wearing a white blouse and skirt," Duncan snapped. "Her name is Moira," he added softly. *And her laugh is as sweet as the summer breeze and her skin as soft as the clouds.*

The trooper spoke into his radio, giving the senator a reassuring smile. "Don't worry, sir. We'll find her." He turned to the task of detailing his men to various duties. A large contingent began to search the house as a medical team arrived to treat the injured.

The police moved everyone into the great hall. Medics packaged Sinead for transport to the hospital, and John Murray's head now sported a white bandage. Deirdre stayed by his side, fussing over him. Anybody looking at him figured he thought his injury well worth the pain to have her fretting over him.

Duncan chafed at the delay. He wanted—no, he needed to be out searching for Moira. The state police separated him from the others, making him sit on a straight-back chair near the door. Two of them eyed him nervously as they fingered the flaps on their holsters.

A deputy sheriff came through the door announcing, "We've found a woman. They're bringing her up to the house now."

He dashed through the door before anyone else could react. Patrick and the Steeles followed closely. The senator caught up to him, and the two of them pushed through the front doors together. Straining to see in the dark, they tried to identify the small figure huddled between two burly policemen.

Margaret recognized her first. "Gemma," she

cried, her voice a mixture of relief and regret.

"Is this one of your guests, ma'am?" a cop asked.

Margaret nodded. "Bring her into the house," she called. As the trio reached the front porch, Margaret went to the frightened woman and put her arm around the shivering woman. "Gemma, are you all right, dear? What happened?"

Gemma had to pass in front of Duncan to reach the front door. She looked at her feet, unwilling to meet his piercing glare. "I was out walking. I heard gunshots and hid in the stable," she mumbled.

"Come inside, dear," Margaret coaxed the young woman. "You must be terrified."

A bright flash and a loud, growling rumble caused everyone to flinch. "Storm's finally here," someone commented.

Duncan stared at the wide expanse of dark forest. Moira was out there somewhere. He could feel her.

DUNCAN!

Moira's voice exploded in his head at the same moment he caught the bright flash low in the tree line beyond the drive. His reflexes took over. Spinning to the right, he pushed Patrick to the ground and stood protectively over him. Searing pain slashed across his rib cage and he was vaguely aware of shouting men as guns fired recklessly.

Pulling himself to his full six feet four inches, he challenged the darkness with his fury. His right hand reached up as if to grab the very fabric of the night and rip it to shreds. "MOIRA!" he roared, but his voice was swallowed up by rolling thunder. "I will find you," he promised the dark night. "I will not lose you again. Not now. Not ever."

Lightning split the sky. Patrick stared up in wonder. Duncan appeared to be bathed in ghostly blue light. The man's face mirrored the anguished fury churning in his soul.

The dark warrior, Patrick's mind whispered, awed by the specter standing beside him.

Four men suddenly swarmed over Duncan. Like a great bear, he tried to shake them off. Two more jumped in and they wrestled him to the ground. After a major struggle, they managed to get handcuffs on him.

"Here, what are you men doing?" Patrick barked, finally finding his voice.

"This man may be trying to kill you, Senator," someone responded.

"Nonsense. Mr. Ross just saved my life. That was a rifle shot, and it came from down in the trees. I saw the flash. Turn him loose and go search down there," he instructed.

"Can't, sir. Orders," another voice countered.

It took all six of the men to drag Duncan back into the house. Under the bright lights of the entry hall, Patrick noticed a slash of red staining Duncan's shirt. "Take it easy," the senator implored. "This man is hurt."

"You can't prove that by me," one of the deputies panted, trying to retain his hold on Duncan's massive arm.

Patrick lost all patience. "Enough," he shouted. "Release this man at once."

"Sorry, Senator. No can do," a cold voice countered from the front door.

He spun around. Two men, wearing black fatigue-style uniforms, Kevlar vests, and armed for war, stood shoulder-to-shoulder in the doorway. He had their flavor immediately.

"Yazkowski, FBI," one introduced himself.

"Curtis, Secret Service," the other added.

"What the hell is going on here?" In no mood for any rhetoric, Patrick stared them down.

The two feds exchanged glances, Secret Service deferring to FBI. "Ross is wanted for questioning in four murders and one disappearance," Ski replied tersely.

"What are you babbling about?"

Yazkowski pulled a notebook out of a pocket. "Let's see." He stared at the unfamiliar name printed there. "Sera? Sha-ee-ra?" He attempted the unfamiliar pronunciation.

"Ciará," Duncan murmured, pronouncing it kehrah.

"If you say so," the FBI agent said looking up. "This Ciará Rafferty person disappeared nine months ago in Montreal."

Patrick watched Duncan closely. "Do you know this woman?"

"I knew of her," Duncan replied. One shoulder lifted in a negligent shrug. "She ran a cell of the IRA in Belfast."

He continued staring at the big Scotsman. "What about the four murders?"

Duncan shrugged again. "They all had ties to the IRA." His voice remained clipped and cold. "Terrorists often reap what they sow." The arch of one brow made the sentence sound cryptic.

After what he'd just witnessed outside, Patrick could believe this man capable of almost anything— even cold-blooded murder.

Curtis looked at the officers surrounding Duncan. "Get him on board the chopper," he ordered. "We're flying him back to Washington tonight."

Before anyone could move, the full fury of the storm erupted. Thunder reverberated through the house as lightning carved the sky with skeletal fingers of jagged fire. Drenched men surged through the front door. Curtis looked out past them. He couldn't see beyond the thick sheets of water pouring off the roof.

"Doesn't look like you'll be flying me anywhere," Duncan commented dryly.

"Put him in one of the squad cars." Ski snapped. "We'll drive to Washington."

Simpson stepped up to the group. "That won't be possible, sir," he interjected, his voice unerringly polite. "The lane between here and the main road washes out whenever we receive a hard rain. Not even a four-wheel drive vehicle will be able to get through."

The agent looked at Allen, who shrugged, and nodded in agreement. "I've had engineers working on the problem all winter," he hastily confirmed at the Fed's skeptical look. "The drive runs through a natural drainage trough. The area ends up collecting runoff from much of the farm, and turns into a small lake."

The two feds exchanged looks again. Curtis turned to Allen. "Is there a secure place somewhere in the house where we can lock him up?"

Allen and Simpson now exchanged looks. "His assigned guest room is as suitable as any," Simpson replied.

"Lead the way, Jeeves," Ski ordered.

"The name is Simpson, sir," the butler informed him curtly as he looked down his nose at the fed.

"Yeah, whatever," Ski muttered.

Gemma and Margaret were coming down from the upper hall, and had just turned onto the landing as Duncan and his guards reached it. His glare pinned Gemma to the spot.

"Where is she?"

Gemma gulped, one hand fluttering to her throat as if she could almost feel his hands on her neck. "I don't know," she managed to choke out.

"Not good enough, Gemma." His mouth curled into a snarl.

She panicked. "O'Rourke," she sputtered. "Ask O'Rourke."

"What do you know about O'Rourke?" Duncan

pressed for answers.

"We did some business together," she admitted. "I accepted some shipments for him when his shop was full."

"What else, Gemma?"

"I...sent some loads to Ireland for him under my name." Her eyes filled with tears as she stammered out the admission.

"Money and guns," he muttered darkly. "I knew he was dirty. Does he have Moira?"

"I don't know," she sobbed. "I don't, Duncan. He wanted me to keep you two separated tonight. That's all I know. Honest." Tears streamed down her cheeks. "Oh, God, Duncan. I swear that's all I know."

Patrick, who'd been following everyone up the stairs, turned his fury on the federal agents. "Did you hear what she said?" he demanded. "Seamus O'Rourke has my daughter."

"They won't get far," Ski guaranteed, his whole attitude arrogant and brash. "We have the entire place surrounded."

Duncan snorted. "It's bloody well flooding out there. Your men will tuck away in their cars snug, dry, and blind."

Ski glared at the big man. "The storm will slow them up, too. As soon as the rain slacks off, we'll make a sweep of the area."

"He'll kill her." Duncan sounded positive. Patrick turned worried eyes to him. "If a large force closes in on him, he'll kill her to escape."

"How do you know?" The federal agent glared at him.

"Because this man cares nothing for any life save his own," he spat back. After studying the other man's face, he realized the feds didn't have a clue. "You don't even know who you're after," he murmured. Louder, he added, "He doesn't care how many innocent people he sacrifices just so long as he is safe." He changed tack. "How many terrorists did you find tonight?"

"Fourteen." Curtis, the Secret Service agent, spat the word out, and then clamped his jaw shut. He hadn't meant to admit the number out loud.

Duncan cocked a knowing eyebrow. "How many were alive?"

Ski and Curtis looked startled. "Just one. A girl at the back of the house."

"She belonged to Simpson," he replied. "I can account for two. One at the foot of the garden."

"Crushed windpipe." One of the officers at the foot of the stairs acknowledged his assertion.

"I found the other at the edge of the terrace, took him out with a knife to the skull." A deputy's nod confirmed his statement. "And the rest?" He stared at the deputy.

"They were all shot."

His face betrayed a momentary sadness before his eyes turned ice cold again. "I'm betting they were all shot at close range." The fed's eyes narrowed in consternation. Duncan smiled, the hard line of his mouth devoid of emotion. "You have a real problem, Agent Yazkowski."

Ski looked at the deputy who only shrugged. "Well? Go check." The deputy trotted down the stairs.

"Go with him, Simpson," Duncan requested softly. "Check to see if one of them is O'Rourke."

"Yes, sir." Simpson stepped out smartly.

"And check for Michael Shanahan," Duncan called after him, his voice terse. "It seems our little professor is missing in action as well."

Patrick and Allen stared at each other. In all the confusion, they hadn't stopped to count noses.

Ski grabbed one of the troopers. "The house has been checked thoroughly?"

"Yes, sir," the man affirmed. "All we found was

the unconscious girl by the back door and the kitchen staff hiding in the wine cellar."

Patrick noticed Duncan's side was bleeding again. "Agent Yazkowski," he snapped. "This man has been injured. I demand that he be given medical treatment."

"'Tis just a scratch, senator." Something in his tone made Patrick back off. "'Twill keep." Duncan's expression warned him off again.

Simpson and the deputy returned. "All shot in the back or head," the officer reported breathlessly. "And at close range."

"Mr. O'Rourke and the professor are still unaccounted for," Simpson added.

Ski glowered at Duncan. "How'd you take 'em all out, Ross?"

Duncan stared at the FBI agent, bitter amusement etched on his face. "I didn't," He paused a beat. "'Twas Brian Boru."

Ski gulped. He didn't like the implication. "What makes you think it was Boru?"

"We both know he's in the U.S., Agent Yazkowski. I've tracked him long enough to know his stench. 'Twas him. And, since both Shanahan and O'Rourke are missing, I'd wager Boru 'tis one or the other."

"No!" The agonized denial came from the entry hall. Ellie stood at the foot of the stairs, dismayed. "Not Seamus," she declared. "Aye, he's a big brute and a bully to boot. And he's full of himself up to here, but he couldn't hurt anybody. Not like that."

"How do you know, Ellie?" Duncan barked the question.

"He's me brother, Mister Duncan," she admitted with a sniffle. Everyone stared at her and she had no choice but to explain. "He changed his name, and then dyed his hair black, and wore them blue contacts so he could pretend to be black Irish. He said it drove the ladies wild. Mister Duncan, please," she pleaded. "I know m' brother. Everything he's done in his life may not have been all legal and such, but he couldn't kill anyone. Especially not Miss Moira. He promised me."

Ski groaned. Things grew more confusing by the minute and he wondered if he needed a program to tell all the players. His main concern continued to be Ross. The man was dangerous—hell, he'd even admitted to killing two people tonight. With two possible terrorists still on the loose and Moira O'Connor in jeopardy, he couldn't spare the six or more men it would take to guard Ross. He jerked his thumb at the big Scot. "Lock him up," he ordered. "I don't care where as long as there's only one door in or out and no windows." He was positive Duncan could escape even from the second or third floor. "You," he stabbed his finger at Gemma, "and you," he pointed to Ellie, "come with me." He sounded like a drill sergeant.

The men holding Duncan looked at Simpson. "Follow me," the butler ordered brusquely. Allen and Patrick started to follow.

"Oh, no you don't," a deputy challenged.

Simpson led them up the left staircase into the family wing. At the end of the hall, he unlocked a door.

One of the guards peered inside. "It looks secure," he said. "No windows and this is the only door."

The two guards holding his arms shoved him inside the storage closet. He stumbled and came up sharply against the corner of a large chest, bruising his shoulder. Before he could regain his balance, the door slammed shut and the lock clicked—an ominous sound.

"I'll take that," one of the cops ordered, taking the key out of Simpson's hand.

"As you wish, sir," the butler acquiesced. He executed a smart about-face and marched down the long hall. All but one officer followed in his wake. The one left behind nervously caressed the butt of his pistol. The guy in the closet was too big and too tough for comfort.

Chapter 22

Abhean sat on his rock staring at the misty, blue mountains on the horizon. 'Twas no natural storm raging in An Domhain. The Harper knew immediately when Manannan Mac Lir appeared behind him.

"You were told not to interfere." Manannan's voice rumbled like the thunder in the world of the living.

The Harper shrugged nonchalantly. "I just nudged a bit here and there."

"Fool," Manannan spat. "You have no idea of the fates you have set in motion."

Abhean wisely remained silent.

"We can only hope they will overcome what you have wrought with your meddling. If not, history is doomed to repeat itself, Abhean."

The Harper was astonished to hear a catch in Manannan's voice.

"I would have spared them this life," he murmured. "But for your interference," he snarled.

Abhean gulped, wondering if he really had mucked up things.

****

Moira's heart had never hurt so bad in all her life. Even the day her own grandmother wished her dead had not pierced her heart like this. The image of Gemma naked in Duncan's arms twisted like a knife in her gut. Blinded by tears, she turned on her heel and ran, wanting only to find a place to hide. She heard Duncan call her name, but his voice just made her put down her head and run harder. Moira would listen to no more lies from him, nor would she ever let him see how badly he had hurt her. Not now. Not ever.

She crashed into something hard and unyielding. Rough hands grabbed her. Thinking it was Duncan, she fought to free herself, flailing clenched fists at the man in front of her. Something cold and leathery caught her by the throat. She blinked her tears away. She wasn't fighting Duncan. The eyes staring into hers were yellowish green— cold and glittering like a reptile's.

She tried to scream but the gloved fingers on her throat choked off all sound. She heard the first explosion, and then gunfire. She had to get away, but she couldn't breathe. Her struggles grew feeble. A thousand stars burst through the clouds over her head and shattered into a million sparks just before she sank into a deep, black pit. Her last thought was of the scent of dying roses permeating the air around her.

****

Oh, this is too good to be true! He chortled out loud. When the first woman had appeared at the stable, he'd watched. Then Ross arrived and went in. He couldn't believe his good fortune. About to make his move, all the lights suddenly blazed on and he slunk back into the shadows, waiting to see what developed. Then the senator's daughter appeared. When she'd come running out a few moments later, he knew the time had come. Indeed, fortune smiled upon him.

Hefting the unconscious girl across his shoulder, he circled around the stable. He was a small man, but fit. He carried her easily. Keeping to the edge of the tree line, he crabbed toward the front of the house. None too gently, he dropped his burden to the ground, and watched the assault with pleasure. His team met with little resistance, and like the well-trained attack group they were, it would be only moments before everyone in the big house became his as well. This was almost too easy, but no more than he'd expected. So much for the bloody rich with their soft hands and softer bodies. They were no match for his team.

He sensed the helicopter before he heard its throaty roar. Far off, he heard the first faint wail of sirens. He'd planned for that expedient as well. He'd captured one prize tonight. Time to move on. He smiled at the unconscious girl, no warmth in his expression. Unless the local authorities took care of his other prize, he'd have that one before too long as well. A huge shadow loomed up beside him. "Watch her," he told the shadow tersely. A moment later, he'd melted into the darkness.

****

Moira was only semi-conscious, but bright lights and a booming voice made her head throb. She longed for the darkness, and slipped back into it, the sickly odor of dead roses still cloying in her nostrils. A soft golden light teased her, badgering her to open her eyes. She swatted at the glowing light, the gesture feeble at best. The glow danced out of her reach, laughing at her. She took a deep breath, filling her lungs with the fresh, clean scent of a spring meadow and green, growing things which exorcised the dead roses. The sound of laughter seemed familiar. She focused on the glow, recognizing the eyes peering from the golden beam.

"Duncan," she murmured. His eyes weren't laughing now. They challenged her, demanding she climb out of the dark pit. "I can't," she cried. *Yes, you can,* the eyes railed at her. In the end, she found it

easier to swim up out of the darkness than to fight
the light that was Duncan.

She opened her eyes. She lay on the ground, but
it spun horribly beneath her. She closed her eyes,
and the ground stilled. Cautious and still nauseous,
she opened her eyes again, willing them to stay in
focus.

A hulking form knelt beside her, holding
something. He raised the thing to his shoulder and
sighted down its long barrel. A rifle. Her fuzzy mind
finally identified the object. He had a rifle. She
raised her head, trying to see where he aimed.

She instantly recognized the tall figure standing
on the front steps of the Steeles' house. *Duncan,* her
heart sang. He was safe. He was alive. Then she
realized the man beside her was aiming at him. She
had to warn him. She opened her mouth. No sound
came out. She tried to swallow, but her throat was
too raw and sore. She watched the man's finger
tighten on the trigger.

"DUNCAN!" She screamed. Did that desperate
shriek came from her mouth or her heart? She saw
him spin, and start to fall. "No!" This time she knew
the sound came from her mouth but it was little
more than a scratchy croak. Horrified by the scene,
she glanced at the monster beside her. "You," she
spat just as his fist slammed into the side of her
head.

Darkness cradled her in its arms again.
Someone sang a lullaby, soft and lilting in a
language she didn't understand. "Nanny?" Moira
asked. "Hush, child of mine, hush," the soft voice
soothed. "Sleep now. Sleep and dream of your faerie
prince."

She looked up into gentle lilac eyes. "Momma?"
"Sshh," the eyes whispered to her. "Sshh, child of
mine." She let the melody waft her along in the dark.
Everything was all right now. She was safe. Just as

she'd wished for as a small child, her mother had finally come for her. 'Twas the sweet scent of the first lilacs in spring filling her nostrils now.

****

Looking more like a dim shadow, he materialized next to the unconscious girl and the big man squatting next to her. "Everything all right?" He kept his voice neutral even though anger surged through him. He would deal with O'Rourke's rash actions later. The people at the house scurried around like ants whose hill had been destroyed. The diversion worked for the moment, though it wasn't an action he would have taken.

The hulk beside Moira shrugged. "She started coming around. I took care of it."

He refrained from comment as he felt for the girl's pulse. He didn't want her to die—at least not yet. "Bring her, Seamus," he ordered.

"What about Ross?" O'Rourke asked.

"Forget about him." He looked down at Moira's inert form, his brow furrowed in speculation. "His time will come soon enough." With any luck at all, that time would come much sooner than later. Once he realized the girl was missing, Ross would come looking, and that would be the end of it. He was tired of the man's interference.

The hulk hoisted Moira over his shoulder, grunting from the exertion. He glared at the noise.

"She's a big girl, Brian," the man lamely complained.

"Yee've been livin' the good life too long," Brian Boru replied sharply. He turned on his heel and melted into the darkness.

Seamus O'Rourke jogged after him, trying vainly not to pant. With every step, he became more aware of the feminine nature of his burden. He still had a personal score to settle with this one and with any luck, he'd have the time soon to do just that.

****

Duncan paced the confines of the linen closet like a caged panther. When Simpson had first mentioned confining him in his bedroom, he'd held some hope of escaping and finding Moira. Now, the only way out of this prison would be through the locked door to the hallway. He could have picked the lock if he hadn't been handcuffed. He smiled wryly. His reputation must have preceded him since the feds weren't taking any chances.

He eyed the door again, gauging its thickness and the strength of its hinges. He'd kick the damn thing down if he had to, even though armed police would be waiting for him. He went back to pacing. The storm sounded less fierce, and he knew they'd move him as soon as the storm abated. He had to get out of this room before it was too late.

****

Simpson stared at the rain from the window in the kitchen. The torrent had slackened, replaced now by intermittent downpours. He needed to act fast before the rain stopped altogether. He crossed the room and descended into murky gloom. Confident of the way, he didn't bother with lights. After gathering a few items and placing them strategically about his person, he returned to the kitchen. He filled several coffee decanters and put them on a tray. Double-checking his appearance, he tugged one corner of his coat back into place. Returning to the great hall, he served coffee. He filled Allen's cup last, whispering, "Thirty minutes."

Allen took a sip of coffee. "Excellent, Simpson," he announced.

He returned the tray to the kitchen. Pausing only long enough to grab a black slicker, he slipped out the back door.

****

Fascinated, Duncan watched a section of the

wall swing away. Tense, he was ready to spring as this might be his only chance to escape.

"'Tis just me, Captain Ross," Simpson whispered. "Please turn around, sir." Duncan watched over his shoulder as the butler fished a small tool out of his vest pocket and picked the locks on the handcuffs. "I'm out of practice," he explained, glancing at his pocket watch. "We need to hurry." He pulled Duncan through the crack in the wall and shut it behind them.

Looking around, Duncan discovered they were in Margaret Steele's dressing room and the door they'd just come through doubled as a large mirror. "Don't tell me you're the White Rabbit," he muttered.

"Not quite, sir." Simpson appeared all business as he shed his coat and quickly unwound the length of climbing rope wrapped around his waist.

Duncan pulled the purloined combat knife from under his shirt. He still couldn't believe he hadn't been searched. A Gerber Mark II was an excellent weapon, though he hoped Simpson had more surprises hidden about his body.

He curled his lips at the corners as Simpson pulled a shoulder holster from the back of his waistband. A very businesslike Beretta 9mm nestled in the nylon webbing. The butler handed the pistol to him, then pulled up his left trouser leg. Two extra clips for the Beretta were tucked into his sock garter. Duncan smiled to show his gratitude as he strapped on the Beretta. "Since you've brought all this, you must have a plan?"

"Of course, sir," Simpson acknowledged. He checked his watch again. "In seven minutes and thirty seconds, there will be a diversion at the front of the house. Go out this window and across the portico to the garage. When you hear the commotion, go down the wall just there and into the woods. After that, Captain Ross, I'm afraid you will be on your own."

"Any idea where they might have taken Moira?" He fought to keep his voice level, to hide the fear constricting his throat.

Simpson nodded. "There are two possibilities if they have reconnoitered the area." He pulled a hand-drawn map from the inside breast pocket of his coat and smoothed it out on the top of Margaret's dressing table. "There are caves here," he said, pointing on the map. "They may have found them in their scouting." He tapped the map again. "Then there is the lodge. Until this house was built, the Steeles stayed there. There is a cabin and several outbuildings."

Duncan stared at the map, memorizing its surprisingly accurate details. "I don't know how to thank you, Simpson." He extended his hand.

To his surprise, Simpson snapped to attention and saluted. "No need, sir. Sergeant Alfred Simpson, Second Royal Scots Fusiliers, Retired, at your service, Captain."

He smiled at the older man and hoped his gratitude showed. "Thank you, Sergeant."

"My pleasure, Captain Ross." Simpson unfastened the window. "Good hunting, sir, and God speed." The butler handed him a black slicker. He shrugged into it, wincing slightly. "Out you go, sir. 'Tis time."

Once Duncan perched on the narrow ledge outside, Simpson refastened the window. He quickly stepped into the bedroom next door and pushed a button on the wall. The silk panels in the wall separated and Simpson stepped into the cleverly concealed elevator. "Bloody Feds don't know everything," he gloated moments later as he stepped out of the doors on the first floor in the room under the stairs.

****

Patrick stared at Deirdre from across the room. She looked to be on the ragged edge, as if she could lose control at any moment. The blusher on her cheeks stood out in stark contrast to her pale face. He cursed this misbegotten plan, and not for the first time. There'd never been any love lost between his daughters. He worried that even with Moira's life at stake, Deirdre might fail to perform her part. His gut clenched. Duncan was Moira's only hope. He hadn't been the only witness as Duncan spit his vow into the very teeth of the storm. For whatever lay between them, the big Scot would find her and bring her home.

****

Duncan flattened against the roof of the portico, holding his breath until the sentry passed below him and turned the corner of the house. Once the guard was out of sight, Duncan continued his sure-footed trek across the mansard roof. In a matter of seconds, he climbed up and over the ridge of the garage roof and stopped, concealed in the shadow cast by a gabled window.

He glanced at his watch. One minute to go. Pulling the rope over his head, he secured one end to an iron ring bolted to the roof. The knot tied to his satisfaction, he scanned the tree line. He gauged the spot where he'd seen the flash from the rifle. That would be his starting point. With any luck and despite the rain, he'd pick up Boru's trail.

****

Deirdre glanced at her father, and he caught the flash of her old spirit in her eyes. As he watched, she patted John's hand. Jerking away from the attorney, she jumped to her feet, and ran from the great hall shrieking like a banshee. Cops appeared from everywhere as her screams echoed throughout the big house. She dashed across the entry hall and jerked open the front doors. Everyone from the great hall spilled into the entry.

Mass confusion ensued. The police on the outside tried to push their way in while the people inside attempted to force their way out. Deirdre managed to squirm through the pack and out onto the front steps. Her shrieks reached a hysterical pitch as she pulled at her clothes and hair. "Blood" was the only word anyone could make out. She ripped the shoulder of her scarlet body suit, exposing one well-shaped breast barely encased in a scrap of lace. She had everyone's attention now.

****

Without hesitation, Duncan dropped the rope and rappelled to the ground. Staying low, he sprinted across the open lawn and dove into the cover of the tree line. Lying still for a moment to catch his breath, he waited for sounds of discovery. After a few deep breaths, he realized he'd escaped.

Staying low, he scrambled to the sniper's position. A flash of lightning revealed a golden glint almost at his feet. He knelt to retrieve the shiny metal—Moira's necklace. "Faerie tear," he murmured, brushing the pad of his thumb over the stone. His sharp eyes scanned the ground for more clues. A scuffed trail led through the thick mulch. Eyes to the ground, he followed it as sure and true as if he'd been a bloodhound. Further into the woods, he tensed when a twig snapped nearby. He dropped to the ground, held his breath, and listened. A soft whinny greeted him.

"Hello, old son," he greeted the big sorrel tied nearby. Simpson had indeed thought of everything. After the heavy rain, wheeled vehicles would have a tough go but four-legged transportation could travel easily. He chased at least two people and they were on foot. Even in the woods, the horse could cover the distance quicker and he would be in better condition for having ridden. He tightened the saddle's girth and untied the reins. Mounted, he could still see the trail and urged the horse to follow the track.

****

John and Patrick finally shoved their way through the throng of cops surrounding Deirdre. Kevin and the other college boys managed to circle around behind the crowd to screen the wide expanse of lawn while everyone's attention focused on Deirdre's show. And what a show it was! She'd snatched off her skirt and the cops didn't know where to look first—at her long, slim legs or that scrap of black lace peeking through the blood-red body suit. Despite their profession, they were no more immune to her ample charms than any other man.

Kevin was the only one who caught a glimpse of the shadow fading into the trees, and only because he'd been watching for it. Still, he wondered if he'd actually seen the dark blotch flitting across the lawn. Waiting a long moment, he nodded to John, who immediately stripped out of his jacket, and tried to wrap it around Deirdre.

John had to stifle his laugher. The madwoman who ranted at him as she struggled to throw off his jacket presented quite a sight. With his best courtroom face, he settled the jacket about her shoulders, pulled her to his chest, and wrapped his arms around her. He almost lost the last shred of his composure when he realized the hysterical sobs she spit against his chest were actually uncontrollable giggles.

Patrick quickly moved beside them and with Deirdre obscured between them, the two men moved her inside, their every movement solicitous to the extreme. The cops quickly rounded up everyone, and herded them back inside. Just to be sure, the FBI agent counted noses. In the great hall, John and Patrick made a big show of getting Deirdre settled

244

on a couch while Margaret fussed over her. When all the officers moved back into the entry hall, Kevin shut the door.

Wiping crocodile tears from her eyes, Deirdre looked up at John. "I need a drink," she calmly announced.

"You deserve an Oscar." His compliment was as heartfelt as her acting was magnificent.

Simpson appeared almost immediately bearing a snifter of brandy. "To settle the nerves, Miss Deirdre," he announced with a wink.

Ski and Curtis entered, and Margaret sailed up to them, a sleek little cruiser intent on a search and destroy mission. Allen and Patrick exchanged a knowing look. The two feds were in for it now.

Pulling herself up to her full height of five feet, three inches in heels, Margaret glowered at the two agents. "Enough of this," she declared, her voice frigid and filled with righteous indignation. "My guests are exhausted. We are not criminals, and you have no right to keep us cooped up here. This is my house. I will not tolerate this abominable treatment any longer." She spun around, pointedly ignoring the two feds. "Deirdre, finish your drink, dear. We're all going up to bed."

"I'm afraid that's not possible," Ski began, sounding reasonable but firm.

Margaret whirled around, her eyes glittering like emeralds. She looked like she might slug the big fed with her petite fist. "I have had it up to here," she pronounced, holding her hand at eye-level, "with you and your heavy-handed tactics. This is the United States of America, Mister Yazkowski, not some fascist dictatorship. Either you let us out of here right now, or I guarantee this fiasco will be the headline of every major newspaper and television station in the free world by tomorrow night."

Ski fixed his most charming smile on his face,

but the petite woman only scowled at him. "You can't do that, Mrs. Steele," he replied, his voice a study in schooled politeness.

Allen came to stand beside his wife. "Oh, but she can." His voice sounded reasonable despite the implied rebuke. "My wife is the CEO of Royce Communications, gentlemen."

The feds gulped. He leaned down and kissed her on the cheek. "And everyone thinks I married you for your looks," he teased the petite spitfire.

Curtis pulled Ski aside. "We don't need this, Ski. Another hysterical scene like we just had, and all the women may lose it."

"So what do you suggest?" Ski countered, keeping his voice low.

"Put everyone in the west wing. The guests can go on the second floor, the kitchen staff up on the third. A man at each end of the hallway, and no one can go anywhere. Besides, we have Ross. That's the important thing." Ski reluctantly agreed.

He turned around and made the announcement. He could tell by the look on Margaret's face she wasn't pleased with the arrangements, but she didn't push for more.

Marshalling everyone, Margaret made room assignments. As they were escorted up the stairs, she confronted the FBI agent one more time. "What about Miss Todd and Ellie, my maid," she admonished.

"They are still being questioned, Mrs. Steele," Ski retorted. He refused to back down on the issue.

John Murray whipped his head around to stare at him. "Are you protecting their constitutional rights?"

"What's it to you?" Ski taunted. He really was fed up with these rich people and their demands. This was a crime scene. Didn't they realize there was an international criminal locked upstairs?

"I'm an attorney, Agent Yazkowski," John replied pleasantly. "If they haven't been Mirandized, I suggest you stop your interrogation immediately until they've had the opportunity to confer with counsel."

Margaret smiled cheekily. "Sic 'em, John."

The attorney rewarded her impudence with a cocky grin. "And, Mr. Yazkowski, I hereby give notice that I represent Duncan Ross. Should you decide to question him, or remove him from the premises, I demand the right to speak with my client beforehand, and to be present during any questioning." Ski muttered darkly under his breath. "Excuse me, Agent Yazkowski?" the attorney prodded. "I didn't quite catch what you said."

Ski glanced up at the man. "You'll be notified." His resigned sigh huffed out before he could stop it.

"If I'm not..." John let his voice deliberately trail off, the threat of legal action ominously implied.

Chapter 23

Moira felt bruised from head to foot, and her head throbbed. Her throat was raw and swollen, but she forced herself to swallow anyway. The searing pain that followed made her teeth hurt. She struggled to sit up, but had to close her eyes to stop the dark room from spinning. When she opened them again, the room tilted a little, but didn't make her dizzy. Her clothes felt wet and clammy, and she shivered.

Details of her surroundings eventually took shape. The dusky gloom didn't reveal much, but the place seemed vaguely familiar. She discovered she sat in the middle of a large bed with four posts resembling small tree trunks. An intricately woven blanket hung on one wall. She focused on the jagged stripes and fantastic animals depicted in the weave even though her throbbing head made it hard to keep her eyes focused. She canted her head gently to shift her point of view. The mouth of a huge stone fireplace yawned at her from the opposite wall.

"The lodge," she whispered with a stab of hope. She was only five, maybe six miles from the main house, even less if one came across country. Duncan would find her. At the thought of him, her gut twisted and she almost cried out from the pain.

Memories flooded her. The stable. Gemma. The man with the rifle. The gunshot. Duncan spinning around and falling. *No!* her mind screamed. He wasn't dead. He couldn't be. It didn't matter what she had seen in the stable. It didn't matter what she had seen from the woods. She loved him, and he loved her. Duncan would come. Like a noisome gnat, a tiny voice tormented her. *If he's alive,* it droned in her head.

Moira angrily brushed at the tears stinging her eyes. She had to keep faith. Duncan would come. He had promised. The image of flames leaped before her eyes, and fear twisted in her gut, its icy fingers freezing her hope. She shook the vision out of her head. *No,* she argued with her doubts. *That was then. Duncan will come.*

She heard the door handle click. Before she could move, a flashlight blinded her. Shielding her eyes with one hand, she squinted to see the person behind the bright beam.

"So, you're finally awake," her captor growled.

He came into the room, shutting the door behind him. Crossing to the bed, he still held her pinned motionless in the flashlight's beam. He switched off the light so she squinted her eyes more, forcing them to quickly adjust to the sudden darkness. She could barely make out the hulk standing over her. She felt the mattress depress as he climbed onto the bed. *Why?* she wondered. Then she knew.

"No," she pleaded.

He barked a guttural laugh. "I owe yee one for Saint Paddy's Day, missy." O'Rourke grabbed her wrists and forced her to lie back on the bed. She twisted and squirmed, fighting to bring her legs up between them. Her struggles only made him laugh again. She jerked one hand free and raked his cheek with her nails. His grunt of pain was immensely satisfying.

"So yee like it rough, do yee?" he snarled, backhanding her across the mouth.

She gasped in pain, but the sting only made her fight harder. He had her arms spread-eagled out to her sides, and his legs forced their way between hers. He kissed her roughly, the whiskey smell on his breath nauseated her as his shadow beard abraded her chin. Without warning, his weight disappeared. She heard a thud followed by O'Rourke's grunting curse.

"Leave off," a cold voice commanded.

"I owe her."

"I said leave off," the voice barked. "'Tis almost daylight and we have work to do."

Still grumbling, the man heaved himself off the floor and left the room. She tried to get a good look at the man who'd interrupted O'Rourke's revenge, but he stayed in the shadows. He appeared much smaller than O'Rourke, but by the way he'd manhandled the brute, he had to be extremely strong.

Before she could say a word, he spoke, his voice cold and emotionless. "Don't be thanking me, Miss O'Connor. If I didn't need his services right now, I would have let Seamus continue. Nothing personal, of course. I have to admit, though, I would have found it rather amusing to inform Mr. Ross he'd been denied that particular pleasure of your company. Virgins are such a rare and refined treat these days." As he talked, he looped a rope around her wrists, and secured her hands to one of the bedposts.

She stayed very still, hoping he wouldn't tighten the ropes if she didn't resist. Then his black-gloved hand stroked her hair. She couldn't suppress the shudder as his hand traveled the length of her body.

"You are a prize, Miss O'Connor," he hissed. "I may decide to have you myself before Seamus has a go at you."

Moira shivered uncontrollably, and even in the

dark, she could see the man's frigid smile. His hand slid into her blouse and he tweaked her nipple between his thumb and forefinger. Bending down, he whispered in her ear, "Just so you don't forget me." He squeezed her breast so hard, tears sprang into her eyes, and she had to bite her lip to keep from crying out in pain. "Let me introduce myself," he whispered seductively in her ear. "The name's Boru. Brian Boru." He leaned back, waiting for her reaction to that bit of news.

Revulsion welled up in her throat, threatening to gag her. The fetid odor reminding her of dead roses washed over her. She fought down the bile in her throat. Staring him straight in the eye, she spit in his face. "I'll see you in hell," she vowed.

Boru wiped her spit off his cheek. "So you shall," he promised. Then he was gone.

She stared at the ceiling. "Oh, God," she prayed, "let him come soon." As the whitewashed ceiling faded into the dark, Duncan's eyes peered back at her and his voice whispered, *I'm coming, bonnie girl. Soon.*

****

He knelt to study the forest floor. The sorrel chewed his bit, setting it to jingling. The trail they'd followed led due northeast almost on a dead line toward the caves. Now the tracks had been completely obliterated, almost as if they knew he followed. Duncan stood up, his posture a study of indecision. He'd been gone almost an hour and the rain had slackened to a cold drizzle. He shivered under the black slicker. If the feds hadn't discovered his escape by now, they would shortly. He was running out of time.

His head told him to go straight to the caves, but his gut pulled him due west, toward the lodge. He stared off in the direction of the caves, undecided. A faint flicker twinkled in the corner of his peripheral vision. He turned his head. A glowing ball danced in the trees, enticing him to play. The sorrel nickered and tossed his head toward the light as he stamped an impatient foot.

"Faerie fire," he murmured in wonder. His brain argued the apparition was nothing more than bog gas but he ignored the scientific explanation. He led the sorrel in the direction of the illusive will-o-the-wisp. The rough ground they traveled began to slant upward. At the top of the small rise, spun gold fluttered before Duncan's eyes. He snagged his prize—several strands of Moira's hair caught in a branch.

The flickering light danced in the hollow below him. The faint radiance of false dawn permeated the darkness, and Duncan could see a wide path leading off to the west. Duncan mounted the sorrel, and nudged the horse onto the path.

"My thanks to the Faerie folk," he called to the light dancing down the path ahead of him. He urged the big horse into a gallop. "I'm coming, bonnie girl. Soon," he shouted into the night.

The sorrel's feet thudded softly on the thick layer of leaves carpeting their way. His powerful legs ate up the distance. A fallen log loomed in front of them and the sorrel sailed over it without breaking stride. Their radiant guide had long since disappeared but he held the horse to a course as sure and straight as an arrow flying to its target. With hands and heels, he beseeched the horse to run even faster. The sorrel strained to do his rider's bidding, his breath coming hard and fast. Duncan's heart knew he rode straight toward his destiny. This time he would not be too late.

****

Moira chewed on her bonds until her jaw ached, but she'd gotten nowhere with them. She heard her kidnappers' voices in the hall and held her breath.

252

"How can yee be sure?" O'Rourke asked. "I saw him fall after I fired. How could it be him?"

"I'm sure," Boru answered flatly. "Just bring the girl."

Her spirits soared. They were talking about Duncan. He was coming. O'Rourke burst through the door, and she met his lascivious leer with a glare. He ogled her for a long moment before putting a noose over her head, and tightening it around her neck. He tied the rope to the bedpost before cutting her hands free. Viciously twisting her arms behind her back, he secured her wrists with another length of rope. He untied the noose at the post, and used it to jerk her off the bed. She landed on her knees— hard. Sharp pain radiated up into her hips. She didn't have time to dwell on it, though as O'Rourke jerked the rope again, and hauled her to her feet. He led her, giggling like some insane child, from the room as if she were a dog on a leash.

****

The big sorrel was tiring. Duncan didn't know how much distance they'd covered, but from the mental map in his head, they must be close. He slowed the fading animal to a walk. As much as he wanted to charge into the middle of things, all his training dictated he remain cautious. He had to scout the enemy before he could act.

****

Boru finished pouring the last can of gasoline as O'Rourke and the girl appeared in the yard. "In there," Boru directed, pointing through the doors of the old wooden barn. O'Rourke dragged her inside and Boru followed. He took the rope from Seamus. "Make sure all the weapons are fully loaded." Boru shoved her toward a sturdy post sunk into the floor at the center of the cavernous interior. He forced her up against it, and roughly tied her, her back to the post. Loops of rope snaked around her, each coil tightening like a constrictor.

She fought down a panicked scream. "You can't do this." She wanted to shout, but the words came out as a whisper.

Boru flashed an evil grin. "But I already have, cailín."

Her eyes grew round with fear as a wicked-looking stiletto appeared in his hand. She tried not to tremble as he caressed her cheek with its sharp tip. He flicked his wrist, and a lock of her hair fell into the palm of his other hand. He pulled a silver locket from under his black turtleneck. Opening it, he coiled the ringlet inside, and snapped the locket shut. She forced herself to keep her eyes open as he leaned toward her, dangling the locket in front of her face like a hypnotist in some backwater stage show.

"Just so I won't forget you," he whispered in her ear.

Boru's face hovered inches from hers. She glowered at him, memorizing every detail of his features. If they met again, she'd recognize him no matter what his disguise.

"Good," he gloated. "I like women with spirit. It's so much more entertaining to watch them die."

She was ready to spit on him when his fist slammed into her jaw. Her head snapped back against the post with a sickening thud. Unconscious, she slumped against the ropes binding her.

"A woman only spits in my face once, witch." His mouth twisted into an ugly snarl. Stepping back to the door, he pulled a wooden match from a pocket in his black jumpsuit. Flicking the head of the match with his thumbnail, he watched as the sulfur tip flared and caught fire. Satisfied, he dropped the burning match into a pile of straw. As he watched, a lazy curl of smoke poked a smudgy finger up through the hay.

****

The sky visible out the wide kitchen window churned with mottled gray clouds. Dawn was still some time away but dark shadows out in the yard took firm shape now. The cook, with Simpson's help, had bullied her way past the guard and now brewed copious amounts of coffee while a batch of muffins baked in the oven. She recognized the deep snarl of the D9 Caterpillar's engine as it pulled around the house. When the back door opened, she presented the newcomer with a steaming mug of her brew.

"Jasper," she greeted him. "You're up early."

"Yes, ma'am." Jasper hitched up his overalls, flashing her a shy smile. He took a sip of coffee and ducked his head in thanks. "Tell Mister Simpson and Mister Steele the road's graded. It's been dry enough lately wasn't much run off. Didn't take long to make it passable." He headed back out the door. "Oh. You might also tell them there's a hint of smoke in the air," he added over his shoulder. "Wind's from the north, northwest. They might want to go over and check the old place."

****

Duncan watched the house. Since the short, stocky man had come out of the barn, there'd been no activity. The front door opened and the same man stepped out onto the porch. He couldn't see his features clearly. The man scanned the woods, his eyes stopping to probe the general area where he lay hidden.

"You're good, but you're not good enough," Duncan whispered.

Like a wisp of smoke, the morning mist swirled between the two men and Duncan shifted his position. Quietly, he moved around to the back of the house. A shotgun blast ripped the branch above his head, sending a shower of leaves and twigs raining down on him. He sighted in the Beretta and squeezed off three quick rounds. He immediately rushed the house. Making a running dive, he crashed through the window. He hit the floor, rolling on impact, and came up in a crouch, firing. His target went down with a groan.

He barely gave O'Rourke a second glance. His prey was the stocky man in black. He prowled through the house, but all the rooms were empty. He found the room where Moira probably had been held, and he winced at the sight of the rope dangling from the bedpost. He swore the bloody bastard would pay with his life for taking her.

When he returned to the first floor, the front door was still open. He sniffed the air, detecting the faint odor of smoke. Then he saw the man in black dart into the open space near the barn.

"Boru!" He shouted, sprinting through the door, firing the Beretta as he ran. Too late, he realized his mistake. Boru had booby-trapped the exit. Twisting to the left, he took the stiletto in his shoulder rather than his heart where it had been aimed. Falling to the porch, he rolled and continued firing as Boru disappeared into the woods. The Beretta clicked on empty. He pulled out the stiletto, and staggered to his feet. With one hand, he dropped the empty clip and reloaded the pistol. Determined to end it here and now, he headed toward the tree line.

"Brian, what about me?" O'Rourke whined behind him.

Spinning, he dropped to one knee. Before he could fire, O'Rourke's body jerked backward as heavy caliber slugs tore into his chest. Boru's maniacal laughter echoed from the woods. He stood up, prepared to follow. Before he could, something exploded inside the old barn, and flames shot through the open door.

"The girl," O'Rourke croaked.

Duncan looked back at him. The man lay spread-eagled in the dirt, his chest stained crimson from four large bullet holes. He gestured feebly with one bloodied hand. "The girl," he wheezed, each breath obviously painful. "Nobody should die that way," he whispered as his eyes rolled back in his head, and he died.

All the dread and agony Duncan had ever experienced welled up from his gut. Yet it was no match for what now clutched his heart, paralyzing him. He peered into the barn, straining to see beyond the flames.

"Moira?" he called, hoping against all hope.

Chapter 24

Why was it so hard to breathe? Moira coughed and raised her head. It was hot. Too hot. She opened her eyes. Her worst nightmare had come true. Flames leaped and danced around her. Sparks showered down from the hayloft above her head.

Where was Duncan? Why hadn't he come? He'd promised. She heard someone calling so she fought down her panic to listen.

"Moira!"

She heard it again. "Duncan?" Her voice rasped out, no more than a whisper. She swallowed hard. "Duncan!" This time she screamed his name.

****

Part of him died when he heard her calling to him. Moira was in there somewhere, and she still lived. But she wouldn't for long. He backed up several yards, and took a running leap at the wall of flames separating them. He was conscious of searing heat, and he thought his lungs were going to burst from lack of air. *Not yet*, his brain screamed. *You can't breathe yet.*

He burst through the flames, and sank to his knees, gulping the relatively cooler air near the floor. Raising his head, he saw Moira slumped against the ropes tying her to a post. Scrambling to his feet, he drew the Gerber and slashed at her bonds. Once free, she slumped into his arms.

He laid her down and shrugged out of the slicker. It wouldn't provide much but was the only protection he could give her. As he wrapped her in it, he thought he heard men shouting outside the barn.

Cradling her in his arms, he took deep gulps of the hot air. Moira struggled, pushing feebly against his chest. "Don't worry, bonnie girl," he whispered. "I'm here." Moira laid still, her fists wrapped in his shirt.

Taking a last gulp of air, he challenged the flames. An ominous rumble followed by a loud crash made him look back. A huge beam caved in, bringing part of the roof with it. Without slowing his stride, Duncan charged into the very heart of the fire. Tongues of flame licked at him, trying to capture him. Moira moaned, and the sound gave his legs new strength.

A great fist of fire loomed before them. He ducked under it and stumbled out into relatively clean air and dingy sunshine. He became dimly aware of flashing lights and lots of noise. Helmeted figures with no faces dashed in and out of the drifting smoke, shouting to each other. Someone tried to take Moira from his arms. He tightened his grip on her and brushed the intruder off with his shoulder.

"Here, Duncan, this way," a voice directed him.

Hands touched his back to guide him. He had trouble focusing on the scene around him. He stumbled on some uneven ground and more hands helped steady him. The air tasted cleaner now, and he filled his lungs deep with gulps of clean air to expel the soot and searing heat lodged in his chest. His vision cleared a little, though it was still fuzzy around the edges and black specks swam in front of him.

"Over here, Duncan," Patrick O'Connor said. "You can put her down here."

He sank to the grass, still cradling Moira. Again someone tried to take her, and his arms tightened instinctively. He wasn't going to lose her now, not to anyone. He felt Patrick pat his shoulder.

"It's all right, Duncan," Patrick said. "These men are paramedics."

Duncan stared up into his face and the older man recoiled. In a voice as fierce and proud as an ancient Highland warrior, he growled, "She's not going to die. I won't let her die."

"No, Duncan," Patrick murmured softly. "She's not going to die. You saved her."

Someone tried to fit an oxygen mask over his face and he realized a man did the same to Moira. "It's okay, pal," a calm voice assured him. "My partner will take care of her. Let's get that shoulder taken care of."

He allowed the men to shift Moira out of his arms. As they laid her beside him, he took her hand. He kissed her palm and her eyelids fluttered.

"Duncan," she mumbled.

"I'm here, bonnie girl," he comforted.

Yazkowski, with two agents in tow, berated Allen Steele as they marched over to the small knot of people. "Why didn't you tell me you had access to a bulldozer to grade the road?" Ski yelled.

"You didn't ask me, Agent Yazkowski, and since I was being held prisoner in my own home, I saw no reason to explain anything to you."

Ski, red-faced and angry, gestured to one of his agents, and the man moved to handcuff Duncan. "And I still want to know which of your people helped Ross escape," Ski barked.

"Whoa, back off, buddy," the paramedic growled at the man.

"This man is my prisoner," Ski snarled. He tried vainly to stare down the medic.

"This man is my patient," the medic replied, his

voice calm. He arched an amused eyebrow at the fuming FBI agent.

A burly man wearing a white helmet bustled up to the group. "Is there a problem here?" he barked hoarsely, his voice used to command and shouting orders in the midst of chaos.

"This man is a federal prisoner," Ski blustered.

"Yeah, yeah. I heard you the first time," the fire chief replied sarcastically. Turning to his paramedic, he asked, "What's his condition?"

"Bad smoke inhalation and his shoulder's bleeding like crazy—deep puncture wound that may have nicked the lung. Without a CAT scan, there's no way to tell what kind of internal damage. He has at least first and second degree burns over thirty to forty percent of his body. Some third degree over ten to fifteen percent." The paramedic looked up at his chief and shrugged. "By all accounts, Chief, this guy should be unconscious. Most people might already be dead in his condition."

"Look, I'm an FBI agent," Ski butted in.

The chief whirled to face him. "You may be a horse's ass for all I care. Let me explain this to you, mister, as simply as I can. This is a fire scene. This is a firefighter. This is the firefighter's patient. I am the fire chief. This is my scene. I am the one in charge. Not the FBI. Not the CIA. Not even the frigging IRS. Me. I'm in charge. You let my paramedics do their jobs, or I'll have you thrown out of here. Is that clear?"

Before Ski could respond, a hose crew doused him and the other two agents. The chief bit his lip to keep from laughing out loud at the astonished looks on the agents' faces. "Just one of the many hazards at a fire scene, gentleman," the chief told the drenched men, struggling to keep a straight face.

Ski motioned for the two agents to back off and the three of them went to dry off somewhere away from charged hose lines. The chief turned to the medic working on Duncan. "Get them packaged and transported ASAP," he ordered tersely. Turning to Allen, he added, "We'll stall the cops as long as possible, Mr. Steele."

"Thanks, Chief," Allen replied, thankful he'd sponsored a new engine for the volunteer fire district that protecting his farm, and also for the age-old rivalry between police and fire.

Duncan flatly refused to be packaged. He surrendered Moira's hand only long enough for the medics to start an IV in her arm, and load her onto a gurney. Still holding her hand, he climbed into the back of the ambulance. One paramedic stayed with them. The other secured the door and motioned Patrick around to the passenger side.

Several fire engines and a water tanker truck maneuvered out of the ambulance's way. As the scene slid past his view out the back window, Duncan realized the rigs had effectively blocked in all of the police cars. Moira stirred so he smoothed her hair back from her soot-scarred face. The paramedic watched him intently, though with a smile.

"She's not going anywhere until we get to University Hospital. Why don't you stretch out here?" The medic motioned to the cushioned bench where the two of them were sitting.

He shook his head. "I'm all right." His voice sounded like it had been dredged up from the very bowels of hell itself, even to his own ears. He caught a glimpse of his reflection the in window. His eyes looked hollow and his face haunted.

"The hell you are," the medic snorted. "The smoke and burns would be enough to knock out most men. Add the blood loss from the shoulder wound and the rib injury you're hiding? You shouldn't even be alive much less sitting here talking coherently to me."

Duncan shrugged. "I've had worse."

Moira mumbled something and both men looked at her. Her face was bruised and swollen and ugly welts ringed her wrists and neck.

The paramedic shook his head and swore under his breath. "Who could tie up someone like that and leave them to burn?"

"A madman," Duncan answered through clenched teeth.

The paramedic leaned over to check her pulse. "It's stronger and her respirations have returned to the normal range. Man, you are some kind of hero," the medic praised Duncan. "We wouldn't have gotten there in time."

"I almost didn't," Duncan whispered, his heart breaking just a little bit more.

The ambulance barely slowed as it encountered Sunday morning traffic in Charlottesville. With deft accuracy, the driver wove through the cars and trucks sharing the roadway. Slowing to a crawl, the vehicle turned into the emergency entrance at the University of Virginia Hospital. Orderlies and nurses appeared as the back doors opened. Duncan climbed out with the gurney, still clutching Moira's hand. People cleared out of their way as the entourage rushed inside. A nurse guided them to an examination room.

"You'll have to come with me, sir," the nurse said, tugging on his arm. He shook off her hands. She grabbed his arm again but the paramedic signaled for her to wait.

Duncan pulled the oxygen mask away from Moira's mouth. Leaning over, he kissed her bruised lips tenderly, then pressed his cheek against hers. "Through the fires of hell," he murmured in her ear. "I'll be back, bonnie girl. I promise." He kissed her again to seal his vow, and replaced the oxygen mask.

As he straightened up, the paramedic took his arm. He shook him off. Reaching into his pocket, he pulled out the fire opal he'd found in the woods and pressed it into Moira's hand. Gently, he fingered the blunt ends where a lock of Moira's hair had been cut. He knew who'd done it. "I promise," he reiterated.

The medic pulled him away again. "This way, pal," he directed. Duncan stumbled and almost went to his knees. The medic grabbed him, grunting as he took most of his weight. Slipping under his arm, he supported him until Duncan regained his balance. "You're done for, pal," the medic advised.

"Not yet I'm not," he argued.

"Yeah, right," the medic agreed jovially. "Let's get you across the hall."

The medic and a nurse got him into a room across the hall, and eased him down on the exam table. He lay back and closed his eyes, his face drawn and ashen. The nurse took his blood pressure, checked his pulse, and then examined the wounds to his shoulder and ribs before checking his burns. The paramedic watched for a moment before turning to leave. "Take good care of my friend there," he told the nurse.

The nurse looked surprised. "You know him?"

The medic shook his head. "Not personally, but I know his kind. I had officers like him in the Army. Real warriors. He's a hellava man."

"We'll do our best," she promised him with a smile as she followed him out to find a doctor.

****

Try as he might, Duncan couldn't keep his eyes open. He felt so tired his body wouldn't obey his brain's commands. A smile tugged at the corner of his mouth. Moira remained safe, but not for long. As long as Boru was still out there, neither of them would ever be safe.

Grunting with effort, he threw his legs over the

side of the exam table, and hoisted himself to a sitting position. If they were to have any chance at happiness, he had to find Boru and finish it. As his feet hit the floor, he had to grab the table to keep from falling over. Still woozy, he stumbled to the door. He had only a matter of minutes before the doctor showed up, or worse, the feds.

The sign on a door down the hall read "Doctor's Lounge." Steeling himself, he moved out into the hall. He managed to walk straight to the other door and get inside. No one stepped into the hallway. No one looked out of the exam rooms he passed. No one came in the doors at either end of the hallway. The lounge was also empty. He found an unsecured locker holding surgical scrubs that would fit, a doctor's ID badge still pinned to them, and he found a set of car keys on the top shelf of the locker. The MG symbol clearly marked an ignition key. He figured not many of the little roadsters would be parked in the parking lot.

He chanced losing some time by grabbing a shower. The fire's stench emanated from every pore, and he wouldn't get too far stinking of smoke. A nurse stuck her head in the door and yelled back to him, asking if he'd seen any strangers lurking about. He answered negatively, and the nurse left. He sighed in relief. That had been too close. He'd left the scrub shirt with the ID lying over a chair outside the shower room and the nurse obviously thought he was the doctor. He dried off and grabbed some 4x4 pads and tape stored in a cabinet. After bandaging the puncture wound in his shoulder and the worst of the burns, he put on the scrubs, grabbed his clothes, and the purloined car keys. Slipping out of the doctor's lounge, he headed for the exit sign at the end of the hall. Just as the automatic door to the parking lot glided open for him, Yaskowski and his bunch marched through the front entrance. Duncan never looked back.

****

Yazkowski breached the Emergency entrance of the hospital, issuing orders as he strode past the front desk. The intake secretary tried unsuccessfully to stop him.

"Out of my way!" Ski glowered at the matronly woman but she didn't back up or get out of his way. She thrust her ample bosom in his direction.

"You can't go back there," she insisted.

"The hell I can't," Ski retorted. "I have a prisoner back there. He waved two of his men forward. "Duncan Ross. Where is he?"

She couldn't hold all three men and check her computer so she simply stepped aside. As Ski and the contingent of agents pushed through the doors, she was on the phone alerting the staff behind those doors.

The agents were searching each ER room when the head nurse confronted them. "Here now. You can't be disturbing patients like this. Who are you looking for?"

"Duncan Ross," Ski demanded.

"Triage room three." The nurse turned on her heel and strode down the hall, her rubber-soled shoes silent on the worn linoleum. She opened a door marked with a red number three and gasped.

Ski followed her in, watching in consternation as she searched the empty room. The nurse snagged the phone receiver next to the door and started snapping out orders. He was not a happy camper.

"What the hell do you mean Ross is missing?" he growled.

"He was in this room not ten minutes ago. I've alerted security. They'll find him. As badly as he's injured, he can't go far."

Ski didn't trust hospital security. He ordered his men to search as well. He dogged the nurse's footsteps, berating her as she made her own search. As reports came in via Ski's radio and face-to-face conferences between the nurse and hospital staff, Ski only became more frustrated and angry. He finally pinned the nurse in a corner near the nurses' station.

"How in the hell do you lose a patient?" he stormed. "How incompetent are you freaking people? That man is a federal prisoner and you left him unguarded?" He was spitting mad.

Before the nurse could muster a reply, an older man in a white lab coat rushed up. "Now see here," the older man began. He all but shook his finger in Ski's face.

"No, you see." Ski cut him off. "I'm going to tear this place apart until you people deliver my prisoner on a tray with a rubber glove balloon stuck in his ass! Who the hell are you?"

The man cleared his voice. "I'm Doctor Adam Wallace, chief of staff of this hospital, and if you do not lower your voice and behave in a manner befitting your rank, I shall be forced to call your Director to apprise him of your behavior."

Ski arched a brow, ready to call the doctor's bluff until the man stared him straight in the eye, reached for his cell phone, scrolled for a moment and then turned the phone for Ski to see the name displayed. He took a deep breath but still glowered. "Why wasn't security assigned to watch him?"

The chief deferred to the head emergency room nurse. She scowled at him, not intimidated at all. "We didn't know he was a security risk. Besides, he was so far gone he shouldn't have been able to sit up without assistance, much less get up and walk out of here unnoticed." Her frigid tone could have caused frost bite but Ski ignored it. He stared unblinking until she dropped her gaze to the clipboard she held. "From the paramedic's report and the initial chart done on him, he should be up in ICU as we speak." She looked up from the chart and shrugged. Her expression indicated she couldn't comprehend how he'd escaped.

"I want to question the O'Connor girl," Ski decreed.

A younger doctor who'd just joined the group shook his head. "I'm Doctor Andrews, chief of emergency services," the man introduced himself. "This is my ER you and your men are disrupting." The doctor stared for a moment before adding, "And you would be?"

"Special Agent Yazkowski. Since you people lost my prisoner, I need to talk to the O'Connor girl." When no one moved, he added, "Now?"

"You can't," Dr. Andrews replied caustically. He started to protest but Andrews cut him short. "Miss O'Connor is in a coma, Agent Yazkowski. I can't tell you when she'll be able to speak to anyone."

He backed down. "I didn't know." His voice and expression were filled with remorse.

"No, you didn't," Andrews pointed out. "She almost died today, Agent Yazkowski. Whoever this big, bad criminal is you're chasing? He saved her life by every account I've heard. The man almost died himself, and as my staff pointed out, we were not informed of any security risk he may have posed. Now, if you will release my staff, we have an emergency room to run." Andrews spun on his heel, and marched down the hall, his rubber-soled Bruno Magli shoes making no sound.

"Will you please notify my office if she regains consciousness? She's our only witness." Ski called after the doctor's rapidly retreating back. He rounded up his men and left. They had other fish to fry. Duncan Ross could not be allowed to flee the Charlottesville area. If he did, they might never catch up to him again.

When the last federal officer cleared the ER, Dr. Wallace pulled Dr. Andrews aside. "How is the girl really?" he asked.

Andrews grinned mischievously. "All things considered, she's in pretty decent shape. Some facial contusions, a concussion. Smoke inhalation and some minor burns. She's sedated right now, but sleeping soundly. I want to monitor the concussion, and the condition of her lungs for a few days. Barring any complications, she should be out of here by the end of the week."

Wallace considered Moira's prognosis for a few moments. As soon as the staff realized she was a senator's daughter, they'd called him, and he'd rushed to the hospital. Once there, he heard all the gossip buzzing around the ER. All things considered, the girl appeared to be in remarkable shape. She would be dead if not for the dark man who'd rescued her. He stared out toward the front doors of the ER, hoping the man was far away by now. Any man who would risk his own life in a fire to save another couldn't be the criminal the feds claimed. He glanced over at his colleague. "Are you going to let the FBI know what her real condition is?"

Andrews shrugged as if to say, "Maybe. Maybe not." His grin widened into a frosty smile. "To tell you the truth, Doctor Wallace, I haven't decided yet. I hate to admit it, but ever since med school, I've developed this perverse streak. I have a hard time dealing with stupid people and jackasses, and Agent Yazkowski qualifies on both counts."

Chapter 25

As Duncan had hoped, the little MGB sportster was easy to spot in the lot. Though the day turned out warm and sunny, the car's owner had left the top up overnight. Duncan climbed in, started the car, and listened as the engine turned over. The motor coughed a few times before it settled into what could only be described as a loud purr. This little car didn't have enough horsepower for a growl. Putting the sports car in gear, he pulled through the lot, even waving jauntily at the guard waiting at the lot's entrance. The guard saluted in return as he merged into the light traffic.

His first priority was to get some real clothes, and a different mode of transportation. With the feds' arrival at the emergency room, it wouldn't be long before they discovered he'd escaped again. Additionally, it wouldn't take too long for the doctor to figure out his car had been stolen, and probably by whom.

He found a mall near the highway running south out of Charlottesville toward Lynchburg and ultimately to North Carolina. The cops would expect him to return to his base of operations in the D.C. area. Boru wasn't headed that direction, and neither was he. He had enough cash on him to buy jeans, a shirt, and a jacket. He still had his boots, along with the combat knife and his *skean dhu*. With his long hair, he could pass for one of the college crowd hanging out in the mall's food court. He overheard two coeds discussing their drive to Florida for spring break, but they needed another passenger to afford the trip. He struck a bargain with them. With a ride out of town, he had one last stop to make, asking the girls to stop at the drugstore perched on the outskirts of the mall's parking lot.

Inside, he stocked up on bandages and antibiotic ointment. He was too familiar with festering wounds, and it wouldn't do to have one now. The clerk who checked him out was an attractive blonde with an unadorned left ring finger. "Could you do me a favor?" he asked, shamelessly playing up a shy reticence.

She smiled at him and giggled. "Is this a pickup line?"

Duncan shook his head, grinning boyishly. "I wish. Actually, I have a chance for spring break in Florida. The problem is, my roommate let me borrow his car, and my ride is leaving right now. I don't have time to take it back to the hospital."

"Hospital?" He'd piqued the blonde's interest now.

"Yeah, he's a doctor in the ER." He flashed his most charming smile. "Could you call him? Tell him his car's here at the mall and you have the keys?" The blonde hesitated. "No girlfriend." He drew the word out into a sly hint.

"Is he cute?"

He handed her the doctor's ID badge. "You tell me," he tempted her. "You keep the keys and the ID so you can recognize him. Call him over at the ER to let him know his car is here. I'll bet he takes you to dinner."

The clerk stared a moment longer at the picture. "Sure," she said, smiling. "I can call this guy for you. Who should I tell him gave me the keys?"

Already headed for the exit, he paused long enough to call over his shoulder, "He'll know."

The blonde looked down at the ID in her hand. The guy's roommate really was a doctor, and very attractive in an Italian sort of way. She slipped the ID into her pocket. She'd call him about an hour before she got off work. Maybe she would get dinner out of this deal.

Duncan climbed into the back seat of the sporty red Ford Mustang. As the girls chatted happily like a pair of magpies, he drifted off to sleep, totally exhausted. His dream started almost immediately.

He stood atop the high ridge of Black Rock Ravine. Below him, the rushing water of the River Glass tumbled over and around the boulders strewn along its bed. At his back, a granite monolith poked a weather-worn finger into a Highland sky the color of Moira's eyes. A lone piper stood next to the rock, his music swirling about him. He recognized the tune, "The March of Earl Ross," Clan Ross's anthem. The piper wore the full Ross kit, a kilt made of plaid with a red ground and blue and green welts, sporran, and jacket. He stared at him trying to decide if he knew him. The piper smiled at him, the tune changing. He recognized this tune as well—the haunting melody that had magically transported him and Moira to the other place.

"Who are you?" he asked the piper. The man never missed a note. Duncan stared into his eyes, suddenly realizing they were the same mystical color as Moira's—that soft radiant blue with mysterious gold and silver swirls dancing in their depths. "Who are you?" Duncan asked again, almost fearful this time.

The music stopped. "Do you love her?" the piper asked in a voice as sweet as spun sugar.

"More than life itself," he swore.

"Then by the gods, bind her this time," the piper

decreed.

Duncan groaned and opened his eyes. He was still curled up in the uncomfortably small back seat of the college girl's Mustang. In moments, his eyes closed again, his mind and body too tired to release him to wakefulness.

****

Moira opened her eyes, blinking against the bright beacon hanging above her. A pair of very serious green eyes studied her. She didn't recognize them. They certainly weren't the golden brown ones watching over her before.

"How do you feel, Moira?" The voice sounded gruff but gentle.

She worked hard to focus her eyes. A man's face finally swam into view. "Duncan?" Her voice croaked and she swallowed. It hurt.

"He'll be fine," the stranger's voice assured her. "I'm more worried about you."

She struggled to sit up, but gentle hands pushed her back. "Who are you?" She stared at the man, her distrust obvious.

He flashed a smile. "I'm Dr. Andrews. Do you know where you are?"

She looked around to get her bearings. Pale green walls and a mad scientist's array of electronic machinery surrounded her. She lay on a bed—a lumpy and plastic bed. An IV bag dangled from a hook above her head. "Looks like a hospital to me," she remarked dryly.

The doctor rewarded her statement with a chuckle. "You're in the ICU at University Hospital. Do you remember what happened? I know this is painful, but I really need to know what they did to you."

She shook her head, wincing as knife-edged pain laced through her head. "My head feels like it's going to explode," she complained.

"I'll give you something for that, but I need to talk to you first." Dr. Andrews remained persistent.

She grimaced. "They beat the crap out of me, Doctor." She swallowed again, her throat still raw. "Is that what you want to hear? I've been slapped, slugged, tied up, and left to burn alive. I hurt in places I didn't know I had, and I can't breathe. And if I don't see Duncan right this instant, I am going to get out of this bed and go find him."

"Whoa, girl." Dr. Andrews soothed her, a big grin splitting his somber face. "I think you're going to be just fine as long as you stay in that bed."

She wasn't about to be put off. The doctor wasn't telling her something. Her stomach turned over, and tied itself in knots. She stared at him, then glanced at the nurse and the paramedic who'd ridden in the ambulance with her standing by the door. They all looked bleak. "Where is he?" she whispered, the fear in her voice palpable.

Dr. Andrews cleared his throat, and she feared the worse. Tears sprang into her eyes. The paramedic rushed forward and grabbed her hand, giving it a reassuring squeeze while glaring at the doctor. "He's okay," he assured her. "Duncan is fine, or at least as fine as can be expected. He got out of here under his own steam anyway."

She stared at him trying to read his expression. "Duncan left? I don't understand."

After the feds left, the paramedic hung around, following when the staff moved Moira to a room. His partner would resupply the unit and flirt with the new nurse down in ER until he returned. For the next few minutes, he related all he knew of previous events to her—how Duncan had rescued her, and had refused treatment until she was out of danger. Chuckling, he told her of the FBI's attempt to arrest him, and how the fire department had foiled them. He told of putting Duncan in a room across the hall from her in the ER, and promising the big man he would look after her.

"The last time I saw him, he was lying on that exam table all but unconscious. Not five minutes later, the big guy was gone. Vanished into thin air." The medic's voice filled with admiration, and he chuckled again. "Man, when that fed came in and no one could find him, I thought all hell was going to break loose."

"You and me both," Dr. Andrews muttered. "Now then, Moira. As for you, young lady, you need to lie back and get plenty of rest. That's the best thing for you right now. Along with a little painkiller for your headache. You took quite a knock on your noggin. We thought it might be a skull fracture, but it's just a concussion. Your father and sister are waiting to see you, and I'm going to let them in, but only for a few minutes." He glanced over at the nurse. "No more than five minutes," he ordered sternly.

****

Walking into Moira's room, Patrick winced at his pinched, haggard look when he caught a reflection of his face. Deirdre didn't look much better. Dark circles under her green eyes stood out in bleak contrast to the redhead's pale complexion. Her tangled hair looked wild, and she obviously hadn't taken any time to fix herself up. Patrick took Moira's hand, fighting back tears. Deirdre hung back by the door, almost as if too embarrassed, or afraid, to come closer.

"I'm okay, Da," Moira assured. She leaned around him to get a better look at her sister. "No offense, Dee, but you look like hell."

"No offense," Deirdre retorted, "but I look a hellava lot better than you do."

Patrick sputtered, offended by Deirdre's retort. He whirled in fury only to discover a giggling

Deirdre. Moira giggled, too. Deirdre flew across the room into Moira's waiting arms. Hysterical giggles gave way to sobs. Stunned, he watched helplessly, then looked to the nurse for enlightenment.

The nurse shrugged. "It's a sister thing," she whispered, nudging him toward the door. "Let them be for a bit. I'm giving Moira a sedative so she'll sleep for several hours. You need to get some rest, too, Senator."

He waited in the hallway outside Moira's room until Deirdre joined him. The redhead wiped tears from her eyes as the door swished closed behind her. Without a word, he opened his arms, and she melted against his chest for a hug. Arm-in-arm, the two of them walked down to the ICU waiting room to meet the Steeles and John Murray.

****

Duncan listened to the two girls talk in the front seat for several minutes before opening his eyes. They were plotting which one would get him into bed first. He smiled. There once had been a time when he'd jump at the opportunity. Now? No way. Not since he'd met Moira. There could never be another for him, now or ever again.

He stretched noisily, and made waking-up sounds so the girls could change the topic of conversation. He didn't want them embarrassed, but he also planned on giving them a stern lecture about taking up with strange men. He recalled their names were Annie and Phoebe, and he'd offered to buy them dinner. They were on the outskirts of Charlotte, North Carolina, and it was coming on dark. He'd slept for three hours. Not that he didn't need it or anything, he reminded himself.

During dinner, he learned the girls planned on driving straight through the night to Daytona Beach. Annie had their route mapped out— Charlotte to Columbia, South Carolina, and on to

Savannah, Georgia. Then they'd follow I-95 down the coast to their final destination. Back at the car, he offered to drive.

"I've had my nap," he joked. "And I'd rather drive at night."

Annie readily agreed. "I don't like to drive in the dark," she admitted.

Phoebe climbed into the back seat, and Annie took up the shotgun position. Even pushing the driver's seat back as far as it would go, and adjusting the steering wheel, he still barely fit. Traffic continued bumper to bumper, and the girls speculated about every college student on the east coast heading to Florida. The drive to Columbia took an hour longer due to the traffic, which suited him. The girls had drifted off to sleep so making his detour was easy. He needed to get to Atlanta.

The girls slept the entire way. About forty miles from Atlanta, he switched from CD to radio. He found an Atlanta station just in time for a newscast. Since the incident at Faerie Glen led the news, he wasn't surprised he was a wanted man. The reporter gave a fairly detailed description of him. Getting to his destination just got a bit tougher, but he'd still make it. The SAS had trained him well. He had gear stashed all over the eastern seaboard, thus the detour to Atlanta.

He pulled into a Motel 6 not far from Atlanta's Hartsfield International Airport. Leaving the girls asleep in the car, he went inside to get a room for them, and a cab for himself. The girls were so sleepy neither protested when he woke them and escorted them to their room. They collapsed on one of the beds, and within moments were gently snoring. He left them a note telling them to be careful of whom they picked up, and left a hundred dollar bill to pay for their gas to Daytona Beach, along with the keys to the Mustang.

Out in the parking lot, he snatched the backpack he'd bought from the back seat, and locked the car. A moment later, headlights flared in the pre-dawn night and a yellow cab pulled up. He climbed into the back seat. "Airport," he ordered tersely. The driver merely nodded.

Ground fog formed, and he worried about delayed flights. As the cab turned into the airport entrance, the driver asked which airline he needed. At the Delta hub, he unfolded his brawny frame from the backseat. He paid the driver and strode inside, unerringly headed to a bank of lockers. Fishing in his pocket for a key, he opened one of the lockers. A small duffel bag was stuffed inside. It contained clothes, money, and identification papers. He checked the papers—a driver's license and passport, both proclaiming him to be Ross Campbell, a Canadian citizen. A small blue folder contained two thousand dollars in traveler's checks. The billfold with the driver's license held five hundred in cash, photos of an alleged family, and other homey touches, including a couple of fake credit cards. A second bag held far deadlier items, but Duncan didn't touch it—instead adding the confiscated Gerber combat knife to the stash.

He caught a shuttle over to the American hub and bought a ticket for the next flight to Boston. He had just over an hour to kill so he found a gift store open 24/7. He asked the clerk if she could mail a package, pleased when she answered in the affirmative. He bought a small doll and managed to conceal his *skean dhu* in the parcel. He also included a card, explaining the significance of the dagger, and what should be done with it. He paid extra for first class postage.

The loudspeaker announced his flight was ready for boarding, and he cleared the security checkpoint easily to join the twenty-odd passengers for the red-eye to Logan Airport. His body still worn out, he fell asleep before the 737 taxied out for take-off.

In Boston, after retrieving other items and a heavy leather jacket from a locker there, Duncan made arrangements to fly out that evening to Edinburgh, Scotland. He had something to do at home before he could continue his search for Boru. With ticket in hand, he caught an airport shuttle over to the Hilton and checked in, paying cash. He showered, dressed his wounds, and shrugged into clean clothes. Repacking his backpack, he slung it over his shoulder, and left the card key on the dresser. With a last look to make sure he'd left nothing behind, including fingerprints, he put the "Do Not Disturb" sign on the door, and shut it behind him. He wouldn't be back.

Duncan caught a cab over to the South Boston area. He had the cabbie drop him off at Broadway and Dorchester. He walked a couple of blocks down East Broadway, and then hailed another cab to Waverly and Commonwealth in Newton. When he got out, he waited until the cab drove out of sight. He found a bar down the street, and slid inside. Like most bars, the pay phones were in a dingy hallway at the back.

He dialed a number from memory. After six rings, he hung up, and retrieved his money. Exactly two minutes later, he dialed the same number again. This time, someone answered on the second ring.

"Yeah?" The voice sounded soft, husky, and definitely feminine.

"Have you got the time?"

"You know where?"

"Yeah." Duncan hung up.

The conversation lasted only seconds. He now had ten minutes to get to his destination. If he didn't make it before his contact arrived, there'd be no meeting. Precisely ten minutes later, he sat on a bench outside the Boston College Library.

A young woman, huddled in a long coat and wearing a floppy wool hat pulled low over her eyes, approached the bench. She sat down on the far end. Ignoring him, she opened a book and began reading. He watched a flock of pigeons fight over some bread an old man tossed to them from his perch on a bench across the walk. The woman pulled a newspaper from her pocket, and laid it on the bench between them.

"I've been expecting you." Her voice sounded as whispery as it had on the phone. She turned to look at him, and Duncan tried not to wince at the sight of the brutal scar ringing her neck. The girl glanced at the paper between them, calling his attention to it. As home ground for both the O'Connors and the Steeles, the story from Virginia would be front-page news here in Boston. The only surprise came from his picture not being plastered on the front page.

"Do you know where he might have gone?" He pitched his voice as soft as hers.

She shook her head. A moment later, she added, "He had an Italian passport."

"That's a start." The girl stood up. "Is there anything I can do for you?" he asked.

Again she shook her head. "I'm fine." He reached into his pocket for some cash, but she stopped him with a look. "Really," she added. She smiled at him finally. "You've done more than enough." She walked away.

He stood up. "Thanks, Ciará," he called after, his voice not much more than a whisper on the breeze.

She stopped dead in her tracks. "Caroline," she told him firmly without turning around.

A group of people emerged from the library, and the girl calling herself Caroline melted into their midst. He watched the knot of people stroll down the walk, obscuring her. He smiled briefly, glad she'd moved on with her life. When he'd found her nine months ago in Montreal, Boru had choked all but the last spark of life out of her, and slit her throat for good measure. He'd revived her, spiriting her away to a small cabin in northern Vermont for safety. For a month he had nursed her. When she was finally well enough to go her own way, he'd made arrangements for her to start anew in Boston. In return, she'd given him the name of Seamus O'Rourke.

He turned on his heel, and started to walk away in the opposite direction. A gruff voice called after him. "I believe you forgot something, young man," the voice barked.

He glanced over his shoulder. The old man feeding the pigeons held out a newspaper. He cocked an eyebrow but warily approached the man. "Pretty girl," the man commented as he retrieved the paper from him. "I wonder if she worked the crossword puzzle."

Before he could reply, the old man turned and shuffled off, pigeons still flocking about him. Duncan stared after him for a long moment before opening the paper to the crossword puzzle page. Squares had been filled in with letters. He crumpled the paper into one hand and stuffed it into his pocket. He would decipher the message later. Since he didn't know who the old man worked for, he needed to disappear quickly.

****

Moira rolled over and blinked her eyes in the wan florescent light. For a moment, she couldn't remember where she was. There were no windows in the ICU, nor a clock she could see. For some reason, she desperately wanted to know the time. A nurse padded in on rubber-soled shoes, and efficiently checked drips and dials, unaware Moira was awake.

"What time is it?"

The nurse jumped, dropping the metal chart holder she had in her hand. The thing clattered noisily across the floor. "Shh," the nurse reminded herself sheepishly as she picked up the chart. "Sorry. You startled me."

"What time is it?" She repeated the question.

The nurse glanced at her watch. "Three," she replied.

"Day or night?"

The nurse checked her pulse, pursing her lips as she watched the second hand on her watch tick off the time. Muttering to herself, she made some notes on the chart. She stuck a thermometer in Moira's mouth before answering. "It's three in the morning and you should be asleep," the nurse chided.

She took the thermometer out of her mouth. "What day is it?"

The nurse snatched the thermometer and put it back under her tongue. "It's Tuesday."

She closed her eyes. She'd been asleep more than 48 hours. Where was Duncan? Had he been caught? Was he still alive? A shudder ran the length of her body. No, she'd know if he was dead. He was out there somewhere. The darkness yawned, ready to swallow her again. She didn't fight this time. There ahead of her, shining like a beacon, were warm brown eyes flecked with gold.

****

Duncan pushed against his plane seat, forcing it back, and squirmed to get comfortable. One of the few direct flights from Boston to Edinburgh, there weren't many passengers. He'd been surprised at the ease with which he'd boarded the plane. With no one seated near him, he took out the paper the old man had given him, and opened it to the crossword puzzle. The first four letters of One Across had been filled in with the letters R-O-M-E. N-I-C-C-O-L-O answered Ten Down. Twenty-three Across had numbers he guessed belonged to a telephone exchange. Nineteen Down looked to be an address.

He remained suspicious of the old man. There'd been too many times in his hunt for Boru just when he'd lost the trail, some new clue putting him back on the scent appeared out of the blue. Not for the first time, he wondered if MI5 had a hand in all this. His lips stretched in a wry smile though the humor didn't touch his eyes. More likely, MI6 pulled his strings without MI5 having a clue. Just like the FBI and the CIA in the States, MI5 and MI6 had their own turf wars.

The cabin attendant brought a tolerable meal, and after she removed his tray, he got comfortable, closed his eyes, and thought about Moira. In moments, her beautiful face and haunting blue eyes swam enticingly in his head. He shifted in his seat to ease the uncomfortable strain against his zipper. Only Moira could make him hot and needy with just the thought of her. He glanced at his watch. Almost 3:00 a.m. EST. He'd reset the time when he landed in Scotland.

Chapter 26

Ski Yazkowski glared at his Secret Service counterpart who sat, complacent and unperturbed, behind his desk. "I don't care what the hospital is telling you, Curtis. I think they're protecting her." Ski growled in frustration. "The senator doesn't want us to question her and the hospital is helping him."

Curtis looked up at him, watching him pace back and forth across the narrow confines of the office. "Relax, Ski. I've got a man posted down there right outside her room. As soon as somebody besides her family or medical personnel goes through the door, we'll be notified."

He stopped pacing for a moment, glaring at some unseen enemy behind Curtis's head. "She knows where he is," he insisted, his frustration boiling over. "That EMT said Ross talked to her the whole way to the hospital, and then again in the ER."

Curtis shrugged. "She was also unconscious at the time, Ski." Ski turned on his heel and marched to the door. "Going somewhere?" Curtis sounded slightly amused.

He wasn't amused at all. "Back to Washington. Call me if you ever get to interview her."

****

Patrick had no chance to open the front door as

Margaret Steel yanked it open before he could even touch the handle. "Bring that precious child in here," the little woman ordered. He ushered Moira through the door, Deirdre and John Murray following with the group's luggage. "You should get right to bed, Moira." He smiled at Margaret's mother hen instincts.

"I've been in bed for a week, Aunt Margaret," Moira replied with a shake of her head. "I'm fine." Mrs. Spencer arrived with a tray of coffee. Moira's expression brightened and she looked hopeful. "Have there been any calls?"

Mrs. Spencer exchanged concerned looks with him and Margaret. They all knew whom Moira was hoping to hear from but there had been no word. Mrs. Spencer finally shook her head. "I'm sorry, pet. Your young man hasn't called."

"He will," Margaret announced to the room.

****

Duncan stared at the phone sitting on the scarred and battered table. He even reached for it once. Only his iron will kept him from picking up the receiver and dialing Washington. Hearing her voice would have him on the next transatlantic flight, and he couldn't go. Not yet. Every law enforcement agency in America, and most of those in Europe were trying to track him. He couldn't afford contact with Moira until he'd hunted down Boru. But once he'd finished? He hauled his thoughts back to the present. He didn't have time to get lost in the future, in the false promise of "what ifs." Hard on Boru's heels, he couldn't lose his focus now. He had to finish it so he and Moira could have a future.

A sharp tap on the door brought him to his feet. "Yeah?" He opened the door a crack. A small man with dark hair and skin and dressed in a military uniform stood there, glancing over his shoulder, his eyes darting nervously.

"This is dangerous, Duncan," the man said in a thick, middle-Eastern accent.

He pulled the man into his room. "I really appreciate this, Saleem. What did you find out?"

"You are very hot, my friend. I cannot believe they have lost your trail."

"As long as I stay one step ahead, they can follow me straight to Boru for all I care. What did you find out?"

The Turkish Army officer shook his head. "This is suicide, what you do, Duncan." He shrugged. "Since I know I will be unable to dissuade you..." Saleem paused to pull a folded piece of paper from his pocket, "...flight number and destination."

He took the paper, unfolded, and read it. "Thanks, Saleem. I owe you one."

Saleem shook his head again. "No, my crazy friend. It is I who owed you my life. I only wish I could stop you from pursuing this madness. I fear for you, Duncan Ross. For your life."

Moira's face appeared in his mind, and he smiled. "Don't worry, Saleem. I have much to live for," he assured the little officer. "I will not throw my life away needlessly, but I will see the end of Boru."

A few hours later, he watched the Istanbul airport fade from view. Not surprisingly, this flight to Moscow was fairly crowded. Purchasing a first class ticket was a foolish indulgence for a man on the run, but he'd done it any way. Two weeks ago, he'd left Moira behind in the ER at Charlottesville. While in Rome, he'd found a copy of the Washington Post with a story about her release and return to Washington. His heart ached for her, even as his whole body came alive at the thought of her. At that moment, he'd give his life to see her just one more time, to hold her in his arms, kiss her, and make her his forever.

"Soon, bonnie girl," he whispered. "I'll come back

to you soon."

****

Life returned to normal despite Patrick's fears to the contrary. Without Moira running his office, day-to-day duties gave him very little time to brood. The puzzle of Duncan Ross continued to confound him. He would have sworn on his own grave the big Scotsman loved Moira. Why the man would go this long without attempting to contact her remained a mystery he would solve sooner or later. For Moira's sake, the senator hoped it came sooner.

The phone at his elbow buzzed. He answered it, listening for a moment before replying, "Yes, Hutch. It is an appropriate topic for the subcommittee, and we need to move it on it fairly quickly. I'm not at all satisfied with the answers I've been getting from the FBI. Or anyone else for that matter."

The voice on the phone rumbled in agreement, and he hung up. He had a serious hunch the FBI, and a lot of other ABC agencies, knew far more about the incident at Faerie Glen than any of them would admit. Patrick grinned coldly. It wasn't nice to fool with a U.S. Senator. Especially if the senator could put a serious knot in an agency's purse strings. He had never made his politics personal, but this time was different. This time, Moira's life hung in the balance.

****

The late model Mercedes sedan squatted amongst its nondescript neighbors, waiting for traffic to start moving along the Kúdamm toward the Tiergarten. Duncan didn't like navigating Berlin. After his flight from Moscow landed at Schonefeld Airport, in what once was East Berlin, he'd rented the car despite his reluctance to do so. Now, two days later, he'd settled into his room at the Savigny. The little hotel was plain, cheap, and close to the Kúdamm, the main thoroughfare through

Berlin. Its location was handy for the few places he needed to go. Like now. He headed toward the Eierschale, a café at the eastern end of the Kúdamm.

The light changed, and traffic pushed forward. A few blocks from his destination, he pulled onto a side street, and found a place to park. After a few minutes' walk, he entered the café. A waiter led him to a small table set back against the far wall of the main room. A tall, black man dressed in a neat suit and tie occupied a table nearby. As soon as the waiter seated him, the man motioned the waiter over to his table. In perfect German, he ordered his lunch. After taking the order, the waiter returned to him.

"I'll have the same as him," Duncan stammered in halting German. The man tipped his glass in his direction.

The two men ignored each other, eating their meals in silence. He finished first, helping his last mouthful down with a swig of beer. He stood up, pulled a wad of euros from his pocket, peeled off several, and dropped them on the table. As he passed the other man's table, he briefly glanced down. The man didn't look up.

Outside the café, he headed east toward the bombed-out bell tower of the Kaiser Wilhelm Gedachtniskirche. The bell tower was the only remnant of the neo-Romanesque church to survive Allied bombing during World War II. A memorial and museum had been built around the base of the tower, and he took a few moments to look at the exhibits. Passing on through, he headed north toward the Berlin Zoo. At the gate, he paid his admission and strolled through the lovely grounds. A few minutes later, he found the bears, all housed in moat-surrounded enclaves. Two Russian bears vied for their keeper's attention as he threw treats to them. Duncan stopped to watch.

"Long time no see," a deep voice with a faint southern accent rumbled at his shoulder.

He turned to stare at the black man from the café. "Rafe." His acknowledgment was short and pointed.

The two men ambled down the broad walkway. "You are in a heap of trouble, old friend," Rafe finally said, glancing over at him. He shrugged, implying *"So what else is new?"* The two men stopped to let a large group of schoolchildren pass in front of them. "I've set up a meet for you tonight," Rafe added, watching the children. "Grosser Stern." His pronunciation sounded perfect.

Duncan nodded, familiar with the traffic circle on the other side of the park from where they stood.

Rafe started forward as the children's chaperons hurried past. "He'll meet you at the base of the Seigessaule. Twenty-one hundred hours."

He nodded again. The monument Rafe mentioned originally stood before the Reichstag, but Hitler had it moved to its present location. Almost 230 feet tall, the granite and bronze structure celebrated three Prussian military campaigns.

The black man moved off down the path away from him. He stopped and turned back. "You owe me," he called.

Duncan smiled for the first time since the two of them had met up. "We're even." Even though said quietly, his words carried above the happy squeals of the children.

A group of people cut between the two men, hiding Duncan for a moment. As the group moved away, Rafe wasn't surprised he'd disappeared. His mouth twisted into a wry smile. The big Scotsman likely remained alive due only to his innate ability to fade into the background. Turning on his heel, he followed the broad walkway until it circled back to the main entrance. Although he watched carefully, he never caught sight of Duncan.

As he exited the Zoo, a pale green sedan rolled smoothly to a stop in front of him. A man in a US Army uniform with lieutenant's bars on the collar jumped out of the front passenger door, and saluted despite the fact he wore civilian clothes. The lieutenant opened the rear door. Rafe halfheartedly returned the salute as he climbed in, his expression and mood somber. There were days he really hated his job. Today was one of them.

****

Duncan watched as the sedan with US Army plates pulled into traffic. Despite rumors to the contrary, he'd suspected Rafe hadn't retired from Army Intelligence. He blended into the early afternoon crowd. He had until nine o'clock tonight. At least Rafe had bought him a little time.

Returning to his hotel, he grabbed a shower in the public bathroom near his room. Wearing only jeans and a tee shirt, he went back to his sparsely furnished room and lay down. He'd be on the move again after tonight, and there was no telling when he'd be able to sleep again. Like the trained soldier he was, he fell asleep moments after his head touched the pillow.

At 6:00 pm, he came fully awake. Most of his gear was already stowed in the Mercedes. He pulled on clean socks and his boots. A denim shirt covered the white tee, and Duncan threw on his worn, leather jacket. Though late spring, Berlin's nights could still be chilly. He took a last look around, checking to make sure he'd forgotten nothing. He debated wiping the room for fingerprints before deciding it wouldn't matter after tonight.

A short time later, he'd parked the Mercedes on a side street off the busy Strasse des 17 Juni. Duncan hiked east to the traffic circle known as Grosser Stern. Even though the Prussian memorial in the center of the circle closed at six, its base and the steep staircase leading to the observation tower at its top already teemed with the night's less savory denizens. As he passed them, they instinctively pulled back from his brooding countenance. He might be a foreigner, but he would not be easy pickings for any such as them.

From the top of the monument, Duncan had a wide view of the surrounding area. He ignored the couple next to him as they did him. They were too busy copulating. At 8:30, two American agents arrived. Though they were supposed to be undercover, he spotted the man and woman immediately. Their body contacts were much too contrived to be natural. He glanced to his right. The woman had a go with a second man while the first caught his breath. He turned back to the scene 200 feet below him, blocking out the panting, sweating bodies just feet away.

By nine, his alleged contact had not arrived, not that he actually expected him to show. He'd come just to make sure. The curve of his lips formed a parody of a smile, his expression cynical and mocking. Rafe still owed him after all.

"You want to have a fuck?" a feminine voice purred in English thickened by a guttural German accent. He glanced at the prostitute. She wasn't bad looking, all things considered. "I have a room," she added, "not far from here."

Her offer piqued his curiosity. "Why do I get a room?" he asked, nodding toward the two drunks now reeling their way toward the steps leading to the street. "And how much more will it cost me?"

The prostitute giggled at him. "For you, it is free," she whispered, her voice and wink meant to be seductive.

He tilted his head like an inquisitive bird, though he likely resembled a raptor far more than a robin. A German prostitute offering her wares for free was a cause célèbre, and he became curious enough to want to find out why. "Lead on."

The frowsy blonde linked her arm through his and led him to the stairs. "There are police waiting below."

"Among others." His reply sounded as cryptic as hers had been conversational.

As they climbed down the long flights of stairs, the woman helped him acquire a new wardrobe—a military overcoat and an officer's cap. With their heads together, kissing and giggling, they walked past several uniformed Berlin police, the two undercover US Army Intelligence officers, and at least one Interpol agent. He'd bet his life one MI6 agent also hung around, if not more. As soon as they turned the corner, she pulled away from him, and broke into a trot. He easily lengthened his stride to keep up. Three blocks away, the prostitute pulled him into a dark, recessed doorway.

"Wait here," she whispered. She stuck out her head, looked both ways, then darted across the street and faded into the shadows.

He listened as her staccato steps faded into the night. With all of his senses on overdrive, he waited. Five minutes later, a voice wafted down. "The door is unlocked."

Try as he might, he couldn't place the accent. It sounded somewhere between Middle Eastern and Yiddish, with a touch of Russian. He pushed open the door, slipped through, and made sure the heavy wooden door shut firmly behind him. That same disembodied voice called down the stairwell, "Come up."

Cautiously, he climbed the steep flight of stairs. At the landing, a little man bearing more than a passing resemblance to a gnome waited. He handed Duncan a thick file tied up with string. "I think this will be what you are seeking," the man told him. Turning on his heel, he disappeared into the thick blackness shrouding the next flight of stairs.

Wisely, he didn't follow. He tucked the file away inside his shirt, and retraced his steps. Out on the street, he hesitated a few seconds to get his bearings. Figuring out his location, he set off for his car, parked only blocks away.

Two blocks from his car, Duncan picked up a tail. Ducking into an alley, he waited. A few moments later, hurried footsteps echoed down the street, slowing as they neared the alley.

"I have a weapon and you don't, Ross," a clipped British voice snarled.

"Are you sure enough to bet your life?" Duncan replied jovially, a cold smile pasted on his lips.

"Don't make this any harder on yourself, Ross. It's time to come in," the British agent replied.

"Not yet."

The blunt barrel of an automatic pistol savagely poked Duncan's ribs. "I said it was over," the man barked.

Acting as meek as a mouse, he allowed the British agent to give his body a cursory search. With the pistol now pointing at the middle of his back, he led the way back to the Mercedes. As he unlocked the passenger side door, the same frowsy prostitute approached them.

"Twenty euros," she offered, giving the two men a leer. "To do you both," she enticed, wiggling her hips in invitation.

"Bugger off," the Brit barked at her. "Get in the car, Ross," he ordered, watching him closely.

"Another time, love," he called after the woman's retreating back. She'd done her job, and he hoped she'd been well paid. That would be some consolation for his stupidity.

Before the woman reached the corner,

something slammed into the back of her head, knocking her off her feet. The world around her turned black, then blazed to scarlet, then back to black as she slammed into the sidewalk all but unconscious. She couldn't hear and she couldn't see. Her last thought, before succumbing to the blackness, was that the bloody bastard had shot her dead.

****

A haunting dirge swirled among the standing stones. Dressed in the Ross kit, Abhean looked for all the world like a Highland piper of old. His lament echoed across the broad plain all the way to the misty, blue mountains and the white-capped sea.

Manannan stared at the Harper, his cold eyes staring out from the carved-granite mask his face had become. "I told you not to interfere."

The weeping wail of the pipes ceased. "But he has atoned!"

Abhean's voice grated in his ears. "Aye, that he has, Harper, but I told you I would have spared them this life. And would have but for your interference. It is not to be."

"Then you would punish her as well?"

The granite mask cracked and a thunderstorm took its place. "This is your doing, Harper!" Manannan roared.

"Am I banished then?" Abhean's voice sounded resigned. When Manannan did not reply, he squeezed the pipes again, his requiem once more filling the sky with its poignant notes.

As Manannan stared across the plain to the mountains, a single tear trickled down his cheek. There was nothing he could do.

Chapter 27

Moira stared out her bedroom window watching the late afternoon shadows march across the small yard. Six weeks had passed since the incident in Virginia. Her smile rueful, she realized she now thought of that weekend of horror in impersonal terms. Calling it an incident made it seem like some sort of diplomatic faux pas, or a minor skirmish in some backwater war. To the press or the FBI, the description might be apropos. To her, though, the weekend had been a cataclysmic event, changing her life forever.

Her physical wounds had healed, leaving only faint traces of the burns, both from the ropes that held her prisoner and from the fire itself. She occasionally suffered from headaches but even those were receding. The constant fear for Duncan's safety and the nagging worry about his continued silence remained the only thing affecting her on a daily basis.

Downstairs, the front door slammed closed and laughter wafted up. A few moments later, Deirdre tapped on the door before pushing it open and peeping in. "Hello, sister mine," the redhead greeted her. She smiled. So much had changed between them. So much about them had changed. "How are you feeling?" Deirdre added.

"I'm fine, Dee."

"Good. We're all going out to dinner tonight," Deirdre announced. She shook her head but her sister held up her hand, palm out to stay any argument. "No ifs, ands, or buts. You haven't left this house since we brought you home from Virginia. It's springtime, Moira. Your favorite season. The dogwoods and cherry trees are blooming. I won't let you sit here brooding and miss it."

Without waiting for her answer, Deirdre went to the closet and sorted through several of the outfits hanging there. From the back of the closet, she pulled out the peach jersey and silk outfit her father had bought Moira in Virginia. "This is perfect," she declared. "Now hurry and get ready. John and Da are starved." She paused at the door, mischievous glints twinkling in her emerald eyes. "If you hurry, I'll give you a surprise when you get downstairs."

She flashed her sister a puzzled look. Deirdre held up a small package wrapped in brown paper. The postmark and stamp looked foreign. Moira's heart pounded, and she blanched. Deirdre ran to her side.

"Moira?" Deirdre winced. "Here, Moira. You can have it." Dee tried to press the box into her hands but she wouldn't take it.

The package showed a postmark from Edinburgh, Scotland, with a return address belonging to a law firm. Her hands shook as she finally accepted the box. Slowly, she unwrapped it. A creamy vellum envelope with her name scrawled across it in a precise but unfamiliar hand fell into her lap. She stared at it as if the paper was something foul and poisonous. "Read it." The words tumbled out in a tortured whisper.

Flinching, Deirdre picked up the envelope and opened it. Her hands shaking, she unfolded the crisp paper, cleared her throat, and tried to speak. She did not want to put voice to the words scrawled on that page, but the sounds finally came out. She tried to keep her voice as cold and neutral as the words themselves. "Dear Miss O'Connor," she read. "I am the solicitor for Clan Ross. It is in this capacity that I write to you. Please find enclosed a ring and a key. Mr. Duncan Ross bequeathed these items to you. In accordance with his last wishes, and to close out his estate, I am forwarding the same to you. Please execute the enclosed receipt, and return the same in the envelope provided at your earliest convenience. Sincerely, Ogden Ogilvie-Smythe, Q.C."

They were both crying but Moira managed to get the wooden box open. A large oval fire opal surrounded by diamonds in an antique gold setting winked up at her. An odd-looking key nestled next to the ring. A folded piece of paper was tucked into the side of the box. She pulled it out.

Written with a bold hand, the words mocked her. "One is the key to the heart of Clan Ross; the other the key to everything else. Now and Forever, bonnie girl. Duncan."

Silent sobs wracked her body. Deirdre folded her arms around her, rocking back and forth with her. "I'm sorry, Moira," Deirdre cried. "I didn't know. I'm sorry."

"No!" She moaned, the sound gut-wrenching. "It can't be. He promised." Her anguish choked her but didn't numb the pain. Deirdre held her and cried, too.

Concerned with the delay, John Murray finally came in search of the sisters. He heard them crying as he reached the top of the stairs, and rushed to Moira's room. There was no doubt something terrible had happened. "What?" he pleaded. Deirdre held out the letter to him. He read it quickly, then took the other page from Moira's limp hand. After reading it, he glared around the room, looking for someone or something to punch. "I don't believe it," he finally spit out. Though flat, his voice carried conviction.

Moira raised her tear-streaked face to look at him. The pain in her eyes hit him like a fist to the gut. He glanced at Deirdre, her helplessness mirroring his own.

Moira took a deep, shuddering breath and swiped at her eyes with the back of her hand. "You two must be starved," she stated calmly, surprising them both.

"No, no. We're fine," Deirdre protested, taking Moira's hands. "Don't worry about us," she pleaded even as she fought to regain her composure.

John recognized the moment Moira noticed the sparkle on Deirdre's left ring finger. "What's this?" she asked, looking first at Deirdre and then up at him. He exchanged guilty looks with Deirdre. Realization dawned on Moira's face. "When?"

Deirdre couldn't look at her sister. "This afternoon," she mumbled trying to hide the engagement ring she wore.

"That's why you were so insistent about dinner tonight. Dee, I'm sorry. You were going to announce your engagement."

"It's no big deal," John interjected.

"Yes, it is," Moira asserted. "It's not every day my big sister gets engaged to the hottest and handsomest attorney this side of the Mississippi." Her voice strengthened as she hugged Deirdre. "I'm so happy for you, Dee, and you, too, John." She attempted a cheeky grin. "I hope you know what you're getting yourself into." She meant to sound teasing. "Your face is a mess, Dee. And mine, too, probably. We can't go out looking like this. Go get ready."

Despite the lightness of Moira's voice, the sadness etched around her eyes tore at his gut and he watched tears well in Deirdre's eyes. She looked up at him for confirmation as she insisted, "We'll eat here tonight."

"We wouldn't think of going out," he added.

"Nonsense," Moira countered. "This calls for a celebration. Now get out of here so I can change clothes." She shooed them out and shut the door firmly behind them.

She walked to the window and threw open the sash. The few puffy clouds floating languid in the sky were tinged mauve and a deep lapis. An early moon rose on the horizon, and the first evening star winked at her. Slowly, she unclenched her right hand. The sharp edges of the opal ring cut an imprint in her palm. She slipped the ring on her left hand. "I'll always love you, Duncan Ross," she whispered to the wind. "Now and forever."

Less than thirty minutes later, wearing the peach outfit, she joined her family in the living room. John had told Patrick, and he was at a loss for words. Like John, he didn't want to believe Duncan was dead. It was ironic the package from Scotland arrived so close to the inaugural session of the Senate Select Subcommittee on Domestic Terrorism. Hearings were scheduled to begin shortly, and he was determined to thoroughly investigate Duncan's status. If Duncan Ross was truly dead, he would have hard proof of it, as well as how the man had died.

The four of them settled into John's Mercedes, each wrapped in their own thoughts. No one noticed the dark sedan parked next to the curb a few houses down street, nor did they see the car pull into traffic behind them. The sedan trailed them to the Bombay Club, the restaurant where John and Deirdre had planned to announce their happy news.

Late that night, when the house finally quieted, Moira stared out her window. She clutched Duncan's note in her hand. The opal and diamond ring winked and twinkled in the moonlight, but the key held her attention. The key was short, wide, and very thick. Numbers and a letter—3366D—were engraved on its side.

"The key to everything else," she mused aloud. She turned the key over and over in her hand. "Tomorrow," she promised. "I'll figure it out tomorrow."

She crawled into bed and closed her eyes, hoping as she did every night that sleep would claim her quickly. It did, but with it came nightmares. In her dream, Moira watched as Duncan loped through a sun-drenched field. She stood at the edge of the meadow, waiting. He kept running, but he never got closer. He never reached her. Something followed him—something omnipresent and terrible, something that wouldn't stop. A huge, roiling wave of fire cascaded behind him, yet he seemed oblivious to his predicament. She screamed his name, but he just kept running toward her, a happy smile on his face. Just before he reached her, the scorching dragon's breath caught up to him and devoured him. As soon as it consumed his body, the flames snuffed out, satisfied by its horrific meal. She could no longer scream, nor did tears blur the awful sight. Nothing blotted out the memory.

She sat up, wide-awake and trembling. She wondered if her dream had indeed just been a nightmare, or if her gift had somehow shown her the reality of Duncan's death. Sleep would elude her for the rest of the night so she curled up in the comfortable chair at her window. She still sat there watching when the pale fingers of dawn touched the night sky, painting the dark with radiant watercolors.

When the senator walked into the breakfast room, Moira already sipped her second cup of coffee. She'd knotted her hair in its old familiar style at the nape of her neck. She wore a linen suit, though only its navy tint proclaimed it to be businesslike. She'd lost weight since Virginia. He suspected she'd slipped into Deirdre's closet early that morning to raid her sister's wardrobe. Deirdre had always leaned toward high style rather than practicality.

Taken aback, he couldn't speak for a moment. "What are you doing?" he finally blurted gruffly.

She looked up and rewarded him with a composed smile. "I'm reading the paper, Da." She arched a brow, which finished her sentence with an implied, "D'uh."

Moira's composure surprised him. He was barely coherent as he sputtered, "I'm not talking about now. Later. I meant later. Why are you dressed for the office?"

"The subcommittee meets next week, doesn't it?" she replied, her voice calculatingly calm.

He didn't know what to say so he poured a cup of coffee, and sat down at the table as an overwhelming sadness enveloped him. He didn't recognize this stranger sitting across from him. She looked like Moira, even sounded like her, but when he looked into her eyes, he found himself drowning in haunting pools of deep cerulean. Far below the surface, there lurked a vast wisdom so sad it should have been far beyond the capacity of any human to endure.

Either Moira didn't recognize or chose to ignore his sadness and reaction to his unanswered questions. "Deirdre wants to get married as soon as possible."

He swallowed around the lump in his throat. Both of his daughters had changed so radically. With John's tutelage, Deirdre had truly learned to love unselfishly. The metamorphosis that began in Virginia had, in the last six weeks, created a lovely butterfly out of his fiery daughter. He sighed as he gazed at his moonchild. She appeared colder, even more distant now, as if she was locked away in some brittle chrysalis.

"We don't have much time to plan, though," she continued, pretending to be oblivious to his silence.

The doorbell rang and a few moments later, Margaret's voice called from the entry hall. "Deirdre, get up, you lazy girl. We have so much to do and so little time." The little woman sailed into the breakfast nook and planted a kiss on Patrick's cheek. Moira grinned at the startled look on his face.

"Look like the Marines have landed, Da," she said brightly. Patrick winced, remembering who'd last spoken those words to him. As she was hugging Margaret at the time, Moira missed his reaction.

Deirdre swept into the room looking as radiant as a spring sunrise. She'd pulled back her rich, red hair with a turquoise headband that matched her outfit. She wore only a dab of makeup and her face looked fresh and youthful. Her eyes shone with happiness.

"How did you find out so fast, Aunt Margaret?" Deirdre demanded, surprised to see the older woman.

Margaret hugged the tall redhead then stepped back to scold her with a shaking index finger. "Phyllis Murray called me first thing this morning. I'm hurt, Deirdre," she pouted. "I had to find out from the groom's mother." She flashed them all an Emmett Kelly face, and the girls giggled appreciatively. Unstoppable, she forged ahead. "Now tell me, darling girl. What kind of wedding do you want, and most importantly, we need the date."

Deirdre glanced at Moira and then her father. "We want something small and simple," she proposed.

"Nonsense, Deirdre," Margaret proclaimed. "This is the social event of the season."

He watched as Deirdre tried vainly to quell

Margaret's zeal, but Moira laid a gentle hand on her arm. "This will be your wedding day, Deirdre. It's the most important day of your life. You and John deserve the most romantic celebration Aunt Margaret can dream up."

"Listen to your sister, Deirdre," Margaret declared guilelessly. "I've always said she was the one with the brains in this family." She pulled a daily planner from her handbag. "First, we have to decide where and when. There are so many parties to plan. Showers. Everything. The Murrays have a cruise planned for late July into August. The weather starts to cool in September, and we'll need time for some prenuptial parties after they return."

"Slow down, Aunt Margaret," Deirdre pleaded. "John and I don't want to wait. We're looking at sometime in June."

Margaret stared at the younger woman, aghast at the proposal. "This June? Deirdre, my darling, you can't possibly be serious."

"June twenty-first," Moira announced softly. He stared at her. "June twenty-first," she repeated, her voice stronger. "A midsummer night's dream."

Margaret and Deirdre gaped at her for almost a full minute. "Oh, Moira," Margaret finally gushed. "That's perfect. We'll have the ceremony in the gardens at the farm."

"No!" Patrick's roaring denial took them all by surprise. The three women stared at him but he only had eyes for Moira. "No," he repeated, his voice a gruff whisper.

"Yes, Da," she asserted, her voice as soft as his. "It has to be."

He knew when he was beaten. This stranger who was his daughter was tougher and stronger than he could ever be. An air of determination surrounded her, and it would not be swept away by mere words. He shrugged, helpless in the face of

303

defeat and now knowing they'd taken the decision out of his hands.

Moira and Patrick left for his office, leaving Margaret and Deirdre to their preparations. As soon as the front door closed, Deirdre turned on Margaret, angry with her adopted aunt for the first time in her life.

"Margaret, I wish you'd be quiet and listen once in awhile," she hissed at the older woman.

Margaret looked devastated, her lip trembling and tears pooling in her eyes. "Gracious, Deirdre, if you don't want my help, just say so. I won't butt in where I'm not wanted."

She reached across the table to squeeze the woman's hand. "It's not that, Aunt Margaret." She sniffled, a tear leaking out of the corner of her eye. "Duncan's dead. We found out last night."

Margaret looked stricken. A long moment passed before she spoke. "Oh, lord," she sighed. "How? Where?"

She shrugged, a gesture more helpless than nonchalant. "We don't know. Da said he'd find out. Moira got a package and a letter from some lawyer in Scotland saying he was closing out Duncan's estate."

Tears trickled down Margaret's cheeks. "One love dies and another begins a new life." Her voice faltered, and she remained silent for a few moments. Then she squared her shoulders, and looked at Deirdre. "Well, Moira is taking the sensible approach, as she has always done, I suppose. We will be sensitive to her feelings, dear girl, but you and John are to be married. I hope this will be your one and only wedding day, and the two of you deserve the best." They both tried to ignore the bleak sadness filling the house and the hearts of all within it.

Deirdre stared out the window and realized

Moira's faerie ring had reappeared. "It's not fair, Aunt Margaret," she whispered.

"No, it's not fair."

****

Abhean plucked the strings of his harp and a sweet note resonated in the air.

"What do you know?" Manannan demanded.

The Harper smiled sadly. "I would but ease their hearts," he admitted. "There is naught else to be done."

Manannan nodded. "One dies. One lives. 'Twas ever so."

The king of Tir Nan Óg disappeared in a rainbow swirl of fog as the little Harper stared off into the distance. "Aye, Mac Lir. 'Twas ever so." He plucked the strings again and the healing notes echoed all the way across the valley. He played for the faerie folk in Tir Nan Óg. He played for the humans in An Domhan. He played for himself, seeking absolution from a soul damned to wander forever, knowing it would never come.

Chapter 28

Every staffer in the senate office turned to stare as Moira stepped through the door with her father. Guiltily, they averted their eyes as she sailed through the outer office into her own, private domain. She shut the door firmly, and sank into her desk chair. Ensconced in the familiar confines of her sanctum, she slipped the oddly shaped key from her pocket. Staring off into space, she mindlessly turned the key over and over in her hand.

"The key to everything else," she murmured, struggling to decipher Duncan's last clue. He would not have sent this key to her if it hadn't been important. She knew his spirit depended on her to exonerate his name, and this key would do that somehow.

She read off the numbers for the umpteenth time. 3366D. A safe deposit box? Or maybe a suitcase? Where would Duncan leave a suitcase so she could find it? The FBI had confiscated everything of Duncan's stored in Gemma's warehouse and at her apartment. She didn't recall any mention of a suitcase in the inventory. Her father had arranged to have the antique weapons sent back to Duncan's family in Scotland.

She put her brain in gear. Okay, she thought. If you traveled a lot, under cover, and might have to leave in a hurry, where would you stash a suitcase?

She stared at the key and the answer popped into her head—a storage locker. At a bus station? Or the airport? She swiveled her chair, grabbed the phone and started dialing.

Late that night, she sat in the middle of her bed with papers and folders fanned out around her. Most of the pages were computer generated. Duncan's bold script scrawled across the one she held in her hand. It was all here—a year's worth of investigation. He had all the names, places, and times, but he'd never had the time to put it together. She stared at the piles of paper. This is what she did best. Duncan had left her the paper trail so she'd follow it for him. She had the time. She had nothing but time now. She would put it together, and would have at least part of it ready to present to the Senate committee when it met.

****

Ski Yaskowski paced the hallway outside of the Senate hearing room. For the third straight day, the committee kept him cooling his heels out here. At the end of the hall, he turned around just in time to see Senator O'Connor slip into the room. He never had figured out just what role the senator played in Duncan Ross's escape. He'd interviewed Moira shortly after she came home from the hospital, though she'd been little help. The doctors had warned him the trauma she'd suffered might leave her memory fuzzy about the details. Despite a great deal of diligence on his part, he hadn't found any conclusive evidence linking the O'Connors to Ross. By all accounts, theirs had been a chance meeting that weekend. Besides, if nothing else, he was smart enough to realize a lowly FBI field agent did not accuse a United States Senator of wrongdoing without definitive proof.

Patrick O'Connor stepped out of the hearing room and came face-to-face with Yazkowski. "Fancy meeting you here, Senator," he quipped, his voice faintly mocking. His lips smiled, but his expression remained cold and calculating. "You know, I'm really curious, Senator. I just can't figure out for the life of me why the O'Connor family has such a compelling interest in Duncan Ross."

Patrick stared down his nose, but Ski didn't let the tactic work. "He saved my daughter's life, Agent Yazkowski," he reminded Ski coldly. "Which is more than the Bureau managed to accomplish."

The door behind them opened, and a page motioned for both men to enter. Patrick took a seat behind the long table at the front of the room. Ski was ushered to a smaller table set in the middle, between rows of chairs and the main table. A microphone, a pitcher of water, and a glass perched on the smaller table's top.

Ski was sworn in and, in a swift series of questions, was asked his full name, occupation, years with the Bureau and other pertinent background information leading up to the incident in Virginia. After that, the questioning, as far as he was concerned, went to hell in a hand basket.

"And what, Agent Yazkowski," the senator from Texas drawled at him, "do you know of the current whereabouts of this Duncan Ross feller?"

Ski cleared his throat, then looked directly at Senator O'Connor. "We received a report from Interpol that he was killed by a car bomb in Berlin."

"That would be Berlin, Germany?" the Texan prompted.

Ski tried to keep the sarcasm out of his voice. "Yes, Senator Hutchinson. Berlin, Germany."

"How did they confirm his identity?" the senator continued. "What I mean is, did they get fingerprints or any stuff like that?"

He became fed up with the Texas senator's good-ol'-boy routine. "No, Senator. They didn't. German authorities estimated the bomb contained in excess of ten pounds of plastic explosives. There wasn't enough left of the body to confirm much of anything. In fact, Senator, there was so little left, the Germans used a baggie instead of a body bag," he snarled.

If he'd been trying to shock the Texan, he failed. The senator merely peered over his reading glasses and asked, "So how did they determine Mr. Ross was indeed the victim in that bombing, Agent Yazkowski?"

He stuck out his chin in adamant support of his testimony. "The rental car was registered to Ross, and they recovered the VIN number plate. They also had a witness who identified a photograph of Ross as the man getting into the car moments before it exploded."

"And this witness was absolutely positive?"

The Texan would worry this bone to death, he decided. "Yes, Senator," he affirmed. "The witness was absolutely positive. In fact, a few moments before the bomb went off, she had tried to solicit him. She was still close enough to be injured by shrapnel from the blast."

"Solicit, Agent Yaskowski? You mean your witness is a prostitute?" The senator did not hide the amusement in his voice. As an aside to his colleagues, he added, "And no one has ever paid for a hooker's..." He paused and cleared his throat before continuing. "Testimony." Everyone on the dais chuckled appreciatively at the double entendre.

Ski got really hot under the collar now. He was just doing his job, dammit, and that job shouldn't involve being the target of an inquisition. He glanced at his watch. Not even an hour had passed. He took a deep breath. Could this day get any longer? He tried to find a more comfortable position in the hard wooden chair, and it squeaked annoyingly. Before he got settled, the chairman addressed him again.

"Thank you, Agent Yazkowski. That will be all for now," Senator Hutchinson said loudly, dismissing him without ever looking directly at him.

The stocky fed stood up and walked to the door. As he opened it, he almost knocked down Moira. He wondered, and not for the first time, just what had happened between Moira and Ross. He decided the time had come to find out. Despite the Senate subcommittee hearing, the FBI investigation of the incident continued.

"Can we talk, Moira?" He tried to sound like the friends they'd once been.

She shrugged. "Do I have a choice?" She nodded to the two men standing with her, and they carried the boxes they held into the hearing room. The hallway was now empty as she eyed him suspiciously.

"This may be painful, Moira, and I'm sorry for that, but I have to know," he began. Moira stared at him, her cerulean eyes threatening to engulf him. He blinked, trying to break the spell her gaze cast. "I need to know just what went on between you and Duncan Ross."

She glanced at the ring on her left hand, and when she looked up to meet his steady gaze, her eyes were blue ice. "That is none of your business." Her voice matched her eyes.

"If he's tried to contact you, it is my business," he asserted. She reminded him of some beautiful ice queen from a fairy tale, and he couldn't look away.

"No, Agent Yazkowski." Her frigid tone matched her icy demeanor. "I have had no direct contact with him."

He'd interviewed too many witnesses and suspects in his career. He could tell she wasn't exactly lying to him, but she wasn't telling him the whole truth either.

"Have you heard from him indirectly?"

As he watched, it seemed her skin took on the luster of Arctic ice—cold, desolate, and unyielding. The color of her eyes deepened, and her gaze turned so cold it actually seemed to burn right through him. "I received a package from his family's solicitor in Edinburgh, who informed me he was closing out Mr. Ross's estate. I was the recipient of a bequest."

He watched as she unconsciously stroked the ring on her left hand. "And what did Ross leave you in his last will and testament?" His voice sounded more sarcastic than he'd intended.

"His mother's wedding ring."

Her voice became so hushed, he had to strain to hear it. He hated his job and himself at that moment. Only a clod would ignore how very much in love she had been with Ross. The anguish on her face was palpable. The letter from Scotland was probably the first she'd heard of Ross's death.

"I'm sorry, kiddo," he murmured.

Her eyes glinted like blue ice as she glared up at him. "Sorry? You wanted him dead as much as they did."

He could no longer stand there and face her wrath or her pain. Ross was a loose cannon, a vigilante, an agent of the law who turned against the very thing he'd sworn to protect. He was nothing but a psycho bent on carrying out his own agenda of destruction. Ski wondered how someone as levelheaded as Moira had been sucked into the man's game. Yet, he admitted to himself, she was partially right. He had wanted Ross, if not dead, at least incarcerated for the rest of the man's life. However, looking down at the torment etched on her face, he felt no victory. Without speaking, he turned slowly and walked down the long hallway.

Her eyes burned into his back the entire way, but he kept his head up and his pace determined. He was not the bad guy in all this. As he turned the corner, he decided it was time the FBI ended their investigation. As far as he was concerned, the case of Duncan Ross was officially closed.

Moira waited until Ski turned the corner before she entered the hearing room. Her two assistants passed out material from the boxes they'd brought in. The committee members leafed through the stacks set in front of them.

Senator Hutchinson looked up at her. "Miss O'Connor, do you wish to explain this?" He sounded brusque and businesslike, but his voice held a touch of curiosity as he waved a sheath of papers in her direction.

She sat down in the chair so recently vacated by Ski it was still warm. She adjusted the microphone and leaned toward it. "Senator Hutchinson, members of this committee," she testified in a voice strong and clear. "I recently came into possession of the information you have in front of you. Copies have been turned over to the Justice Department. I am in possession of the originals and will retain such until ordered by a court of competent jurisdiction to surrender them. Gentlemen, and lady, as you can see, there is a great deal of information contained in those papers. There is evidence affecting national security. I also have data pertaining to the breakdown of intelligence which includes evidence citing the complicity by members of the intelligence community in this country and by other allies in a duplicitous conspiracy. I would make the suggestion you adjourn, Senator Hutchinson, until such time as the committee members have had time to study this information. Many of the questions you have asked in these hearings very likely will be answered."

The tall Texan cleared his throat, then leaned forward so he could peer up and down the table at his colleagues. As he looked at them, each senator nodded in agreement with his unspoken question.

"Miss O'Connor, this subcommittee will not look a gift horse in the mouth. You stated the Justice Department has copies of all this?"

"Yes, sir. I delivered copies to the Attorney General and his staff this morning before my arrival here."

"Let us hope, then, that they have a better idea of what to do with this than they did the last time." Senator Hutchinson snorted, scoffing at the idea. "At this time, I hereby declare this subcommittee in recess until further notice."

Over the next month, the committee's investigators pieced together the saga of Duncan Ross and Brian Boru. One grizzled veteran reached out to touch an old friend. Following up on the information he gleaned, he confronted a crime analyst at Interpol.

"Wait. You mean to tell me you suspect Ross killed Boru's operatives simply because he contacted them shortly before they were found murdered?" Jack sputtered as an affirmative answer crackled through the trans-Atlantic static on the phone line. "That's a crock of shit and my twelve-year-old granddaughter is a better analyst!"

The more Jack learned about the illusive Boru and Duncan's unrelenting pursuit, the more questions he had concerning Great Britain's intelligence agencies, MI5 and MI6. He wasn't new to the intelligence community. This wouldn't be the first time an agent was betrayed in the name of the "greater good."

Jack found the paper trail Duncan had compiled linking a number of domestic and international corporations with various terrorist groups most interesting. He dug deeper and then met an analyst from the Treasury Department for lunch.

"These companies have supplied everything from money laundering services to computer components and weapons to the terrorists."

"I know," his companion replied. "We're already drawing up subpoenas. Is it true Senator Hutchinson is about to reconvene the Senate Intelligence?" She looked around then leaned closer. "I can't believe how deep this runs. It's scary!" She dropped her voice even lower, all but whispering. "You're going after the FBI files on this Duncan Ross guy, to find out where he is now."

Jack nodded. Keeping his voice soft to match hers, he said, "I heard they managed to track him from Atlanta to Boston and then to Scotland."

The analyst nodded. "I've seen the file. Interpol picked him up in Rome and followed him to Istanbul, Moscow, and Berlin." She took a thumb drive out of her pocket and placed it next to her plate. Louder, she added. "Time to get back to work. It was good to see you, Jack. My regards to the family."

A few hours later, Jack faced Senators Hutchinson and O'Connor over a conference table. "Yessir," he replied to Hutchinson's question. "I'm sure. He met with a high-ranking Army Intelligence officer. There's no doubt the Army was involved in the Berlin fiasco. Interpol and MI6 were stirring up the shit, too." He glanced at Senator O'Connor. "Various agencies have continued to track Boru. He's damned lucky he managed to stay one step ahead of Ross. It was a close thing, according to the info I have. Since Berlin, rumors have him all over the map, from Argentina to Libya to Iraq and Afghanistan."

A tap on the door interrupted his narrative. An aide opened the door, handed Senator Hutchinson a fax, and slipped out. The senator read the paper in his hand, smiled coldly, then passed it around. Bradford Williams had been arrested at the Miami Airport and would be sent to Washington ASAP. His name led the list on an indictment for the sale of banned or restricted material and items to terrorist groups.

"Good." Senator O'Connor spoke for the first time. "Hutch, you know Ellie O'Bannion was questioned extensively and cleared. Allen Steele paid for her to fly home to Ireland with Seamus O'Rourke's body." He turned to Jack. "What about Gemma Todd?"

"She remains under surveillance, just in case. It seems Agent Yazkowski learned his lesson." He paused, swallowed and decided to go for broke. "Your daughter, Moira? She's gone back to work in your office, right?" He watched an array of emotions flit across Senator O'Connor's face. When the other man nodded, Jack continued. "She did a hellava job putting it all together, Senator."

Senator Hutchinson reached over to pat O'Connor on the shoulder. "I'm sorry, Paddy, that the news couldn't be better. As near as we can figure, this Ross fella died in that explosion." He cleared his throat. "How is Moira doin'?"

Patrick shrugged. "She does her job, a bit more relentlessly than she did before. The only time I see her relaxed is when she and Deirdre have their heads together talking about wedding plans." His expression hardened. "So, this is it then? The end?" He stared at Jack, who met his gaze steadily.

"I'm afraid so, Senator O'Connor. Not much in the way of personal closure, but Moira managed to bring down some bad folks."

Later that evening, Patrick stared out the window of his study at the Georgetown house, lost in thought. Glancing at his watch, he was surprised to discover how much time had passed. Mournful ruminations usually left one with too much time to think. He pushed out of his chair. At the door, he turned to gaze at Maeve's portrait. For a long moment, he became lost in the lilac serenity shining from the portrait's eyes.

"He was a good man," he whispered to his wife's memory. "You would have liked him, Maeve. And he truly loved our girl. I know he did. I owe him for her life. Without him, she surely would have died."

Though probably a trick of lighting, he could have sworn Maeve's portrait winked at him. Bemused, he went in search of his daughters. He found them curled up on Deirdre's bed, their heads bent over a magazine. Moira's hair hung loose for once, and the silken tresses fell across Deirdre's shoulder to crown her fiery locks with a golden halo.

As he stood in the doorway watching, Deirdre said something and Moira giggled. He smiled when they looked up. His heart was almost full. His two beautiful daughters were finally sisters. He ignored the sadness bullying its way into his happiness. One would be married in two days' time, the other still mourned her true love.

****

The man standing across the street from the Goergetown house pulled down his hat brim and hunkered deeper into his coat as the light drizzle turned to rain. His eyes never left the square of light in the upstairs window. A car turned the corner and slowly cruised down the street, its headlights sweeping across the gloom. He shrank further back into the shadows, cursing Washington's finest. The squad car stopped in front of the senator's house, and he could clearly see the two officers silhouetted inside. After a long moment, the police car slowly pulled away. He sighed in relief. 'Twouldn't do to get caught now. 'Twouldn't do at all. He still had much to do.

Chapter 29

By noon on the twentieth of June, the O'Connors were ready for the trip to Faerie Glen. Darrell drove the Lincoln with Mrs. Spencer, the housekeeper, riding in front with him, while Deirdre and her father sat in the back. Moira followed in a rental sedan. The two cars cruised down the block, the Lincoln in the lead.

A man watched until the two cars were out of sight. He knew where they were going. There was time enough later to deal with them. Before he could indulge in that particular pleasure, he had to take care of another piece of unfinished business. With purpose in his walk, he hurried down the street in the opposite direction.

Moira drove through the Washington traffic with one eye tuned to her rearview mirror. She'd gone to bed the night before with a vague sense of dread. The bright June morning to which she'd awakened didn't do much to dispel the feeling. She followed Darrell onto the Arlington exit, memorizing the cars following them. As they headed west on I-66, Moira continued to check the vehicles around them. Once they cleared the I-495 loop exchange, traffic thinned. At Warrenton, Virginia, the two cars turned south toward Culpepper and Charlottesville. They were just over an hour away from Faerie Glen.

When she realized her knuckles were white from

gripping the steering wheel, she forced herself to relax. Since leaving the outskirts of Washington, the knot of trepidation lodged in the pit of her stomach unraveled slightly. Though her chest still felt constricted, she could breathe easier now.

The massive stone gateposts of Faerie Glen loomed up. She let the car roll to a stop. That feeling of dread had returned, but with it came a sense of peace. She'd met Duncan here. This is where they'd discovered their entwined destinies. She could almost feel him beside her, his voice whispering in her ear, "Now and forever, bonnie girl."

Patrick, watching out the back window of the Lincoln, was concerned when Moira's car stopped at the gate. He feared all the horror of that night in March would come back to haunt her. After a moment though, her car rolled forward and he relaxed. She was strong, his Moira, just like her mother.

The cars rounded the wide curve and pulled up to the house. All the damage from the gun battle had been repaired. Margaret, John, and his parents waited on the front steps. As Deirdre emerged from the Lincoln, John ran to her and swept her into his arms. Moira smiled, her expression wistful. Her time had come and gone. Now it was Deirdre's. As the greetings progressed at the Lincoln, she climbed out of her sedan.

"May I be of assistance, Miss?"

Moira smiled at the angular butler. Everyone had filled her in on Simpson's part in Duncan's escape. "You already have been." She kissed the startled man on the cheek.

Simpson's formality melted away. "He was a good man, Miss Moira," he declared in stout defense of Duncan. "We shall all miss him."

She squeezed his hand, then opened the back door of the sedan to retrieve a satin dress bag from the back seat of the car. She bestowed the bag on Simpson by laying it across his outstretched arms. "Deirdre's wedding dress," she announced.

"I will ensure it is aired and hung properly, Miss," he replied, the model of efficiency once more. "And your dress, Miss Moira?"

She smiled as she took out the other bag. "It should be fine, Simpson. Thanks."

"I'll see it is hung in your room then, Miss."

"Moira, come inside," Margaret called. "Simpson will see to the luggage."

The next few hours whirled by as the wedding party got into full swing. Deirdre and John beamed at each other throughout the rehearsal and the sumptuous dinner that followed. Ward Winston, as John's best man, paid dutiful attention to her, but she barely noticed his presence. Memories of Duncan echoed around her, and she tried to grab their gossamer threads to weave a protective veil around herself.

Just before ten, Allen asked her to come into his study. He closed the door behind them and gestured for her to take a seat. Mystified, she sank down onto the leather couch. He crossed the room and opened a small safe in the wall. He came back and placed a tartan-wrapped item in her lap. Perplexed, she looked to him for explanation.

"Unwrap it, Moira, and then I'll explain." He answered the question in her eyes with a little nod of encouragement.

The tartan had a red ground with blue and green welts running through it. The item it held looked to be about eight inches long and hard. Carefully, she let the folds of soft wool fall away, revealing a magnificent dirk. Its handle, an intricate Celtic knot, topped its Damascus steel blade etched with Celtic fretwork. Near the hilt, Moira could just make out the words, 'Success Nourishes Hope.'

"Do you know what it is, Moira?" His voice, soft and reverent, belonged in a cathedral. She shook her head. "It's a Scottish *skean dhu*. This is a very personal weapon, worn inside the boot or hose, next to the skin. Because of that, when a Scotsman gave his *skean dhu* to another, it meant he offered his life."

She stared at him for a long moment, and then picked up the dirk. Though metal, it felt warm in her hands. "This belonged to Duncan, didn't it?"

Allen nodded. "It arrived while you were in the hospital. The Feds were still hanging around, so I didn't want to take any chances. Back then, we had hopes he would come back to claim it and give it to you himself. Obviously, that won't happen now. Moira, you do understand the significance of this gift, don't you?"

"His life for mine," she murmured.

He shook his head. "No, my dear. It means he loved you more than life itself."

He returned to the party, leaving her alone with her thoughts. He wasn't surprised when, a few minutes later, Simpson reported Moira had retired for the night.

In the refuge of her room, she mechanically prepared for bed. After tossing and turning for almost an hour, she got up and went to the window. Pulling the curtains back, she stared out into the woods, straining her eyes against the dark. The sky was so cloudy no stars twinkled above. No faerie lights danced in the indigo blackness. No haunting melody sang its way into her heart. She curled up on the window seat, her cold cheek pressed against the warm glass. She dozed off listening for something her heart knew it would never hear again.

"Moira?"

She opened her eyes and for a moment, two golden brown eyes gazed at her. "It's after midnight, child. In to bed with you."

"Da?" She blinked a few times and sighed. That beloved voice and those loving eyes had been only a dream.

She allowed her father to coax her into bed. He pulled the coverlet up to her chin, and bent to kiss her on the forehead. "Sweet dreams, love," he whispered.

"Sweet dreams, bonnie girl," the voice whispered in her heart.

****

Where is the blasted man? He checked the glowing dial on his watch. He'd watched all day and now, most of the night as well. He forced himself to calm down. He hadn't waited this long to botch it up at the last minute. There was time. He would wait. He hated unfinished business.

****

Midsummer's day dawned bright and clear. Even before daylight, the big house at Faerie Glen turned into a beehive of activity. Thanks to the effects of a copious amount of champagne the night before, the bride slept away the morning. In the room across the hall, her sister finally did the same. After a dark night filled with haunting images and whispers, Moira fell into a deep sleep as the first fingers of the sun's rays chased the demons back into the dark recesses of her mind.

****

At ten o'clock, a maid appeared with a tray. Moira nibbled Cook's hot cinnamon rolls and savored the cup of café au lait the maid poured for her. "Luncheon will be served at noon in Mrs. Steele's sitting room," the maid informed her.

She smiled. Margaret was a traditionalist, and would not allow John and Deirdre to see each other before the wedding ceremony late that afternoon.

Finishing the roll and coffee, she padded into

the bath for a long, hot shower. She stripped down and stared at her reflection in the full-length mirror. She'd lost weight and her high cheekbones stood out prominently above her hollow cheeks. Faint circles left smudges under her dark lashes. Her long neck seemed almost too thin and her ribs were visible. Her dress had been refitted twice already, and she hoped it wouldn't hang off her today. Turning on the shower full blast, she stepped into its stinging spray. Scrubbing vigorously, she tried to scour away the cobwebs left from the night filled with demons.

As soon as she stepped out of the bathroom, she saw her sister on the foot of her bed waiting. Deirdre wailed, "Aunt Margaret won't let me see John."

She stared wide-eyed at her sister, then burst out laughing. Deirdre's tangled hair and leftover mascara gave her a frightful appearance. "I don't think you want John to see your raccoon eyes right now. Trust me, you'd scare him away before the knot could be tied," she giggled.

Deirdre glanced at the mirror on Moira's dressing table and yelped. Then she started to giggle, too. "I can't believe how nervous I am," she finally choked out, wiping tears from her eyes. "I just know if I could see John, he'd tell me everything will be all right."

Sitting on the bed, she took both of Deirdre's hands in hers. "No one else can tell you that. You have to know it in your own heart." She tilted her head, staring into her sister's emerald green eyes. "Deirdre, do you love John?"

"Oh, yes!"

"Can you imagine living your life without him?"

Deirdre's eyes grew as round as saucers as she thought about the unimaginable. "No," she whispered. "John is my life now."

Moira squeezed her hands. "Then you have nothing to be nervous about."

Deirdre searched her face for a long moment. "I know things haven't always been easy between us."

She shook her head gently, hoping her sister wouldn't continue. She did anyway.

"It's just not fair, Moira. You were always the good one. The quiet one. The one everybody loved."

Moira looked up quickly, shocked by Deirdre's words. She'd always felt Deirdre had been the favored child.

"It's not fair that I have John and you..." Deirdre gulped back tears. "I saw his face, Moira," she continued. "When Da said you were missing. He loved you so much. As the hours ticked away and we thought you might be dead..." She paused to clear the lump from her throat with a hard swallow and cough. "I'm sorry, Moira. Sorry for everything."

She leaned over and hugged her hard. "Your time will come, little sister. There will be another," Deirdre tried to promise.

Moira gently disentangled herself from Deirdre's arms. "Let's get you cleaned up. You can't go to lunch looking like this—even if John has been banned for the duration." The last thing she wanted was to believe. There would never be another. Ever.

Lunch was a cozy affair, just Margaret and the two sisters. Deirdre's nerves got the best of her and she only picked at her food. For the first time in months, Moira's appetite had returned and she ate everything on her plate and then some. At two o'clock, Margaret shooed the girls back to their rooms to rest before it was time to dress.

At 4:30, Moira pulled the peach silk gown over her head. She zipped it up and adjusted the neckline. Softly shirred straps accented the sweetheart neckline, and the fitted bodice showed off her narrow waist. Layers of iridescent silk made the full, tea-length skirt shimmer with a life of its own. She wore her mother's necklace and Duncan's ring with matching fire opals shimmering in her ears.

She brushed her hair up on top of her head, secured it with some pins, and crowned the cascading curls with the circlet of fresh flowers the maid delivered. Using just a dab of makeup, she touched up the dark circles under her eyes, finishing with a brush of shimmering peach lipstick across her lips. Ready, she stepped across the hall to Deirdre's room.

As the maid fussed with the train on Deirdre's gown, she stared in awe. "You are beautiful, Deirdre." Her words sighed out, heartfelt and admiring.

Made of creamy, antique silk moiré, the gown set off Deirdre's skin to perfection, and its Victorian style was perfect for her tall figure. The Irish lace of her flower-bedecked veil didn't even come close to containing the radiance of her blazing hair. The maid handed them their bouquets, and hand-in-hand, the two sisters walked down the hallway, then regally descended the grand staircase.

Patrick awaited them on the last step. *My sun and my moon,* he thought, gazing up at them. *And you are my guiding star, Maeve.*

With Moira in front and Deirdre on his arm, they waited at the French doors leading to the terrace. Simpson nodded approvingly at Deirdre and flashed Moira an almost paternal smile as he spoke softly into a walkie-talkie. A string quartet in the garden below began to play, the sweet notes drifting up to the terrace. Simpson threw open the doors.

Moira stepped onto the terrace and the late afternoon sun embraced her with its soft radiance. The guests assembled in the garden released a collective sigh. Moira's pale skin seemed translucent under the softly filtered light and, as light played on the opalescent sheen of her dress, a golden aura surrounded her. She looked fragile, and as beautiful as some ethereal creature captured in a land of mystical mists.

A woman leaned over to her young daughter. "You asked if there were really fairies here," she whispered to the child. "There's your answer. If you squint your eyes and look just right, you'll see her gossamer wings." The little girl could only stare in wonder as Moira floated by them.

John, standing at the front of the gathering, let out a sigh. He thought his new sister-in-law was the most beautiful woman he'd ever seen. Then he saw Patrick with Deirdre on his arm. His heart caught in his throat. Under the late afternoon sun, Deirdre's hair took on a life of its own, shimmering and dancing with red and gold sparks. Her green eyes glimmered like the emeralds she wore around her neck, and the smile on her full red lips was meant only for him.

Margaret watched Moira as the young woman drifted down the white satin aisle cloth. Her eyes held a faraway look as a secret smile hovered about her lips. Margaret refused to turn around to look at John and the priest. If she did, the spell would be broken. Margaret knew in her heart the ghost of Duncan Ross awaited his bride, just as surely as John awaited his.

Patrick gave Deirdre's hand to John and sat down beside Margaret. As the priest recited the vows, a voice as sweet as spun sugar crooned a Gaelic love song. When the priest pronounced them husband and wife, John kissed his bride to a thundering ovation, but Moira's ears still echoed with the refrain from the poignant melody.

Following the ceremony, the wedding party posed for the inevitable pictures and, as twilight caressed the garden with gentle fingers, the group joined the rest of the guests in the great hall for the reception. After the initial flood of well-wishers and most everyone in the room had a glass of some sort in their hands, the best man claimed the microphone.

"May I have your attention," Ward announced. "I'd make a toast to the bride, but she is so beautiful I'm left speechless." He paused to let the laughter and jovial murmurs of agreement die away. "Seriously, folks, this is a happy occasion. My best friend has gotten married. The problem is, this is the only toast I can remember." He held up his fluted champagne stem. "John, Deirdre, may the road rise to meet you, may the wind be always at your back, and when the time comes, may you both be in heaven an hour before the devil knows you're dead."

Ward gulped his champagne and grinned sheepishly as he was hooted from the microphone. "Hey, I did my job," he insisted. "I got the groom here on time and sober. What more do you want?"

The crowd laughed appreciatively. Now they looked to Moira, as maid of honor, to make the next toast. She took Ward's place at the microphone.

"I usually write the speeches," she began, "not deliver them." She paused a beat as the guests chuckled. "A long time ago, I read this in a romance novel, and I've saved the words ever since." She held up her flute. "Deirdre, John, to love is nothing. To be loved is something. To love and be loved is everything. Here's to everything, now and forever."

"Hear, hear," someone shouted.

"Now and forever," the crowd echoed.

She raised her glass in salute. *Now and forever, Duncan Ross,* her heart whispered.

The small orchestra struck up an Irish jig, and John and Deirdre led the first dance. Patrick claimed Moira and whirled her away. She was barely aware of her surroundings as she danced with one partner and then another. Somewhere, just on the edge of the music, she kept hearing the echo of that magical voice and the words captured in her heart and mind. *By the life that courses in my blood and the love that resides within my heart, take thee to my hand, my heart, and my spirit to be my chosen one.*

****

Manannan could not be angry with the Harper. He, too, had wanted to bless the union of the two humans. Allowing Abhean to sing the binding song seemed simple enough. He knew the truth now. For a brief moment, he wondered if he would have changed things had he known before. He shrugged. Probably not.

Chapter 30

Michael Shanahan pushed open the door to his darkened apartment. He flipped the light switch. Nothing happened. Muttering curses under his breath, he put down his overnight bag and briefcase. Cautiously stumbling across the room, he tried a lamp near the sofa. It, too, didn't work. Puzzled, he peered around.

A metallic click echoed behind him and he froze. That chilling sound was all too familiar. A good ten feet from the front door, he still might make it out if he stayed low. He gathered himself to try but never got the chance. An orange tongue of flame spit at him from a dark corner and he crumpled to the floor, his left kneecap shattered by the bullet.

He stared up at the dark figure looming over him. "I've been waitin' a long time for that, Michelean O'Shaughnessy," a cold voice informed him. He closed his eyes as the pistol boomed again, groaning as the bullet blasted through his other knee. "That was a present from Belfast," the cold voice hissed. The black shadow pulled something from his waist and through the red mist of pain clouding his eyes, he saw the wicked-looking blade of a knife gleam dully.

He had no doubt his tongue was about to be cut out, but he would have the last word. "I'll be seein' ya in hell." He spit at the man.

"He'll be there long before you, Mick," a calm voice announced from the doorway.

The man standing over him whirled, bringing his gun up to fire. He reacted too slow. The man in the door fired one shot. A look of surprise flitted across the shadow's face as he crumpled to lie next to him on the floor. Michael fought to stay conscious. The man he stared up at had to be a dream—or a nightmare. Then he looked at the man stretched out beside him. Even as he watched, the sinister greenish-yellow light faded from Brian Boru's eyes.

"And that's the end of the bloody bastard."

"If you say so," his spectral savior replied.

The dark man leaned over Boru's body, rummaging through all the pockets. Whatever he searched for wasn't there so he turned to the body itself. He found his prize at last, dangling from a chain around the dead man's neck. As Michael watched, the man brutally jerked the chain, breaking it. A silver locket came away in his clinched fist. He turned to look at him. "I need a favor, Mick O'Shaughnessy."

"Anything," he answered, gritting his teeth against the pain.

"Tell them the game is over."

"That it is, my dark friend." He groaned. "For all of us," he tried to add, gasping from the pain. He took a couple of deep breaths. "You can't be real," he mumbled, beginning to lose his hold on consciousness.

"Help is on the way," that calm voice reassured him. "They'll be here soon, Mick."

"Don't be worryin' 'bout me," he replied groggily, and then promptly passed out as the scent of dead roses filled his nostrils.

When he awoke, he listened to the voices floating somewhere over his head. A man he presumed to be a paramedic worked diligently. His quiet voice soothed Michael. Two other voices sounded sharp and discordant to the floating feeling in his brain and extremities.

"An anonymous 9-1-1 call. The first unit on the scene found this guy unconscious with a 9 mm pistol clutched in his hand, and two shattered knees. They also found that guy dead, shot once, just like you see. The knife is still clutched in one hand, and the Beretta pistol over there is within reach, like he dropped it when he was shot. Forensics will confirm if the Beretta was fired and who pulled the trigger."

Michael heard shuffling and the rustle of clothing. He pictured the two detectives squatting down to examine the body.

"Holy crap. That bullet hole is dead center between the eyes." A low whistle accompanied the exclamation. When the voice spoke again, speculation hovered around each word. "If I read this right, the professor here came home and the guy in black confronted him."

"Pretty damn good shooting for a man who's been knee-capped."

"If you disagree, give me your version."

Michael winced. He needed to find his voice, explain what happened. He swallowed and tried to speak.

"Easy now, guy," the paramedic said.

The voice of the second police officer overrode the paramedic's comfort. "I think there was a third person here and that was the shooter."

"No," Michael croaked. He swallowed, working up enough spit to speak clearly. "Is he dead? He shot me. Stood over me with the knife to cut out my tongue. I shot back. No one else. There was no one else."

He forced his eyes open, his stomach roiling as the scene swam before him. Had he actually seen that specter? Heard that damnable voice?

"Are you guys done? We need to transport Mr. Shanahan."

Michael closed his eyes against the bone-jarring pain as hands rolled him and lifted him onto a gurney. He swallowed the bile erupting in his throat. Damn but it hurt.

As they wheeled him out into the warm June night, a shadow flitted across the lighted doorway across the street. He tensed. Had anyone else seen it? Before he could decide, shooting stars exploded in his head and the darkness swallowed him once again.

****

When he next regained consciousness, Michael realized he was in the emergency room. Frantic activity seeming to have very little to do with him surrounded him. He recognized the voice of the doubting cop above the hubbub.

"What do you mean the case is closed?" The man all but shouted into his cell phone. "Wait. Run that by me again? Who called?" He gulped several deep breaths. "Who the hell is this Colin Keller character that the British Embassy and the FBI would yank the chief's chain?" He listened for a long moment. "Terrorist? Interpol most wanted list under the name Brian Boru? Who the hell is this professor that some international assassin came to take him out?" He snorted. "Need to know basis. Fuck that. This is an on-going investigation."

Michael had been right. His attacker had been Boru. He'd recognized the voice, remembered it from the dark days he'd spent in Belfast as an informant.

The cop barked again. "What the hell? I mean..." His voice trailed off, his dismay evident in his tone. "So the official damn version is that Keller was the perp, Shanahan killed him in self-defense, and fuck the evidence?"

Michael sympathized. Confronted with the same

set of circumstances during his career, he'd been bloody well brassed-off, too. When he was back on his feet, he'd send the cop a bottle of good Irish whiskey. The pain ebbed and flowed through him and then something sharp and burning hit his circulatory system. Suddenly pain free, he drifted back into the darkness, thinking he owed someone else a bottle of whiskey as well.

****

Michael's savior waited in the shadows nearby until he knew the little British Intelligence agent, alias Professor Michael Shanahan, would survive. Turning sharply on his heel, he slipped out of the hospital, strode around the corner, and climbed into the small, Rover sedan that was Shanahan's pride and joy. He turned the ignition key and the engine coughed to sullen life. He had to pump the gas pedal several times before the engine leveled out to run smoothly.

He pushed the little Rover to its limits, leaving the lights of Washington far behind. This was Midsummer's Night, and he had a promise to fulfill. He refused to be late. Not this time.

****

Simpson took the phone call in the butler's pantry. No, he told the caller, he would not disturb Senator O'Connor during his daughter's wedding reception to take a call. He listened intently for several minutes. "Yes, sir," he vowed into the receiver. "I will give him the message personally." The butler's mouth formed a grim line on his face as he hung up the phone. He had never claimed to be more than a former soldier and now a butler. He'd never wanted to be a judge or an executioner, but the news he'd just received made him want to be both. Served the bloody bastard right.

He checked on the kitchen staff. Glancing out one of the kitchen's wide windows, he saw a pale figure drift into the garden. His heart went out to the wraith gliding through the fragrant flowers.

****

With the coming of darkness, the garden transformed into a wonderland. Twinkling lights festooned every tree and shrub. Flowers in full bloom perfumed the soft summer air with a potpourri of fragrances. Moira wandered through the fairyland until she came to the arbor where she and Duncan had first discovered their entwined lives after learning of that other Moira and her fairy lover. In this place, she'd felt hopeful and filled with the wonder of new love. Now draped with delicate wisteria blooms, it provided a secluded hideaway. She settled on the bench and tried to relax. A couple, unaware of her presence, strolled by hand-in-hand. They stopped in front of the arbor, embraced, and kissed.

The icy lump that was her heart had thawed from the happy events, but watching this couple? Her heart froze even harder than before. Clearing Duncan's name and planning Deirdre's wedding had given her something to think about, something to divert her focus away from her own misery. In an hour or so, the festivities would end. Her life now stretched out interminably before her—a life bleak and empty.

The couple moved off, whispering and clinging to each other. She watched their departure through misty eyes, and shivered in the chilly night air. Laughter floated down from the terrace. She closed her eyes and sighed, wondering if she'd ever laugh again. When she opened her eyes, a little girl stood staring at her.

"Are you a fairy princess?" the child asked.

Moira felt her soft smile almost reach her eyes as it settled around her mouth. "No."

"You look like a fairy princess," the little girl

persisted.

"Why aren't you at the party?"

The little girl shrugged elegantly. "I got bored. Do you know any stories?" The ingenious child gazed at her hopefully.

Moira studied her a moment. "What kind of stories?"

"I like fairies. My mother told me you were a fairy." The little girl wasn't giving up on the idea. "If you don't know any stories, I could tell you my favorite," she offered. She sat down beside Moira and gazed up at her earnestly. Moira smiled back and nodded. "Long ago and far away, far over the ocean in a land called Eire, there lived a girl," the child began.

"Not a fairy princess?" she interrupted with a smile.

The child frowned at her. "No, just a girl. One day, she was out in the woods and met a handsome stranger. They fell in love, and planned to live happily ever after. But, a terrible ogre..." The girl paused and gave her a meaningful look, "You do know what an ogre is, don't you?"

Moira nodded solemnly, trying vainly not to smile.

"Anyway, this ugly, horrible ogre found the two of them. There was a great battle. The ogre killed the handsome stranger and kidnapped the fair maiden."

"How awful." She hid her smile.

"Definitely," the child agreed before continuing. "The ogre took the maiden to his dark castle, and kept her prisoner for years and years. No one ever came to rescue her. Then, one night, when the moon was full..." She looked up at the sky and noted, "...just like tonight. Anyway, a dark stranger on a blood red horse rode up to the castle gate. He knew the ogre could be defeated in battle only on

Midsummer's Night and only when the moon was full. The battle was awful, but the dark stranger finally killed the ogre, and he claimed his prize—the fair maiden. The dark stranger swept her into his arms, jumped onto his horse, and galloped away into the night. When the horse stopped, the maiden realized she was in the exact same place where she'd met her own true love. The place where the ogre had killed him all those long years ago."

The little girl paused to catch a breath. "The dark stranger threw off his hood and cloak, and the maiden knew he was her true love, alive and well. He was a fairy prince and the ogre hadn't really killed him, only placed him under a horrible spell. The fairy king and queen finally broke the spell so the prince could rescue the maiden, and make her his bride."

"And they lived happily ever after?"

"Of course," the child asserted. "Isn't that the way all fairy tales end?"

"Maeve!"

Startled, Moira and the child both flinched. An attractive woman, hands on her hips scowled down at the little girl. "Maeve Brown, where have you been? I've been looking all over for you."

"I've been right here, Mummy," Maeve answered matter-of-factly. "I've been telling the fairy princess a lovely story."

Maeve's mother turned to her. "I hope she hasn't been bothering you." Her voice held a hint of apology.

Moira hastened to reassure the woman. "Not in the least. I enjoyed her story." She then smiled at the little girl. "My mother's name was Maeve."

The woman took Maeve's hand and led her off. Suddenly, the child darted back to her and planted a kiss on her cheek. "Your fairy prince will come back soon," the little girl told her solemnly, her eyes wise beyond her years.

Before she could respond, little Maeve skipped back to her mother, and the two disappeared up the path. Moira stared after them. "I only wish that was possible." The breeze caught her whisper and whisked it off into the night.

Back in the great hall, Simpson found the Senator talking with Allen. In his clipped accent, he informed the two men of the attack on Michael Shanahan and the death of Brian Boru. Patrick searched the room for Moira but she was nowhere to be seen. *Tomorrow,* he thought. *I'll tell her tomorrow. There will be time enough then, and she'll have peace at last knowing that monster is dead.*

Simpson returned to the kitchen to marshal his forces. The buffet table was running low, and more champagne needed to be chilled. His curt orders sent the staff scurrying. Deep inside, he hoped Boru's death had been long and painful. It was the very least the bloody SOB deserved for all the suffering he'd caused to so many people, especially those dear to his heart.

All too soon, John and Deirdre were ready for their departure. The crowd gathered on the front steps and lined the drive. Darrel pulled the Lincoln around and waited with the back door open. The newlyweds appeared at the door. Deirdre paused long enough to throw her bouquet. A young woman standing next to Moira caught it, much to the embarrassment of her escort.

Deirdre kissed her father, then Moira, and John bundled his bride into the back seat. After the car vanished around the bend, the party began to break up.

An hour later, when all the guests had departed, John's parents retired to their room, and Margaret headed to her suite for a long bubble bath. Allen and Patrick disappeared into Allen's private study for their customary nightcap. Simpson dismissed most of the exhausted staff and supervised the rest in their clean-up efforts.

Moira strolled out onto the terrace for a breath of air. Jasmine and honeysuckle mingled with the spicy-sweet scent of magnolia. As she watched, the lights in the garden winked out one by one. The full moon cast a soft, opalescent glow over the landscape. Dew formed and the droplets glittered like tiny diamonds in the moonlight. Taking a last deep breath to savor the scented air, she went up to her room.

Once there, she started a hot bath before stepping out of her gown. As she sank up to her chin in the hot, steamy embrace of the bathwater, she closed her eyes and her shoulders relaxed. Tension oozed away. When she next opened her eyes, Moira wasn't sure how long she'd dozed. The water was tepid, and the air chilled her skin as she stepped out. Wrapping a huge, fluffy towel around her, she went into the bedroom.

She stopped dead in her tracks. The door to the hall had just clicked shut. She nervously scanned the room, all of her senses alert. The coverlet had been turned down with her nightgown draped across the foot of the bed. She rolled her eyes, tickled by her own foolishness. The maid had obviously come in, and likely left just as she got out of the tub.

After drying off, she slipped the nightgown over her head. Made of white lawn, it felt smooth against her skin. Cut like an old-fashioned petticoat, the fitted bodice tied with satin ribbons and lace edged the full skirt.

She brushed out her long hair and climbed into bed. Switching off the lamp, she lay back against the pillows and tried to sleep. Her right hand slipped under her pillow. Her fingers curled lovingly around the hilt of Duncan's *skean dhu*.

Lying there in the dark, she imagined music playing very faintly. With a start, she realized the music was real. Drawn to the window, she pulled back the curtains and opened it. She heard the music more distinctly now—pipes, a flute and some stringed instrument she couldn't identify.

As she watched, a glowing orb danced through the woods, a troop of fluttering fireflies following. The music swirled around her, tugging and pulling her. Entranced, she snatched a soft cashmere throw, tossed it around her shoulders, and hurried out. Her bare feet made no sound as she skipped down the stairs and out into the night.

Insistent now, the music plucked at her soul, and the distant faerie lights beckoned to her, their dance seductive and beguiling. Without hesitation, she followed the summons into the woods. The music swelled around her, carrying her along a path farther and farther from the main house. The lights twinkled about her, teasing and tantalizing just out of her reach. She longed to capture one of those orbs, to hold its soft glow in the palm of her hand.

The music faded on a last discordant note, and the lights winked out. Bemused, she blinked. The moonlight, so bright before, seemed dim here as it filtered through the canopy of branches above her head. She shivered. Her hand clutched Duncan's *skean dhu*. She gripped it tighter, a bit surprised. She didn't remember picking it up. As if a cloud had suddenly cleared the face of the moon, the gloom brightened. Ghostly moonlight now illuminated a wide path stretching deeper into the forest. Moira looked behind her. Threatening shadows reached out to engulf her. Squaring her shoulders, she set her feet on the path, following its faint beacon.

She lost all sense of time. It seemed as though she had been walking this dim trail forever. A night bird called off to the side, its voice mocking her. She gripped the *skean dhu* tighter, holding it before her like a talisman. Behind her, the darkness still reached out to trap her. Ahead of her, the path dipped into a small hollow. The sound of running water sang to her. No longer afraid, Moira ran up the path, sure of her location now.

Chapter 31

Simpson, his shirtsleeves still rolled up, hurried across the entry hall. He must stop that infernal pounding before it woke the entire household. The massive wooden doors actually shuddered with each battering blow. He wondered if a drunken guest had returned after realizing he was in no shape to drive home. In deference to his position, Simpson straightened his tie and buttoned his vest before opening one of the doors a crack.

"It's the middle of the night, you bloody fool," he growled before the apparition standing in the door froze the words in his throat.

The phantom, who by all rights could not exist, shouldered his way through the door and stared, wild-eyed and frantic, around the entry. "Where is she?"

Still speechless, Simpson could only point up the stairs. The man took the stairs three at a time. The butler stood rooted to the spot, watching as the rippling muscles in the man's legs carried him up and out of sight.

He sprinted down the hallway and threw open the door to Moira's room with such force the door banged hollowly against the wall. The bed was empty. With long, purposeful strides, he crossed the room and checked the bath. Turning back to the bedroom, he saw the curtains flutter gently. Drawn to the open window, he stared out. Faerie fire danced in the woods below.

He bounded down the stairs, brushing by the bewildered Simpson. At a dead run, he hit the front door, knocking it open, and was gone.

Simpson stared at the door as it slowly swung back and forth on its well-oiled hinges. Out of long-practiced habit, he rolled down his sleeves and buttoned the cuffs. He shut and locked the front doors. Retreating to the pantry, he snagged a bottle of Scotch from the liquor cabinet. After twisting off the lid, he took a long swig of the fiery liquid. Recapping the bottle, he turned on his heel, marched to his room, and went to bed.

****

Leaving the house, the man who was no longer a ghost sprinted down the path to the stable and burst through the door. Spooked, the horses stamped and whinnied. He grabbed a bridle and strode to a stall. The big, red horse with liquid brown eyes nickered to him.

"Hello, big un." He soothed the horse as he slipped on the bridle. He led the horse out, mounted bareback, and put his heels to the horse's sides. The big sorrel leaped forward and galloped down the road. The horse shortened his stride as his rider guided him onto the narrow path leading into the woods. Leaning low over the animal's neck, rider and horse became one.

Thorny branches grabbed at his hair and shirt, trying to pull him from his mount. Oblivious, he urged the big horse to greater speed. A large branch stretched out and snagged the rider's shirt, ripping the buttons from it. His long, dark hair mingled with the blood red mane of the sorrel. With a final burst of power, the horse crashed through the ring of trees and slid to a stop.

The brook sang its melody in the moonlit glen.

Sleepy flowers nodded in the gentle breeze. The horse blew softly and stamped a foot, sending the perfume of crushed flowers wafting through the air. Fireflies of every shape and color danced across the meadow. Enthralled, the rider gazed at the golden vision sitting across the glade.

****

Moira stared at the phantom rider, her heart barely beating. Like some ancient highland warrior, he had galloped into her dreams. "What are you looking at, sir?" she called, her voice ringing clear in the warm, summer air.

"I'm looking at you, miss," he answered, his voice husky. The expression on his face, visible in the pale moonlight, reflected both longing and admiration.

He slid off the horse. Letting the reins trail, he strode across the space separating them. She flew to him, and he caught her about the waist, lifting her high and spinning them both around. He slowly lowered her to his chest, her arms curling around his neck.

She looked deep into his honey-brown eyes. Her fingers wove through his long hair as he kissed her, his mouth tasting her with a slow, almost hesitant nibble. Their hearts beat madly as his arms tightened around her.

"I've missed ye, bonnie girl," he whispered against her lips. He let her slide slowly down the length of his body to stand on her own feet. Stepping back, he reached into a pocket of his jeans. He pulled out a silver locket and opened it. A curl of golden silk lay inside. "I believe this is yours," he whispered. She shivered, remembering how that lock of hair had been taken from her. He gathered her into his arms and kissed her harder, his tongue parting her lips so he could sample her mouth. Sweeping her up, he carried her back to the square of cashmere she'd dropped near the brook. Kneeling, he set her down on it.

She traced the angles of his face with her fingers, memorizing every detail. Taking her wrists, he stilled her hands so he could kiss each fingertip. She studied the feathery tracings of hair on his chest, longing to kiss the sculpted muscles they covered. She nuzzled his chest, and he groaned. Her tongue traced the hard ridges of his muscles down toward more feathery hair. His breath caught in his throat.

"No," he whispered, "not yet, bonnie girl." He gently pushed her away and stripped off the remains of his shirt.

With one finger, Moira gently traced the white scar grazing his rib cage. With soft lips, she kissed the puckered skin on his shoulder. He crushed her to his chest, kissing her lips, her throat, her eyes. One arm circled her waist, holding her to him while his other hand tangled in her hair.

Like a starving man desperate for food, he covered her body with kisses, leaving her breathless and aching for more. Her breasts strained against the smooth material of the gown's bodice. He tugged at the top ribbon and then the next, continuing until the material parted to reveal the soft fullness of her breasts. With what felt like agonizing tenderness, his hands caressed her arms from wrists to shoulders. His fingers flirted with the straps of her gown, finally coaxing them down to her elbows.

"Please," she whispered, swaying toward him. She gasped as his strong, hard hands cupped her breasts. She pressed her hardened nipples into his palms as the warmth from his fingers spread across her body, sending shock waves into the very core of her being. Her fingers dug into his muscled biceps as she arched toward him.

"Slow, bonnie girl, slow," he implored. He pulled

away from her and turned his back. As he tugged and jerked to get his boots off, the muscles bunched and rippled across his broad back. Standing up, he stripped off his jeans and tossed them aside. Turning, he gazed down at her. Golden lights danced in his eyes.

She smiled.

He smiled in return. As he watched, her skirt hiked up, revealing long, lithe legs. As that sight teased him, she lay back on the grass, her hair fanning out like a golden nimbus. She was almost too beautiful to touch. Kneeling beside her, he gathered her into his arms to cradle her in his lap. With a deft motion, he flipped the flimsy nightgown over her head. Still holding her, he shifted positions so they lay side by side. Her fingers drew small circles through the hair on his chest. While one arm cradled her, his free hand explored the silky skin of her thigh and hip.

His hand slipped between her thighs, testing her readiness. Hot and slick, she pushed against his hand. Kneeling between her legs, his strong hands rested softly on her hips. "'Tis time, bonnie girl." He lowered himself to cover her.

His erection, thick and hard with need, pressed against her. She gasped as he pushed into her depths, tears glistened at the corners of her eyes.

"Shh, bonnie girl," he soothed, kissing away her tears. "Lie still and relax for me. 'Twill pass soon enough." He kissed her deeply as he slowly pushed further into her very center. With aching gentleness, he pulled back and her body arched against him, as if his withdrawal left her feeling bereft. She wrapped her arms around his back, attempting to hold him inside her. Smiling against her lips, he pushed back inside, deeper still. With a leisurely rhythm, he moved within her—in, out, back again. He could feel rippling waves spread out from deep within her, and she matched him move for move. The waves built. Harder. Faster. Deeper. His hands and mouth were everywhere as his body claimed hers for eternity. Her hands kneaded the hard muscles of his buttocks as she tried to force him deeper inside her. He groaned. Deep within his soul, words formed and he whispered them into the night.

"By the life that courses in my blood and the love that resides within my heart, I take thee to my hand, my heart, and my spirit, to be my chosen one. To desire thee and to be desired by thee. To possess thee and to be possessed by thee. I promise to love thee wholly in life and beyond where we shall meet, remember, and love again. Our love is a beginning without end, until the end of time. You are chosen."

The words he vowed danced on the gentle night wind and the sound of pipes playing off in the distance lent wings to his vow. He felt her tense as she arched to meet his thrust, her inner muscles clenching around him, both caressing and gripping his shaft.

"Duncan!" She screamed and he recognized all the agony and longing, all the fear, all the love that had been locked away in her heart.

"I'm here, bonnie girl," his voice whispered in the dark.

****

The warm fingers of the sun's first rays danced across her face, teasing her eyes open. Faeries had painted the glen in pastel shades of pink and gold. She stretched beneath the soft cashmere throw she'd slept under. Naked, she lay on her nightgown.

The rising sun poked a bright finger through a break in the trees, blinding her with its intensity. Blinking away the brightness, she realized a dark figure loomed over her. Dark hair spilled across his wide shoulders. His broad chest tapered to a narrow waist and long muscular, jean-clad legs. She blinked again as Duncan knelt beside her. She propped herself up on one elbow, her eyes wide with wonder.

"It wasn't a dream," she whispered, afraid her voice would break the spell.

He cupped her cheek in his big hand. "It definitely wasn't a dream, bonnie girl," he drawled. A wicked grin crinkled his cheeks, and his brown eyes twinkled with devilish amber lights as he leaned over to kiss her.

Her pulse raced to keep up with the rapid increase in her breathing. The cashmere throw slipped off her shoulder but she didn't care. She wanted this man more than she had ever wanted anything in her life. She reached for the top button of his jeans.

She made her intentions plain enough for him to read. He playfully swatted away her hands. "Oh, no you don't," he chided, even as he squirmed to ease his obvious erection. "I've got to get you home before the whole house turns out looking for you."

He swiveled around and reached for his boots. His hand closed on thin air as she pulled him over backwards. Before he could react, his arms and hands were full of naked skin and golden hair. Laughing, he tried to fend off her seductive attack. Then she started kissing him—on the pulse point of his neck, the hollow of his shoulder, and finally his mouth.

Moira's inexperienced hands fumbled with his buttons so he brushed her hands away. "I'll do that," he growled. His jeans constricted him to the point of pain now so he squirmed out of them and clasped her to him. Her mouth found his and she kissed him. Her tongue pushed into his mouth, dueling with his.

His arms bound her to his chest, then one hand found the damp curls at the top of her thighs. She was hot and ready. He pushed a finger into her.

When her hands found his heavy erection and

her fingertips danced along the length of him, he groaned. Her mouth trailed kisses from his chin, down his neck, across his chest, and... He gasped when he realized her intentions. Her tongue swirled across the smooth tip of his shaft and the shudder that ran through him rocked his very soul. When she took him into her mouth, he came close to losing all control.

Almost roughly, he dragged her head up so he could kiss her mouth, and his tongue replaced his erection. He pushed her back on the grass with her legs spread wide. His body fit so perfectly in the soft cushion of her hips as she arched to meet him. He entered her and pushed all the way to her core.

The sensation of having him inside her forced a sigh of pleasure from Moira. Duncan was so rigid and thick, he filled her completely. The friction of his movements caused volcanic ripples deep in her center as he stroked hard and sure, and she matched him thrust for thrust. She wanted all of him buried deep within her. He kissed her long and hungrily, his tongue and lips tasting her as if she were some succulent treat. His hands cupped her breasts, his thumbs polishing her nipples. He broke off their kiss, lavishing attention on one of her nipples.

As he pulled her nipple into his mouth, Moira thought she might faint from the sheer pleasure of it all. His shadow beard rasped against her skin, heightening her pleasure. Then the first contraction hit, rippling out from her core. His hands cupped her buttocks, tilting her hips so he could drive deeper into her. She panted, murmuring his name over and over like a prayer—or a plea. Her whole body shuddered as he took her up and over the edge while she clung to him, her body rippling around him, milking him. He pumped his life into her.

Exhausted, she lay back on the grass as he collapsed on top of her, totally spent. After a long moment, he started to roll away. Her arms tightened across his back and her legs wrapped tightly around his hips, holding him in her.

"I'm afraid my weight will crush you."

"Don't worry. I'm sturdier than I look." She never wanted him to move, never wanted to be away from him again. "Who are you, Duncan Ross?" she whispered.

This time, when he moved to roll off her, she didn't stop him. He pulled her to him so his shoulder cradled her head, and his legs entwined with hers. The soft sound of his breath in her ear left her question unanswered.

A few minutes later, he rolled her away from him and playfully swatted her bare bottom. "We have to go," he growled. The look on his face left no room for argument. She slipped her nightgown over her head. He reached over to tie the ribbons on her bodice, giving her breasts a fond caress as he tied the last one.

He pulled on his jeans and buttoned them. As he shrugged into his shirt, he realized most of the buttons had been torn off the night before. He tucked the tails into his jeans, and hoped for the best as he stamped his feet into his soft, leather boots.

The big sorrel grazed contentedly across the glen. He snagged the horse's reins and led him back to where Moira waited. He adjusted the bridle, then vaulted gracefully to the animal's back. He caught her with one arm and swung her up behind him.

As the horse picked his way through the trees to the path, she let her fingers play across the muscles of his stomach. His big paw caught both her hands.

"Be still, woman, lest I take you here and now."

She giggled and pressed against his broad back. She felt his muscles ripple and a shudder surge through his body. He grabbed her, and swung her around in front of him so her round bottom sat snuggly between his thighs, and her legs trailed over his right leg. He kissed her soundly with a loud smack.

"Enough, woman. Time to get you home."

She gazed deeply into his warm brown eyes for a long moment. Her arms circled his waist as she laid her head against his shoulder. "I am home."

He kissed the top of her head and rested his chin on the spot. "I'm the man who loves you, Moira O'Connor. Loves you now and forever," he murmured into her hair, finally answering her question.

Silver James

Epilogue

The King of Tir Nan Óg glared at the Harper. "You are incorrigible," he declared, his voice booming like distant thunder heralding a summer storm.

Abhean continued playing his pipes, a lilting tune that had the flowers dancing in the breeze. He finished the ditty, laid aside his instrument and faced the other fae. "Would you have me do other than I did?"

His expression revealed nothing to Manannan Mac Lir, not that it mattered. His king knew exactly what concession he sought and hence refused to answer, replying instead with a question of his own. "Are you ready to leave well enough alone?" Abhean laughed. "Just as I thought," Manannan sighed. With a clap of his hands, the king disappeared in a rainbow swirl but his voice echoed among the standing stones. "When will you stop then?"

Abhean said nothing and long after the king's departure, he continued to play happy tunes and ballads of love. As the sun set and stars emerged to dance among the heavens, in a voice as sweet as spun sugar, he crooned a lullaby. When the song ended, he whispered to the darkness finally answering Manannan's question, "As long as the mortals need me."

350

A word from the author...

At the age of four, I lined up my stuffed animals and told them stories I made up. At thirteen, I committed my first "novel" to paper—in a black-and-white-plaid spiral notebook. "The Talisman" had a decent plot along the lines of "Connecticut Yankee in King Arthur's Court" though processed through the brain of an adolescent girl. Needless to say, it was abysmal.

I've been married to my best friend, who also happens to be an attorney, for twenty-five years. Our wonderful daughter is in college, majoring in museum studies and history, a love she came by honestly from her dad and me both.

Over the course of my lifetime, I've been a military officer's wife, state appellate court marshal, airport rescue firefighter and forensic fire photographer, crime analyst, and technical crime scene investigator. I've since retired from the "real world" and live in Oklahoma. I spend my days at the computer with my two Newfoundland dogs, the "lolcat" who rules us all, and myriad characters all clamoring for attention. Eventually, I'll get around to telling each of their stories.

Be sure to visit me at www.silverjames.com

Thank you for purchasing
this Wild Rose Press publication.
For other wonderful stories of romance,
please visit our on-line bookstore at
www.thewildrosepress.com

For questions or more information,
contact us at
info@thewildrosepress.com

The Wild Rose Press
www.TheWildRosePress.com

www.ingramcontent.com/pod-product-compliance
Lightning Source LLC
Chambersburg PA
CBHW070155260626
47160CB00002B/351